PASSAGE OF
DISCOVERY

PASSAGE OF
DISCOVERY

The American Rivers Guide to the
Missouri River of Lewis and Clark

DANIEL B. BOTKIN

Sponsored by and written in cooperation with American Rivers

Foreword by Stephen E. Ambrose
Afterword by Robert Redford
Illustrations by Garry Pound

A PERIGEE BOOK

A Perigee Book
Published by The Berkley Publishing Group
A division of Penguin Putnam Inc.
375 Hudson Street
New York, New York 10014

First edition: July 1999

Published simultaneously in Canada.

The Penguin Putnam Inc. World Wide Web site address is
http://www.penguinputnam.com

Library of Congress Cataloging-in-Publication Data

Botkin, Daniel B.
    Passage of discovery : The American Rivers guide to the Missouri
River of Lewis and Clark / Daniel B. Botkin. — 1st ed.
        p.   cm.
    ISBN 0-399-52510-6
    1. Missouri River—Guidebooks. 2. Missouri River Valley—History,
Local. 3. Lewis and Clark Expedition (1804–1806) 4. Historic
sites—Missouri River Valley—Guidebooks. I. American Rivers
(Organization) II. Title.
F598.B72 1999
917.804'33—dc21   98-56643
                                                                        CIP

Printed in the United States of America

10 9 8 7 6 5 4 3 2 1

To my mother, Gertrude F. Botkin, who believed that each of us should be innovative, creative, and leave the world a better place than he found it

LITTLE BLUESTEM

HAIRY GOLDEN ASTER

"One of the most butifull Plains, I ever Saw" where "nature appears to have exerted herself to butify the Senery by the variety of flous" which "profumes the Sensation, and amuses the mind."

—WILLIAM ROGERS CLARK, JULY 4, 1804, IN THE PRAIRIES ALONG THE MISSOURI RIVER AT THE LOCATION OF MODERN ATCHISON, KANSAS

Contents

■　　■　　■　　■　　■　　■　　■　　　■

Contents

CONTENTS

Maps

■　　■　　■　　■　　■　　■　　■　　■

Foreword

■   ■   ■   ■   ■   ■   ■   ■

by Stephen E. Ambrose

Dan Botkin's book takes us on two intertwined journeys.

As historian, Botkin retraces the steps of Lewis and Clark, one of the greatest adventure stories of all time. Although we are inspired by their courage and determination, we are also overwhelmed by Corps of Discovery's detailed descriptions of the Missouri River valley and its human and wild inhabitants. Far more than explorers, Lewis and Clark were pioneering naturalists who recorded dozens of species previously unknown to science, ranging from coyotes to prairie dogs to cutthroat trout.

As naturalist, Botkin describes the meandering Missouri—destroying banks, creating islands and sandbars, continually changing its channel—and considers the bargain we struck when we converted much of the Missouri into a canal and six enormous reservoirs. The Missouri that Lewis and Clark knew featured thousands of islands and sandbars separated by two constantly shifting channels. Dense forest, shallow wetlands, and endless prairie bordered the river. Botkin recaptures this wilderness as Lewis and Clark saw it—a land filled with thousands of buffalo, elk, antelope, and grizzly bears.

Today, Lewis and Clark would hardly recognize much of the Missouri River. The river is 127 miles shorter, one-third as wide, and far deeper and faster. One-third of the river's banks are plated with rock and lined with two thousand miles of levees. Botkin also captures this river—a wild river tamed to meet human needs and wants.

We have, in his words, struck a Faustian bargain with the river.

As we converted the meandering Missouri into a canal, we robbed the river of the ability to build the sandbars and side channels that support river wildlife. By eliminating the variability of the Missouri, we believed we could aid river commerce and floodplain agriculture. But, as Botkin shows, neither has flourished. In the final accounting, we sacrificed one of the world's most biologically important and aesthetically pleasing rivers—and a commercial fishery that once supported thousands—to move a handful of barges.

The problem, of course, is that natural systems, once taken apart, are difficult to put back together again. By taking us to places where we are trying to restore some small piece of the river of Lewis and Clark, Botkin helps us to better appreciate the awesome task of repairing our tattered natural resources.

In a few places, the river is being rehabilitated. Resource managers and private organizations like American Rivers are struggling to restore some dynamism to the Missouri River. At places like Lisbon Bottoms, river managers are letting the river spread out across a portion of its floodplain, allowing the Missouri to re-create a maze of side channels separated by islands, sandbars, wetlands, and forest.

Ultimately, Botkin's book teaches us how rivers work—a remarkable achievement—and captures the struggle to balance our needs with the needs of our natural resources. From St. Louis to Three Forks, we see the Missouri River—past, present, and possibly future—through the eyes of a trained historian and naturalist. For those who know the Missouri, you will never see the river the same way again. And for those who are now discovering the Missouri, Botkin's guide is the perfect blend of ecology, history, and seasoned reflection on our two-hundred-year relationship with the nation's longest river.

In the next few years, millions of people will retrace Lewis and Clark's Passage of Discovery. Today, there are few places that the explorers themselves would recognize. But, if we begin today, we can repair much of the Missouri River. We can create a Missouri River Lewis and Clark would recognize.

In particular, riverside communities and resource managers can create a string of natural places along the Missouri—including pockets of floodplain forest and prairie, side channels, sandbars, and islands—where river wildlife can feed, conserve energy, and reproduce, and where people can see a semblance of what Lewis and Clark saw. We can reform dam operations to meet the needs of riverside communities and recreation, create riverside parks and trails to revitalize our riverfronts, and reduce the impact of grazing on cottonwoods in Montana and the Dakotas.

The two-hundredth anniversary of the Passage of Discovery creates an unprecedented opportunity to repair the nation's longest river. In many places, this process of renewal has already begun, as Botkin's book demonstrates. But in too many places we continue to turn our backs on the Missouri. Unless we act now, a rare chance to reconnect to our natural heritage will be lost.

Acknowledgments

■　　■　　■　　■　　■　　■　　■　　■

I wish to acknowledge the assistance and comments of many people who helped me in the preparation of this book. John Schline, vice president and corporate director of business affairs of Penguin Putnam Inc., who did double duty as my editor, provided invaluable suggestions about the basic structure and organization of this book, and was always a source of enthusiasm and support for the work that I did. The idea for this book arose from conversations with Rebecca Wodder, president of American Rivers, and she played a key role in the evolution of the book and its connection with American Rivers. Many staff members of American Rivers provided assistance with sources of information and help in locating people I could visit along the route of Lewis and Clark, especially: Scott Faber, who played a special role by providing much background information about the Missouri River, helping to contact experts and organizations, and assisting with the accuracy of the manuscript; Chad Smith, who provided additional sources of contacts and information; and Barbara Matos, who helped with the coordination of art, expertise, and communication.

I am forever grateful to Garry Pound for his beautiful illustrations that suit the style of the book; to Joan Melcher, who reviewed and edited drafts of the manuscript and provided literary guidance in many ways; to Susan Day, who also reviewed and edited drafts of the manuscript, helped organize my trips, maintained communication with the many people I visited, and assisted me with the entire process of the production of the manuscript; and to Karen Redden, who helped in making contacts with people I visited and did literature and Web research that provided essential information.

I thank Peter H. Raven, director of the Missouri Botanical Garden in St. Louis, for his help and support for the book, especially in establishing communication with others in the St. Louis area; George A. Yatskievych, botanist of Missouri flora with the Missouri Department of Conservation and the Missouri Botanical Garden in Saint Louis, who provided much detailed information about the vegetation, both past and present, along the Missouri River; and Robert Archibald, director of the Missouri Historical Society in Saint Louis, who provided helpful information about historical collections and plans for exhibits related to Lewis and Clark.

I am indebted to each of the people I visited during my trips along the Missouri River and who guided me and provided invaluable information. These include: Mark A. Brohman, environmental analyst supervisor with the Nebraska Game and Parks Commission, who took me on a wonderful full-day outing to see many of the restoration projects on the Missouri floodplain and was a continuing source of valuable information; Professor Thomas Bragg of the University of Nebraska at Omaha, for sharing his insights about the Allwine Prairie and on the general status of prairie in Nebraska; J. C. Bryant, refuge manager (retired) of the Big Muddy National Wildlife Refuge, U.S. Fish and Wildlife Service, Columbia, Missouri, and Jim Milligan, project leader of the Columbia Fishery Resources Office, also of the Big Muddy National Wildlife Refuge; William Glenn Covington, environmental research specialist with the U.S. Army Corps of Engineers, Kansas City, who spent a Sunday morning showing me Benedictine Bottoms and subsequently provided much helpful information about Kansas City and the Missouri River; Stephen R. Earl, Missouri River project engineer with the U.S. Army Corps of Engineers, Omaha, who made it possible for me to travel on the boat *Mandan* for a day on the Missouri River; Gary Garabrandt, chief ranger of the Fontenelle Forest Association, Fontenelle Forest and Nature Center, Bellevue, Nebraska, who has taken me on many field trips over the years and has been a great source of information about the natural history of Nebraska and Iowa; Mimi Jackson, director of the Lewis and Clark Center, St. Charles, Missouri, for her stories about the floods on the Missouri and her kind help during my visit to the museum; Rob Leonard, wildlife management biologist at Grand Pass Wildlife Conservation Area, Missouri Department of Conservation, Miami, Missouri, who took me on a tour of Grand Pass and explained the practices, policies, and ecology of the region; Dr. David Glenn-Lewin, dean of Wichita State University, Fairmount College of Liberal Arts and Sciences, Wichita, Kansas, for many discussions about the prairie and for taking me on several field trips to see prairie lands, including Loess Hills and Ledges State Park; Gerald Mestl, Missouri River program manager in the Fisheries Division of the Nebraska Game and Parks Commission, who took Mark Brohman and me out on the river to visit Hamburg Bend and explained the ecological dynamics of the river; Larry Mason and his family at Tarbox Hollow Living Prairie Ranch, Dixon, Nebraska, for the tour of their bison ranch and helpful discussions about bison and prairies; Tom Motacek, superintendent of Niobrara State Park, who was an informative and congenial host to a wonderful park; and Rick Plooster, assistant superintendent of Niobrara State Park, who took me on a beautiful boat ride on the Missouri River.

I thank Jane Weber, director of the Lewis and Clark Interpretative Center, U.S.D.A. Forest Service, Great Falls, Montana; Martin Erickson, editor of *We Proceeded On*, Great Falls, Montana; and Sammy Meadows, executive director of the Lewis and Clark Trail Heritage Foundation, Great Falls, Montana, for helpful information and support for the idea of the book.

I extend special appreciation to Gary E. Moulton, editor of *Journals of the Lewis and Clark Expedition*, University of Nebraska, Love Library, Lincoln, Nebraska, first because his excellent edition of the journals provides an essential background to this book, second because he has always taken time from his crowded activities to answer specific questions, and third because he has provided additional enthusiasm about the work I have attempted. All quotations from Lewis and Clark are from Gary Moulton's definitive edition of their journals.

I also extend special appreciation to James M. Peterson, past president of the Lewis and Clark Trail Heritage Foundation, who, in his role as a retired professor, read and made helpful comments and corrections to the entire manuscript and, in his role as "Missouri River Rat," took me on a beautiful and informative trip on the lower wild-and-scenic portion of the Missouri River. Finally, I thank Jane O'Brien for her support for the process of writing the book, enthusiasm for the project, help during travel, and suggestions about making contacts with people along the trips.

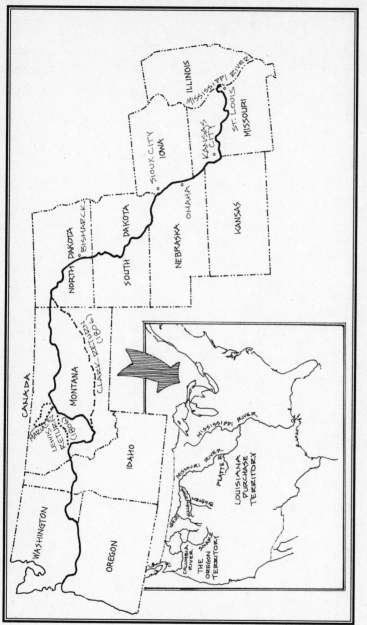

Outbound, Lewis and Clark traveled up the Missouri to its headwaters in Montana, over the Bitterroot Mountains to the Columbia River. On the return, after crossing the Rocky Mountains, Lewis and Clark divided the expedition. Clark took some of the men and followed the Yellowstone River to its confluence with the Missouri (dashed line on map) while Lewis took the others and went up the Marias River and then retraced the expedition's outbound journey. The two groups met and followed the Missouri downstream to St. Louis, their starting point.

Introduction

■ ■ ■ ■ ■ ■ ■ ■

How to Use This Book

This is a different kind of travel book. It is intended for two types of travelers, actual and vicarious, to find out about Lewis and Clark, nature, and ourselves. It has two brief introductory chapters, forty-two main entries about places to visit, and a list of more than eighty other travel destinations. Each main entry tells some of the things that happened to Lewis and Clark and relates a unique story about nature, natural history, and the environment. As a set, all the entries paint a picture of the entire Missouri River and its landscape, both at the time of Lewis and Clark and as they have changed and are today.

There are hundreds of interesting locations to visit along the Missouri River and its surrounding countryside related to the Lewis and Clark expedition. So that you can design your travel plans to visit the places whose topics interest you, the list of additional entries is cross-referenced to the main ones. Each entry provides travel directions.

Travelers can use the book in several ways. For those who have picked destinations, they can refer directly to the main entries. Each is about one aspect of the natural history of the Lewis and Clark expedition and the changes that have occurred since the expedition. Each includes relevant experiences from the Lewis and Clark journals: what they did and what happened to them at the location. These are augmented by modern experiences of myself and others to suggest what you can discover and do there.

A second way to use the book is to select a general route and then refer to the main and short entries on that route to make a list of places to visit. Take the book with you and read each main entry at its location. A third way to use this book is to read it from beginning to end. Taken together, the introductory chapters and major entries form a whole story of nature, Lewis and Clark, and us.

CLARK'S NUTCRACKER

LEWIS, CLARK, NATURE, AND US

In preparation for the Lewis and Clark expedition, President Jefferson wrote to Meriwether Lewis that he should "record the mineral productions of every kind . . . Volcanic appearances . . . Climate, as characterized by the thermometer, by the proportion of rainy, cloudy, and clear days, by lightning, hail, snow, ice; by the access and recess of frost; by the winds prevailing at different seasons; the dates at which particular plants put forth or lose their flower or leaf; times of appearance of particular birds, reptiles, or insects." Throughout their historic journey, Lewis and Clark faithfully followed President Jefferson's instructions—recording the condition of rivers, prairies, forests, mountains, and wildlife, without romanticism, without ideology.

LEWIS' WOODPECKER

Lewis and Clark were careful and accurate observers, skills learned as outdoorsmen, as military men on horseback, and as young men full of curiosity. To these abilities, President Jefferson added modern scientific training. He sent Lewis to Philadelphia, then to the center for learning about "natural philosophy"—the term of that day for all natural sciences together, not yet divided into the narrow disciplines they are today. There, within the city of Benjamin Franklin, one of the young nation's centers for rational thought, Lewis took crash courses in botany, zoology, and geology. This study reinforced and deepened the knowledge that he and Clark shared of wildlife and countryside.

It is common knowledge that the journey of Lewis and Clark was an incredibly successful and fascinating epic, full of adventures, near disasters, amazing coincidences, and replete with tales of courage and bravery. But it was more than that. It was a journey to discover the natural history of an unrecorded continent. As a result, it can be modern society's window on a nature we know little about but discuss often, believing that we do know it. On their way west, Lewis and Clark measured the distance they traveled; paced off the feet between river meanders; shot the sun with a sextant; looked at, touched, and tasted minerals; collected, described, and pressed new species of plants. They ate, wore, and wrote about wildlife. Their records tell us what nature was like before modern technology changed it; they have become a yardstick against which we can measure what we have done to the rivers and landscapes of midwestern and western North America.

Seeking to find the right route across the continent and to survive in the process, Lewis and Clark were not just keen observers but also willing participants in an attempt to generalize successfully from a series of observations. It is a skill we are seldom taught and few of us learn: how to make reliable inferences from a selection of facts. More typically, we cannot believe that an event that we see in detail once may not be true in general. We fall into the unscientific trap of indefensible generalizations from too few observations. Lewis and Clark traveled up the river, but when they could, they strode on shore and climbed hills, bluffs, and mountains to get a view, to see a broader perspective. They measured and counted, they mapped and studied. In my experience, three decades of trying to piece together an understanding of the process we call nature, I have found a great irony of our times. In this information age, we rarely obtain the information we most need about ourselves, our civilization, and our surroundings. Over and over again I have discovered that Lewis and Clark, two centuries ago, put a yardstick or sextant to things that we no longer seek to pace or measure.

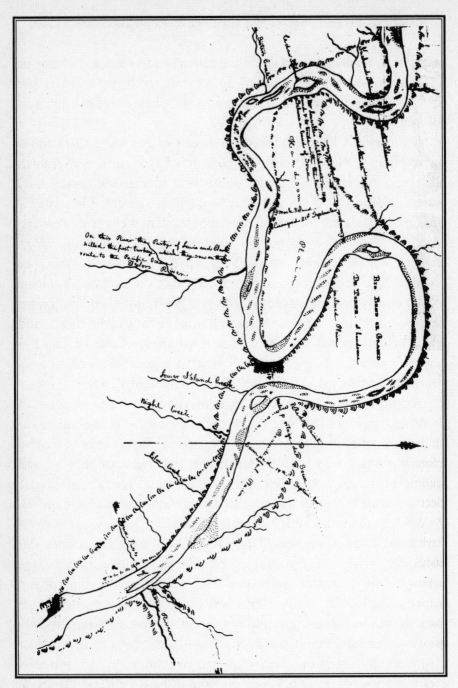

A section of a map drawn by Lewis and Clark

And so by experience, necessity, and Jefferson's plan, Lewis and Clark are our best external window on the reality of nature in the American West before it was altered by modern technological civilization. Their journey epitomizes our struggle to understand our effects on nature and nature's effect on us. Their journals provide clear and vivid insights into the past.

What is remarkable, and I believe unique, to the expedition of Lewis and Clark is that these two men took on the role of naturalist-recorders as seriously as they did their tasks of finding a route to help open up the West and making contact with and learning about Native Americans along the way. Human beings have long altered nature, but our knowledge of this is obscured by failed memories, confusion between myths and realities, and a loss of written historical accounts.

The Missouri River and its landscape exist for us at two levels. The first level is that of external knowledge: natural resources, environmental issues, the names of animals, plants, and minerals; and rational inferences about how the landscape and its life came to be and how it might be in the future.

It is the level of detailed observation and records of natural history. The second level is internal; it is the level of feelings: how the countryside affects us and how we feel we fit into that countryside. Like Lewis and Clark, we begin with the first, external level; these experiences lead us to the second.

So I invite you to come with me on this journey with this guide in hand to see, touch, smell, and feel the countryside of Lewis and Clark and the landscape of today, and to find a path to a connection between oneself and nature.

The Missouri River:
Nature's Landscape Painter

The river is the central fact [of one-sixth of the United States]. In its twisting and turning, ever easterly, from Three Forks to the Mississippi, the Missouri has succeeded in carving a crude but large question mark across the surface of one-sixth of the Nation. The mark readily symbolizes the great array of problems which await satisfactory solution in the Basin.

—Missouri Basin Survey Commission, 1953

Thousand years. All this here water just a-going to waste.

—Woody Guthrie

Rocks are nature's books; minerals are its words.

Rivers are nature's landscape painters, brushing rocks and minerals, books and words, on the landscape. Rivers have a beginning; a young river cuts steeply through the book of rocks, creating cliffs.

Rivers mature; they erode cliffs back into gentle hills; they create wide floodplains and meander through them. Life responds to this painted landscape. In the soils, microbes and plants read the words and push through the pages, abstracting life-giving nutrients. The river creates a landscape with flowing water, backwaters, side channels, stream-side zones, and uplands. Each is a different habitat to which a different collection of creatures has adapted. In the United States, one of the greatest painters of landscapes is the Missouri River.

THE MISSOURI RIVER IS THE GREAT PLAINS

> Some people would think it was just a plain river running along in its
> bed at the same speed; but it ain't. The river runs crooked through the val-
> ley; and just the same way the channel runs crooked through the river. . . .
> The crookedness you can see ain't half the crookedness there is.
>
> —A RIVER MAN WHO RACED BOATS ON THE RIVER, COMMENTING A CENTURY AFTER
> LEWIS AND CLARK HAD TRAVELED UP IT (S. VESTAL, *THE MISSOURI*, 1945)

The Missouri is one of the Earth's twenty longest rivers, extending 2,315
miles from its origin at the confluence of the Jefferson, Gallatin, and Madison
Rivers in Montana to its mouth, where it meets the Mississippi at St. Louis. It
flows eastward from its origin, through Montana into North Dakota, then
makes a big bend southward into South Dakota down to Nebraska. From
there, it flows southeast and east for a way, forming part of the boundary
between the two states, South Dakota and Nebraska, then turns south once
again to form the boundary between Nebraska and Iowa, then Nebraska and
Missouri, and part of the northern border between Kansas and Missouri.
Finally the river turns generally east and southeast, flowing through the state
of Missouri to its confluence with the Mississippi near St. Louis.

The Missouri is not just a river that happens to flow through the center
of North America; it drains more than five hundred thousand square miles,
or about one-sixth of the continental United States. Along with the Arkansas
to the south and the Saskatchewan River in Canada, the Missouri drains the
Great Plains, an area that makes up one-third of the United States: all the
land between the Rio Grande in the south and the Mackenzie River's delta at
the Arctic Ocean in the north, from the Rocky Mountains on the west and
the lowlands on the east—an area some three thousand miles long and three
hundred to seven hundred miles wide, part of which is in Canada. The Missouri collects waters from the Bad, Blackwater, Cannonball, Cheyenne, Gas-
conade, Grand, Heart, Judith, Kansas, Knife, Little Missouri, Moreau,
Musselshell, Niobrara, Osage, Platte, White, and Yellowstone Rivers, all of
which flow into it from the south and west. Meanwhile it also picks up

waters from the northern plains that extend into Canada, from its other tributaries—the Bad Teton, Big Sioux, Chariton, James, Little Platte, Marias, Milk, Sun, and Vermillion Rivers, rivers that enter from the north and east.

The Missouri drains waters that fall on mountains fourteen thousand feet high in the Rockies, and it ends its journey near St. Louis at an elevation of only four hundred feet above sea level. What goes into this huge area of the United States— the central part of the Great Plains, its main prairie states—comes out the

Meriwether Lewis

Missouri. Drop a bottle with a message in it in a stream in eastern Montana or in southern Canada north of Nebraska and, unless it rafts up on some sandbar or snag, it will float out at St. Louis.

The Missouri flows from a major mountain range through comparatively dry country that has been greatly altered by the glaciers. The Great Plains give up their waters to the Missouri. In turn, the great river, with the help of vegetation, paints the surface into prairie.

William Clark   The Missouri picks its pallet from the slopes, from the mountains and the wind-formed hills. It carries these earth colors downstream and dabs the landscape with floodplains, terraces, and bluffs.

On the surface of our planet, the Missouri River acts as an irresistible force against which there is no immovable object. All earthly things that confront the Missouri, all that attempt to surround it, to seize it and hold it back, give way. If not now, then later. The mountains fall before it as do the more meager works of mankind—levees, houses, and bridges.

President Jefferson

The simplest way to understand the Missouri is to consider that it has four major geographic sections. The first section is from its headwaters to near Great Falls, Montana. The Madison, Gallatin, and Jefferson headwaters are in the Rockies, where rain and snowfall greatly exceed evaporation, and these rivers accumulate water and sediments, which the Missouri River carries onto the plains. The second section is from Great Falls, Montana, to where the Milk River joins the Missouri near the Montana–North Dakota boundary. Here the river flows through semiarid plains along a geologically new pathway, formed when ice-age glaciers changed the Missouri from a river whose outlet was at Hudson Bay to one that flowed into the Mississippi. The third is from the Milk River to Yankton, South Dakota, where the river joins its ancient bed, the bed of the preglacial-age Missouri. Here evaporation exceeds rain and snowfall and the river deposits sediments. In dry years, the river can lose water faster than it accumulates water from its tributaries. The fourth is the last 825 miles from Yankton to St. Louis, where the river flows through a humid region of higher rainfall and low relief. Each section has its own scenery, its own hydrology, and its own characteristic, dominant species.

The Painter and the Carpenter

Without the Rocky Mountains there would be no Missouri River. The river is a necessary consequence of a mountain range adjacent to a large plain. Mountain ranges are created when huge masses of the Earth's crust, called plates, collide through a process called plate tectonics. The word *tectonics* comes from a Greek word meaning "carpenter" or "builder." As the river is the painter, the continents are the carpenters, creating the mountain ranges on which rain and snow fall, from which water drains and erodes, creating channels that dig deeper and deeper into the rock—creating a river.

From the mountains, a river erodes away pieces of different sizes: clays, silts, sands, gravels, pebbles, and, for short distances, rocks and boulders. With these, it cuts through the rocks and, downstream, colors the landscape: With the help of wind it colors the land the burnt-wheat brown of loess hills; with bacteria, algae, sedges, rushes, and cattails it paints wetlands a Swiss-chocolate brown; with prairie tallgrass and flowers, the best soils in the world become a gingerbread brown; and with the dry-land plants of sand-bars and sandhills, the shores are tinted a creamy lemon-white. The river is the master painter; its journeymen are living things. To these it gives habitat, nutrients and water, a place to stand, a place to grow, a place to color with a much brighter, broader palette—if much more fleeting and occasional—from the brilliant white of migrating pelicans to the rich blues of prairie asters.

It is my hope that the essays that follow will help the reader come to know the natural history of the Missouri River both externally and internally, and that with this knowledge and appreciation we can move forward to a better use of our natural resources—for nature and for people.

The Natural History of Special Locations Along the River

■ ■ ■ ■ ■ ■ ■ ■

1. Camp Dubois: Preparing for the Journey

Take Interstate 270 from St. Louis east across the Mississippi River, then take Route 3 north to the exit for State Route 203. There is a sign before the exit that directs you to the Lewis and Clark Memorial Park. Go left (west) over Route 3 to the frontage road, then follow the sign to the park, making a right turn and following the road onto the floodplain. At the end of this road is a parking area, the Mississippi River, and a circular structure that marks the location for the restoration. Directly across the river is Columbia Bottom, an area undergoing environmental restoration. Upstream (to your right) on the opposite bank is the mouth of the Missouri River. In 1998 the state of Illinois allocated several million dollars for an interpretive center at Camp Dubois—or Site 1, as they call it.

From December 12, 1803, until May 14, 1804, Lewis and Clark stayed at Camp Dubois—also called Camp Woods—on the Illinois side of the Mississippi River at the mouth of the Dubois River. They built cabins just downstream and in view of the mouth of the Missouri River. Here they made their final preparations for the expedition. The exact site of their camp no longer exists, but a replica of Camp Dubois is being constructed at a location on the Mississippi River with the same relative position to the mouth of the Missouri River as the original one.

I visited this replica on a raw, cloudy spring morning when the combined Mississippi-Missouri River channel was so wide that the line of trees on the far shore looked no taller than the short hairs on a beaver's head. It seemed a humble location for the beginning of a great expedition. The replica had not been built and was marked by flat cement pillars holding up a disk-shaped roof. Only a set of plaques on each pillar, one for each state through which the expedition passed, gave the location any historic aspect. Haze hung over the Mississippi. The road to the replica snaked through a bottomland forest where the water stood among the trees and spilled onto the roadway. Recent flooding had scattered leaves, twigs, and limbs across the road. From the shore we could see in the distance where the Missouri emptied its churning, dangerous currents into the Mississippi channel. The threatening sky and dark forest accentuated the speed of the rolling waters. Here nature loomed large in width and power if not in height and beauty.

As I stood on the shore beside the wide river, I wondered, as have many others who have followed the Lewis and Clark journey, how two young men, Meriwether Lewis and William Rogers Clark, managed to lead a small corps of tough, resilient men more than twenty-three hundred miles up the powerful, forceful river, over the Rocky Mountains, down the Columbia River, and return. The trip lasted from May 14, 1804, to September 23, 1806, a total of 864 days—two years and four months—and, from start to finish, covered approximately eight thousand miles. From April 1805 through August 1806, all communication with their civilization was suspended, and in this sense they were truly in the wilderness. Many are familiar with their story, but we can only wonder at their success.

Their journey fascinates us on two levels. There is the surface level of the events of the expedition and of the expedition's contact with a little-known landscape. This is the novelistic story of their experiences, sometimes truly stranger than fiction. It is the story of how they survived the journey up a river that was constantly threatening them with sandbars, snags, and tumbling cliffs; how they overcame grizzly bears, hailstorms, blizzards, and food scarcities. This surface level is the one at which we discuss societal and political topics; it is the level of discourse about natural resources and land-use issues—how we can combine the various uses people want for the Missouri River and its valley: safe navigation on the river; freedom from the threat of floods; the opportunity to farm, build homes, see and conserve wildlife and fish and the natural ecosystems of the river, and enjoy the river and its countryside.

But that was only part of how the view from Camp Dubois affected me. I was much more strongly involved with another, much deeper level, one that I believe moves our curiosity even more strongly toward these two men and their expedition. The flat landscape at Camp Dubois, a view without distant vistas, obscured by vapors evaporating from the rivers, symbolized for me the unknown that confronted Lewis and Clark at the beginning of their expedition and that confronts us still today. Standing at this location, viewing a river that seemed ominous in the gray light beneath a threatening overcast sky, I could think only of the way that Joseph Conrad expressed such a trip on a wilderness river into an unknown continent by a solitary, independent man. Conrad wrote, "Going up that river was like traveling back to the earliest beginnings of the world, when vegetation rioted on the earth." It was a trip into the "heart of darkness," but not the darkness of the land. Rather, the darkness within a person's soul, known and knowable only from a direct confrontation with nature, brought to light by the river journey.

Conrad knew that deep within us is a connection with that nature, a connection that is a longing, a desire, a process, and a continuation. Within our modern world, in our cities, our suburbs, our automobiles, we are linked indirectly to that nature; it is a permanent fact of humankind, but it is also a connection not usually on the surface of our lives, not within the range of our daily vision. Like the nutrients necessary for life suspended in the swirling, rushing reptilian gray of the Missouri's waters and therefore not visible to the naked eye, it is not usually apparent to us, but it is essential.

How did they succeed? The view of the big rivers from Camp Dubois raises the question but does not give the answer. For that we must delve into their journals and into the records of others. The first among many remarkable things to notice about this expedition is that the members did keep records. It was the greatest wilderness trip ever recorded in pen on paper. A sobering thought about their success is that they were not the first but the third expedition sent out by Jefferson to find the best route west. The two before had simply disappeared, perhaps because their leaders lost interest or courage and turned away.

It seemed to me, contemplating the question at Camp Dubois, that several important factors, in addition to fortune and good luck, make for a successful expedition. I reflected on my own experiences, spread over thirty years discovering and studying nature, and knew that one of the first elements of a successful expedition is careful planning and preparation. President Jefferson sent Lewis to Philadelphia to take crash courses in botany, zoology, and geology so that he could identify, collect, and report on the natural resources he encountered.

An important aspect of this planning was the careful selection of the participants. Lewis began by telling Jefferson that he would only lead the trip if his good friend in whom he had great faith, William Clark, could accompany him as coleader. Lewis and Clark then selected the men for the expedition carefully. "Accept no soft-palmed gentlemen dazzled by dreams of high adventure," Lewis had told Clark when they were interviewing people to make up the crew in 1803. "We must set our faces against all such applications and get rid of them on the best terms we can. They will not answer our purposes," he wrote.

A second aspect of good planning is choosing the right equipment, and one important part of good equipment is simply good maps. Much of Lewis's winter of 1803–1804 was spent talking in St. Louis with those who had traveled up the Missouri. Lewis copied and created maps as far as the land was known—from the mouth of the Missouri all the way to its middle portion, the present location of Bismarck, North Dakota. To put this in perspective, when the astronauts landed on the moon, there were much better maps of the moon's surface than Lewis and Clark had available to them of the American West when they began their journey.

Lewis was occupied for months with selection, as well as invention, of devices to take on the journey. He brought the best equipment available, purchasing only the best, including imported gunpowder, since at that time American-made powder was not of as good a quality. He brought the latest in technology, including a newly invented air rifle. He prepared for danger, and he brought equipment as gifts or to impress the Native Americans he would meet. In addition to the air rifle, Lewis brought three cannons mounted on the boats—not so much to win battles as to deter them—plus small flintlock pistols, muskets, blunderbusses, tomahawks, and scalping knives.

He purchased the best clothing available for the members of his expedition, along with blankets, hooded coats, some clothing of a water-repellent material, thirty yards of flannel with which to make new clothing, and needles and awls to make the clothing. He brought a wide array of tools, so that everything that was needed could be repaired or made along the way. His medicine chest included the best available pharmaceuticals of the day.

On the Missouri, the expedition traveled on a sixty-foot keelboat, called a bateau, and a large wooden canoe, called a pirogue. An iron-framed canoe that Lewis had tested especially for the trip was assembled after the group made its way past Great Falls. However, because they did not have the correct materials to seal the skins that covered the iron frame, the metal canoe sunk. Wooden dugout canoes were built and used instead. In all, the equipment for the trip weighed thirty-five hundred pounds.

When appropriate equipment was lacking, Lewis invented new devices. He designed a rifle especially for the expedition, a design that became the model for the first mass-produced rifles of the U.S. Army. He packed carefully, making the most efficient use of the limited weight and space available to him. He designed watertight containers, made of lead, to hold gunpowder. When a container was emptied of its powder, it could be melted down to make bullets. He brought fifty-two of these, and they worked exceedingly well. Even his estimate of the number of these turned out to be quite accurate. Twenty-seven were used on the outward journey and only five of the remaining ones had cracked and allowed water to reach the powder by the time they were ready to return home.

How could Lewis know that fifty-two canisters of gunpowder were enough? Experience in the field was part of the answer, and this too is an important quality for such an expedition. Both Lewis and Clark were experienced soldiers and outdoorsmen, accustomed to the hardships and practiced in good observation of the countryside.

Beyond these characteristics, these men also possessed the vitally relevant inner human qualities of commitment, responsibility, and perseverence. As Joseph Conrad was to explain through his many novels a century later, the essence of human existence within nature and within society is in making a commitment and accepting the responsibility to see things through.

These are not qualities that come easily to mind in our modern world; they are not something that a cozy seat with a remote control for the TV brings to mind. They are deep and dense and, like boulders and water-saturated logs, they rarely come to the surface. Perhaps we feel a fascination therefore with these qualities in Lewis and Clark. Another important attribute is simply the willingness to do plain hard work, which Lewis and Clark as well as the other members of the expedition showed repeatedly.

Finally, there are the elusive qualities of leadership, which the two men had in great abundance—an ability to command and lead, to make people want to go where they had not gone before, and still to have them singing and dancing in the evenings, as happened upriver on numerous occasions later in the expedition.

Some of the writings in the early portions of the journal might make you think that Lewis was not a tough outdoorsman and leader, but rather an urbane gentleman. When Lewis and Clark left Camp Dubois, Clark took the boats and sailed to St. Charles, just up the mouth of the Missouri. There, taking care of the last of the preparations, he waited for Lewis to come overland from St. Louis. On his way between St. Louis and St. Charles, Lewis wrote that the "morning was fair, and the weather pleasant," and that he was "joined by Capt. Stoddard, Lieuts Milford & Worrell together with Messrs. A. Chouteau, C. Gratiot, and many other respectable inhabitants of St. Louis." He bid "an affectionate adieu to my Hostis, that excellent woman the spouse of Mr. Peter Chouteau, and some of my fair friends of St. Louis," as if he were off on a spring picnic with the highest society of the town, not off into the wilderness of a continent. And he "arrived at half after six and joined Capt Clark, found the party in good health and sperits, suped this evening with Monsr. Charles Tayong a Spanish Ensign and late Commandant of St. Charles, at an early hour I retired to rest on board the barge," as if this were a well-organized tourist holiday for which he was just another passenger. But do not be fooled by this bit of an aside, nor by Lewis's ability to move at several levels within society and without, for he could be both a gentleman of St. Louis and a rough-and-ready, experienced, thoughtful and curious, tough, committed, knowledgeable leader of men.

It is with these things in mind that I left Camp Dubois and began to search for the natural history of the Lewis and Clark expedition. I invite you to join me on this journey, as we seek to find what nature was like before it was changed by European civilization, how we might restore and conserve nature, how we might achieve simultaneous uses of the river and its surrounding landscapes, and how we can find a place for ourselves and our civilization within that landscape.

2. Cahokia: Clark Discovers an Ancient Indian Mound

From St. Louis take Interstate 55/70 east to the exit for Route 111. Go south on 111 about one-quarter mile and turn left (east) onto Collinsville Rd. Follow this to the sign for the Cahokia Mounds Historical Site. You will see the largest mound, Monks Mound, on your right.

Lewis and Clark spent the winter of 1803–1804 building Camp Dubois and preparing for their journey. In midwinter, despite sleet and snow, Clark explored the surrounding countryside. He often made trips out into the countryside, sometimes to hunt for game, which was plentiful; sometimes for purposes related to the preparations for the expedition; but sometimes, it seemed from his journals, just to explore, to get away from the humdrum of the daily chores of the preparation.

On Monday, January 9, 1804, he took Collins, one of the men hired for the expedition, and "went across a Prary to a 2nd Bank." On the Illinois side of the river, Clark came to a curious place. "I discovered an Indian Fortification," he wrote. "This fortress is 9 mouns forming a Circle." Confronted with something new, Clark responded by making measurements—a habit that would follow him throughout the journey. "Two of them is about 7 foot above the leavel of the plain," he continued. Looking around the mounds, he found "great quantities of Earthen ware & flints" and a "Grave on an Emenince." The mounds were not in use. They were ancient and abandoned.

He had unwittingly stumbled onto what we now call Cahokia Mounds, the remains of the largest prehistoric earthen construction in the New World, built, according to discoveries by modern archeologists, between A.D. 700 and 1400. Looking back from our perspective, it was an ironic and curious discovery. He and Lewis were about to embark on a journey into what was perceived as wilderness, and Clark finds, quite accidentally and without any guidance, evidence that they were in the backyard of Native Americans who had affected that countryside for much longer than anyone understood. It demonstrated unequivocally that the lands along the Missouri River had long been settled by Native Americans who had selected where to live carefully in regard to nature's resources, and who had lasting effects on the countryside. And just as the mounds formed a base on the level plains, the Indian cultures would provide a foundation for the expedition. The help that the contemporary generation of Indians would give to the Corps of Discovery during their trip would be invaluable. It is fair to say that the expedition would not have succeeded without that help.

We visited the mounds on a cool, drizzly April day, driving from the center of St. Louis; past the Gateway Arch, celebrating the Lewis and Clark expedition and the city as the gateway to the West; past abandoned, brick-fronted industrial buildings with broken windows and cracked pavement; over the river on the interstate, in the company of trucks and commuting passenger cars; past fast-food restaurants among a mixture of suburban development and farmland.

As we approached the modern town of Collinsville we saw a tall mound rising surprisingly high above the level farmland, back behind fences in a large open field. A large sign directed us to the well-maintained Cahokia Mounds State Historic Site. We found a beautiful modern facility in a park setting, with wide lawns, gardens of prairie grasses and flowers clearly labeled, and paths to the mounds.

Modern archeological studies tell us that, at its peak, the great mound city held about twenty thousand inhabitants living in an urban population density similar to that of modern St. Louis. Cahokia was surrounded by a two-mile-long stockade of twenty-foot-high logs built from about twenty thousand trees. At the height of its development, Cahokia included 120 mounds, all of earth, and these made Cahokia the largest site of earthen structures in the New World. A large ceremonial mound reached one hundred feet high, with a base of fourteen acres and a building on top more than one hundred feet long and forty-eight feet wide, and another fifty feet high.

Archeologists estimate that more than fifty million cubic feet of earth was moved for the construction of the mounds.

It was like discovering Mayan temples in our backyard. Although the mounds have been designated a United Nations World Heritage Site and therefore recognized to have international significance, few people I met along our journey to rediscover the travels of Lewis and Clark knew about the mounds, and few we have spoken with since have heard of them. But there they are, just outside St. Louis, not far from the famous Gateway Arch—the largest prehistoric city in the New World north of Mexico.

The sophistication of the culture that developed here was revealed by archeological finds in the 1960s, spurred by a plan to put the interstate through this location. An archeologist, Warren Wittry, discovered oval-shaped pits the size of posts, made from trees and arranged in arcs of circles. These appear to have served as celestial calendars, much as Stonehenge did in England, and have become known as Woodhenge. The posts mark the winter and summer solstices and spring and fall equinoxes. As with other early agricultural people, the Cahokians were dependent on the seasons for planting and harvest and needed a method to predict when changes would come.

A densely populated, defended city was possible here near the confluence of the Missouri and Mississippi Rivers because the rivers and the surrounding countryside provided abundant natural resources. The floodplain's soil was frequently re-enriched when the rivers flooded and deposited new soil carried from far upstream. Fish, freshwater shellfish, migrating and nesting water birds, and native mammals, including deer, were abundant in the complex habitats along the river and over the wide floodplain. The location of the largest prehistoric city in North America was not accidental, but was a direct product of the natural resources.

Living close to the land and depending on it, the people of Cahokia responded to local differences in their natural resources. They farmed the eastern floodplain of the Mississippi, but not along the western shore. At the time, the western shore was a series of bluffs and valleys, comparatively poor land to farm. Today, you would not notice this difference because the bluffs have been removed and the land leveled, as part of the development of St. Louis.

The city of Cahokia began a gradual decline around 1300 and was abandoned by 1500. Nobody knows the fate of its people. The Indians Clark met with around St. Louis knew no more than he did about the mounds. The history of the greatest city of ancient times in North America had been lost.

Did the mound builders overuse their natural resources, or destroy their local environment, and die off or migrate away? Did climate change around 1400 make it impossible for them to live? Or did politics and war put an end to their culture? Nobody knows. Bones of the dead suggest some malnutrition and disease, so perhaps there was an environmentally related decline in this civilization. Perhaps it is a history lesson we should pursue to see if there is any warning or message to help our civilization sustain itself and also sustain its natural resources. Our trip from downtown St. Louis that morning seemed to warn of a need to understand the decline of Cahokia. Although St. Louis had made civic attempts to redevelop and improve its waterfront and its center, we saw the signs of urban decay everywhere once we were away from the publically funded projects symbolized by the famous arch. Would St. Louis survive as a viable city or decline as Cahokia did? The parallel seemed unavoidable and was a little disturbing, not the least because the park around Cahokia was one of the more beautiful landscapes we had seen in the St. Louis area.

3. St. Charles: Floods, Levees, Towns, and Wetlands

St. Charles is just across the Missouri from St. Louis, and historic Main Street is easily reached from an exit off Interstate 70.

> There is only one river with a personality, habits, dissipations, and a sense of humor . . . a river that goes traveling sidewise, that interferes in politics, that rearranges geography, and dabbles in real estate; a river that plays hide and seek with you today and tomorrow follows you around like a pet dog with a dynamite cracker tied to its tail. . . . It cuts corners, runs around at night, lunches on levees, and swallows islands and small villages for dessert.
>
> —G. FITCH IN THE *AMERICAN MAGAZINE*, 1907

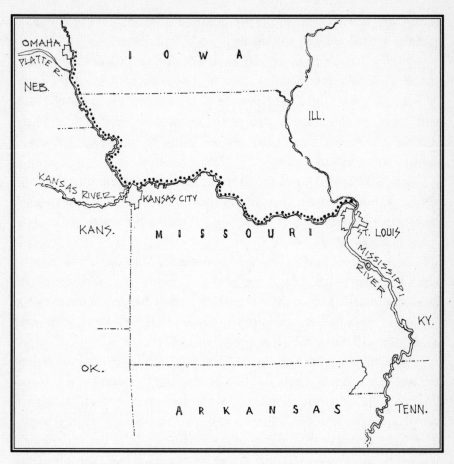

The first part of Lewis and Clark's journey along the Missouri River took them west from St. Louis to the Kansas River and the present location of Kansas City, then northerly to the Platte River and the present location of Omaha. During this phase, they traveled from European settlements to the unsettled prairie, but were still in countryside that had been traversed and mapped by people of European descent. This part of the journey took from May 14 to late July 1804.

Clark set out with most of the men of the expedition from their winter camp at the mouth of the Dubois River on May 14, 1804, and noted in his journal that the mouth of this river should be considered as the Corps of Discovery's point of departure, although citizens of St. Charles claim their town as the starting point for the expedition as a whole. "I determined to go as far as St. Charles a french Village 7 leags Up the Missourie, and wait at that place untill Capt. Lewis Could finish the business in which he was obliged to attend to at St. Louis and join me by Land," Clark wrote.

On May 16, the boats arrived at St. Charles, and Clark noted that "a number of Spectators french & Indians flocked to the bank to See the party." On May 20, Lewis joined them from St. Louis and on Monday, May 21, the party set off on the boats "at half passed three oClock under three Cheers from the gentlemen on the bank," wrote Clark. The entire expedition, with its two leaders, was underway.

Gary Moulton, editor of the definitive edition of the journals of Lewis and Clark, notes that "St. Charles was the earliest white settlement west of the Mississippi and north of the Missouri," having been surveyed in 1787 and settled soon after.

The location of St. Charles had been selected with care. "The plain on which it stands," wrote Lewis, was "sufficiently elivated to secure it against the annual inundations of the river, which usually happen in the month of June." The town had one main street, parallel to the Missouri, with about 100 houses and 450 inhabitants, according to Clark.

This main street has become the location of a private historical restoration and is a series of lovely old houses now used as stores and bed-and-breakfast hotels catering to tourists. We arrived there in early spring and went first to the Lewis and Clark Center, a small but excellent museum. Mimi Jackson, one of the curators of the museum, told us that, as originally planned by its surveyor, Auguste Chouteau, the town had been sufficiently above the river to never suffer a flood for more than two hundred years. But then, in 1993—the year of the great floods on the Missouri, the Mississippi, and the Red Rivers—water began to move up toward the museum building. The curators went out to watch the water rise, expecting the worst: that the exhibits would soon be destroyed by the floodwaters. But just before the water reached the edge of the museum building, they heard a *whoosh* like the flushing of a toilet, and the floodwaters quickly abated.

They soon found out that a levee had given way in Chesterfield, about ten miles downstream, and this allowed the floodwaters to move into the countryside there and away from St. Charles. With the release of the waters into the floodplain, across the levee, the water level dropped fast and no

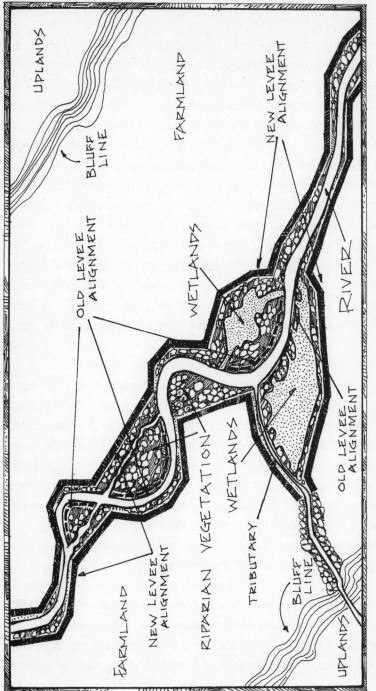

Two ways to use levees. The old way: force the river into a single, comparatively narrow main channel. This requires high levels and leads to the kinds of severe flooding that occurred near St. Louis and St. Charles in 1993. The new way: place levees at the edge of the flood-plain, allowing the river to flood and form wetlands as it did in the past. These wetlands can be used for many purposes when the river is not in flood.

longer threatened the museum or the historic main street of St. Charles. This was a clear example of how an alteration of one part of the river—the nearby levees—had effects on another—the waterfront of St. Charles.

Over the fifty years prior to the 1993 floods, the U.S. Army Corps of Engineers, along with state and private efforts, had spent $25 billion on a system of levees, walls, and other flood control measures on the Missouri-Mississippi River system. Ironically, the impression these actions created of a calm and peaceful river led to some complacency: The greater the apparent control over the Missouri, the greater the faith people had in their own effectiveness and the less alert they were to possible dangers.

Chesterfield responded to the break and failure of its levees by building bigger, higher ones, which are supposed to be resistant to a flood so great that it is likely to occur only once in five hundred years. Some of the St. Charles businesses and some of the government agencies near St. Charles propose to do the same, so that there can be more development on the floodplain.

The more the river is crowded in by taller levees, the faster it flows and the more erosive and dangerous it becomes. The result is a war of levees. A town or house with no levees or lower levees suffers the flooding that is being avoided by the places with levees. The alternative is to create sections of the floodplain that are allowed to flood naturally. Columbia Bottom, a large wetland being developed into a nature preserve from farmland (discussed in the next entry), could be one of these areas. At Columbia Bottom there are more than four thousand acres to absorb floodwaters. Similar projects are found at other locations along the Missouri.

There is no better place than St. Charles to become directly acquainted with the dilemmas raised by a river that continuously changes its depth and is affected over its twenty-three hundred miles by changes in seasons, changes in snowfall and rainfall—by a dynamic and variable array of climate and geology. We walked along the waterfront park, just slightly below the elevation of the Lewis and Clark Museum, and thought about the choice confronting the citizens of Missouri: to resist and fight against the forces of the river, or to develop a regional design that allows for nature's continuous changes by providing some locations where floodwaters can spread out and, in this way, not flood the towns along the river. The latter is a natural approach because the bottomlands have always been wetlands that flooded now and again, and they contain plants and animals adapted to these variations and able to recover from them.

4. Columbia and the Big Muddy National Wildlife Refuge: Approaches to Meeting All the Uses of the River

To reach a view of Overton Bottoms and Diana Bend, and the Interstate 70 bridge over the Missouri River, drive to Columbia, Missouri. From Columbia, take Interstate 70 west about twelve miles to exit 115, then drive west on Route BB to Les Bourgeois Wine Garden and Bistro (on your left, on a bluff overlooking the Missouri River). From there you can see Overton Bottoms and Diana Bend, which are part of the Big Muddy National Wildlife Refuge, the Interstate 70 bridge over the Missouri, and the effects of the 1993 and 1995 floods.

To see the bottomlands close up, go to the small towns of Boonville (another tourist destination) and Overton, the Katy Trail, and the old river town of Rocheport, a few miles from the winery.

> [The Missouri River] makes farming as fascinating as gambling. You never know whether you are going to harvest corn or catfish.
>
> —Fitch, 1907

One of the best ways to understand the lower Missouri River valley is to see it from the top of one of the nearby limestone bluffs. Lewis and Clark often climbed these bluffs on their way up the river, especially between the locations of modern-day Jefferson City, the state capital, and Columbia, Missouri. From these heights they could read the countryside to see what its natural resources might be and judge its potential for farming, settlement, and defense.

One of the most spectacular views of the river valley is from the Les Bourgeois winery near Rocheport, Missouri, just west of Columbia. We stood on the top of the limestone bluff with J. C. Bryant, manager of the newly

BLACK WILLOW

developing Big Muddy National Wildlife Refuge, and Jim Milligan, project leader of the Columbia Fishery Resources Office. Far below us we saw the wide river valley and the narrow, engineered main channel maintained at a minimum of nine feet deep and three hundred feet wide, cut deep enough for barge navigation. Alongside the main channel were rows of cottonwoods and willows, highlighting the levees built to protect farmland on the bottomlands beyond the channel.

"I like to bring people up here and show them the view of Overton Bottom and tell them that the Missouri River drains one-sixth of the United States, and all that water has to flow right *there*, under *that* bridge on Interstate 70," J. C. Bryant said as we looked down at the beautiful landscape. From the top of the Overton bluff, all appeared placid, almost gardenlike—a mosaic of bottomlands: dark soils of the few remaining active farmlands, grays of last year's weeds in abandoned farmland, stands of cottonwoods and willows greening the sands and silts.

The Missouri River valley provides people with many benefits, and Lewis and Clark took advantage of many of these as they passed along the limestone bluffs between the modern locations of Jefferson City and Columbia, Missouri. On June 5, 1804, York "Swam to the Sand bar to geather greens for our Dinner and returnd with a Sufficient quantity wild *Creases* or Tend grass," Clark wrote. Wild cresses remain common along the Missouri floodplain. On June 10, 1804, Clark wrote that the country was "roleing open & rich, with plenty of water" and an abundance of plums, "Verry full, about double the Sise of the wild plumb Called the Osage Plumb & am told they are finely flavored," Clark wrote. They harvested these fruits and, in this way, participated in the harvest of crops on the floodplain. Clark also saw "great quts of Deer" that provided much of their food.

Near the modern location of Columbia, Clark described a salt creek about thirty yards wide, which had "so many Licks & Salt springs on its banks that the Water of the Creek is Brackish," and the water in one spring was so strong that "one bushel of the water is said to make 7 lb. of good salt." Salt was an important and limited commodity, and this site was later used by the sons of Daniel Boone to produce salt as a commercial product.

Lewis and Clark enjoyed the sounds and sights as do travelers along this part of the river today. Repeatedly they referred to "butiful" prairies approaching the river and extending back from it. Near Overton, Clark wrote that there was "delightfull land." Near Jefferson, where the expedition camped on June 4, 1804, Clark named a small stream Nightingale Creek because of the beautiful sounds of the birds calling all night—though he was probably hearing the whippoorwill, which you can still hear echoing in this region on a spring evening. They saw goslings on the river and large cottonwoods on the sandbars.

But in this reach of the Missouri the expedition continued to struggle against the dangerous river. On June 9, 1804, as they passed Arrow Creek just across the valley from Overton, "The Sturn of the boat Struck a log which was not proceiveable," Clark wrote. The current quickly turned the boat "against Some drift and Snags," which it hit with "great force." They

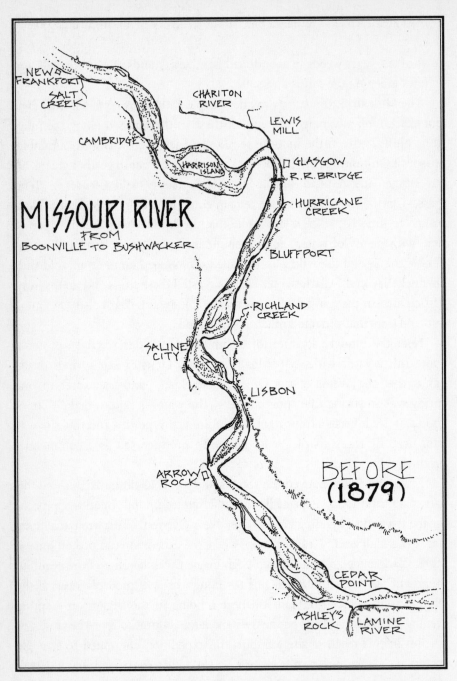

The Missouri in the region of the new Big Muddy National Wildlife Refuge before and after channelization. In the map before 1879, the river meanders through many channels and there are many islands and sandbars. After 1954 the river flows through a single main channel.

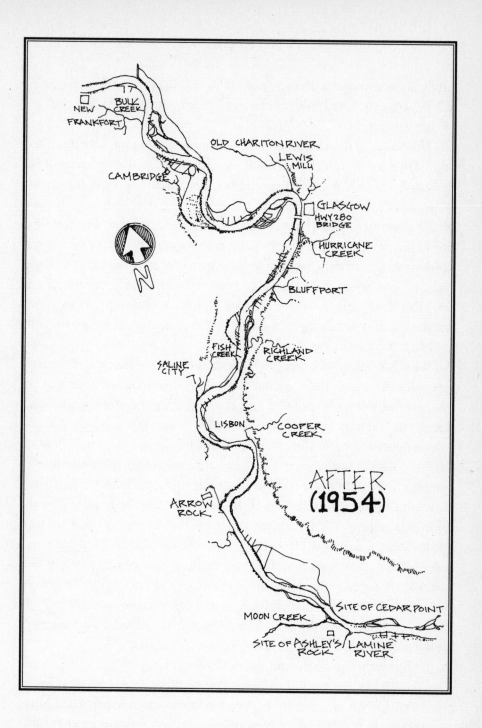

NEW FRANKFORT
BULK CREEK
OLD CHARITON RIVER
LEWIS MILL
CAMBRIDGE
GLASGOW
HWY 280 BRIDGE
HURRICANE CREEK
N
BLUFF PORT
FISH CREEK
RICHLAND CREEK
SALINE CITY
LISBON
COOPER CREEK
AFTER (1954)
ARROW ROCK
SITE OF CEDAR POINT
MOON CREEK
SITE OF ASHLEY'S ROCK
LAMINE RIVER

handled the situation when some of the men "leaped into the water Swam ashore with a roap, and fixed themselves in Such Situation, that the boat was off in a fiew minits."

The power of the Missouri's water was made clear to me later that afternoon when we drove down to the floodplain, through the remnants of the tiny hamlet of Lisbon and out onto Lisbon Bottom and Jameson Island, two sections of the new wildlife refuge, and crossed the river and the floodplain on a bridge near a railroad bridge that had to be reconstructed after the 1993 flood. The flood occurred when the descending bank of a levee broke west of Glasgow: floodwaters took out about one mile of levee, one mile of Highway 240, and one mile of the GM&O railroad bed; created a scour hole of 100–300 acres; and flooded thousands of acres of farmland. Flood flows returned to the river above Lisbon and cut the pilot channel for a new chute at Lisbon Bottoms.

We saw a line of rock that Jim Milligan said "follows the path of the river before the '93 flood. There are one hundred or two hundred acres that are now riverine habitat behind that line, that was dry ground before the flood. The Corps had put riprap—big rocks—there. When that flood came across Lisbon Bottom, it came with such force that it knocked the whole nose off Jameson Island. And what helped this happen was that there was a levee completely around Lisbon Bottom. When the upstream levee broke, Lisbon Bottom filled up with water and then the water blew the levee out on the lower side getting back in the river." J. C. said that "the water came out with such a force that it was like a fire hose." Jim noted that "local observers reported that there were one hundred dump trucks running twenty-four hours a day for two, three months"—that's close to one hundred days—to bring in enough rock to rebuild the levee, Highway 240, and the GM&O railroad crossing across the scour hole. "About three million dollars' worth of rock reportedly went into that hole," he said.

"Why won't it just blow out again?" I asked.

"The idea is that it will hold next time because there is no fill between the rocks; the whole structure is pervious to the water. When floodwaters come they can pass through it now. About eight feet down is another highway—the one that was flooded and silted over." However, Jim noted, "because of local landowner complaints about water coming through the permeable dike, there are plans to seal it up."

When the twentieth century opened, about three-quarters of the flood-plain vegetation was in forests, and prior to European settlement there were 160 species of birds, reptiles, amphibians, and mammals that lived on the floodplain or used it during migration. There were also 156 native species of fish. But most of this complexity is gone. It is estimated that more than 90 percent of the floodplain wetlands, forests, and prairies have been converted to agriculture or made no longer functional as a result of channelization of the river.

Throughout most of the twentieth century, the pendulum of use swung to navigation and agriculture, leaving little habitat for fish and wildlife. Now the pendulum is swinging back slightly the other way, and the development of the Big Muddy National Wildlife Refuge is an indication of the shift. The Army Corps of Engineers is participating in a series of mitigation projects to restore fish and wildlife habitat to compensate for losses that have occurred. Some of the mitigation projects are the combined effort of the Corps and the U.S. Fish and Wildlife Service, along with state agencies. I came here to learn about these projects and the reasons behind the establishment of the Big Muddy Refuge.

The Fish and Wildlife Service's major effort between Kansas City and St. Louis is the Big Muddy National Wildlife Refuge. It is a different idea than what we are used to thinking about as a national park or nature preserve, which have almost always been a single, contiguous piece of land. The Big Muddy Refuge will be a series of floodplain units spread across the lower Missouri in the state of Missouri like beads on a necklace of river.

At present, the Big Muddy consists of seven identified areas that occupy sixteen thousand acres, of which approximately seven thousand acres are currently public lands. The plan is to purchase more land from willing sellers and to eventually establish twenty-five to thirty areas covering sixty thousand acres. From Arrow Rock State Park, we could see two areas already established: Jameson Island and Lisbon Bottom.

Some bends or units of the Big Muddy Refuge will have restored or newly created side channels, called chutes, cut through them to allow some of the river's water to flow away from the main channel and form quieter side-channel backwaters, wetlands, and other pieces of the complex set of habitats that used to be there.

The idea for such a refuge had been discussed for many years, but the great flood of 1993 revived interest in it, in part because after the flood there were some willing sellers among the landowners—those who had suffered from the flood because the Missouri had deposited coarse sandy soil, impossible for the farmers to use, on many acres of land. The primary purposes of the refuge are to restore natural river floodplain structure and function and to allow better management and conservation of fish and wildlife habitats, with public use—where it is compatible with these purposes—as a secondary goal.

Only portions of the land need to be returned to the original complex and dynamic habitats to provide enough spawning, nesting, feeding, and migratory habitat for a large abundance of fish and wildlife. A lot of bottom-land is magnificent, rich farmland; it is not necessary, useful, or in the greater public interest to return it to these kinds of complex habitats. According to Jim, the "most desirable refuge lands are those containing some remnant floodplain habitats and/or are subject to periodic flooding or drainage problems—rendering them less valuable to agriculture."

The idea is to let the river manage itself—for people to manage with a light touch. The river remains the landscape painter; we provide only a little nudge, a little color, a little material here and there, perhaps a line drawn through a bottom to start a new path for the water, which the river will then mold and continue molding as it weaves and wanders its way across the valley.

5. Arrow Rock State Park: Cottonwoods and the Resiliency of Life

Arrow Rock is reached most easily from Interstate 70. Take this interstate about thirty miles west of Columbia and turn north on Route 41; follow this until you reach Main Street of Arrow Rock, which you take east. To reach Arrow Rock State Park, continue east to the end of Main Street, then turn right and follow the road as it winds around and down a small hill and passes over a small stream. The road continues up the hill to the park.

While the Missouri River was treacherous, it also created a well-watered and fertile bottomland where trees adapted to these conditions grew in great abundance. On June 9, 1804, Clark wrote that they passed a place called "Praire of Arrows," which was below a bluff called "arrow rock" and where there was a stream called the "Creek of Arrows" flowing into the Missouri. Clark observed a "Delightfull land" on the south side of the river. The next day he noted that they "passed a part of the River that the banks are falling in takeing with them large trees of Cotton woods which is the Common groth in the Bottom Subject to the Flud."

The bottomlands were full of cottonwoods, and these came and went at the will of the river, sprouting after a flood, dying when the current cut the soil out from under them. We saw these same natural processes working at the same location, as we stood on a bluff overlooking Arrow Creek and the Missouri River. After the time of the expedition, Arrow Rock developed as a crossing point on the Missouri River because Arrow Creek provided a way up and over the steep bluffs. The Santa Fe Trail, which originates in Independence, Missouri, came this way. This charming, small town blossomed briefly. Now a small village of about seventy residents, it is registered as a national historic landmark.

We visited Arrow Rock on a beautiful spring day. We walked down the main street through the town, past pleasant, well-maintained houses surrounded by shade trees and blossoming redbuds, some of the houses converted to bed-and-breakfast hotels, past a summer stock theater well known in the region. Stores on Main Street have wooden sidewalks and wooden porch-fronts, like a movie-set western frontier town. The movie *Tom Sawyer* was made here years ago, the local people told us. Walking through Arrow Rock was like walking into the past and into the perfect image of small-town America. It made us aware of how villages have waxed and waned, with just a few, like Arrow Rock, maintained as reminders of the past.

At the foot of Main Street we turned right and followed the road down a short slope. In a short time we reached Arrow Rock State Park, with its large, manicured lawn of playing fields and a few trees—oaks and other upland species. The park stands on the edge of the bluff, providing a magnificent view of the Missouri River. Below us flowed the Creek of Arrows, much as Clark had described it.

Beyond the creek and far below us was a vast field of young cottonwoods, light green against the black bottomland soil. Beyond the first field of trees was a wide expanse of open soil and then another field of cottonwoods mixed with willows. In the middle distance were the levees along the channelized Missouri River, and beyond them the main channel flowed—as straight as an arrow, as straight as Main Street—reflecting the blue of the sky. In the distance, limestone bluffs could be seen.

The day before, Jim Milligan, fisheries biologist for the U.S. Fish and Wildlife Service at the Big Muddy National Wildlife Refuge, had told me that hundreds of acres of young cottonwoods had sprouted up on former agricultural lands after the 1993 flood, creating stands so dense they were almost impossible to walk through now and, if you succeeded, hard to keep your sense of direction in unless the sun shone brightly. These trees were now five years old. Remarkably, some were twenty and twenty-five feet high and up to five inches in diameter—as thick as a wrist. I had seen trees that had grown that fast on only two other occasions. One was on the Tanana River outside of Fairbanks, Alaska, where, in a similar situation, on sandbars on the floodplain, balsam poplar (a relative of these cottonwoods) had also grown five feet a year. The other was in Costa Rica, where we went to the tropical rain forests with a local forestry expert. We ate lunch under several balsa trees (not related to these cottonwoods) about thirty feet high, and he told us that those trees had sprouted five years before.

Under good conditions, trees of the upland forests of Missouri and the states to the east—like the oaks growing near us on the top of the bluff in the woods bordering Arrow Rock State Park—grow a foot or maybe two taller and a half inch in diameter a year. In a poor year upland trees, especially those adapted to the deep shade of older forests, increase in diameter hardly at all, a hairbreadth, just enough so you can see a growth ring when you look at a stump. Some trees, including some of the oaks, can persist for years with this kind of small growth. Cottonwood is a fast-growing tree, characteristic of what ecologists call the early successional stage in the development of a forest—the time soon after a disturbance, like the 1993 flood, when light, water, and nutrient elements are in great abundance and there is little competition. Willows are much the same, germinating and sprouting on newly formed floodplain soils. Sometimes the willows come in first, especially on

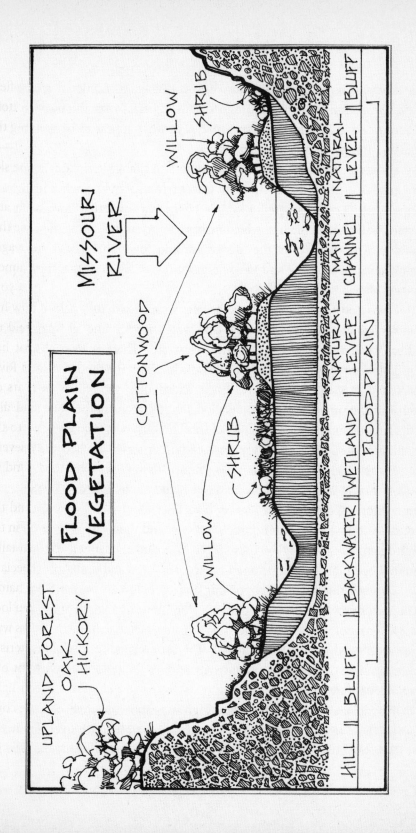

FLOOD PLAIN VEGETATION

MISSOURI RIVER

UPLAND FOREST OAK HICKORY

COTTONWOOD

WILLOW

SHRUB

WILLOW

WILLOW

SHRUB

HILL || BLUFF || BACKWATER || WETLAND || NATURAL LEVEE || MAIN CHANNEL || NATURAL LEVEE || BLUFF

FLOODPLAIN

the coarser soils of sandbars, followed by cottonwoods. Sometimes, as in our view, the cottonwoods sprout immediately, especially on the heavier soils. Cottonwood is also the dominant species in what appear to be mature bottomland forests on the Missouri River.

Lewis recognized this process of the natural change in dominant species. On June 14, 1804, a little farther upriver from Arrow Rock and toward Kansas City, Lewis gathered a sample of the narrow-leaf willow, which he noted "is invariably the first which makes it's appearance on the newly made Lands on the borders of the Mississippi and Missouri." These, he wrote, "grow remarkably close and in some instances so much so that they form a thicket almost impenetrable."

Lewis also observed that, once the trees were rooted, they helped build up the floodplain soil. "The points of land which are forming all ways become eddies when overflown in high water," he wrote. "These willows obstruct the force of water and makes it more still which causes the mud and sand to be deposited in greater quantities." Lewis added that "the willow is not attal imbarrased or injured by this inundation, but (the moment the water subsides) puts forth an innumerable quantity of small fibrous roots from every part of its trunk near the surface of the water which further serve to collect the mud."

He also observed that the trees thinned themselves over time. "As the willow increases in size and the land gets higher (and more dry) by the annul inundations of the river, the weeker plants decline dye and give place to the cotton-wood which is it's ordinary successor, and these last in their turn also thin themselves as they become larger in a similar manner and leave the ground open for the admission of other forest trees and under brush."

This self-thinning was happening already below us on Jameson Island. The faster-growing trees shaded out the slower-growing ones, and the slower-growing ones died. The dead organic material from these thinned trees improved the already rich soil. The cottonwoods and willows were a clear example of life's great productivity and its ability to restore itself when conditions were right.

Floodplain forests have declined greatly since the time of Lewis and Clark. These forests covered three-quarters of the Missouri River floodplain in 1826, but only 13 percent by 1972. During that time, clearing the land for farming was a major cause of this decrease. Land in crops increased from 18 percent to 83 percent of the floodplain lands. But channelization also had its effect. Sprouting and survival of cottonwoods and willows declined greatly because of the reduction in spring flooding. The habitat had been changed and was no longer available or suitable to these trees.

The view from Arrow Rock State Park illustrated a general rule about life: Most species do well as long as their habitats are in good condition. It is better to have a small population in a good habitat than a large population in a poor habitat. And here the habitat for cottonwoods was near to perfect—a floodplain whose soil was just renewed, laid bare of other vegetation that could compete with the cottonwood sprouts, which do poorly when shaded by other trees.

Jim Milligan said that one of the farmers along the river valley, seeing the great productivity of the cottonwoods since the flood, is using these as crops. A five-year-old tree that was twenty-five feet high and five inches in diameter could be sold for fiber if a timber processing plant were near enough to make it economically feasible. This was intriguing because I had just completed an analysis of the world trade in timber products with an economist. We had calculated that all of the world trade in timber for fiber and construction could be met with plantations on good land that would require less than 10 percent of all the forest land in the world. Here was an example of what we had proposed: Use land subjected naturally to frequent disturbances, whose trees are resilient and productive and respond well to frequent harvests. A field of cottonwoods, natural in this location, would benefit wildlife and fish as well. Here was a way that farming and conservation could come together.

The scenery at Arrow Rock was not a duplicate of what Clark saw, in part because of natural changes in the location of the river channel and backwaters, in large part because of the channelization of the river. It was an exact replication of the ecological processes he observed. Cottonwoods grew in the same abundance and after disturbance to the bottomlands just as Lewis and Clark had described them almost two hundred years before, and the species of trees changed with their elevation above the river, just as Clark had said. These patterns and processes are gateways to opportunities to restore the landscape. Given a good habitat, a small number of mature cottonwoods can provide the seeds to fill a valley.

COTTONWOOD

G. POUND

6. Pelicans and Grand Pass: The River and Migrating Birds

From Arrow Rock take Route 41 west to Marshall where 41 joins 65. Continue on 65 west to State Route N, and take that north to the end of the road, which is the entrance to Grand Pass. The office is to your left.

Well upriver, in the general vicinity of present-day Onawa, Iowa, forty miles south of Sioux City, the expedition saw a strange sight on August 8,

1804. Lewis wrote, "I saw a great number of feathers floating down the river," covering sixty or seventy yards of the river's width. "For three miles after I saw those features continuing to run in that manner," he continued. "We did not percieve from whence they came." It was as if the river had painted itself white. "At length we were surprised by the appearance of a flock of Pillican at rest on a large sand bar," Lewis wrote. Almost three months into the journey, you might think that Lewis was becoming used to strange and extraordinary sights, but miles of white feathers amazed him. There were so many birds that he did not even try to count them, merely writing that the numbers "if estimated" would "appear almost in credible."

He shot one bird as a specimen and made an accurate, written identification of its features, as Jefferson had instructed him to do. The beak was "a whiteish yellow" and the pouch under the beak was so big that they filled it with five gallons of water. It had yellow feet, mostly white feathers except that the "large feathers of the wings are of a deep black." Lewis recognized these as the same pelicans that are found in Florida and the Gulf of Mexico— the white pelican. The birds were "no doubt engaged in procuring their ordinary food," Lewis wrote, "which is fish."

The pelicans were all the more remarkable because Lewis noted that "We had seen but a few aquatic fouls of any kind on the river since we commenced our journey." He listed a few geese, wood ducks "common to every part of this country," and cranes. The expedition had left too late to see the spring migration of waterfowl, which occurs generally in March or April, and saw primarily resident water birds.

Starting one of our trips along the Missouri River in late April, near the end of migration, we had better luck. One of the best places to see waterfowl during their migration along the Missouri River is at Grand Pass Wildlife Conservation Area, five thousand acres managed by the Missouri Department of Conservation. Pelicans pass through and stop here, just as they do along other parts of the Missouri where habitat is suitable.

We visited Grand Pass Wildlife Conservation Area with Rob Leonard, the top wildlife management biologist there, driving along gravel roads past many kinds of artificial wetlands developed to provide habitat for different species of wetland wildlife. Rob, a direct descendant of William Rogers

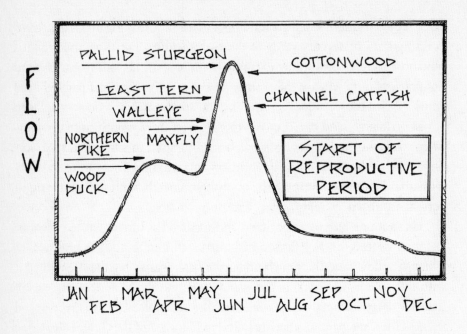

F
L
O
W

PALLID STURGEON

COTTONWOOD

LEAST TERN

CHANNEL CATFISH

WALLEYE

NORTHERN PIKE   MAYFLY

WOOD DUCK

START OF REPRODUCTIVE PERIOD

JAN FEB MAR APR MAY JUN JUL AUG SEP OCT NOV DEC

Many plants and animals have evolved and are adapted to the different stages in the natural flooding of the Missouri River over the seasons. There is a first, early flood and a second, higher flood. Without these variations and seasonal high waters, habitats may not be right for the reproduction of fish such as the pallid sturgeon, birds like the wood duck, and trees like the cottonwood.

Clark, had the same red beard for which Clark was famous and the same outgoing manner and ready smile.

Grand Pass is one of many bottomland areas being restored for fish and wildlife habitat between Sioux City and St. Louis. The challenge at each of them is to find the best and most economical way to re-create the muted mosaics of backwaters, oxbows, perennial wetlands, seasonal wetlands, wet prairies, and floodplain forests.

One approach is to do as much as possible to speed up natural processes. This is the approach of the Missouri Department of Conservation at Grand Pass. Rob explained that Grand Pass is intensively managed to create wildlife habitat, by creating many artificial wetlands and by carefully timing when these are filled and emptied to try to match the natural, prechannelization seasonal patterns.

We drove first to a pumping station, where Rob told us that the pumps are capable of pumping 250 acre-feet a day—enough water to cover 250 acres a foot deep and enough to provide a day's water for more than 800,000 people—more than twice the number of people in St. Louis—at the liberal but average U.S. water use of one hundred gallons per person a day. Water pumped into a wetland is not lost to public use, rather it is enhanced and then returned to the river. Rob commented that "wetlands should be viewed as a part of public infrastructure in much the same way as roads and highways. Wetlands are nature's way of providing clean water and flood control."

The water is pumped into a set of large ponds and wetlands separated by levees of different heights, forming an artificial network. About one-third of the area's five thousand acres is in a status Rob referred to as "refuge," meaning once a pond or wetland is constructed there is a "no-touch" policy—no other actions are taken. Refuge areas of no disturbance provide habitat to migrating waterfowl. The refuge wetlands are juxtaposed with actively managed areas where much more is done. Some are flooded only in the spring and the fall and then pumped dry in the summer and winter, to mimic seasonal wetlands as they used to be on the river. Others are flooded for shorter periods. Still others are restored as wet prairie, planted with switchgrass to protect levees. According to Rob, "switchgrass was selected because of its ability to hold soil, while providing wildlife habitat."

Many kinds of waterfowl depend on the Missouri River and its backwaters for nesting, breeding, rearing, and migratory feeding. Today there are eighteen species of ducks that use the river. Of these, wood ducks remain the most common nesting species, just as Lewis reported in his time. There are three geese: Canada, snow, and white-fronted. There are ten species of wading birds and twenty-five species of shorebirds. A total of two hundred species of migratory birds use the floodplains.

Some birds are threatened or endangered, or have become locally extinct along the Missouri. The birds whose situation is of concern live in many of the kinds of habitats once common along the Missouri floodplain. Restoring the floodplain for migrating birds means restoring many kinds of habitats— putting the mosaic back together. In addition, wetlands are important for many species, as well as waterfowl.

An alternative to the intensive, active management at Grand Pass is a light touch, do-as-little-as-possible-and-let-nature-heal-itself approach. This is one of the policies of the U.S. Fish and Wildlife Service at the Big Muddy National Wildlife Refuge. The light-touch idea is that a few smartly selected and well-executed actions could allow the river to repaint the landscape in the most natural way—a break in a levee at just the right location, for example, to form a single new chute. Then the river would be left alone to erode a complex maze of channels the way it always had and, given the opportunity and following the laws of physics, always would.

The two policies, at Grand Pass and at the Big Muddy, are two different approaches to designing landscapes. It is as if two different landscape painters were set before a large canvas. We tend to view environmental issues as a matter of a single truth whose identification is our goal and the solution. But I have found that environmental issues are often a question of the best design. The path to the best design is to try several, just as major buildings are often the focus of a design contest. Lacking precise information and having only poor understanding of how nature worked in the past, we have no "silver bullets," and it is wise to let a number of approaches bloom on the river.

The intense management at Grand Pass seems to be working. As we walked by one of these ponds, two sandhill cranes rose majestically into the air, banked and turned, and flew away from us, their wings the warm brown of loess soils, to settle in a distant pond. To our right several hundred ducks—shovelers and blue-winged teal mostly—swam among rushes and sedges and wetland grasses. Here and there in other immense ponds and wetlands we saw great blue heron, cormorants, mallards, Canada geese, snow geese, coots, and the American white egret. A blackboard at the headquarters listed more than 150,000 ducks having stopped at Grand Pass this spring and more than 50,000 snow geese.

And all this is relatively new. Grand Pass land was purchased by the state of Missouri in the early 1980s, but the intense management did not start at Grand Pass until Rob arrived there in the late 1980s.

If you want to see migrating water birds that are characteristic of the Missouri River in Lewis and Clark's time, you can do no better than to stop at Grand Pass. But if you want to see 150,000 ducks and 50,000 snow geese, then you have to pick your time carefully—March/April or November. The

THE WHITE PELICAN

migration timing varies somewhat from year to year, so you may also need a little luck or flexibility.

I was impressed with both approaches I had seen, the intense management and the light touch, and glad that we had a landscape large enough to allow both to be happening at this time, in my lifetime, when I could see it. Later in our trip, far upriver, we came across the last of the migrating pelicans. When we stopped to watch them, they flew as a flock into the air and circled high above us in a pure blue sky. When they flew one way, only their white wings reflected the sun, and we saw a brilliant white spiral moving above us. When they flew in the other direction, their black feathers caught the sun. The alternating white and dark-gray spirals in the air illustrated the complexity of natural patterns and seemed to symbolize the multiple plans underway to try to restore the Missouri River's habitats.

7. Kansas City: Where the Kansas River Meets the Missouri—City Plans and River Pollution

The confluence of the Kansas and Missouri Rivers is just across the Missouri River from the Kansas City Airport, to the southwest. Railroad tracks run along both sides of the Kansas River near the confluence and on the south shore of the Missouri River, while the north and east shores of the Missouri at the confluence are near the boundary of the airport. On the south shore of the Missouri River near the mouth of the Kansas River, Market Street is near, but not at, the junction of the rivers. A new Richard Berkeley Riverfront Park opened in late 1998 that can be reached from the Interstate 29/35 Front Street southbound ramps.

On June 26, 1804, the expedition camped just above the mouth of the Kansas River, at the present location of Kansas City, Kansas. They spent several days there because they had to repair the pirogue, which they emptied, brought up on land, and turned over. During this work, on June 28, 1804, the expedition saw its first buffalo, which they did not kill. These animals would soon become a principal source of food.

Clark praised the location for its beauty and its opportunity for defense. He wrote that the Kansas Indians lived "in a open & butifull plain" and that "the high lands come to the river Kanses on the upper Side at about a mile" which made "a butifull place for a fort, a good landing place."

Just downstream on June 25, 1804, the expedition camped in what now is Sugar Creek, a suburb of Kansas City, and there saw great numbers of deer "feeding on the young willows & hearbage in the Banks and on the Sand bars in the river." It was a productive location, with "Plumbs, Raspberries & vast quantities of wild (crab) apples." The next day they killed seven deer. Near there the next day they also saw "a great number of *Parrot Queets*," the Carolina parakeet that is now extinct, but for which Lewis and Clark provided the first written observation west of the Mississippi. It was a place of appealing biological diversity.

Kansas City was an important location for a geographic reason: Downstream, the Missouri runs east and west; above the Kansas River, it runs north and south. This was the farthest west one could go on the Missouri below Sioux City, where the river once again turned west. The choice of a traveler at the Kansas River mouth was to take that smaller river, which few did; go north to Omaha and take the Platte River west, which became the major route west; follow Lewis and Clark and continue up the Missouri; or begin travel by land. This made the location a natural one for a city as well as a fort.

When we visited Kansas City, we tried to find an easy way to the mouth of the Kansas River and to get a sense of the geography of the city as Lewis and Clark might have seen it. It is a large city, with more than one and a half million residents and a metropolitan area said to be larger than Connecticut. I looked forward to visiting Kansas City. Although my professional work has often focused on wilderness and endangered species, I like cities. Kansas City is famous for jazz, and I looked forward to a break in our work to listen to jazz in the evening. Reading up on this city before our visit, I found that it had been called "an exemplary model of urban planning." The Web site for the city's Chamber of Commerce said that it had "more miles of boulevards than Paris and more fountains than any city but Rome," and that "a careful regard for beauty is evident throughout the city's boulevards, lavish fountains, spacious parks and attractive business centers."

Unlike so many American cities at the end of the twentieth century, it seemed to be prospering. Many Fortune 500 companies have manufacturing plants or offices there; it is one of the nation's centers for flour production and marketing, for railroads, and for many kinds of manufacturing.

So we arrived in Kansas City on a warm summer afternoon with considerable enthusiasm, stayed in an attractive redevelopment area of high-rise hotels, and listened to jazz in a small place in the evening. The next day we set out to try to find either of the rivers, the Kansas or the Missouri. Not an easy task, we discovered. There wasn't a major park along either river that we could see from a map. So we left our hotel and walked to an outdoor Sunday public food market that was near the Missouri River. Once we were out of the hotel area, we walked through a seemingly empty city where there were few other pedestrians, where empty storefronts confronted us as we approached the market. The market was busy and interesting, but it had no view of the river and was not in a particularly comfortable part of the city.

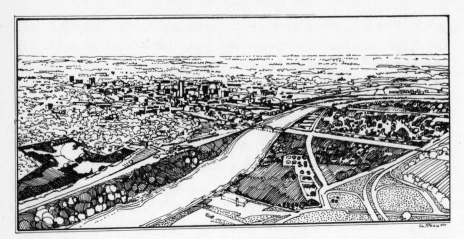

Cities connected to their rivers, with parks along the riverfront, generally do better than those whose roads, railroads, airports, and other constructions separate the river from the rest of the city. Here, parks along a city's riverfront benefit the river, the people, the environment, and commerce.

Environmental concerns seemed to be valued here—the Chamber of Commerce had also noted that "greater Kansas City was the first major city to have earned clean air status from the EPA." But in spite of pride in its urban planning and clean air, Kansas City seemed to have disconnected itself from its major rivers.

I couldn't help comparing Kansas City with another Lewis and Clark city, Portland, Oregon, at the confluence of two other major rivers—the Willamette and the Columbia. Portland had been blighted by Interstate 5, which passed between the downtown and the Willamette River. The city had found funds to move the interstate across the river and to build a beautiful riverfront park. The park is heavily used; it is a fashionable location for upscale condominiums, and a wonderful setting in which to walk from an urban desk to a view of a great river. The new Riverside Park in Kansas City, planned but not built during our visit, may be a step in the right direction.

It seems to me that cities that are well connected to their waterfronts tend to do better than those that are not—at least better culturally and as a place to live. This is not a new discovery. There is a history of formal, written city planning that extends back more than two thousand years in western civilization. And there are two traditional goals in all of that history: military and aesthetic—to build a city that is at the same time defensible and beautiful. A great emphasis was placed on the planning of cities because it was long believed that cities were the center of civilization—of creativity, innovation, and commerce.

Settlements along the trail of Lewis and Clark did not develop in a way that suggests a recognition of that long history of city planning. Towns and cities grew quickly after Lewis and Clark, as the West opened up and there was a need for places to buy supplies and centers to buy and sell the products of the land. Cities grew up, used and converted the river's resources, and forgot the ancient—and I believe hard-learned—lessons of city planning.

Kansas City, Missouri, began as a trading post in 1821, only fifteen years after Lewis and Clark returned past the mouth of the Kansas River on their way back, and only two years after the first steamboat sailed on the Missouri River. The town grew as steamboat activity increased. Other towns and cities along the Missouri developed with similar speed and without the late-twentieth-century concern for the environment that we take for granted.

In the first half of the nineteenth century, rivers provided transportation and took away wastes. The river was a thing you traveled on and dumped into, but otherwise you might pay it little attention.

Perhaps this attitude began to change a little in 1910 when there was a serious increase in deaths from typhoid fever in the towns along the Missouri River, and in 1913 when the U.S. Public Health Service identified sewage as a major factor in these deaths. Typhoid is spread through contaminated sewage and wastewater. But not much happened to reduce water pollution for many decades. It was not until the 1960s that construction even began for primary sewage treatment.

Pollution of the Missouri River got worse before it got better. Fish started to taste bad, and PCB levels were identified in 1969 as posing a potential health threat. In 1970, one-quarter of the fish sampled from a bay in the reservoir behind Oahe Dam, one of the great dams on the Missouri River, were found to contain unsafe levels of mercury from a mine on a tributary stream. In the early 1970s, PCBs and the pesticides Aldrin and Dieldrin in fish reached concentrations that were determined to pose potential health threats. Then in 1972 the Federal Water Pollution Control Act was passed, establishing national standards for wastewater effluents. This was followed by the construction of secondary treatment plants. But Aldrin and Dieldrin, from non-point-source runoff from farmlands, continued to increase in fish, exceeding safe limits on the Missouri River by 1976.

In 1989 more stringent limitations were imposed on discharges of toxic wastes from the major cities on the lower Missouri, including Kansas City. In the 1940s, a downtown Sioux City hotel, *the* meeting place for visitors to the city, had a large restroom open to the public. It contained this sign: "Please flush the toilets, Omaha needs the water." Water quality has improved much since then.

The United States numbered about five million people at the time of Lewis and Clark, with a density of just over five people per square mile—a density we call rural today. By 2004, the bicentennial of the Lewis and Clark expedition, the United States will number almost 300 million, with a density of more than seventy people per square mile. Most of those people will live in metropolitan regions.

Although it is common today to believe that cities will disappear or become unimportant in the future—as our computerized society moves to the suburbs and rural lands, and we all telecommute—this is not the actual trend either in the United States or elsewhere around the world. Urbanization continues with a relentless momentum. Those with the right kind of training can live where they want, but most people will continue to go to a regular workplace, and these will continue to be in cities.

The future of our environment lies as much in the way we treat our cities as it does in the way we treat our wildernesses—perhaps even more so. The more pleasant our cities are to live in, the more people will want to live there; the more people want to live in cities, the less the human pressure will be on outlying areas for development and the more likely we will be to share the landscape with other creatures. Wilderness, wildlife, prairies, and forests will benefit if our cities prosper. So will we.

8. Weston, Missouri: Where the River Meandered Away, Leaving the Town Without a Waterfront

Weston is north of Kansas City, Missouri, and south of Atchison, Kansas. From the west side of Kansas City take Interstate 435 north to exit 22 to Route 45 north. Follow Route 45 north, and just north of Waldron turn left on County Route P, which takes you into the town. Alternatively, from the east side of Kansas City take Interstate 435 west to Interstate 29 north. North of Platte City take Route 71 southwest to Route 273 west. Route 273 takes you to Route 45, which you take north and follow the directions above to County Route P.

> [The Missouri River is] eating all the time—eating yellow clay banks and cornfields, eighty acres at a mouthful.
>
> —S. VESTAL, *THE MISSOURI*, 1945

As the expedition moved up the Missouri River past the mouth of the Kansas River—the present-day location of Kansas City—Lewis and Clark and the men accompanying them found many beautiful areas along the shore and suggested some as fine locations for settlements or forts. On July 2, 1804, George Drewyer, one of the major hunters for the expedition, told Clark that the lands he passed through that day and the day before on the south side were "generally Verry fine." On July 2, 1804, the expedition camped opposite an old Kansas Indian village where there was a large island in the river and "extensive" prairie beyond it. The island, Clark wrote, appeared to have "thrown the Current of the river against the place the Village formerly Stood" so that the current washed away the bank, forming an arc or natural harbor. "The Situation appears to be a verry elligable one for a Town, the valley rich & extensive, with a Small Brook Meanding through it and one part of the bank affording yet a good Landing for Boats," Clark commented. He also noted that the French had once located a fort there.

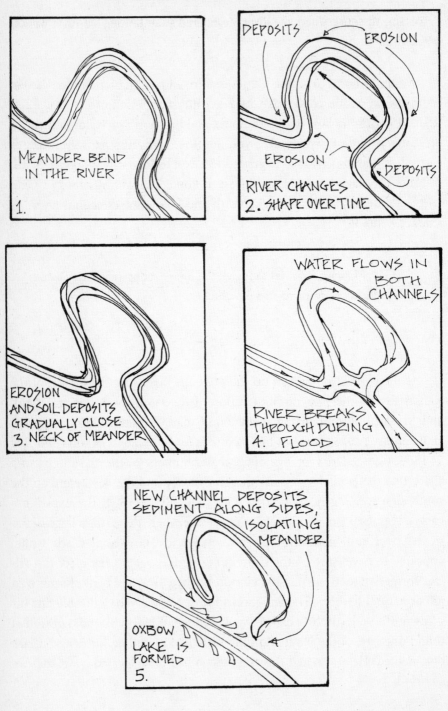

1. MEANDER BEND IN THE RIVER

2. RIVER CHANGES SHAPE OVER TIME — DEPOSITS, EROSION, EROSION, DEPOSITS

3. EROSION AND SOIL DEPOSITS GRADUALLY CLOSE NECK OF MEANDER

4. RIVER BREAKS THROUGH DURING FLOOD — WATER FLOWS IN BOTH CHANNELS

5. NEW CHANNEL DEPOSITS SEDIMENT ALONG SIDES, ISOLATING MEANDER — OXBOW LAKE IS FORMED

In 1837, Weston was established at this location as predicted by Clark. Soldiers from nearby Fort Leavenworth saw the potential of the location, bought the land, and began to develop it. Weston's natural bay made a good port for boats to tie up, and there was good land nearby for farming and good upland locations—dry and well-drained for basements but with good water supply—for houses. The soldiers established a dock and a main street that led from the dock away from the river. Settlers moved in quickly and set up a variety of shops and activities. The countryside was rich for farming. Tobacco farms were established and their products shipped downstream on boats that tied up at Weston's harbor.

A severe flood in 1844 damaged farmlands near Weston, and this was followed by outbreaks of diseases carried by water, such as typhoid. But the town continued to increase: By 1850 there were five thousand residents. But in 1881 a bad flood occurred, and the Missouri cut a new main channel two and a half miles to the southwest of Weston. In this one event, the river meandered away from the town, leaving Weston high and dry, no longer with a harbor at the foot of Main Street.

This event was natural for the river. It is natural for any river in a valley wide enough to allow meanderings, but the Missouri is especially famous for such meanderings. "Some people would think it was just a plain river running along in its bed at the same speed; but it ain't," a river man who raced boats on the Missouri River said a century after Lewis and Clark had traveled up it. "The river runs crooked through the valley; and just the same way the channel runs crooked through the river. . . . The crookedness you can see ain't half the crookedness there is." The Missouri became known as the hungriest river ever created, "eating all the time— eating yellow clay banks and cornfields, eighty acres at a mouthful" (Vestal 1945).

A river on a wide and generally smooth floodplain does not flow in a straight line—or if it does, it does not maintain that straight line for long, especially if it is carrying a heavy load of sediment. Meanders are a natural form of a river, in part because the meander form keeps an even slope as the water flows downhill, minimizing the energy used by the river. In addition, even in a straight path, eventually some chance occurrences cause a difference in where material is deposited and other material is eroded—a log catches on the bottom, a pebble is pushed into the riverbed by the whirling water and catches hold. If the riverbed and its borders had been smooth, they were no longer. Because flowing water takes the path of least resistance, it begins to assume a sinuous shape around small obstacles, and the river begins to form a meander, creating shapes something like the reaction of spring steel that has been pulled straight and then released.

Although scientists can be sure that a river like the Missouri will meander, the exact location of any meander is influenced by chance events and cannot be predicted with complete accuracy. That is to say, the river wanders. It is also to say that the river is neither completely chaotic nor completely fixed.

Geologists who study rivers and how they affect the land tell us that over time, the arc of a meander becomes sharper and sharper, so that the river forms a shape like the wishbone of a chicken or a sharply curving bow, usually called an oxbow. Always seeking the path of least resistance, the flowing water will cut across the bottom of the bow when conditions allow.

This hydrologically natural event was a disaster for Weston. The fickleness of the Missouri led to a decline and almost an end to the town. For years, Weston was a tiny village where little happened.

In the 1960s there was renewed interest in Weston because of its historic buildings. The town began to redevelop as a tourist attraction and as a bedroom community for Kansas City, a short commute by today's standards. In 1998 the population had risen to fifteen hundred. Weston is nestled among the bluffs west of the Missouri River, a picturesque location. We spent a pleasant night there in a bed-and-breakfast and thought that it was one of the prettier places for a traveler to stay along the Missouri River. Like many other visitors, we walked down Main Street, only a few blocks long from where it begins in the hills to where it used to end at a dock on the Missouri River. Across the railroad tracks at the bottom of the street, we could see the broad flat lands where the main channel of the Missouri River once flowed, now good bottomland agriculture.

Bruges, Belgium, has a history similar to Weston, Missouri's—it is also a town separated from water transportation. Bruges, however, suffered from a change in its location relative to the sea. Once a port city, Bruges had canals like those in Venice and was an active transportation center. But over the centuries the land slowly rose and the Atlantic Ocean was forced away from the city. Bruges ceased to be a major port. But, like Weston, Missouri, because of this abandonment by water, Bruges became a settlement where old buildings were not replaced over the years as rapidly as elsewhere. Today these settlements make for modern tourist attractions.

Most major cities of the world are located on rivers—at crucial locations on those rivers—or on the ocean. The quality of life in those cities is strongly affected by the quality of the waterfront and the way that the city is connected to the waterfront. When the riverfront is a park and connected to the city, the city often flourishes. But rivers have traditionally been used as an easy way to rid a settlement of its wastes. The old stories are that a river will clean itself in one mile, or two miles, or four miles, meaning that you could dump whatever you liked into the river and it would remove it for you locally and transform it into something harmless for the next town downstream.

When populations were low and towns scattered widely, and when technology consisted of materials made of wood and stone, and wastes were natural organic ones, perhaps this belief could survive. But with an increase in the density of human habitation and with the rise of the technologies of steel, aluminum, chrome, lead, and other heavy metals, and a technology of thousands of artificial chemicals including long-lived plastics, this old tale has lost all of its credence. But practices deep within cultures disappear slowly, and it is common that we continue to use our rivers as dumps and to ignore them as important to life in a city or town.

Weston's fate illustrates the variableness and changeableness of the river, and the importance of such changes to the fate of human settlement. It has survived because its residents have understood the beauty of historic buildings in a lovely setting. The river wandered but the town remains. When you visit Weston, walk down to the bottom of Main Street and consider what might be done elsewhere to improve the fate of our towns and cities, to make them more vibrant and livable.

9. Benedictine Bottoms: Pollution As a Problem of Landscape Design

Benedictine Bottoms is best observed from the campus of Benedictine College. Route 59 is the main highway to Atchison, Kansas, passing through the city from east to west. To reach the college campus, take Sixth Street north from Route 59, then turn right (east) onto Commercial Street and follow that to Second Street. Take Second Street north (left) up the bluff to the campus. Drive through the campus to a lookout from the bluff over Independence Creek, Benedictine Bottoms, and the Missouri River. To go to Independence Park, take Commercial Street past Second Street to River Street. Turn left (north) to the park.

On July 4, 1804, the expedition reached a tributary that entered the Missouri at the location of modern Atchison, Kansas. Here they camped in what Clark wrote was "one of the most butifull Plains, I ever Saw, open & butifully diversified with hills & vallies all presenting themselves to the river covered with grass and a few scattering trees." The Creek was "handsom" and "The Plains of this countrey are covered with a Leek Green Grass, well calculated for the sweetest and most norushing hay," suggesting that Clark was thinking of uses to which the land might be put. Here, there seemed a wonderful potential for farming. The land was already producing much to eat. "Groops of Shrubs covered with the most delicious froot is to be seen in every direction, and nature appears to have exerted herself to butify the Senery by the variety of flous Delicately and highly flavered raised above the Grass, which Strikes & profumes the Sensation, and amuses the mind." The grassland was "interspersed with Cops of trees," and the trees spread "ther lofty branchs over Pools springs or Brooks of fine water."

The country was so beautiful that Clark wrote that it "throws into Conjecterng the cause of So magnificent a Senergy in a Country thus Situated far removed from the Sivilized world to be enjoyed by nothing but the Buffalo Elk Deer & Bear in which it abounds." It was one of the few times that Clark departed from his usually direct reporting style and list of measurements and waxed philosophical.

Since it was Independence Day, Lewis and Clark "ussered in the day by a discharge of one shot from our Bow piece," the cannon, and named the tributary Independence Creek, a name that it still carries.

Today Atchison, Kansas, is heavily developed and the surrounding countryside has been primarily in farmland for a long time. We visited Atchison with Glenn Covington, environmental research specialist with the U.S. Army Corps of Engineers office in Kansas City. Trained in biology, Glenn is in charge of Benedictine Bottoms, one of the Missouri River mitigation projects, across Independence Creek from Atchison. At the mouth of Independence Creek is a narrow but pleasant park and boat ramp. The tributary, like many along the lower Missouri, has been channelized and levees have been built along its edges to protect farmland that developed in the bountiful landscape so appreciated by Clark. Glenn said that the mouth had been straightened so that the creek no longer entered the Missouri River exactly where Lewis and Clark saw it do so.

On July 4, 1804, Lewis walked up a "high mound" from the top of which he had an "extensive view." After viewing the park, we did the same, and traveled up the bluffs on city streets to the campus of Benedictine College. Along the edge of the bluff of this pleasant campus, probably the same summit where Lewis stood, we sat on a park bench and we looked out to Independence Creek and Benedictine Bottoms and the Missouri River beyond. Benedictine Bottoms consists of a large section still in row-crop agriculture on the bottomland that Clark so admired as a site for farming, and another that is in an early stage of restoration to wildlife habitat. The view from the college is a good place to compare the two uses of the land.

Since the time of Lewis and Clark, the Missouri River basin has become one of the nation's major agricultural areas; about 95 percent of the basin's use is for agriculture. The emphasis on the lower Missouri downstream from Gavins Point Dam is on row crops; west and upstream, past the hundredth meridian, the predominant farming shifts to grazing. This large-scale agriculture has been a great benefit to the United States, but it also has brought changes of an invisible kind not imaginable to Lewis and Clark or their contemporaries: the introduction of artificial chemicals used as pesticides and the increase in levels of nitrate and phosphate from widespread application of fertilizers.

Before the channelization of the Missouri River, measurements of water quality were few and scattered, but provide some baseline measurements. These suggest that by 1984 nitrate and phosphate concentrations in the Missouri River waters below the big dams had increased to four times the baseline level. Meanwhile, upstream in the reservoirs, nitrate and phosphate seemed to have decreased.

This downside of agriculture became apparent in 1964, when a fish kill extended more than one hundred miles downstream from Kansas City, Missouri. Monitoring of pesticides remained spotty, but between 1968 and 1976 fish flesh at Council Bluffs, Iowa, had concentrations of the pesticide Dieldrin that exceeded public health standards in 13 percent of the samples, and DDT and its breakdown products exceeded public health standards in one-third of the samples. In the early 1970s, the levels of PCBs, Aldrin, and Dieldrin in fish analyzed at Hermann, Missouri, posed a potential health threat. In the mid-1970s Dieldrin levels were high enough in catfish that the Missouri Department of Conservation issued warnings. People stopped buying catfish, affecting commercial fisheries.

Pesticides were arriving in the river not just from agriculture but from urban, suburban, and industrial use. By 1984, chlordane, commonly used at the time against household pests such as termites, exceeded established safe levels in fish in the lower Missouri. In 1987 the Missouri Department of Health advised against consumption of specific commercial fish species from certain areas of the Missouri River because of contamination with toxic compounds.

When I returned from this trip I began to look into more recent information about the levels of pesticides and fertilizers in the Missouri River. About 700 million pounds of pesticides of more than one hundred compounds are applied nationwide, and herbicides account for about 60 percent of the total pesticides found in the nation's waters. Public health standards and environmental effects standards have been established for some but not all of these compounds. I searched the scientific literature, the World Wide Web, and called many of my scientific colleagues who study rivers or organic chemicals, and scientists I had met while exploring the Missouri River countryside. Surely, I thought, people have done experiments to determine what happens to pesticides put onto row crops—how fast they decay, how fast they are transported to the river by water flowing on and below the surface. Surely they have done experiments to determine what scientists call the "dose-response curve"—the curve showing effects on a species as the concentration of a toxin increases. But I could not find such studies for actual locations in the Missouri River valley or for fish and wildlife species found there. All my colleagues agreed that the necessary research to determine the effects of these chemicals on fish and wildlife in the Missouri River had not been done.

Some studies are being done. Monitoring for the levels of these chemicals in the waters has increased greatly. The U.S. Geological Survey has established a network for monitoring sixty sample watersheds throughout the nation. One of these is for the Platte River, one of the major tributaries of the Missouri River. The most common herbicides used for growing corn, sorghum, and soybeans along the Platte River are alachlor, atrazine, cyanazine, and metolachlor, all organonitrogen herbicides. Monitoring on the Platte near Lincoln, Nebraska, suggests that during heavy spring runoff, concentrations of some herbicides might be reaching or exceeding established public health standards. But this research is just beginning, and it is difficult to make definitive conclusions about whether present concentrations are causing harm in public water supplies or to wildlife, fish, algae in fresh waters, or vegetation. The advances in knowledge tell us much more and on a more regular basis about how much of many artificial compounds are in the waters, but we are still unclear about their environmental effects.

My search for adequate information was frustrating. Here was a potentially major national problem receiving relatively little attention; most of the focus on pollution has been on urban, industrial, and feedlot contributions, much less on pollution from row-crop agriculture. We are conducting experiments with nature without the usual qualities of the scientific method: treatments and controls, adequate monitoring, and adequate long-term experimentation in laboratories.

The view from the bluff at Atchison was a mixed one. It was not my purpose in traveling the Lewis and Clark country to simply add another lament for the loss of the beauty of the past countryside; many have done that well before me. Here I was seeking to understand *how* we go wrong, not merely that we may or may not have gone wrong. The scene below us was a combination of farm-

BEAVER

lands, wetlands, streams, rivers, and heavy land development. It was no longer a scene to rhapsodize about, the way Clark did in 1804. It was not that the land had been converted to uses with human benefits that was the problem for me. It was that these changes seemed to have been done in large part without the kind of care for design and beauty that should have been taken in the garden-like surroundings that Clark had found. So it seemed with the invisible effects our activities were having on the river. It was not so much a matter of absolute rights or wrongs, of winner and loser, but of an overall perspective. What was needed was a connection between people and their natural resources, one that would lead us to be careful in causing novel changes in nature, to follow the best scientific procedure to assess their effects before putting them into use.

10. Atchison, Kansas: Commerce in Beaver

See the previous entry for directions to Independence Park.

Beaver were an important part of North American fur trade long before the Lewis and Clark expedition. Jefferson had a scientific curiosity about wildlife, plants, and geology, but he was also interested in the commercial potentials of natural resources. Two questions Lewis and Clark sought to answer were whether beaver were abundant along their route and, if so, whether the United States might begin to take over from Great Britain some of the beaver trade with the Indians.

In spite of their interest in this species, Lewis and Clark did not record any observations of beaver until July 3, 1804, when they reached the neighborhood of Leavenworth and Atchison, Kansas. On that day Clark recorded that they stopped at a deserted old trading house where they "found a verry fat horse, which appears to have been lost a long time," and passed a large island called *Isle <la> de Vache*, or *Cow Island*. On the shore was "a large Pond containg beever." The presence of the trading house marking the first observation of beaver suggests that Lewis and Clark were still within countryside known and used to some extent by trappers, who had exploited and pretty much eliminated beaver downstream. Beaver, like other wild living resources, were generally perceived at the time as things to be exploited but not conserved, harvested but not sustained, and beaver were disappearing before the inroads of European-based settlement.

Lewis and Clark saw beaver next near Council Bluffs, just north of modern Omaha. Afterward, they saw these animals frequently. They caught a few in the fall when they had reached the Mandan villages where they would spend the winter. The next spring, beaver were common among the cottonwoods and willows of the floodplain woodlands. Lewis and Clark's observations are so good that they tell us that beaver were once plentiful on streams that, as one writer put it, "have not know(n) them for so many years that it is hard to believe they were ever present."

Today much of the habitat along the Missouri that beaver might have used is gone—the backwaters and the bottomland forests. Even many of the tributaries have been channelized and have levees along them. When beaver do return, they are considered pests whose dams flood land that people want for other uses. So to see beaver on a Lewis and Clark journey, you will have to travel farther upstream to less intensively developed areas. We saw a beaver house and a large cottonwood partially chewed through by beaver on our Zodiac boat trip from Niobrara State Park; both were on a large island in the Missouri River just upstream from the mouth of the Niobrara River. We saw other signs of beaver in the wild and scenic–designated portion of the Missouri River near Vermillion,

South Dakota. Such are the places, away from human settlement, where a traveler in 1804 and today would be likely to see these once common animals.

11. Hamburg Bend: The River Farms the Prairie and the Prairie Feeds the Fish

There are many habitat restoration projects on the Missouri River floodplain—some in operation, some in progress, and others planned. Most are set up primarily as fish and wildlife habitat improvements and are not usually provided with tourist facilities or easy access. Hamburg Bend is on the west (Nebraska) bank of the Missouri River six miles south of Nebraska City. You can approach Hamburg Bend on the Nebraska side by taking County Route 66 from Nebraska City south and then heading east on County Route N. Hamburg Bend is directly east of the small village of Minersville.

You could instead go south from Nebraska City to the intersection of Highways 2 and 75. Follow 75 south one mile and drive east (left) on paved County Road K (marked by an Omaha Public Power District sign) four miles. Before entering the power plant, drive south (right) on the gravel county road one-half mile, then drive east (left) one mile on a gravel road until you reach the parking lot adjacent to the levee. You can walk along the levee above the bend by taking County Route N east to its end and parking.

To see Hamburg Bend from the Iowa side, or to put a boat in, take Interstate 29 to the exit for the town of Hamburg, Route 333, and County Route J-64. Take J-64 west (it's a gravel road) to the river's edge and a parking area. Hamburg Bend is across the river.

The easiest of the restoration areas to visit is Boyer Chute, which has visitor facilities. Boyer Chute is north of Omaha and east of Fort Calhoun, Nebraska. Take Route 75 north from Omaha. About one mile north of Nashville turn right (east) onto County Route P338, then left (north) on County Route P236, left (north) again on County Route 151, and right (east) on County Route 234. Follow this route to the visitor facilities.

You could instead take Route 75 north from Omaha to the southern edge of the city of Fort Calhoun. Drive east on Madison Street until you reach Fort Atkinson Historical Park and go south (right). On Seventh Street go east (left) for three miles and you will reach the Boyer Chute entrance.

On Tuesday, July 24, 1804, Clark wrote that "one of the men cought a *white Catfish*, the eyes Small & Tale reseumbing that of a Dolfin." This was probably the channel catfish, and Clark's observations provided the first written description of the species—a new species to western science. The expedition was camped on the eastern, Iowa side of the river across from Bellevue, Nebraska—a suburb of Omaha and the location of Fontenelle Forest Preserve. "Cat fish is verry Common and easy taken in any part of this river," the journals noted at the end of July 1804.

Fish and fishing were not a major focus of the expedition. Lewis and Clark's eyes were on the lands along the river—their wildlife, vegetation, and potential for settlement and development, and they were on the surface of the river whose treacherousness demanded constant alertness. Most of the expedition's protein came from four-footed game, especially buffalo, deer, elk, and antelope. The murky waters of the Missouri made it less likely that they would see fish unless they tried to catch some, and not too many of the men seemed to be fishing enthusiasts. This is not inconsistent with the economics of development since their time. Fish can be an important source of protein, but usually, around the world, fishing is a minor part of the economy.

With settlement along the river, catfish became a highly desired catch. They were an important food for those going west on the Sante Fe, Oregon, and Mormon Trails and they were important to the early homesteaders. In the twentieth century, catfish were the focus of commercial fishery on the Missouri River and continued to be a prized recreational catch.

But like fisheries around the world, commercial fish catch on the Missouri declined in the twentieth century. Commercial catch of catfish declined steadily after the Second World War, decreasing by 61 percent between the 1940s and 1983. Also, the average size of catfish decreased, meaning there were fewer mature adults. Channel catfish can grow to four feet and sixty pounds, and blue catfish can grow to one hundred pounds, but by the 1980s channel catfish caught in the Missouri were less than seventeen inches long and most were smaller.

In 1992 the Nebraska Department of Game and Parks closed all commercial harvest of catfish. In part this decision was to help support recreational fishing, which ranked as the major public activity on the river.

Although in Lewis and Clark's time there were many fish in the main channel of the Missouri, these depended on quieter backwaters and on the small tributaries for many parts of their life cycle. In those quiet waters it was also sometimes much easier to catch fish, as the expedition discovered. On August 15, 1804, Clark took ten men to a creek along the Missouri River where they found a beaver dam and started to fish. "With Some Small willow & Bark we made a Drag and haulted up the Creek," Clark wrote, "and Cought 318 fish of different kind." He listed pike, bass, perch, catfish, something he called "salmon" but was probably a brook trout, since there are no native salmon on the Missouri, "red horse," and "a kind perch Called Silverfish on the Ohio."

On July 29, 1804, when they were north of Omaha, Clark wrote that "we Stoped to Dine under Some high Trees near the high land" and "in a fiew minits Cought three verry large *Catfish* (3) one nearly white." He noted that "those fish are in great plenty on the Sides of the river and verry fat, a quart of Oile Came out of the Surpolous fat of one."

The channelization and conversion of much of the floodplain from woodlands and wetlands to farming since that time has reduced the area in the backwaters and the diversity of floodplain habitats. Along with overfishing, these habitat alterations caused the decline in many species of fish. Today more than ninety species are found on the lower Missouri, including some introduced species that were not there at the time of Lewis and Clark. Of these, the pallid sturgeon is listed as endangered under the U.S. Endangered Species Act and other species are listed as of special concern to the U.S. Fish and Wildlife Service because of their low abundance.

In recent years, work has begun on an extensive project to restore the Missouri River's habitats for fish and wildlife. Some of these are in the planning stage, others in development. One of the currently active and most successful is the Hamburg Bend Wildlife Management Area of the Nebraska Department of Game and Parks. I went to Hamburg Bend to learn about the habitat of the fish and see an active restoration project. The area occupies 1,637 acres of prime hunting and fishing land and waters. It is the first of six such areas planned in Nebraska and one of twenty-five or thirty planned between Sioux City and St. Louis, being undertaken by the U.S. Army Corps

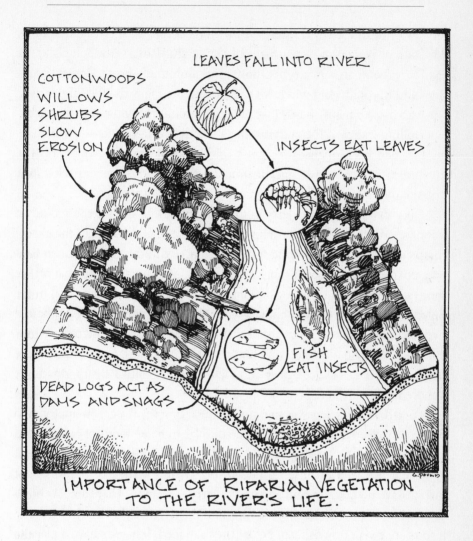

COTTONWOODS
WILLOWS
SHRUBS
SLOW
EROSION

LEAVES FALL INTO RIVER

INSECTS EAT LEAVES

FISH EAT INSECTS

DEAD LOGS ACT AS DAMS AND SNAGS

IMPORTANCE OF RIPARIAN VEGETATION TO THE RIVER'S LIFE.

of Engineers in cooperation with state and other federal agencies (as first described in the entry on the Big Muddy National Wildlife Refuge).

Mark Brohman, an environmental scientist and lawyer with the State of Nebraska Department of Game and Parks, took me to see a number of these mitigation sites. We viewed Hamburg Bend from the levee on the Nebraska side of the river, where I could see down to the almost hemispheric shape of the bend's floodplain lands. Then we went to a boat launching area on the Iowa side of the river, where we met Jerry Mestl, a fisheries biologist for the State of Nebraska Department of Game and Parks. He took us to see Hamburg Bend in a wide, flat-bottomed aluminum boat. Under cloudy skies and in a stiff, cold wind, we sped across the main channel of the river. Once across the main channel we slowed, carefully moving over the turbulent, rolling waters at the entrance of a recently created chute—a side channel that had been opened up across the floodplain by the Army Corps of Engineers. The chute was meant to maintain a steady but controlled flow into the floodplain and reestablish some quiet backwaters.

Once inside the chute, Jerry put the engine at idle and we coasted down this new side channel. The current was so gentle that he soon cut the engine completely. The boat moved at a pleasant pace with the current, often rubbing up against the eastern shore of the chute. Mark pushed the boat off the shore as we chatted. Large logs were scattered all along the chute and in the water. The recently created chute was beginning to mimic some of the old river channel structures. Jerry said that the river used to be incredibly productive of fish. An old-timer told him recently that before channelization the reach of the river between Blair and Plattsmouth, Nebraska, supported one hundred commercial fishermen.

I asked what the key was to restoring the fish in the river. This appeared to be a complicated task because there used to be so many kinds of habitats and kinds of vegetation. But Jerry said that the key was surprisingly straightforward.

Many fish feed on insects, but in the swirling waters of the Missouri, insects have no place to gain a foothold, Jerry explained. There are few boulders or places where bedrock outcrops into the riverbed. Without a foothold, insects are swept downstream before they can feed. If insects have a place to stand and feed, they can become food for fish. In this constantly changing environment, snags—logs that are caught in the bottom, hung up on a sandbar, or tangled in a group—provide the main stable surface in the river. They provide a place for insects to stand, and they catch prairie grasses that fall into the river—becoming food for insects.

Snags have been notoriously dangerous to navigation—the killers of steamboats since they first ran on the Missouri River, and destroyers of motorboats in the twentieth century. Lewis and Clark were well aware of them as

Snags—dead trees that lie in the river—are a key to a healthy habitat for the fish of the Missouri River (based on a watercolor by Karl Bodmer).

a danger that they encountered frequently. On July 5, 1804, when they were near Atchison, Kansas, Clark wrote that "the Boat turned three times" on some driftwood.

And so there was an early movement to clear the river of these hazards. Congress first authorized the removal of snags from the Missouri River with an act passed in 1832. By 1838, more than 2,000 large trees had been removed from the channel along the lower 400 miles of the river. Between 1885 and 1910, these activities increased. In 1901, along 528 miles of the river, more than 17,000 snags were removed, along with more than 6,000 trees whose limbs hung over the river. Snag removal was completed about 1950. As a result, insects became less abundant. In one part of the unchannelized section of the river in Nebraska, from Gavins Point Dam to Ponca State Park, the annual production of river insects declined between 1963 and 1993 to one-quarter of its former value.

The snags that kill boats are the saviors of the fish. But the snags need not be in the main navigation channel. Even confined to side channels and backwaters, they still provide the necessary habitat for insects that the fish depend on. In this way, two uses of the river—navigation and fisheries—can coexist.

A wonderful thing about the Missouri River is the resiliency of its life, because, when the habitats are available, the river provides plenty of water and nutrients. We can think of it as a kind of natural aquaculture. Create a few, limited kinds of backwater channels on the river and fish production goes up. The river is so fertile, the soil so rich and well watered, that not much else is needed.

WHITE CATFISH

In this way, the river farms the land. It deposits fresh soil in some places, and there trees or prairie grow. Elsewhere, the river undercuts and harvests. The prairie feeds the river, but the river harvests the prairie, it harvests the floodplain forests.

12. Shilling Wildlife Area: How the Platte Changes the Missouri

Shilling Wildlife Area is on the Platte River within view of the confluence with the Missouri. To reach this wildlife area from Omaha, take Route 75 south to Route 34. Follow the business loop of 34 through the town of Plattsmouth and then follow signs to the Shilling Wildlife Area. From there you can go to the Plattsmouth boat ramp from another perspective. Exiting the Shilling Wildlife Area, follow the road left (east) to that ramp.

From Iowa take the exit on Interstate 29 to Route 34. Cross the Missouri River and follow the Route 34 business loop north through Plattsmouth. On the main street you will pass the county courthouse and a sign that says "Historic Plattsmouth Welcomes You." Follow signs to the Shilling Wildlife Area.

On July 21, 1804, Lewis and Clark had reached the mouth of the Platte River, at the time a well-known tributary of the Missouri. It was a big river, one of the largest of the Missouri's tributaries, and it was fast and full of large, sandy sediment. The sand was "remarkably small and light" and "easily boiled up and is hurried by this impetuous torrent in large masses from place to place with irristable forse." If Lewis needed any more evidence that rivers, as with all of nature, are in constant flux, he found it in the Platte, even more turbulent than the Missouri. The sands were collecting and forming sandbars in the course of a few hours, which "as suddingly disapated to form others and give place perhaps to the deepest channel of the river."

The Platte flowed, Lewis wrote, with "a boiling motion," which he speculated was the result of "the roling and irregular motion of the sand of which its bed is entirely composed"—a good insight. The bottom of the Platte, like the Missouri, is formed of its own sediment rather than bedrock or large boulders. These bottom sediments are moved along by the water in much the same way that wind drives sand. Sediment dunes form just as sand dunes form by the wind. These little hillocks force the water up and over, creating turbulence. The resulting motion flows downstream and upward, reaching the surface as large bubbling bursts that look just like boiling water in a kettle. You can see this motion in the Missouri River when you stand along the shore.

Lewis and Clark measured the speed of the rivers and found the Platte the fastest, running "at least" eight miles an hour. The Missouri above the Platte was running about three and a half miles an hour in its widely dispersed, complex floodplain of many channels. Below the Platte and influenced by that river, the Missouri was running five and a half miles an hour. The faster a river flows, the heavier and coarser the material it can carry, so the Platte could carry a sandy load, while upstream the Missouri could lift only smaller silts. Also the two rivers drained different kinds of countryside. The Platte watershed is mostly sandy soils long ago eroded from the Rocky Mountains and deposited in western Nebraska, only to be picked up again and transported by the Platte. The Missouri drains a landscape where the ice-age glaciers created soils of many sizes of particles, including small silts and clays.

At the mouth of the Platte the two kinds of sediment loads came together but did not yet mix. The Platte was so swift and powerful that its current, having entered the Missouri River channel, forced the Missouri's waters against the far bank "where it is compressed within a channel less than one third of the width it had just before occupied," Lewis wrote. The currents could be distinguished by their colors. The Platte did "not furnish the missouri with it's colouring matter as has been asserted by some, but it throws into it immence quantities of sand." Lewis claimed that the separation of the currents "abates but little until it's junction with the Mississippy."

Both rivers were so full of sediment that neither was clear, but there was a difference. The Platte deposited "very fine particles of white sand while that of the Missoury is composed principally of a dark rich loam—in much greater quantity." The Platte's waters were "turbid at all seasons of the year but is by no means as much so as that of the Missourie." These two painters of landscape had different palates and different styles of painting.

The Platte has a great effect on the Missouri in other ways than shoving its current to one side of the channel. Above the Platte and below Gavins Point Dam—the farthest downstream of the dams on the Missouri—the channel is eroding and deepening—but this erosion is only in the main river channel, not in the surrounding floodplain. The river is incising itself into the engineered floodplain.

Below the mouth of the Platte, the river is depositing material on the bottomlands. The floodplain is accumulating material, while the main channel, functioning as designed by the Army Corps of Engineers, is not changing its depth; it is neither eroding nor sedimenting.

The accumulating material on the Missouri River floodplain below the Platte has an important effect on floods. This accretion is raising the level of the floodplain relative to the artificial levees, shrinking the height of the levees relative to the floodplain. The total volume of water that can be held back by the levees is therefore less. It is like a stream carrying sand and silt into a swimming pool and depositing those sediments in the quiet waters. Over time the sediments build up on the bottom and the pool can hold less water. This was a factor that made the large floods of the 1990s so catastrophic. In 1998, the Army Corps of Engineers reduced the flow from Gavins Point Dam, claiming bottom aggradation below Omaha was causing lowland flooding.

The aggrading land below the Platte has a biological effect as well. As the floodplain builds up, its soils become drier; there are fewer wetlands but the soil becomes better for farming, at least where the deposits are not heavy sands. Overall the floodplain habitats become fewer and simpler.

The Missouri is a complex system; fingers of tributaries feed waters of different colors, qualities, speeds, and amounts into the main channel. In this sense, the Missouri is many rivers, not one. What happens on the tributaries affects the Missouri, and many of these have been channeled and controlled to prevent flooding. Water from channelized tributaries flows faster and adds more quickly to the floodwaters of a rising and dangerous Missouri. The quality of the water from tributaries affects the Missouri, as does the chemical runoff from farms, industries, and houses. Remember, the Missouri drains one-sixth of the continental United States; that land affects the quality of the Missouri's waters.

Mark Brohman and I drove to the Shilling Wildlife Area at the mouth of the Platte. Mark is the environmental scientist and lawyer with the State of Nebraska Department of Game and Parks who had taken me to Hamburg Bend as well. Here, we watched people fish and tow their boats out of the Missouri as dusk fell. The tumbling, mixing currents of the Platte and the Missouri still rushed together, still boiled, and still were able to evoke in us the feel of prairie and river countryside, and remind us of the importance of the intimate linkages between rivers and their landscape and the constancy of change in nature.

13. Along the Platte River: The Great Prairie River—Once the Route West, Now Isolated from People

You can view the Platte at its mouth, as described in the Shilling Wildlife Area entry. But the Platte is an interesting river to follow. Many roads cross the Platte through central Nebraska and it is often easy to find a place along one of these to stop and see the river. Some Nebraska state parks are on the Platte, but few have direct access to the river. As practices change for the Nebraska state parks, it is advisable to contact the state offices for updates on access to the river, which will most likely increase in the next few years. Grand Island is a major town and travel stop on Interstate 80, particularly because it is a major stopping location for migrating birds. Mormon Island State Recreation Area is just off the interstate. Audubon and other organizations have tours during the sandhill crane migration seasons.

On July 21, 1804, after they viewed the mouth of the Platte River and measured the flows of the Platte and the Missouri, Lewis and Clark traveled a ways up the Platte and found it shallow—not more than six or seven feet deep anywhere. One of the men of the expedition had spent two winters along the Platte and told Clark that the Platte "does not rise seven feet, but Spreds over 3 miles at Some places." Later pioneers would say the Platte was "a mile wide and an inch deep."

And the pioneers followed the Platte. Although Lewis and Clark—as well as Jefferson—hoped and assumed that the Missouri was the best way west, expecting there to be an easy portage between its headwaters and the Columbia River, in fact the better route was along the Platte. Ironically, if the Lewis and Clark expedition had headed west at this location, they would have had an easier trip to the Pacific coast. The Platte became the river of the Oregon, Missouri, and Mormon Trails.

Today the Platte is worth seeing as part of a Lewis and Clark rediscovery trip because it is one of the few major rivers of America that has not been greatly altered by channelization and dams. Although the North Platte is dammed, it is one of the least altered of the major tributaries.

If you want to see a river that resembles the original lower Missouri before its channelization and before its levees, then one of the best things you can do is travel along the Platte. And the Platte River's Big Bend in the center of Nebraska is one of the most important habitats for migratory birds. More than 240 species have been seen there, including sandhill cranes, whooping cranes, piping plovers, and the least tern, species listed as endangered or of special concern.

The Platte is one of my favorite rivers—an odd, shallow, sometimes dried-out-looking waif of a river, meandering along a wide and sandy floodplain where scattered and usually half-starved-looking cottonwoods struggle to survive on its banks and sandbars or, having lost the battle, lie as snags in its shallow current. Between towns, the Platte and its countryside have a lonesome, open feel that is for me the character of the American West—open country, open sky, dry land.

It was the shallowness of the Platte that probably saved it from channelization and dams. "An inch deep"—or the real average depth of the Platte—isn't enough for a steamboat. The Platte became the way west for those in Conestoga wagons, on horseback, or on foot, guiding the way and giving enough water to drink but never enough for navigation.

This is not to say that the Platte is without alteration. Its waters were first diverted in 1838, and by 1885 the demand for Platte water for irrigation exceeded the average flow. There are thousands of diversion structures and nearly 70 percent of the flow is used; what you see along the Platte is a river much closer to being an inch deep than it was at the time of Lewis and Clark. Present flows on the Platte are about one million acre-feet a year, 4 percent of the water that flows down the Missouri River. As a result of water diversions, the proportion of open areas, wetlands, and forested floodplains have changed, leading to concern about whether enough bird habitat remains.

Over the years, I have liked to travel along the Platte farther upstream, where it retains its prairie character. But unfortunately it is not easy to get near the Platte other than at the places mentioned in the previous entry. The State of Nebraska has a fine series of parks along the Platte River, but they are designed for recreation away from the river.

When I first began to explore the Missouri River country, I talked with ecologists and botanists about getting on the Platte River. They assured me that this would be easy because of all the Nebraska parks that fronted the Platte. They assured me I would find outfitters who would rent canoes. But I found nothing like this. One day we traveled east from Lincoln, Nebraska, on Interstate 80 to State Route 370 and then to Route 50, and crossed the Platte River at Louisville, Nebraska. From there, we went south through Springfield to Schramm Park State Recreation Area.

Along the way, we stopped by a bridge over the Platte. Here the river was much wider than it had seemed farther to the west, and the water was high. A log floated past quickly, revealing a strong current. Debris, mainly floating timber, had built up against the pilings of the bridge. There were islands in the river and wetlands along the shore.

The Platte was so heavy with sediment that we could not see into the water at all. Across the river was a large rock quarry, where big trucks were moving and stirring dust into the air. We drove across the Platte and stopped at the Louisville State Recreation Area located adjacent to the river. Ironically, we could see the quarry buildings from the recreation area, but not the Platte. We drove down to the end of the road in the park and found that the Platte was just barely visible through cottonwood trees; the river was not included in a scenic part of the park. Between the major usable land in the recreation area and the river was an asphalt car-trailer parking area; beyond, at the very end, hidden by the cottonwoods, was my favorite prairie river.

We visited Mahoney State Park, a beautiful facility with many kinds of outdoor recreation and a pretty lodge. The lodge was the one place where you could see the river, but that building imposed itself between everything else and the river. You could only view the Platte from inside the lodge or on its porch.

It was a shock to find that the Platte River, one of the major rivers of the Great Plains, was so hard to get to and seemed never to be the center of attention or, even worse, seemed to be obscured in every possible place by buildings. This is representative of how our society has approached the relationship between human beings and nature throughout much of the twentieth century: as separate things not to be connected.

Pursuing the Platte at the right time of year is worthwhile in spite of these kinds of limitations and obstructions. And the design of Nebraska parks is improving with the growing interest in the state's rivers. One of the best and most famous places to visit is Grand Island, a good two-hour drive west of Lincoln. Grand Island is one of the most important locations on the Platte River bird migratory routes, especially for sandhill cranes. In the spring and the fall more than 500,000 of these large and magnificent birds stop for four to six weeks to feed and rest before continuing to their breeding grounds in Canada, Alaska, and Siberia. Lewis and Clark saw this bird during their trip up the Missouri, and it is a characteristic bird of the central United States. Its wingspan reaches six and a half feet, making it one of the largest birds of North America. Several parks at Grand Island are near or on the river, and from these you can see the incredible abundance of the sandhill crane.

On the whole, the crane is an example of a success in biological conservation. It was the first bird ever protected by international treaty, the 1916 bird migration treaty between the United States and Canada. Protected from hunting, its numbers expanded to the point that in the 1960s farmers found these birds to be pests, because they migrated as a huge unit and ate grain from farm fields. Hunting was proposed as a solution, but this bird has never attracted a great many hunters. Once numbering as few as fifteen or twenty thousand, it has expanded greatly, repopulating the prairie.

SANDHILL CRANE

The sandhill crane, the sandy flood-plain, and the Platte create a quality of the prairie countryside that was familiar to Lewis and Clark for many months. Travel along the Platte brings back these qualities no longer accessible along most of the lower Missouri.

14. Omaha, Nebraska: Down the River with the Army Corps of Engineers

A few commercial boat companies operate on the Missouri River, such as Belle Riverboat Cruises, which runs trips that leave from Abbott Driver at Freedom Park Road in Omaha, Nebraska (402-342-3553). It is likely that, as interest grows in the Lewis and Clark expedition and in recreation on the Missouri River, more boat operations will develop, so you should check in the major cities—especially Omaha but also Yankton, South Dakota.

Anybody can build a bridge that will stand up; only an engineer can build a bridge that will just barely stand up.

—ANONYMOUS

Before its valley was settled, the Missouri's floods were not destructive, as they are now viewed, but beneficial events that rejuvenated the river.

—KEN BOUC, IN "NEBRASKA LAND," A PUBLICATION OF THE
NEBRASKA GAME AND PARKS COMMISSION

From the beginning of the expedition, Lewis and Clark found that navigating the Missouri River in their boats was difficult, to say the least. On May 15, 1804, Clark wrote that they went nine miles and that "the Boat run on Logs three times to day." On May 23, 1804, Clark wrote that they "Set out early run on a log: under water and Detained one hour." And on the next day Clark reported that they passed through a reach called "Devils race Grounds," and as they were passing a small island the boat struck the sands "which is continerly roaling (& turned) the Violence of the Current was so great that the Toe roap Broke, the Boat turned Broadside, as the Current Washed the Sand from under her She wheeled & lodge on the bank below as often as three times, biefore we got her in Deep water." This was accomplished "by mean of Swimmers."

Boat transportation developed rapidly after the Lewis and Clark expedition, always meeting with the same difficulties, and it was not long before people traveling on the river began to petition Congress to do something to improve the safety of the navigation and to protect the increasing number of settlements from the river's floods. By 1884 Congress established a Missouri River Commission to improve navigation of the river by stabilizing the channel, protecting banks from erosion, and removing snags. In 1912 Congress authorized a 6-foot-deep, 180-foot-wide channel to be constructed between Kansas City and St. Louis, extended to Sioux City in 1927. But the big changes in the engineering of the river began during the Great Depression. The Flood Control Act of 1936 authorized "works of improvement" on more than fifty rivers, and in 1937 the first of the six big dams on the Missouri, Fort Peck, was completed in Montana. The Pick-Sloan plan was authorized by Congress in 1944 for the construction of the six big dams as well as bank stabilization, hydropower generation, and maintenance of the navigation channel. The next year the Rivers and Harbors Act authorized a much deeper and wider channel: 9 feet deep and 275 feet wide.

With the rise of the environmental movement in the 1960s, concerns grew about the loss of wildlife and fish habitat on the Missouri from these alterations. Between 1975 and 1980 the U.S. Army Corps of Engineers built "environmental notches" on more than one thousand wing dikes between Sioux City and St. Louis to provide fish habitats. In 1978 two portions of the river, 149 miles in Montana and 59 miles below Gavins Point Dam between South Dakota and Nebraska, were made part of the National Wild and Scenic River System.

Naturally, because Lewis and Clark traveled on the Missouri River, I wanted to travel the same way whenever possible to view the river from a similar perspective. But I discovered early that it is not easy to get on a boat that travels a good distance on the lower Missouri River below Gavins Point Dam. There are a few commercial tourist boats, one leaving from Omaha. If you are curious about the river, it is well worth it to search out these few opportunities. I had tried for several years to get onto the lower Missouri, without success.

Finally, I had the good fortune to arrive in Omaha in April, the day before the Army Corps of Engineers was to send its large boat, the *Mandan*, down the river to St. Louis to check the condition of the river channel. The *Mandan* makes this trip once or twice a year. There was room on the boat for a few passengers and I was able to squeeze on board.

It was a raw, windy day with heavy clouds threatening rain when we walked up the gangplank at 7:30 in the morning, our feet clanging against the cold metal. People from several state and other federal agencies, some from wildlife refuges, were also on board to see the landscape and the river.

As the boat powered down the river, I talked with several of the engineers, starting with the tough question: "How does it feel to work for the agency that is enemy number one for many environmental groups?" Steve Earl, the head of the Omaha Army Corps of Engineers office, responded, "You have to understand that we are just the tool of Congress. In the last century and the first part of this one, Congress wanted the river safe for navigation and told us to do that, and we did. Now Congress asks us to restore wildlife and fish habitat. We can do that, and we are."

"We are caught between a lot of desires for different uses of the river," another engineer added. "You could say that whatever we do makes somebody unhappy. But to understand our job, you have to understand the river as a huge hydrologic system, and you have to understand our responsibilities."

I learned that, in an average year, the water that flows down the Missouri River is enough to cover 25 million acres a foot deep—8.4 trillion gallons. The average water use in the United States is one hundred gallons a day per person; this is very high compared to the rest of the world—in some countries, people make do with ten gallons or less a day. With each person using one hundred gallons a day, the Missouri's flow is enough to provide water for domestic and public use for about 230 million people. With a little water conservation and reduction in per capita use, the Mis-

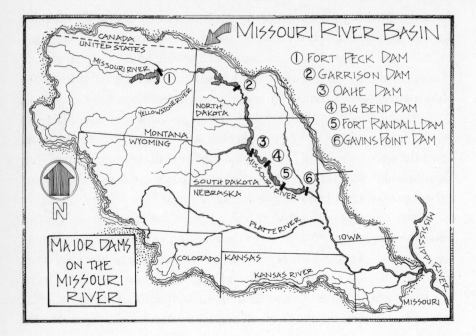

souri provides enough water for all the people of the United States, so great is its flow.

The six major dams on the river were designed for several purposes: to hold back and control floodwaters; to release water so that there would always be enough in the channels for safe navigation; to keep enough water in the reservoirs to provide that flow in years of drought; and to provide water for irrigation.

There are two kinds of dams on the Missouri: big storage dams and control dams. The storage dams are the ones farthest upstream: Fort Peck, Garrison, and Oahe, each of which can store approximately 25 million acre-feet; together they store a three-year supply of Missouri River water flow even if there were no rain or snow.

"Under perfect conditions, the storage drops to 50 million acre-feet—a two-year supply—in March, just before spring runoff from the mountains," another engineer chimed in. "Then we hope that the spring runoff will just be enough to fill the reservoirs back up to a three-year supply." As the upper dams fill, water is released to the three lower dams, which then release water so that the channel is maintained as close as possible to desired steady-state conditions.

"But when the weather doesn't cooperate, then somebody is bound to be unhappy. If there is a drought, then the storage may fall below two years," one of the engineers continued. "If there is a very wet year, then the dams reach their maximum capacity and water has to be released, with flooding the result. One of the things nobody planned on originally is that a lot of recreation grew up on the reservoirs. Now in a drought year, when we have to let the water level fall in the dams, a lot of people complain that we are ruining the recreation. People come from all over the West now to fish in the reservoirs. Upstream people have become used to the reservoirs and want them at a high level. Downstream they want no floods. The farmers want land that is farmable. . . . We can't solve everybody's problem at the same time."

The construction of the dams also meant that large areas of land would be covered by the reservoirs and lost as fish and wildlife habitats. The big three of these six impound almost a million acres: Fort Peck 249,000 acres; Garrison 368,000; Oahe 371,000. The three smaller dams downstream impound just under 200,000 acres: Big Bend 61,000; Fort Randall 102,000; Gavins Point 32,000.

Channelization of the river shortened it by 127 shoreline miles below the dams, by cutting off meanders—a loss of about 5 percent of the length.

Today, the idea of altering so much of a major river seems strange to many of us, but during the 1920s and 1930s, with the Dust Bowl and the Depression, our society embraced the idea that we needed big dams on our big rivers to provide water for irrigation and electricity for power. During the same era that the big dams were being built on the Missouri, they were also being built on the Columbia, the other great river of the Lewis and Clark expedition. Woody Guthrie was one of the first employees of the Bonneville Power Administration, set up to build the Columbia River dams. He was hired to write songs about the huge projects and popularize dams for irrigation and power, and he believed in it.

"Roll on Columbia roll on, Roll on Columbia roll on, Your powers are turning the darkness to light, So roll on Columbia roll on," Woody wrote.

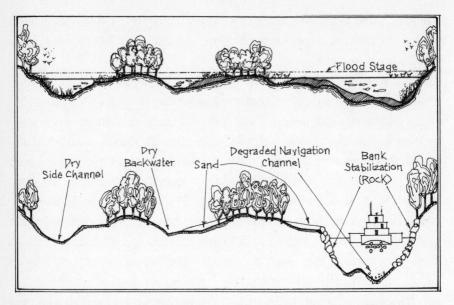

A floodplain before channelization (upper drawing) and after channelization (lower drawing). Stabilizing the river's bank and creating a single navigation channel has many effects on the habitats along the river.

About the Grand Coulee, he wrote it was "the biggest thing ever made by a man, to power our factories and water our land, so roll on Columbia roll on."

Woody Guthrie was a social activist, a union organizer, a political radical; his support of these projects and his songs about their benefits show how different our society's attitude was about the rivers. They were just "a thousand years of water going to waste," he wrote in another song.

To understand the dilemmas that face us—our society, the people of America—we have to understand that social context about the environment. In a time of desperation for many people, turning to the power of the rivers to create jobs and better the lives of the poor was seen as a social good and an important political movement.

The irony from our perspective now is that these dreams of social good came at the price of a high environmental cost, familiar today. Not only were large areas of floodplain habitat lost, but the control of the flow removed seasonal patterns of change. Before channelization and control of the flow, there was a natural hydrological seasonal pattern, with two floods in the spring. The first was in March, when the ice melted on the river and snow melted on the plains, as Lewis and Clark saw during their winter with the Mandans. The second came in June, when the snow melted in the Rockies and there was rainfall in the river basin. Usually the June flood was higher. Fish and wildlife had adapted to these seasonal variations, some requiring it as part of their life cycle.

Around lunchtime the *Mandan* was offshore from Hamburg Bend, one of the fish and wildlife mitigation projects mentioned in an earlier chapter. The chute that the Corps had created there—a straight channel that allowed some of the river's water to pass across the bend and create new fish and wildlife habitat—was a new thing. Some of the engineers wanted to check that the chute was functioning as designed and wanted to walk its entire length. The *Mandan* slowed and came to shore.

About a dozen of us got off with the engineers and walked three and a half miles along the chute. It was designed to allow some water to pass through the bend, but not too much. If the river were running free, it might switch and make that cutoff the main flow. But the corps wanted the chute to remain a shallow side channel.

The wind was blowing so strong that we had to lean against it to stay upright. We hiked across a mosaic of dry, caked silt and silty sands the river had recently laid down. Here the powerful winds blew sand and silt into our faces. We hiked quickly for about an hour, part of the time on the levee, part of the time right along the chute, then waited for the *Mandan* to find us where the chute emptied into the main channel. The engineers were satisfied; the chute was flowing freely and hadn't begun to dam up and spill over its banks, nor had it started to erode the bottom to the point that it might become the main channel. It was precision engineering. By the end of the hike along the chute at Hamburg Bend, I felt somewhat envious. I compared what these engineers could do to achieve a goal in their work compared to what I and my colleagues tried to do in applying the science of ecology to solve environmental problems. Once in a while we succeeded, but mostly our proposed solutions didn't achieve the desired goals. We were driven by myths about nature, ideologies, oversimplifications, lack of understanding.

Out west on the other Lewis and Clark river, the Columbia, the Bonneville Power Administration had spent more than $1 billion on salmon research and restoration without a single sign of improvement, and the estimates I had heard suggested $3 billion total had been spent for salmon there without success. As we waited along the shore of the Missouri River for the *Mandan* to pick us up, I tried to think why there was such a difference between our ability to deal with the physical aspects of our environment and the biological. Too often we made widespread policies for fisheries, forests, and wildlife, based on what seemed plausible, without tests and observations—without the equivalent of walking the side of Hamburg chute to find out if what we were doing worked. I wished that we had the understanding, knowledge, facts, tools, and skills for the restoration of ecosystems that the Corps had for water, rock, and sand. Engineering, grounded in well-understood physical principles, had a sound basis for understanding how a river works as a hydrological system. Our understanding of biological systems lagged far behind, and had not caught up with our social goals. At Hamburg Bend, at Grand Pass, and at the Big Muddy, other places I had visited and written about, beginning experiments in the design of landscapes were starting to give an understanding of how these river and floodplain ecological systems work.

Back on board the *Mandan*, someone called to say that three deer were swimming across the Missouri. We rushed to the bow, and the pilot slowed the boat. Everybody watched. The current here was seven to nine miles an hour, yet the deer seemed to be swimming strongly straight across, not being dragged very much downriver by the current. Not much more than their heads and backs were visible. They made it across in a surprisingly short time; then, having struggled onto the muddy edge of the floodplain, they tried to jump a steep rise, about four or five feet high, to take them into the woods.

Perhaps the major mistake our society made in engineering the Missouri was to believe that there were simple direct solutions to our use of natural resources. The warning from this experience is not simply that these past approaches were wrong, but that the entire set of natural systems are complex and that any of our actions will have many effects.

We all watched as one after another of the deer kept sliding back, the soil rolling away under their hooves, only to try again. The smallest gave up at the first spot and moved away, looking for a break in the bank. The animals looked tired and I thought they must be cold from the strong wind and the water. Meanwhile the largest made it over with a struggle, shook itself, and moved into the brush. The second found an old creek bed and jumped it. Finally the little one, seemingly abandoned by the others, made it up a shallower bank a little farther down. If anything symbolized the resiliency of life and the ability of life to deal with complexity, it was those three deer on that windy, cold day, swimming an icy Missouri that would have drowned a human being quickly. Perhaps if we could only give life a chance, to do a little but not too much, to learn from our mistakes, some of the troubled landscapes along the Missouri could restore themselves.

15. Fontenelle Forest Preserve: Killing Nature with Kindness

Fontenelle Forest and Neale Woods are two segments owned by the same nonprofit organization. The larger and main facility, Fontenelle Forest, is in Bellevue, a suburb south of Omaha, at 1111 Bellevue Boulevard North, Bellevue, Nebraska 68005 (402-731-3140). Neale Woods Nature Center is to the north of Omaha, at 14323 Edith Marie Avenue, Omaha, Nebraska 68112 (402-453-5615).

To get to Fontenelle Forest, go south on Thirteenth Street in Omaha (an exit off Interstate 80); drive to Bellevue (a short distance); look for signs that direct you to the left onto Camp Brewster Road, which ends at a T intersection. Turn right, following a sign to the forest, and the entrance is on your left within a city block.

On July 22, 1804, the expedition reached the vicinity of modern Bellevue, Nebraska, just south of Omaha, on Papillion Creek. Lewis and Clark decided to camp here on the Iowa side of the river for several days, to dry out some of their provisions that had gotten wet and to see if they could find Indian chiefs and set up the meeting they would have soon afterward, at the place they called Council Bluffs.

The eastern white-tailed deer was common here, as it had been thus far on the journey; it was a common source of meat for the expedition. They brought in five deer on this day, five the next, and two on the twenty-fifth.

Deer were so common and readily taken that Clark noted on July twenty-sixth that "only 1 Deer Killed to day." On July twenty-seventh, the expedition moved on upriver, and Clark observed that on the Nebraska side there was "high land covered with timber."

Today the Nebraska side of this location is the setting for Fontenelle Forest, the premier conservation organization of Nebraska. It is one of the best places to see the upland woods and forests along this section of the Missouri. I had been there several times and enjoyed the well-maintained paths through the woodlands and down into hollows, the view of the river through the trees, and the knowledgeable staff. It is also one of the few places directly on the lower Missouri River where you can take natural history field courses and participate in guided hiking trips.

Fontenelle Forest has 368 species of flowering plants, including 38 species of native trees, 17 species of shrubs, and 13 woody vines. The woodlands are good habitat for birds, and more than 300 species have been observed in Fontenelle Forest and its surroundings. Just as it was good deer habitat when Lewis and Clark were here, so it continues to be today. In fact, it has become too good a deer habitat.

At Fontenelle Forest the latest scientific approaches to conservation and management of wild living resources are attempted. So it was ironic and intriguing that the forest would be subjected in recent years to a problem with deer not of the staff's own making. In the 1980s the deer population increased noticeably within the preserve, on both the upland loess bluffs and the large wooded bottomland. The problem continued into the 1990s; the deer, feeding on young trees, reduced saplings by 70 percent, a potentially serious decline in the ability of the forest to regenerate. Deer, so much loved by people, were becoming a serious problem.

The rapid rise in deer population appeared to be in part the result of the suburbanization of the land adjacent to Fontenelle Forest. The surrounding high bluff was becoming an attractive place to build homes. And with the best of intentions and the desire to have a pleasant setting, homeowners planted gardens and put in trees. Many of the plants they grew were typical of young woodlands—low shrubs and small trees—just the kind of vegetation that deer love to eat.

From a distance the Fontenelle woodlands resemble the wooded river-side seen by Lewis and Clark, but up close the forest has become denser and shadier. Deer are animals of young woodlands. They cannot reach very high, and in a very old, very shady forest there are few leaves they can reach. The kinds of trees and shrubs they prefer grow primarily in open areas or young forests, and this is what the suburban landscape was providing in abundance. The human neighborhood created a cafeteria of great interest and benefit to the deer, and the deer population soared.

The staff at Fontenelle Forest thought the problem over. The first important point to consider was that deer depend on certain kinds of changes in nature, contrary to the usual assumption that nature left alone by people remains constant. Although a local 1959 publication by the Omaha Botany Club called the woodlands a "virgin forest," this is not so. Photographs from the turn of the twentieth century reveal much more open woodlands, with oak and hickories scattered among prairie grasses, than occur now. These oak openings are a product of frequent fires that occur naturally on prairies. Oak openings develop on the wetter sites. On the drier sites, prairie grasses return after fires. Deer prefer acorns and require leaves and twigs of shrubs and trees; they need young forests and therefore are adapted to and require a landscape that changes, that is subject to natural fires.

So deer depend on changes occurring in forests. Nature does not paint the landscape once, but continuously revises the canvas. If there were never any disturbance, never fire, then the forests would develop into closed woodlands of large trees, dense shade, and little that the deer could reach and eat. The deer themselves are a force of change. Given young forests and a high density of deer, these animals can convert woodlands to grasslands.

Deer hunts were organized in the early 1990s. The hunts were restricted initially to where the deer seemed to congregate most—on Gifford Point, the bottomlands within the preserve. The assumption was that the deer herd moved about freely, and removing the deer from one part of the preserve would reduce the population density everywhere. This seemed obvious, I thought, remembering the three deer I had seen swim the Missouri River on a cold April not far from this location. It seemed obvious that the deer moved rather freely about the countryside as their need for food, habitat, cover, and breeding required. But often the obvious, the plausible, isn't true about wildlife.

These first efforts had some effect, but not as much as was expected. In 1994 Fontenelle Forest began a cooperative research program with faculty at the University of Nebraska, Omaha. As part of the study, fifty-one deer were tagged to learn about their movements within and outside the preserve. To everybody's surprise, the deer maintained very small home ranges—often less than one-half square mile. So the deer "do not act like gas molecules," said Gary Garabrandt, chief ranger of the Fontenelle Forest Association. They do not fill a vacuum of deer. Removing deer from one location does not result in immediate replacement by deer from elsewhere.

So the practice of harvesting deer from one part of the preserve was not having the desired effect. Deer were not moving in at the rate expected from areas of high density to those whose density had been lowered by hunting. In 1995 there were 495 deer in the seven square miles of the preserve, a density of 70 deer per square mile. The staff at the forest determined that there should be no more than 20 deer per square mile. At this density or lower, the forest could withstand deer browsing and regenerate.

Taking this new finding into account, the forest association adjusted the allowed hunting so that it could occur in more locations but remain carefully managed. Along with the new hunting policy, the staff encouraged local homeowners to plant less palatable plants and provided information about these. In 1997 the overwintering population of deer in the preserve had been reduced to 316, or 45 deer per square mile, and by 1998 to 256, or 36 per square mile. The program appeared to be working toward the desired level.

The approach to deer management at Fontenelle Forest, with changes in policy made as new information develops, is known as adaptive management. Scientific research is integrated into the management and conservation practices; nature is monitored and experiments set up. As part of this process at Fontenelle, exclosures were established within the preserve. Four of these have been set up, each almost a quarter of an acre in area with eight-foot-high fences to keep out the deer. These quarter acres serve as controls to compare growth of young trees where deer cannot reach with growth of young trees on land subjected to deer browsing. The exclosures are part of a guide to whether the population of deer has been sufficiently reduced.

The experiences at Fontenelle Forest reveal the naturalness of certain changes but also help us separate desirable from undesirable changes. For Fontenelle Forest, whose goal is to maintain representative forests much as Lewis and Clark saw them, desirable changes include frequent light fires and some browsing by deer, but not too much. The experiences at Fontenelle Forest also reinforced for me that we have to look beyond what seems obvious and plausible, and continually test our knowledge against observations. Here at Fontenelle Forest people are learning to refine a general concept of natural change into practices of adaptive management that will maintain the countryside in ways that people want to see it. When you visit the forest you can see another kind of countryside that is reminiscent of the landscapes Lewis and Clark saw. And while you are there you can look at the forest for signs of deer, their browsing, and fires past and present.

16. The Allwine Prairie: Once-Vast Prairies Are Now Rare

At 144th and State Streets, Omaha. From downtown Omaha, you can take Route 64 west to 144th Street and go north on that street to the intersection with State Street. Or you can take Interstate 680, the beltway, to exit 6 and go northwest on Route 133 to the intersection with State Street. Take State Street west to 144th Street. Permission is required; contact the biology department of the University of Nebraska, Omaha.

We were standing at the corner of 144th and State Streets in Omaha, Nebraska, looking for a prairie. It was a sunny late afternoon in August, and we had left a large, sprawly Ramada Inn on the west side of Omaha, driving for more than an hour through dense rush-hour traffic. The air was hot, the paved landscape busy.

Following the directions we had been given, we reached the outskirts of the city, where the land opened into active farms, suburban homes, and tree-shaded roads. We had been told to look past the intersection where we were and that we would see a sign. There it was, attached to a tall chain-link fence: "This is the Allwine Prairie Preserve, a Research Area of the University of Nebraska, Omaha."

We parked on the side of the road and got out to stare at the peculiar sight. The fence protected the prairie preserve from us and us from the prairie. For the past week, we had been searching the Nebraska and Iowa countryside, with advice from many friends and prairie experts, for remnants of the tallgrass prairie, and here was one, but locked away, protected, preserved.

It was an ironic sight. In the pre-European settlement landscape, the landscape of Lewis and Clark, prairie once covered more land in the United States than any other kind of vegetation—more area than the green deciduous forests of the East that spread from Maine to Georgia; more area than the deserts of the Southwest; more than that of the boreal forests that covered our northern border from Maine to Minnesota and spread into Canada to Hudson Bay.

Prairies dominated the landscape where it was too dry for forests, but not so dry as to allow cacti, coyote bush, and sagebrush. Here, most of the rain occurs in the spring and summer—from April through September—and averages about twenty-nine inches a year—wet for prairie land. In this wetter end of the prairie, fire keeps forest out, and in this experimental preserve, fires were lit regularly to maintain the grasslands.

At the time of Lewis and Clark, the prairie reached from the middle of Minnesota and the western side of Iowa to the Rocky Mountains. Prairie reached north to the tundra in Canada, covered much of Saskatchewan and Alberta, covered eastern Montana, the Dakotas, Minnesota, Nebraska, Iowa, Indiana, western Illinois and western Ohio, eastern Wyoming and Colorado, Kansas, western Missouri, the eastern edge of New Mexico, and spread into Oklahoma and Texas, ending at the edge of the desert in New Mexico and Arizona. Separate outliers were in the far West: the Palouse grasslands of Washington and the grasslands of California's Great Central Valley. These vast and often seemingly empty lands were the home of the Apache, Assiniboine, and Cheyenne; the Chippewa, Comanche, and Crow; the Kiowa, Mandan,

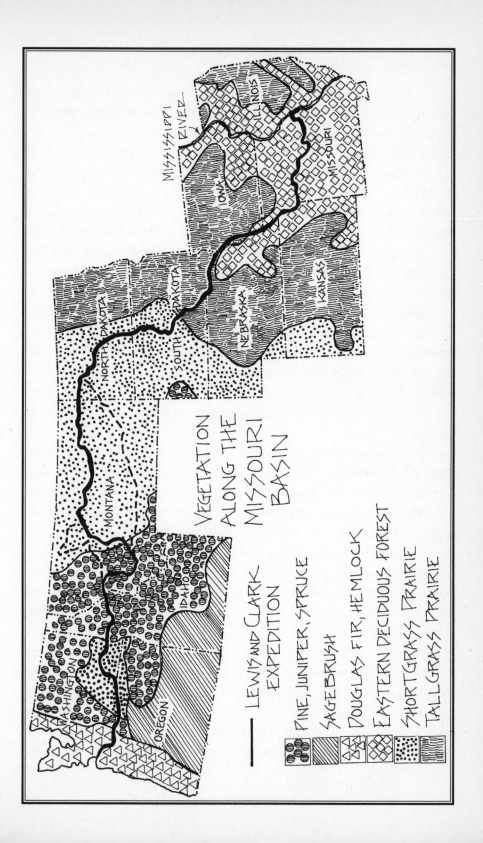

VEGETATION ALONG THE MISSOURI BASIN

—— Lewis and Clark Expedition

Pine, Juniper, Spruce

Sagebrush

Douglas Fir, Hemlock

Eastern Deciduous Forest

Shortgrass Prairie

Tallgrass Prairie

Omaha, and Osage; the Oto, Pawnee, Ponca, Sioux, and Wichita. Prairies at one time covered one-fourth of the Earth's surface: the steppes of Asia, the pampas of South America, the veld of South Africa.

I stared at the fence and the sign. Why look for a prairie within a great city rather than in the countryside? Because it is only in tiny remnants, like the Allwine Prairie Preserve, that prairie exists today. I thought about the typical impression of the Midwest by those who do not live there and only pass through it. Easterner friends always say to me "drive as fast as you can from the mountains of the East to the mountains of the West; get past all that corn and soybeans, it's so flat and boring." But originally prairies did not simply cover vast areas; they were, in that vastness, beautiful, over-whelming. Staring at the locked-up prairie, I could only think about the early impressions the tallgrasses must have given Lewis and Clark. It was in the prairies that Lewis and Clark began the transition from the civilization they knew to the land unsettled by people of European descent, and it was through the prairies, on their return, that they reentered their civilization. So it was the prairies that gave them their first sensations of wild America.

Reading accounts of early travelers across America had fascinated me for years, and I remembered the descriptions of these travelers. One was Josiah Gregg, who traveled the prairie by horseback some decades after Lewis and Clark and wrote that the land of tallgrasses was "as level as the seas" and was so immense and wide that "the compass was our surest, as well as our principal guide." It was the big sky country.

"North America's characteristic landscape," Walt Whitman wrote of the prairie scenes, "while less stunning at first sight" than Yosemite, Niagara Falls, and the upper Yellowstone, "last longer, fill the aesthetic sense fuller, precede all the rest."

But the American prairies contain some of the best farmland in the world—wonderful soils under a good, if fickle, climate—and the land first opened up by Lewis and Clark was rapidly converted to corn and wheat and other small grains, and later to soybeans. There was so much prairie that it seemed not a valuable commodity by itself, and few paid attention to its rapid disappearance. In the nineteenth century, this vast, fertile, and beautiful landscape had no hero, no John Muir, no Aldo Leopold. And so the prairie all but disappeared.

We parked and got out and walked over to an interpretive sign that told us that the Allwine Prairie Preserve was "a reestablished bluestem grassland research area" on 140 acres that had been previously farmed. The land had been donated to the university in 1959 and seeded in 1970 with native grasses—mainly big and little bluestem (known to botanists as *Andropogon gerardii* and *A. scoparus*), with smaller amounts of sideoats grama (*Bouteloua*) and Indian grass (*Sorghastum nutans*), all major grasses of the eastern prairie.

We walked over to the restored prairie and saw some tall forbs (tall flowering plants that are not grasses) about six feet high, scattered among the grasses that grew about four feet tall. Above, swallows swirled over the prairie. Beyond, to our right, there was a large farm field where a John Deere tractor was pulling a hay harvester. The tractor growled and shifted gears. The harvester-bailer opened its huge jaws and vomited out a great cylinder of brown hay, neatly tied. The jaws clanked shut and, almost with a smack of lips, settled down as the tractor began to mow once again, driving through a perfection of geometric uniformity. In contrast to the farmland, the prairie vegetation appeared very patchy—a bunch of tall forbs in one place, some patches of grass, then a bunch of another flower; upslope the grasses had the reddish hue of little bluestem.

Seeing little bluestem was like visiting with an old friend, because this prairie grass found its way east thousands of years ago—during an especially warm period after the end of the last glaciers—in a tongue of prairie that stuck out from Iowa into Ohio, Pennsylvania, New Jersey, and New York, east past New York City and all the way to eastern Long Island where, if you look carefully, you can see its pretty, rusty hue on the slopes along the Northern State Parkway as you drive to Orient Point, the far end of that island.

So here we were, viewing a *restored* prairie, and a tiny patch of one at that. It was better than not seeing prairie at all, but there was none of the sense of vastness, of that special wind-wavy wildness. Standing between farm field and restored prairie, we could see that the two fit together easily. Unlike a lot of other conservation issues, there wasn't a conflict here except for space. Prairie and farmland can exist side by side.

In our century, the novelist Wallace Stegner, who grew up in the northern remnants of the prairie landscape, called it "this grand ocean of wind-troubled grass and grain," which had "the biggest sky anywhere" and "a light to set a painter wild, a light pure, glareless, and transparent." He wrote that "the drama of this landscape is in the sky, pouring with light and always moving . . . looked at for any length of time," he wrote, the sky, the terrain, the grasses "begin to impose their aweful perfection on the observer's mind." It was that feeling of the big sky and the big grasses as far

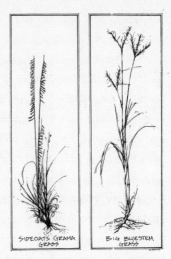

SIDEOATS GRAMA GRASS   BIG BLUESTEM GRASS

as the eye could see that I was searching for, a kind of wildness unfamiliar to modern America. We returned to our car and set out once again to look for a larger patch of that "aweful perfection," somewhere to the north, perhaps.

17. Fort Atkinson State Historical Park: The River Shapes the Floodplain, Creating Good and Poor Sites for Settlement

Take Route 75 north from downtown Omaha, Nebraska, past the Interstate Beltway 680, to the town of Fort Calhoun. A sign on Route 75 clearly marks the road to Fort Atkinson State Historical Park.

One of the most famous incidents of the Lewis and Clark expedition was their meeting on August 3, 1804, with the chiefs of the Oto and Missouri tribes on bluffs along the shore of the Missouri River just north of modern Omaha, Nebraska.

On July 23, 1804, Lewis and Clark sent two men, Drewyer and Crousett, "with Some tobacco to invite the Otteaus if at their town" and "if they Saw them to Come and talk with us at our Camp." The search for the Indians continued for more than a week, because the buffalo were in abundance and the Indians were hunting and away from their villages. Meanwhile, the expedition sought a good location for a camp where they would meet the Indians.

Lewis and Clark named the meeting site Council Bluff, to commemorate their first major council with the Indians. Historians have established that the town given that name in Iowa is south of and across the river from the actual meeting place. The real Council Bluff was probably at or near the site of Fort Atkinson State Historical Park, near what is now an interstate beltway around Omaha. And the river has meandered enough since Lewis and Clark passed this way that it may no longer exist as a bluff overlooking the river. We decided to visit Fort Atkinson State Historical Park because this is at least very similar to the original location in its environmental attributes. I was curious what kind of place Lewis and Clark chose as their first major meeting with Indian tribes. To this point in their journey, they had encountered Indians but not held a formal interchange.

On July 30, 1804, the two captains left their camp early and walked three and three-quarter miles west, through "the most beautiful prospect imaginable." Between the river bottom and the prairie, Clark distinguished several distinct levels. At the lowest level, along the river, Clark saw a "beautiful bottom land . . . interspersed with groves of timber" containing willow, cottonwood, mulberry, elm, sycamore, and ash. These are floodplain species. If bottomland habitats along the river were restored today, this layering of various kinds of trees would reappear.

Above that was a "lower Prarie" situated "above high water mark at the foot of the riseing ground & below the High Bluff." This was a river bench— a term geologists use for a kind of natural terracing. Today, geologists have come to understand that river benches are the result of past changes in river flow and floods, deposition and erosion. Finally, at the top, were the uplands of prairies interspersed with groves of trees.

At the top, Lewis and Clark were in a "Clear open Prarie," which they estimated was "about 70 feet higher than the bottom." Clark wrote that the prairie extended as far as they could see and was "covered with grass about 10 or 12" inches high, interspersed with groves of walnut, oak, hickory, Kentucky coffee tree, and basswood. These are the trees characteristic of the upland forests in the better-watered locations and on the best soils within the prairie.

Clark wrote extensive and detailed notes about the countryside he saw on that day, notes that are fascinating in the precision of his observations of the countryside. He provides an accurate description of the physical shape of the landscape near the Missouri, before it was channelized in the twentieth century, as geologists understand these formations today. He also accurately described the different sets of vegetation found according to their nearness to the river, and therefore the frequency of flooding and the kind of soil. With this description of the landscape on so large a pallet, Clark shows himself to be an interested and careful observer of natural history, one whose records I felt I could trust to be good depictions of the environment before major changes took place. It was a big landscape, a big river valley where the river had deposited and eroded the land for a distance that Clark estimated "to be from 4 to 20 ms" from bluff to bluff. It is a landscape big enough that most of us would drive through it without noticing these subtle differences in the countryside.

Clark thought the location seemed ideal not just for a one-day council with the Indians, but for future settlement. "Perhaps no other situation is as well Calculated for a Trading establishment" Clark wrote of the site they selected. Clark was right about this site. A fort was established here in 1819, but the designers did not have Clark's eye for the landscape: They made the mistake of putting the fort along the river, on the bottomland. This created two problems: the dampness and abundance of insects can be unhealthy, and there is always a chance of floods. A Yellowstone party—a group of travelers/explorers—spent the winter of 1819–20 at this fort, and sickness and bitter cold took the lives of more than 160 members of the expedition. A disastrous spring flood prompted the move from the bottomlands to the present site on the valley terrace above the floodplain. When you walk around this location, consider its advantages in contrast to other locations.

Clark was aware of the importance of what geographers call site and situation, an idea about the location of forts, towns, and cities that we have all too often forgotten. The *situation* is a location's relationship to transportation and resources. The situation of Fort Atkinson was excellent, near to the Missouri River as well as to wood, clay for bricks, and excellent soil for farming. The *site* is the physical, chemical, and ecological conditions of a location. Down by the river, on the floodplain, is a notoriously poor site, while up on the prairie, on the bluffs, where the clean wind blows and there is no danger of flooding, the site is excellent. As we live through the floods on the Missouri at the end of the twentieth century, we should relearn the concepts that came so naturally to Clark, an experienced outdoorsman who was fascinated with the countryside and its potentials.

18. Fort Atkinson: The Badger and Discovery of New Species

See previous entry for directions.

On July 30, 1804, when the expedition was near Fort Calhoun, the location Lewis and Clark were to call Council Bluffs, Joseph Fields, a member of the expedition who often hunted, killed a badger and brought it back to the camp. The animal was new to western science; it had never been described and was little known. Neither Lewis nor Clark had seen one before. Following the charge given to them by President Jefferson, Lewis and Clark wrote a description of this animal, providing the first written, scientific description. Clark noted that the animal "burrows in the ground and feeds on Flesh (Prarie Dogs), Bugs & vigatables." He described the badger as having the size and shape of a beaver, a "head mouth & c." like a dog "with Short ears," hair and tail like a groundhog, intestines like a pig. Thus he described the different parts of the strange animal in terms of others that he knew. This description sounds peculiar to us. But all Clark was doing was describing something new in terms of things he and others were familiar with. This is the way we always describe something new.

Lewis wrote a somewhat more detailed and scientific description, noting first that it was a "singular animal not common to any part of the United

States," that it was carnivorous and had "one long and sharp canine tooth on both sides of the upper jaw," that its eyes were "small black and piercing," and that it weighed sixteen pounds.

This badger was the first animal that Lewis and Clark preserved, skinned, stuffed,

BADGER

and later sent back to President Jefferson with the soldiers who accompanied the expedition as far as Fort Mandan. Along the way they would identify many new species of animals and plants. They were the first to describe the mule deer, the pronghorn, the prairie dog, and the black-footed ferret. They found the rattlesnake, garter snake, the horned lizard, and various snails.

Lewis and Clark were outdoorsmen, familiar with wildlife and with the preparation of skins. Both were excellent naturalists, with curiosity about their surroundings and the ability to see what was new and different. To fulfill Jefferson's charge to them, they did elsewhere as they did with the badger: shot or otherwise caught an individual of each species of wildlife, and measured and described the specimen. They collected sample plants and pressed them and sent these back also with the returning soldiers. Their plant collection still exists at the Philadelphia Academy of Science, with most of the material intact and available on microfilm.

Most familiar with wildlife, their descriptions of mammals, birds, and snakes are generally accurate and homey. Lewis, with his crash course in Philadelphia before the expedition, learned how to provide a formal description of plants and to press them for preservation. Their observations are therefore helpful to us in considering one of the environmental issues that receives the greatest attention in the media today—conservation of endangered species, and, the more general term, conservation of biological diversity.

19. Ledges State Park: Reading Ancient History in Tiny Grains of Pollen

From Ames, Iowa, follow Route 30 west to Route 164, just south of the town of Boone. Take this route south to Ledges State Park. From DeSoto Bend National Wildlife Refuge, take Route 30 east to the same junction with Route 164.

Although the main body of the expedition traveled by boat on the Missouri or alongside it by foot and horseback, Lewis and Clark took turns exploring the land back from the river. Often they sent a few men out to hunt for food. Those who hunted often roamed widely and sometimes—not too infrequently—became lost and returned to the expedition after a hiatus long enough to cause some concern.

Because the river and the surrounding land are intimately linked, exploration away from the river was necessary for the expedition to understand the natural history of the newly purchased lands. So it is today. The best way to get the feel of the Missouri River as countryside is to go back from it into the prairie and woodlands. With this in mind I set out from Ames, Iowa, to explore the countryside between that city and the Missouri River with two ecologists from Iowa State University, David Glenn-Lewin and Tom Jurik.

From Ames we took State Route 30 west to Ledges State Park, where beautiful sandstone ledges thrust out of soils deposited by the great continental glaciers more than 14,000 years ago. The Peas and Des Moines Rivers sculpted these ledges through sandstone on their way downstream.

We walked through the park on trails to admire the view of bottomland woods; even on a cloudy, cold day the scenery was dramatic as we stood on the ledges and looked at the Des Moines River beyond. This was not the Iowa of urban stereotypes, not miles upon miles of flat fields of corn, but a steeply rolling countryside of water, hills, and forests. The scenery was all the more striking because the forest on the hills obscured the steep descents along the bluffs until we walked out to an edge to make a sudden discovery of flowing water below and sandy cliffs beneath our feet.

Tom and David told me the ancient history of this landscape. All that we saw from these bluffs was under hundreds of feet of ice 14,000 years ago and for many thousand years before that, the time of the last great continental ice age. Those masses of ice bulldozed the landscape, tearing rock and stone, pebble and crystal, with an awful force and momentum, grinding rock to stone and stone to soil, tumbling clays and sands and pebbles and rocks together into a jumble we call *glacial till*, sandpapering the hills and filling the valleys with masses of this till.

Then the climate changed and the ice melted back, and torrential rivers began to flow, cutting through the till and into the bedrock sandstone that had resisted the icy mass for thousands of years. Warmer and warmer it became; by 10,000 years ago elm and ash grew near these rivers, floodplain species then just as now. For several thousand years, the landscape must have looked quite as we saw it this April day. But then the climate grew even warmer, too warm for trees, and the climate and winds pushed the prairie ever eastward. By 7,000 years ago the climate was the warmest it would become after the ice ages, and prairies pushed their way through these ledges and east, all the way to the Atlantic coast. Then the climate cooled again and the prairies retreated westward; about 3,000 years ago the forests had fully returned, to cloak the hills as we saw them that day.

The history of the vegetation is learned from the study of one of the unlikeliest products of plants: their tiny pollen grains. From them scientists have painstakingly reconstructed an ancient history, never available before. This knowledge of the countryside is something new; it is a late-twentieth-century item, the result of medium and high technology. The people who uncovered the history of the migration of trees and grasses needed fine microscopes to examine pollen grains. Each pollen grain has a hard outer coating of silicon; the grains, under a microscope, are elaborately patterned, like Victorian Christmas tree ornaments. Each genus has its own character-istic pattern and overall shape and, for many plants, each species within a genus can be distinguished. The patterns seem as various as snowflakes. Cores taken with long metal tubes driven into mud on the bottoms of lakes and bogs provide the primary material. This is subjected to strong acid washes to clean out everything but the resistant casings of the pollen.

But how to date the deposits? That had to await the nuclear age and the invention of carbon dating. Organic material in the muds, with the pollen casings, are removed and the amount of radioactive carbon is counted. This decreases over time at a rate that is calculated and carefully calibrated. It is the ticking of the Pleistocene clock. From this knowledge of the atomic age, scientists date the layers of pollen grains and then know what was growing when. With these technologies, we have a moving picture of natural history not available to Lewis and Clark nor to any people before. It is a grand cin-ema, deepening our understanding of nature.

Standing on these lovely ledges, we were awed by the history revealed to us, a time before civilization and agriculture, before Babylon. Learning this history of the land and vegetation has changed the way I look at countryside and the way I feel about countryside. Now I see this land as clothed in glacial till, its bare bones of bedrock arching in a few places above the fill; the deep, U-shaped, glacier-cut valleys hidden beneath rock and stone, silt and clay— the product of climate changes, migrations of species, and great forces beyond our imagination, acting over thousands of years.

20. Loess Hills State Recreation Area: To Keep a Prairie, Disturb It with Fire

There are a number of parks, preserves, and wildlife management areas in the Loess Hills of Iowa east of Onawa, Iowa. The best way to see them is to obtain the "Loess Hills Scenic Byway" brochure from Iowa Welcome Centers by writing to the Harrison County Museum Welcome Center, RR #3, Box 130A, Missouri Valley, Iowa 51555.

You can reach several of these areas as follows: From Interstate 29 take exit 112 and go east on Route 175 through Onawa. Just east of town take County Route L12 northeast to the Loess Hills Wildlife Management Area. Or continue on 175 to Turin and go north to Turin Loess Hills State Preserve. Other Loess Hills public areas can be reached from exit 95 on Interstate 29 by going east through the town of Little Sioux on County Route F20 to Pisgah and going north or south on Route 183.

On July 16, 1804, Lewis and Clark were near today's Iowa-Missouri border, on the river near the present location of Peru, Nebraska. Clark wrote that the river was about two miles wide, but it was not deep, because he could see snags scattered across it, and on the far shore "about 20 acres of the hill has latterly slipped into the river above a cliff of Sand Stone for about two miles." Looking beyond the river, Clark saw "a range of Ball [bald] Hills parrelel to the river & at from 3 to 6 miles distant from it, and extends as far up & Down as I Can See." He was viewing a special kind of prairie that grows on a strange and rare kind of soil, called loess. "This prarie I call Bald pated Prarie," Clark wrote, seemingly because the brownish color of the soil and grasses made the hills look hairless at the top.

One might in fact call them tonsured hills, because the summits are clothed in grasses, while trees and shrubs surround the bases near the water, giving the hills the rounded appearance of a monk's head with the hair shaved above the ears. The next day, July 17, 1804, Lewis rode out into this prairie and along a stream that passed through it, which he referred to by its Indian name, Neesh-nah-ba-to-na Creek. Along this stream he found "Some few trees of oake walnut & mulberry." The hills were not as barren as they looked; several of the men went out hunting and one of the best hunters, Drewyer, "kill'ed 3 deer, & R. Fields one," Clark wrote.

I had long wanted to visit loess hills in a place where the prairie still existed on them, because this is a strange and unusual formation. Waubonsie State Park, Iowa, is the nearest to where Clark first walked through loess hills, but opportunities did not come up for me to go there. My first chance came when I visited Iowa State University, and I told my hosts, Tom Jurik and David Glenn-Lewin, about my desire to visit natural areas related to the Lewis and Clark expedition. We agreed to an exchange: lectures to their classes for a natural history tour.

From Ames, Iowa, we took State Route 30 west, passing the farm town of Grand Junction and miles of farmland. We stopped by the side of the road to look at some prairie potholes that remained in the fields. "Best soil in the world," David said as I took some photographs and we looked at the black, wet prairie soils still bare of crops.

As we continued on Route 30 farther west, the landscape suddenly changed. The relatively flat land with its black soil gave way to a strangely abrupt rolling landscape of a browner and finer soil. We had come to the loess hills, the same kind of strange, wind-formed landscape that Clark had walked on almost two hundred years before.

Loess is a material found in only a few places on Earth; the American Midwest and China have the two largest parcels. Loess hills are a product of the glacial ages, created by water and wind between 30,000 and 17,000 years ago.

Loess began as silt eroded from the Rocky Mountains by the ancient Missouri River and by the Platte River to the south. The faster a river flows, the heavier the material it can carry. A mountain stream pushes boulders during storms. Rivers separate material they carry by size, leaving the heaviest material behind near the mountains when the water first begins to slow down. Silts are fine particles and are carried a long way downstream to where the quieter waters can no longer carry them. As the Missouri and Platte meandered across their floodplains over the centuries, they spilled their silt wide and deep.

Toward the end of the last ice age, intense winds developed, a result of the great difference in temperatures and reflection of light between the ice and the warmer bare ground. The great winds created silt storms that piled the soil into steep silt dunes. Like sand dunes, the silt dunes formed a rolling countryside of uniform material, without any apparent layers. Seen from the side, especially along a road cut, the soil is deep but not layered. Here in Iowa the loess sits on top of glacial till and on top of bedrock that is much, much older. The cliffs that Clark saw when he first viewed the loess hills were laid down in the Pennsylvanian period, more than 286 million years ago—the age of coal formation.

Two days after Lewis and Clark first saw the loess hills, Clark went for a walk onshore after a breakfast of roasted ribs of deer and a little coffee. He began to follow fresh tracks of elk, and "after assending and passing thro a narrow Strip of wood Land, Came Suddenly into an open and bound less Prarie" where trees were "confiend to the River Creeks and Small branches" and the prairie "was Covered with grass about 18 inches or 2 feet high and contained little of any thing else." The grass was shorter than on the tallgrass prairie that grew on other kinds of soil. "This prospect was So Sudden & entertaining that I forgot the object of my prosute, and turned my attention to the Variety which presented themselves to my view," he wrote. He continued up a hill toward a "line of woods" where he found "a butifull Streem," which he followed for three miles where it flowed into the Missouri River "between 2 clifts." He was near the location of modern Nebraska City, probably on Table Creek.

Loess makes poorer soil than till, partially because the soil is made up of particles of one size. The best soils in Iowa are to the east, the poorer ones along the Missouri where Lewis and Clark passed. This was one of the things that struck Clark about his "Bald pated Prarie": The grasses on these hills were short—eighteen inches—unlike the tallgrasses of the eastern prairie, some of which reached six feet. As a result, he could get a view of a long distance, and that view was pleasing. Reading his accounts, and driving toward the loess hills, I thought of the irony of this landscape. It was created by ice and wind, during episodes that people, if present, would have found terrible

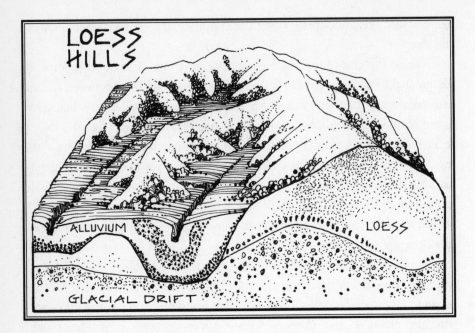

and destructive. This seemingly peaceful landscape would not have been here without an environmental disaster, next to which the dust storms of the 1930s would have seemed like small dust devils.

We passed the town of Denison, Iowa, and saw a sign on Route 30 stating that we had just crossed the divide between the Mississippi and the Missouri Rivers. East of this point, all the streams flowed to the Mississippi; west, all the streams flowed into the Missouri.

At the recreation area, we parked and began to walk into the short, steep, rounded loess hills. David told me that this is an actively managed area with the goal of returning the vegetation on the hills to the way that it was before European settlement—the way Lewis and Clark saw the loess countryside. The way to accomplish this goal was to burn.

In our century, wildfires have been considered bad—we all know the Smokey Bear advertisements of the U.S. Forest Service. With the suppression of fire, the vegetation on the loess hills changed. The most impressive plant we saw was eastern red cedar, a small tree that reaches twenty or so feet high. The seeds of red cedar are eaten and excreted by birds, which spread the seeds widely. Red cedar grows rapidly in bright sunlight, when it is not shaded by taller trees. If the seeds fall on bare soil, they can germinate and survive. But if there is a dense cover of grasses, then the seeds land within the grass and do not reach the soil. So there are two major intervals following a fire when red cedar can get established: soon after a fire, before the grasses are well established, and ten or twenty years later, after the grasses have matured and some of the grasses die back and expose bare soil. Where rainfall is high enough, cedar can survive past the seedling stage and grow for forty or fifty years. Without fire, in this eastern edge of the prairie, in locations where the rainfall is relatively high, the cedars grow well.

In the distance we could see unburned hills that were dark green from a dense cover of red cedar. But the first hill we walked up had recently been burned to clear it of cedars and restore the prairie. The vegetation we walked through was burned to the ground or to the low mounds of bunch grasses, except for two or three rosettes of prairie forbs that had already sprouted since the fire. The grasses we saw included big bluestem, prairie grass, Indian grass, foxtail grass, as well as little bluestem, a prairie grass common in the East.

After we walked through the first, burnt row of hills, we could see that the unburned hills had a distinct pattern. On the south slopes the vegetation was almost all prairie grasses, while the north slopes were heavily wooded. As a result, when I looked south and saw only north slopes, I saw only a wooded countryside. If I had no other view, I would have believed myself in forest land. Then I turned and looked north and, seeing only south slopes, saw hill after hill of brown grasslands. If it had been a sunny day, I would have taken two photographs, one north and one south, and could have shown it to my friends and made them believe they were from two completely different areas. It was the clearest illustration of the effect that the direction a hillslope faces has on its vegetation. A south-facing slope in the northern hemisphere gets sun most of the day, and sun dries out the soil. The drier, south-facing slope is more likely to burn. A north-facing slope is shaded a good part of the day, so it stays cooler and retains its moisture. The steep, short hills formed by loess accentuated these differences in this transitional countryside.

The south-facing slopes of these loess hills looked like the drier land-scape far to the west; the north slopes, on the other hand, looked like the moister countryside found east of here. Because the entire prairie land is in the rain shadow of the Rocky Mountains, the average rainfall is lowest just east of the Rockies. In the high plains one hundred miles east of Denver, for example, it averages twelve to sixteen inches a year. The rainfall increases eastward—twenty inches per year at Dodge City; twenty-eight inches near Lincoln, Nebraska; thirty-six inches east of Kansas City.

We walked through these steep, strange hills for several hours. It was a satisfying day in spite of the clouds and drizzle; we saw one of the stranger but pleasing landscapes of the Missouri River drainage, saw constructive activities to restore the large natural area to the way Lewis and Clark had seen it, saw the effects of ancient glacial and river events on the modern land-scape, and smelled the sweet and sharp scents of prairie plants. I had learned, paradoxically, that the countryside Clark found "Sudden & enter-taining" to the point that he forgot what else he was doing, was the product of cataclysmic forces of fire, ice, and winds.

21. DeSoto Bend National Wildlife Refuge: What Happens When We Stop a River's Meandering

DeSoto Bend National Wildlife Refuge is north of Omaha, Nebraska, in Iowa. From Omaha take Route 75 north to Fort Calhoun (you can then stop at Fort Atkinson on the way) to Blair, Nebraska. Go right (east) on Route 30 over the Missouri River. The refuge is off of Route 30. Turn right at the signs to the refuge.

You can also reach the refuge by taking Interstate 29 in Iowa north to Route 30, then left (west) on 30 to the refuge.

With a series of cries and the beat of wings, snow geese rose from the icy waters and faded in and out in the falling snow, white upon white, up against down, birds swirling to the right, counterclockwise, snow angling left, clock-wise, in the winter wind. An icy blast burnt my fingers and stung my eyes. Everything seemed to move and the world lost its color. It was November, but the early snowstorm and blast of Canadian arctic air made it seem like

January. Lewis and Clark had passed this spot in the late summer, but they had known this kind of prairie winter when they wintered with the Mandan Indians near modern Bismarck, North Dakota.

This was my third visit to DeSoto Bend—whenever I came to Lewis and Clark country, I ended up here. This time I had come out to give a talk at the Fontenelle Forest Preserve. Gary Garabrandt, chief naturalist at the forest, had agreed to take me on a field trip to see more of the Lewis and Clark countryside in exchange for my talk.

It was my first view of snow geese and about as dramatic as I could imagine. The scene was like a Japanese watercolor—muted hues blended together. It was worth fighting upwind against a cold that made blue jeans feel like thin cotton; it was so cold that I could only take my fingers out of my gloves long enough to take two snapshots—any longer than that and the cold metal started to feel like it was freezing my fingers up to the knuckles.

We parked in a tarmac lot and walked upwind to a bird-viewing blind on the oxbow lake for which the refuge is well known. This was not wilderness, but in the winter air there was a feeling of wildness created by the swirling images and blasting wind. A few other people braved the cold, but it was hard to see them.

The wildlife refuge had changed greatly since my first visit, the result of the 1993 floods on the Missouri River. The first time I visited DeSoto Bend had been in early spring a few years before that flood, when the work of the Army Corps of Engineers was intact and the wildlife refuge was one of the most accessible places to see effects of channelization on the Missouri. On that first visit, with Iowa State University professors Tom Jurik and David Glenn-Lewin, we saw a Missouri River very much tamed—an Army Corps of Engineers' canal, with broken rocks set along the shores like an ocean breakwater, and the sides cut away and made uniform. On this third visit, the river's edge was in disorder, the floods had scattered the rocks and unstraightened the channel. I thought about the great differences between the tamed Missouri, the Missouri in disarray, and the river that Lewis and Clark observed when they reached this area.

On August 4, 1804, Lewis and Clark were a little north of the present location of DeSoto Bend National Wildlife Refuge when the variableness and fickleness of the river became dangerously apparent to them. They wrote that the riverbanks were "washing away & trees falling in constantly for 1 mile." The next day the boats followed a large meander in the river upstream. In the evening Clark walked on the shore. "In Pursueing Some Turkeys" he went on foot downstream 370 yards and found himself at the beginning of the meander, a distance he had measured to be twelve miles by river. "In every bend the banks are falling in from the Current being thrown against those bends," he wrote. "Agreeable to the Customary Changes of the river I Conclud. that in two years the main current of the river will pass through"—it will cut off the meander. Clark recognized the river's natural tendency to change its channel, to meander across its floodplain, to create sandbars and then erode them away, to deposit soil on the edges and then undercut them into unstable cliffs.

It was just the kind of dangerousness that Lewis and Clark observed that the Army Corps of Engineers projects were supposed to remove—to make the river safe for people who lived and farmed on the floodplain, to provide a constant, reliable source of irrigation water from dams, and to make navigation safe and simple for boat traffic, with the belief that barges would be a major mode for transporting goods through the Midwest in the late twentieth century. But other forms of transportation—railroads, interstate highways, big trailer trucks, and air freight—interfered, and the channelized Missouri never became a big moneymaker for the transportation industry. Today barges carry only 1.5 percent of the agricultural products of the region.

At this refuge in 1960 the U.S. Army Corps of Engineers constructed a channel that cut through a meander to shorten river travel by seven miles, avoiding the DeSoto Bend of the river. They built levees to cut off the meander, thus forming an oxbow. In this case, the oxbow lake had an artificial original; but long before channelization, natural oxbow lakes were continually being formed by the Missouri as it cut off meanders. These are scattered over the countryside and many are recreational parks, such as Lewis and Clark State Park in Iowa.

A meander begins as a small bend in a river. Over time, the shape of a meander becomes more extremely arced, with more material deposited on

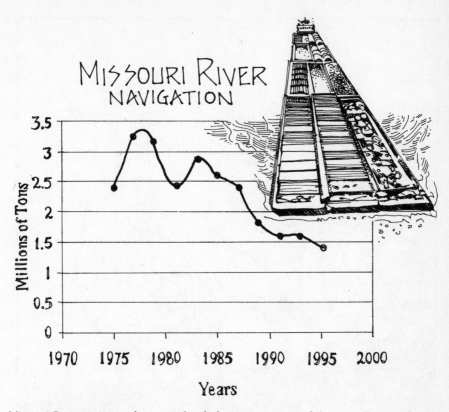

MISSOURI RIVER
NAVIGATION

Missouri River navigation has carried a declining percentage of the agriculture production from the Missouri Basin.

the inside of the curve, where the river runs slower, than on the outside. The river erodes the outer, longer bank and deposits along the shorter bank nearer to the main channel. Eventually the meander takes on an extreme shape of a near circle, called an oxbow. A flood carries the waters across the short bank at the inside of the meander, cutting off the meander. This short channel becomes the path of the river; beside it remains a lake with the shape of a crescent moon, called an oxbow lake. Meanders of the Missouri have been measured to migrate across the floodplain at an average rate of about 250 feet a year.

SNOW GEESE

Over the years, the meanders themselves migrate back and forth across the river valley. Over thousands of years, the river has wandered across the plains, eroding and depositing, like an artist working his oils over and over again on his canvas. On this sculpted, painted landscape, Lewis and Clark pushed their small river crafts upstream, through the meanders, through the fallen sands, through the snags. They saw the river's sandy, silty painting at one moment in time. It has become a common belief of our age that nature undisturbed by modern civilization was fixed, constant, steady, perhaps reliable and trustworthy. But the real Missouri changed before Lewis and Clark passed its way, kept changing under their feet, and changed after they left. The countryside, as a result, was also always changing.

During my first visit to DeSoto Bend, it seemed that the channelization of the river had extinguished the wonderful wild Missouri of fact and folklore. In its place was a placid, tamed stream. My reaction was not so much sentimental as it was a recognition that we had made a Faustian bargain with the river, gaining short-term stability—a chance to build and live on the floodplain, to farm that floodplain for a number of years without worrying about dreadful floods—in exchange for a loss of the renewing sediments that had created the fertile farmland in the first place, and in exchange for rarer but more dangerous floods that could occur in the future.

During that first visit, we strolled from the channelized banks back to low wetlands. We saw large willows and cottonwoods, which are so characteristic of these habitats. But these willows were much larger—probably much older—than I was familiar with. There was also a dense understory of flowering dogwood. David suggested that such an understory would never have existed with the natural flooding of the river, because dogwood cannot withstand flooding and the floods would bulldoze the small trees away. He believed that the presettlement floodplain forests would have had a "cathedral" look—tall, arching trees, but little understory. We saw there were few dead logs on the ground. This also David thought unnatural; there would have been many dead logs on the natural bottomland, some washed there from upstream by the river, the rest from trees that fell and remained in place. Although a few floodplains trees were there, others that we expected to see were not, including elm and ash; the elimination of flooded areas seemed to have eliminated many kinds of trees adapted to those wet, frequently flooding habitats.

These images of the wetlands and tamed river I had seen before the 1993 floods came to mind as we walked through the drifting snow to the edge of

OXBOW LAKE
AT DESOTO BEND,
IOWA

the river's main channel. The well-intentioned works of human beings on the river were in disarray. The neat, straight banks were gone, washed away; the even line of boulders a jumble of rocks.

Since the time of Lewis and Clark, the Missouri River has been teaching the same lessons, but rarely have we listened; rarely have we learned. We thought that our mechanized projects were a rational approach to the river, but it hasn't worked out that way. There is a rational approach we can take to living with the river, benefitting from its waters, conserving its living resources, enabling it to fertilize and help restore the land.

DeSoto Bend National Wildlife Refuge provides an example of how we can accomplish this today. One of five hundred U.S. Fish and Wildlife Service refuges throughout the United States, DeSoto Bend is actively managed to increase production of wildlife. This management is part of the reason that DeSoto is such a good place to see many of the water birds that were here when Lewis and Clark passed this way. With much of the surrounding countryside under cultivation and many of the prairie pothole ponds and wetlands drained for farming, there are fewer places for migrating water birds to stop and feed. At DeSoto, about 1,500 acres have been planted in grasslands, including big and little bluestem, switch grass, Indian grass, sideoats grama, and wheat grass—classic grasses of the tallgrass prairie. These are burned on a three-year rotation to prevent trees from entering, as are the loess hills. Other fields are cultivated in crops, and the crops not harvested provide additional food for birds.

The snow geese swirling in the November snow created one of the most beautiful scenes I have ever witnessed on the Missouri River. DeSoto Bend left me with a mixed message. Channelization had caused many problems, but that didn't mean all human attempts to improve nature were bad. The planting of prairie grasses and of crops that were left for the wild birds was a natural resource management action that worked. As Gary and I went on to view other natural areas along the Missouri where prairie restoration was in progress, I was convinced that we could learn the difference between those actions that can be beneficial and those that are likely to fail. This was worth the walk in the cold and the snow.

22. Sergeant Charles Floyd Monument: Medicine and Nature

From Interstate 29 take exit 143B, the first exit south of Sioux City. The sign for this exit says Route 75, Industrial Road. Take that exit and go north, and then turn into the parking area for the Floyd Monument.

The death of Sgt. Charles Floyd, the only member of the expedition to die during the journey, is one of the best-known events in the Lewis and Clark journals. The monument to him, completed in 1900, stands on top of a bluff above the Missouri River, clearly visible from Interstate 29. Visiting it is a pilgrimage for most Lewis and Clark buffs, and the monument is listed on the National Park Service map of the Lewis and Clark expedition as one of about eighty recommended places to visit. What could be easier to find, we thought.

We set out on a beautiful summer day to see the monument, driving south from the center of Sioux City, Iowa. There, ahead, stood the monument, a miniature Washington Monument and therefore unmistakable. But the road to it was not marked on any of the standard road maps we had with us, including the AAA map. We circled around on various roads without success. It was time to ask directions. But people we stopped did not know about the monument. I wondered that such a famous and visible landmark seemed so unknown to the residents of this city. It was a bit of an Alice-through-the-looking-glass experience; for a while, the harder we tried to reach the monument that was clearly visible to us, the farther we found ourselves from it. Eventually, we wandered onto the road that led to it, came across a sign (the first we had seen) about five hundred feet before the entrance, and drove into the parking lot.

It was Monday morning and we were the only visitors. The monument to a death on the prairie was surrounded by a large lawn of introduced grass. The view from the bluff was a pleasant one of trees lining the Missouri River and of fields of hay, interspersed with highways and grain elevators, all beneath a cloudless sky—a peaceful setting with a view of the great agricultural bounty of a prairie state, a place on this quiet day for contemplation, but not a setting in which one expects a sudden death.

The expedition may have had the same impression when they arrived here. On August 15, 1804, Floyd was one of three men sent out by Lewis and Clark to examine a prairie fire "at no great distance from the camp," which they found had been set by Sioux Indians. Activities seemed more or less normal, except that Lewis and Clark had to deal with two attempted desertions. Floyd was just another healthy, productive member of the crew. But on August 19, 1804, Clark wrote that "Serjeant Floyd is taken verry bad all at onc with a Beliose Chorlick" and that they tried "to relieve him without Success as yet, he gets worse and we ar much allarmed at his Situation, all attention to him."

On the next day, August 20, 1804, Clark wrote that they made him a warm bath "hopeing it would brace him a little," but "before we could get him in to this bath he expired, with a great deel of composure, haveing Said to me before his death that he was going away and wished me to write a letter." Death came quickly and with little expectation.

The symptoms suggest a burst appendix, a rapid death in any century. That only one man died on the expedition, and his death was from causes not related to the travel itself, is often remarked upon. It is a demonstration of the remarkable leadership of Lewis and Clark, who persevered through dangerous encounters with grizzly bears; intense storms; the terrible cold of the first winter near Bismarck, North Dakota; cold, wetness, and lack of food during the second winter near the mouth of the Columbia River in Oregon; canoeing down rapids on the Columbia River—a feat never attempted by the local Indians; and an attack on the return trip by a hostile Indian tribe.

Floyd was buried at "the top of a high round hill overlooking the river & Country for a great distance," long since washed away by the Missouri River, but similar to the location of the modern monument. They named a river after him, and moved on toward greater unknowns.

A two-year expedition into the wilderness required especially thoughtful consideration of medicines. Needing to keep materials to a minimum, Lewis selected carefully, including in his medicine chest the best available pharmaceuticals of the day. It is interesting that these were derived from plants or were simple minerals. Here is what was in Lewis's medicine chest: Balsam, from the tree; Borax, a mineral compound still in use today; Calomel, a mercury compound in the form of a white, tasteless powder, used then as a purgative and used in the twentieth century as a fungicide; Camphor, used to treat pain and itching—it is the whitish and translucent crystalline from the camphor tree that today provides the clean scent in many public bathrooms; Cinnamon Cloves, which relieve toothache; Copperas, which is iron sulphate, then used to treat anemia; Ipecac, a dried root of a South America shrub, used as an emetic; Jalap; Laudanum, which is opium in a solution of water and drinking alcohol; Niter, which we call saltpeter, an ingredient in gunpowder that was also used to treat many diseases, especially asthma; Nutmeg, which in small quantities is a familiar spice but in larger quantities can have some mood-altering effects.

Many modern medicines have the same origins as those Lewis brought on the expedition. Antibiotics, the products of fungi, are arguably the most spectacularly successful of mid-twentieth-century medical discoveries from natural products. The list of plant-derived medicines has grown tremendously, and the potential for new medicines is an argument conservationists frequently put forward as one of the main utilitarian reasons we should conserve rare and endangered plants. Taxol, a product of the comparatively rare Pacific yew tree, found useful in therapy for some cancers, is one of the better-known recent examples of such a find. But aspirin is also a natural plant derivative, from the inner bark of willow. It was well known to the Indians.

It is interesting to consider why plants might produce compounds that are helpful in curing diseases. One reason is that plants produce many chemicals to ward off and kill organisms that feed on them or cause diseases. Unable to strike back with a club, plants have evolved chemical methods to fight their predators and parasites. These are therefore useful to us, in small doses that are not toxic to ourselves but toxic to disease organisms.

Although the interior of a modern hospital or physician's office appears to be quite divorced from the raw nature Lewis and Clark confronted, in fact many of the medicines your physician prescribes come from that nature, or had their original source there. It is another sobering way that we are closely connected to our surroundings, yet rarely aware of them.

Our modern medical care—available just up the highway in Sioux City—would seem to protect us from such incidences. But in spite of the tremendous medical advances made since Lewis and Clark stood by Sergeant

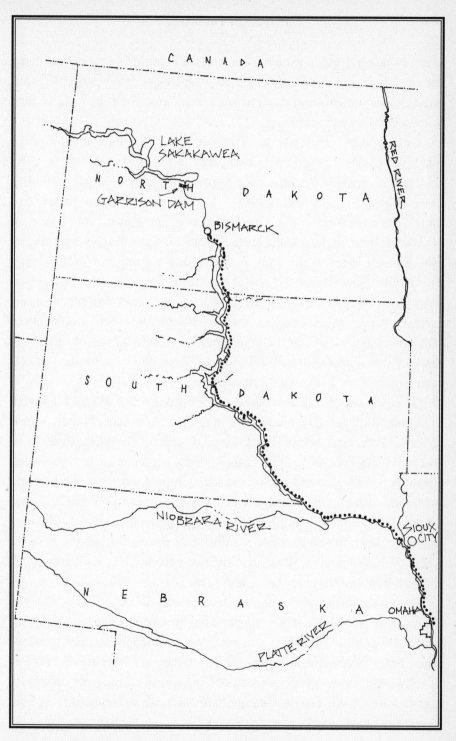

The second part of Lewis and Clark's journey along the Missouri River took them from the present location of Omaha to that of Bismarck, ND, where they spent their first winter.

Floyd as he lay dying, a wilderness hiker today would fare no better from a ruptured appendix. That event requires a timely operation performed with sterilized instruments and modern anesthetics in at least the kind of field hospital used by a modern army,

As I stood in contemplation of this sad event, I thought about modern hikers who often seek to find an experience as much like those of the early explorers as possible. On any hiking trip or expedition, what first aid to bring is always a question. Usually, casual hikers carry less rather than more—sometimes nothing. I remembered two young men I met hiking up Mount Washington, New Hampshire, famous for some of the worst weather ever recorded in the world, with snow recorded in every month of the year. That day had started like the one at the Floyd Monument, warm and perfectly clear. The two men were clad only in shorts, socks, and hiking shoes. "Where are your shirts?" I asked when we stopped for a brief conversation. "Oh, it was so hot, we left them on a tree down below," one of them said, unaware that storms with hail and snow had been known to descend on this mountain in a few hours with little warning.

If you choose to seek a wilderness experience as close as possible to that of Lewis and Clark, you would have to forgo the availability of modern medical assistance, and accept Floyd's risk of death. The alternative, often accepted today even among the most physically rugged of us, is to have society support the search and rescue of sick and injured mountain climbers and wilderness seekers. Increasingly, hikers equipped with GPS satellite positioning devices and cellular phones have been calling in to ask for helicopter assistance when they find it nearing dusk and themselves not yet home or lost. This have-it and not-have-it wilderness experience is spiritually much different from the travels of Lewis and Clark.

As I stood near the monument and looked out at the peaceful scene below, I contemplated a nature that heals us in ways we have generally forgotten and confronts us with risks we think our modern technology eliminates. Like the monument to Sergeant Floyd, these qualities are there before us to see, but are as often passed by, and are just as surprisingly difficult to approach as was our bungled attempt to find a quick and smooth route from a great prairie city to this historic marker.

Since our visit, the grounds at the Floyd Monument have been reno-
vated. The area at the base of the monument is known as the Dr. V. Strode
Hinds Memorial Plaza. Strode was a past president of the Lewis and Clark
Foundation. On the evening of August 20, 1998, the new lights illuminating
the monument were turned on. I am told the lights make the monument
seem to glow against the night sky—truly a lovely sight and site.

23. Sioux City, Iowa, Waterfront Park: Highways and Riverfronts

Sioux City is easily reached by Interstate 29.

As the expedition moved up the Missouri River near the location of
modern Sioux City, Iowa, Lewis and Clark found the river and the prairie
rich with meat, fur, and fruits—a bountiful land. On August 12, 1804, he
noted that beaver were "verry plentiful on this part of the river." On August
15, 1804, Clark saw "Verry fat ducks" and plovers "of different Kinds" on
the river. On August 21, 1804, in the vicinity of modern Sioux City, Clark
discovered "a very excellent froot" like a currant, growing on a shrub
"about the Common hight of a wild plumb." This is the first record of buf-
faloberry, one of the small bounties of the prairie. And so their journals
continue.

The biological richness of the prairie and the river provided a foundation that continues today. The surrounding rich prairie soil is the basis
for grain and meat production. And Sioux City, population 80,000—
120,000-plus including suburbs—is a prosperous center for grain and
meat processing. Located at the confluence of the Big Sioux River, the
Floyd River, and the Missouri River, Sioux City is a natural location for a
city to rise. At this junction farmers could easily bring their produce and
transport their purchases upriver to the northeast and to the west, or
downriver to the south.

We came to Sioux City to use it as a central jumping-off place: to visit
the only downriver portion of the Missouri that has not been channelized
or dammed, which is best visited at Ponca State Park, a thirty-minute drive
from here. We came here also to see how the rest of the river and the countryside had been transformed by human actions since Lewis and Clark

passed this way. We stayed at an inn in South Sioux City, Nebraska, across the river from Sioux City, Iowa, where we could view the city within its environmental setting. "Sioux City" can and does confuse visitors because Sioux City is in Iowa, South Sioux City is in Nebraska, and North Sioux City is in South Dakota.

We had spent the day before driving through a lonely countryside of crops and few people. Here, on the banks of the Missouri, the financial prosperity of the city and its suburbs was evident at a crowded bar at the inn, where businesspeople, vacationers, and military personnel on leave from an airbase talked at a high pitch.

From the bar, we could see a pleasant park across the river. There, a large pavilion stood on a wide lawn, and within it a wedding was taking place in the lazy, late-summer cocktail hour. The bride came down with her entourage, then the groom and his friends. Gradually, the ceremony colored the green lawn with white and black and pastels, a moving tapestry. Between us and the wedding, small outboard motorboats buzzed upstream and floated downstream, sometimes in twos, with people conversing between boats and sharing beers. There was a sense of prosperity and fun. Bicyclers, walkers, and joggers moved past the wedding scene on a cement path along the river.

The inn was separated from the river shore by a wide, irrigated lawn. We strolled outside down the lawn as near to the river as we could get. Here the channelized Missouri River flowed straight. The buzz of conversations was replaced by the murky rumble of outboard engines. The current was swift enough that boats coasting downstream seemed to go almost as fast as those motoring upstream.

I decided to measure the speed of the river. I paced off a distance parallel to the river on the lawn of the inn. From my surveying days I knew that I could walk a measured pace that was close to five feet long. I paced off one hundred feet. There was quite a bit of small flotsam in the river: small tree branches, soda bottles bobbing in the boat wakes, fast-food restaurant plates. I focused on one of the branches and, with my stopwatch, timed how long it took to float the distance. Distance divided by time equals velocity. I picked out a plastic soda bottle and timed its transit. Pretty consistent: The river along its channelized shores was running between five and six miles per hour. Interesting, because on July 17, 1804, Clark made the same measurement when the expedition was south of here, near the Iowa-Missouri border. He recorded in his journal that the river took forty-one seconds to run fifty fathoms. A fathom is six feet, and so his measure worked out to five miles per hour. The Missouri River I stood by at the end of the twentieth century was running just about the same speed as the Missouri River Clark had stood by almost two hundred years before. That's a strong current for a river, I thought, and it would be hard to row upstream against that current. Difficult today if I could find such a boat, and difficult when Lewis and Clark came by here with their pirogues.

I looked again at the entire scene. In the setting sun it was pleasant, and clearly people were enjoying it here. Otherwise the bride would not have picked the waterfront park for her wedding, the bar would not have been so full of conversation, the river not so dense with motorboats. There was prosperity, but not much of a sense of place, of what was special about this setting. This was unlike many famous cities around the world, where people go to see not only architecture, but also the connectedness between artifice and landscape.

Standing along this altered shore, I thought about the experiences of the past weeks, when we had sought to find remnants of the natural landscape and a sense of place for people within the prairie and along the river. The second we had not found. In nearby Gayville, South Dakota, a large billboard said, "Hay Capitol of the World," and I wondered why Sioux City lacked a sign that said "Prairie City of the World" or "Missouri River City."

We had found this indifference to the prairie heritage and prairie river everywhere we had visited over the past weeks. What was missing here seemed to be missing throughout our nation in our approach to environmental issues, which are phrased mostly as "problems" rather than in terms of a natural heritage. Beer drinkers on a noisy outboard on a channelized Missouri River would be condemned by puritanical environmentalists, while those enjoying the boats, disconnected from the very heritage surrounding them that gave rise to their prosperity, would dismiss the accusations and the accusers. Within one landscape, the two sides passed each other by, much as did the downstream and upstream boaters on the Missouri River, each with their own conversations, concerns, assumptions, and focus. The environment was a "problem" viewed within our society as having defenders and opposers—both abstracted from the local natural heritage. Why not seek to integrate a sense of natural history heritage into this setting in which the idea of an "environmental problem" would dissolve into an environmental heritage? Here was one place to do it, with the discretionary income to make it possible.

In a few places, this is happening, as Bill Stevens of the *New York Times* wrote in his book, *Miracle Under the Oaks*. Near Chicago, prairies are being restored as part of volunteer community projects. People are enjoying their natural history heritage and celebrating it by restoring their connection to nature. With that restoration, people can once again feel a place within nature, and once again become a part of nature.

24. South Sioux City and the Bluffs on Fire: Lewis and Clark Learn About the Geology of the Missouri

From Sioux City, Iowa, take Interstate 29 south to Interstate 129 west. This becomes U.S. Route 20. Or, from South Sioux City, Nebraska, take U.S. Route 75 south to U.S. Route 20, then turn right. Watch for roadside historic markers on U.S. Route 20, past Martin Airport to the west of South Sioux City. The signs are located just west of Jackson, Nebraska. One, about one mile west of Jackson, locates the campsite of August 21, 1804; a second, the campsite of August 23 through 25, where Lewis and Clark saw the blue clay bluffs that appeared to have been on fire, with the ground too hot to touch.

From here you can reach Ponca State Park by continuing on U.S. Route 20 to the junction with Route 12, at Willis. Take Route 12 northwest (a right hand turn) to the town of Ponca, then follow Route S26E to the park. Weather permitting, you can see these bluffs across the river from Elk Point, South Dakota, which is on the Missouri floodplain to the north of the river's course.

On August 24, 1804, Lewis and Clark saw "rugged bluffs" on the southwestern shore of the river rising "about 180 or 190 feet high." These bluffs are northeast of present day Newcastle, Nebraska, and six miles southeast of Vermillion, South Dakota. Today they are known locally as the Ionia Volcano. Clark wrote that the bluffs had "lately been on fire and is yet verry Hott." They examined these rocks and tried to ascertain what they were, referring to them as having a "Great appearance of Coal & imence quantities of Cabalt in Side of the part of the Bluff which sliped in." They were studying the geology of the Missouri River, as President Jefferson had commissioned them to do in his letter to Lewis before the journey began. Jefferson instructed them to pay attention to "the mineral productions of every kind, but more particularly metals, limestone, pit coal & saltpeter; salines and mineral waters."

They also studied the geography of the river, each day recording the direction of the river and the distance traveled, making measurements, winding the chronometer, wherever possible determining their latitude and longitude using a sextant. Every day at noon they took a temperature reading. During the day and at the end of each day they estimated the distance traveled. Their measurements were incredibly accurate. And so the days continued. Breakfast, break camp, move upriver, measure the distance, observe the countryside—its rocks, animals, and plants—record these observations, hunt for food, keep the men of the expedition at their tasks, make camp, eat dinner, sleep, and begin again. A measured journey, a scientific expedition—remarkable for its time, for any time.

And so when I was preparing to set out and learn the natural history of the Lewis and Clark expedition, I thought it would be easy to find information about the geology of the Missouri River. After all, they had started this study almost two hundred years before. Just think what scientists ought to know now after that length of concerted effort. I began a search for scientific papers and books about the subject. I readily found information about most of the other great rivers of the world. There were many books and papers about the Amazon River's geology. So too for the Columbia River, the Hudson, the Mississippi. But, oddly, I couldn't find much about the Missouri River. Surely this can't be right, I thought. I had years of experience doing this kind of search for information. What was I doing wrong now?

I decided I had better call my friend and colleague Tom Dunne, one of the world's experts on how rivers and landscape interact. A geologist, he specializes in what is called *geomorphology*, the study of the shape and form of the Earth's surface.

"No, you're not making any mistakes," Tom said over the phone. "You're right. There is not much written about the geomorphology of the Missouri. This subject went out of fashion in the middle of the twentieth century," Tom said. "Then the big construction projects started on the Missouri—the dams, the channelization. When geologists accepted the idea of plate tectonics [in the late 1960s], geomorphology came back into fashion. But by that time, there wasn't enough of the original Missouri left for geologists to get really interested in it. So there hasn't been as much done on that river as on the other great rivers."

And so geology, like other sciences I am acquainted with, has its fashions, with a given topic coming in and out of popularity. Perhaps as the Lewis and Clark expedition becomes more and more popular and the concern for our rivers grows, the geomorphology of the Missouri will come back into fashion.

25. Ponca State Park: Rocks Tell Stories and Soils Are Nature's Braille

From Sioux City take U.S. Route 20 to Nebraska Route 12 and on to the entrance of Ponca State Park. From Gavins Point Dam take County Route 26E south to Nebraska Route 12 and then east to the park.

Early in 1998 a new overlook was built on a bluff in the park. A state and National Park Service project, it contains four excellent interpretive signs. Three states—Nebraska, South Dakota, and Iowa—are visible from these bluffs.

On August 22, 1804, Lewis and Clark "landed at a Bluff" where they got out and examined the exposed minerals. They thought that these included "alum, Copperas, Cobalt, Pyrites." Lewis examined these closely—perhaps too closely. "In proveing the quality of those minerals [Lewis] was near poisoning himself by the fumes & tast of the Cobalt," Clark wrote. Later when they camped for the night, Lewis "took a Dost of Salts to work off the effects

of the Arsenic." As this episode makes clear, theirs was a hands-on expedition. They not only saw, but they touched, tasted, and smelled. In this way
they came to better read and know the countryside.

The next day, August 23, 1804, Lewis and Clark did not have to reach
out to the countryside; it came to them. "The Wind blew hard West and
raised the Sands off the bar in Such Clouds that we Could Scerely See," Clark
wrote, "this Sand being fine and verry light Stuck to every thing it touched,
and in the Plain for a half a mile the distance I was out every Spire of Grass
was covered with the Sand or Dust." They were not just passing through
nature, they were in it. The expedition and the land at this time were not two
things, but one.

I am told that in China, where fish have been farmed in ponds for several thousand years, the farmer tends his ponds in a similarly intimate way.
In the morning he will go out to his pond, kneel on his haunches, take a
palmful of pond water, and smell it. Depending on the smell, he will know
what to do that day. One smell tells him to add a little fertilizer; another, to
get more air into the pond. It is a knowledge handed down among generations and learned by each through touch and scent, senses intimately connected to motion, to change.

Today, accustomed as we are to learning about nature from vision—from
television programs and a quick view from a moving vehicle—we tend to
think of nature somewhat abstractly—as a view more than an experience.

I thought about these experiences when I went to Ponca State Park, near
the bluffs where Lewis tasted and smelled the fumes. This park marks the
southern limit of the unchannelized and undammed stretch of the Missouri.
It is the most accessible location to experience this reach of the river and its
nearby forests, the landscape and river as Lewis and Clark might have experienced them.

The road into the park had taken us through pleasant, shady forests to a
picnic area along the shore. There we saw floating and half-sunk logs interspersed with sandbars. The river meandered, cutting away at the bank. On a
sandbar on the far north side of the river, a family had beached their outboard
motorboat. The mother was sitting on a lounge chair on the sandbar while the
father and the children were walking on the sandbar and swimming and

splashing in the river. The steep, almost vertical cliffs next to the river were pockmarked with swallows' nests. These bluffs, I thought, must be the ones mentioned by Lewis and Clark when they passed this way. They were generally light colored, but had bands shading into dark, almost coal-like rocks.

Cottonwoods, willows, and ash lined the shore. Across the river on the far shore a herd of cows came down a bare-soil trail to the river to drink. It was quiet and peaceful, a pastoral scene. The breeze rustled through the cottonwoods, but there were few other sounds. Quiet was not the way we had been seeing the Missouri River, crowded in by highways and railroads, by industries and cities for most of its length downstream, or its surface resonating with the sound of motorboats.

We drove inland, following meandering roads within the park that led to a series of summits. The bluffs descended steeply to the shore and were wooded with eastern deciduous forest vegetation: eastern white and red oaks, eastern red juniper, basswood, and dogwood. These were the best-developed, richest woodlands we had seen on our journeys into Lewis and Clark country. Unlike most groves of trees that we visited along the Missouri, where grass grew beneath the trees and the woods seemed recently formed or replanted, these woodlands had a rich, dark surface of humus and leaf and twig litter and were dense with shrubs and saplings.

We stopped and strolled into the woods, where I picked up some of the rich organic soil, smelling it and then rubbing a little between my thumb and first finger. I could feel the slickness of fine silts and clays, the grittiness of a little sand, and the soft and pliable bits of leaves and twigs. This handling of the soil, a standard practice among field soil scientists, is one of nature's communications with us, a kind of braille. It might seem crude, but if you do it enough you get to tell one kind of soil from another quickly.

We returned to the river shore, where we sat and ate a picnic lunch. I knelt down by the shore and picked up some sandy soil, rubbing it between my thumb and first finger, to compare this with the soil of the woods. I could feel the individual grains as they spilled back to the ground. Nearby, where there was some vegetation, I did the same thing with the soil. Between my fingers I could feel the slight stickiness of silt and the graininess of sand. Three kinds of soil in three kinds of habitats, distinguishable by touch.

We were careful about where we chose to touch soils and rocks, because at Ponca State Park there is an official concern with endangered species. Walking to the base of a steep bluff, we read a sign posted by the Army Corps of Engineers warning: "Attention boaters and recreationists; least terns and piping plovers are protected by State and Federal Endangered Species Laws. Both species nest on sandbars and beaches on the river. Some of these nesting areas are posted as closed to all access. Do not disturb these birds."

Returning to the shore with a good view of the sandbar in the middle of the channel, we sat back and took in the scent of the river and the downslope breezes carrying the scent of the forest. I was reminded that knowing our surroundings requires more than seeing them. It is common to think of human activities as separate and outside of, or above, nature. It is also common to believe that the activities of scientists separate them from nature. Some believe that these activities are even bad for nature. I thought about the field research I had done in forests in many places. Our measurements often included the diameters and heights of trees, which put us into constant contact with the vegetation, struggling through dense stands of shrubs and saplings, brushing aside the sweat and the mosquitoes, insects that frequently bothered Lewis and Clark. Putting a measuring tape around a tree trunk, we felt the differences among the species, the rough bark of a cottonwood, the smooth alder—another of nature's brailles. Sometimes we collected leaves and soils for analysis, to see how rich they were in nutrients for wildlife. At times we would pick up a little soil and rub it between our fingers.

I found that the process of making these measurements, of touching and smelling, led me to see things I had never noticed before. In a natural area, each creature has a story to tell us. Sometimes in the quiet I would notice a bird flying by that I would have missed if I had been hiking and talking with a companion in the woods. Sometimes I would come across a species of tree I hadn't expected to find and would have missed if I hadn't been out taking measurements and following a systematic process that forced me to examine each tree within a specified area. And I would ask myself what story this tree could tell me. How did its seeds arrive? Why, if this species isn't common here, has it survived? Is there something different about the soil? Or was there some event that allowed it to persist and flourish?

To know the nature of the American Midwest, of the river, the prairie, and the forests, is to do more than see it and pass it by. There is another level of experience, entered into by naturalists like Lewis and Clark through their senses, that sometimes manifests as an intuitive knowledge or understanding, nonverbal and nonvisual. This is how to read nature, to learn nature's stories.

26. Vermillion, South Dakota, and Dixon, Nebraska: Buffalo Demise and Recovery

From Sioux City, Iowa, take Interstate 29 south to Interstate 129 west. This becomes U.S. Route 20. Take Route 20 west past the junction with Route 9 to Tar Box Hollow Road. Take this road south to a mailbox, in the shape of a buffalo, for the Tar Box Hollow Living Prairie Ranch, owned by the Mason family. For brochures and directions, write to Larry Mason, 57957 871st Road, Dixon, Nebraska 68732.

Other places to see buffalo include: Fort Niobrara National Wildlife Refuge in Valentine, Nebraska; the National Buffalo Range; the Little Missouri Grassland and the Theodore Roosevelt National Monument in South Dakota; Custer State Park, South Dakota. At Fort Belknap Indian Reservation of the Gros Ventre and Assiniboine Tribes there are Tribal Buffalo Tours (call the Tribal Visitor Center 406-353-2205). At Custer State Park there are guided jeep rides into a buffalo herd. Fort Niobrara has a fenced-in, self-drive wildlife viewing area. An increase in interest in buffalo has many private ranches developing tourist facilities, so it is worthwhile to seek local information as you travel in Nebraska, the Dakotas, and Montana.

On August 25, 1804, Lewis and Clark along with nine men went north from the Missouri River to visit a place the Indians referred to as a mountain of evil spirits and which has become known as the Spirit Mound. From the top of this hill, about seventy feet above the plains, they had a

A MOTHER BUFFALO AND HER CALF

view of the river valley, which is wide at this point, and Clark noted that he saw upwards of eight hundred buffalo and elk feeding. "From the top of this Mound we beheld a most butifull landscape: Numberous herd of buffalow were Seen feeding in various directions," Clark wrote.

He was north of the location of modern Vermillion, South Dakota. Although they had first seen buffalo when the expedition reached Kansas City, they did not shoot a buffalo until they neared present day Vermillion on August 23, 1804. From this location until past Great Falls, Montana—until July 15, 1805—they saw herds of buffalo on many occasions, and these animals became one of their principal sources of food.

Sometimes they saw large numbers—on June 30, 1805, when they were portaging around the falls downstream from modern Great Falls, Montana, Clark wrote that he thought they could see ten thousand buffalo in a single view. After this they left the buffalo country and saw no more of these animals for the rest of their outbound journey.

Over the numerous trips that I made into the landscape where Lewis and Clark passed, I sought places where buffalo could be seen within a landscape as similar as possible to what Lewis and Clark might have experienced. There are several national wildlife refuges, parks, and grasslands that maintain buffalo, and I tried several of these. At the Little Missouri Grassland and the Theodore Roosevelt National Park, I looked for buffalo but on a hot August day saw only one. I had read on a Web site that a visitor to Fort Niobrara National Wildlife Refuge, near to where the expedition passed, was pretty much assured a view of buffalo. But what I found was buffalo in a paddock— a large pasture and a high fence. Jim Garrett, a Sioux Indian who had studied with me, told me that there were some on his reservation and discussed with me over several years a plan to develop a wildlife migratory corridor from the reservation to Canada, one in which the Sioux would once again be able to follow the big game. But this has not become a reality. Fort Belknap Indian Reservation of the Gros Ventre and Assiniboine Tribes conducts buffalo tours.

As I continued to search for the best place to see buffalo, I thought about the demise of this once-major species of our continent. We think of buffalo as creatures of the American West, but at the time of early European discovery and exploration of North America, they were found over a much wider range. By the time of the Lewis and Clark expedition, the geographic range of the buffalo had been greatly reduced—a fact few Americans know.

Lewis and Clark's first sighting took place once they were past settlements of Europeans, where buffalo had been before but had already been eliminated. This was the characteristic pattern: Buffalo were hunted to local extinction or driven out, as farms with fences and grazing lands with European cattle were established. The plow and the buffalo were considered incompatible.

It is little known how widely dispersed buffalo were at the time of European discovery and early settlement of North America. Cabeza de Vaca, the famous Spanish castaway who spent eight years with the Indians and later recounted his experiences when he returned to Spain, saw buffalo in southern Texas in the 1530s. In 1612, explorer Samuel Argall, sailing on the Chesapeake Bay, saw "a great store of cattle," which were "heavy, slow, and not so wild as other beasts in the wilderness." He had seen buffalo. In 1701 there was an attempt to domesticate buffalo in a new settlement on the James River in Virginia. Near Roanoke, Virginia, buffalo were common at a salt lick until the mid eighteenth century. One herd was reported in southwestern Georgia in 1686. Buffalo were killed off in Georgia by 1780, in South Carolina by 1775. Some evidence suggests that the buffalo had only recently reached the East Coast when Europeans began to settle and explore that area.

These records and others suggest that before the arrival of Europeans, buffalo may have occupied one-third of North America, reaching their northern limits in the boreal forests of Canada and their southwestern limits in the chaparral of southwestern Texas. Buffalo were found in Canada as far north as Great Slave Lake in the Northwest Territories—at latitude 60 degrees north, just north of the present Wood Buffalo National Park, which lies in northern Alberta and the boundary of the Northwest Territories. Fossils of bison, some from as long ago as 40,000 B.C., have been found from New Jersey to California.

The buffalo continued in great abundance for many years after the Lewis and Clark expedition—until after the Civil War. Gen. Isaac I. Stevens was surveying for the transcontinental railway in North Dakota. On July 10, 1853, he and others climbed a high hill and saw "for a great distance ahead every square mile" having "a herd of buffalo upon it." He wrote that "their number

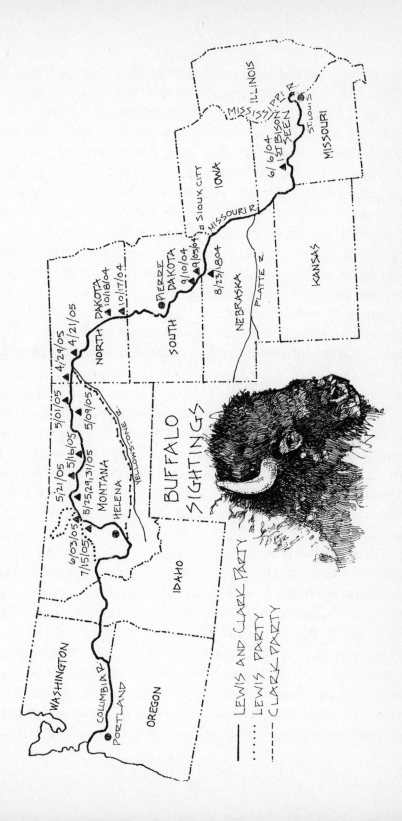

was variously estimated by the members of the party—some as high as half a million. I do not think it any exaggeration to set it down at 200,000."

One of the better attempts to estimate the number of buffalo in a herd was by Col. R. I. Dodge, who took a wagon from Fort Zarah to Fort Larned on the Arkansas River in May 1871, a distance of thirty-four miles. For at least twenty-five of those miles he found himself in a "dark blanket" of buffalo. Dodge estimated that there were 480,000 in the mass of animals he saw in one day. At one point he and his men traveled to the top of a hill, where he estimated that he could see six to ten miles, and from that high point there appeared to be a single solid mass of buffalo extending over twenty-five miles. At ten animals per acre, not a particularly high density, there would have been between 2.7 and 8 million animals.

Just before and just after the Civil War, reports suggested that there were always buffalo somewhere along the tracks of the Kansas Pacific Railroad. In the fall of 1868, "a train traveled one hundred twenty miles between Ellsworth and Sheridan through a continuous, browsing herd, packed so thick that the engineer had to stop several times, mostly because the buffalo would scarcely get off the tracks for the whistle and the belching smoke." That spring a train had been delayed for eight hours while a single herd passed "in one steady, unending stream." At a density of ten buffalo per acre (again, not an especially high density in a migrating herd) there would have been at least 750,000 animals, and quite likely many more—many millions more—depending on the shape of the area covered by the entire herd.

The destruction of the buffalo took place with a rapidity that is hard to grasp. They were killed for two reasons: profit and to eliminate the food of the Indians, and therefore to kill the Indians—an ecological warfare. Col. R. I. Dodge, the same who made one of the estimates of the numbers in a herd, was quoted in 1867 to have said, "Kill every buffalo you can. Every buffalo dead is an Indian gone." In 1864 buffalo robes and tanned hides began to be shipped from St. Louis eastward. New technologies made it possible to increase the use of buffalo. Modern rifles made it easy to kill the animals. Trains made transport of hunters and hides easier. A new tanning process, developed in Germany, allowed the treatment of many more hides, and the finished hides provided a better, more desirable grade of leather. A European market opened for the improved hides.

In the first half of the nineteenth century, the animals were seen as a commodity, like gold, to be removed as quickly as possible for individual profit. Railway construction crews spent their winters—when it was not possible to work on the railroads—hunting buffalo. Although many saw buffalo as a way to riches, ironically few of the buffalo hunters got rich.

The Civil War had its effect on the buffalo. During the war, buffalo hides were used by the military, increasing the market. After the war, army veterans, skilled in shooting rifles, headed west, where they used these skills against the buffalo. A major increase in exploitation of many of America's biological resources occurred just after the Civil War, as new lands opened up in the West, as displaced Southerners found their way westward, and as our nation shifted away from war to the development of transcontinental railways and the settlement of the West. Wild Bill Hickok became one of the major buffalo hunters, along with Buffalo Bill Cody.

Records of the number of buffalo killed were neither organized nor all that well kept, but enough are available to give us some idea of the number taken. The Indians were also killing large numbers of buffalo for their own use and for trade. Estimates range to 3,500,000 buffalo killed a year during the 1850s. In 1870 about 2,000,000 buffalo were killed. In 1872, one company in Dodge City handled 200,000 hides. Estimates based on the sum of reports from such companies, and guesses at how many more would have been taken by small operators and not reported, suggest that about 1,500,000 hides were shipped in 1872 and again in 1873. In these years, buffalo hunting was the main economic activity in Kansas.

As this high harvest continued, concern about the possible extinction of buffalo grew. In 1871, the U.S. Biological Survey sent George Grinnell to survey the herds along the Platte River. He estimated that there were only 500,000 buffalo there, and that at the present rate of killing the animals would not last long. As late as the spring of 1883 a herd of an estimated 75,000 crossed the Yellowstone River near Miles City, Montana, but fewer than 5,000 reached the border. By the end of that year—only fifteen years after the Kansas Pacific train was delayed for eight hours by a huge herd of buffalo—only a thousand or so buffalo could be found: 256 in captivity and about 835 roaming the plains. A short time later, there were only 50 buffalo wild on the plains. The great era of the buffalo was over.

The incredibly rapid demise of these animals demonstrates the power of nineteenth-century technology when put to a destructive purpose. But societal attitudes change. With the rise of the environmental movement in the 1960s, concern with endangered species increased. In recent decades a revival of interest in buffalo on the plains has begun. People began to see profit in running buffalo. One of these families, the Masons who live near Dixon, Nebraska—not far south of where Lewis and Clark shot their first buffalo—started ranching buffalo in 1993. The Masons are returning the land to prairie—in one area they have planted some prairie grasses and forbs, on most of the land they have let the grass go, and as the buffalo graze, their grazing favors prairie grasses, which are reinvading.

Today Larry, Rose, and Monty Mason have 210 buffalo on 480 acres. Their primary business is selling young buffalo—calves born in the spring are sold in the fall—to people who want to have these animals on their own land, to produce buffalo meat or to just have buffalo on the range. But once the business started, people like me began to visit and ask to see the buffalo, so a tourist operation began as an afterthought. Today you can ride in a "hay-wagon"—a comfortable tractor-pulled wagon with seats for twenty or more people, and an arched awning reminiscent of a Conestoga wagon—out into land that is being returned to prairie. We visited the Mason ranch and went out with them. "You don't want to walk among them," Larry said. "They look peaceful, but they are wild animals." We drove out on the track where the buffalo were and watched them graze, push at each other to assert their position in a pecking order, and nurse calves.

I had heard that few ranches were going into the buffalo business because the animals were too strong and agile and it took expensive eight-foot fences to keep them in. I asked Larry Mason about this. "Don't need a high fence," he said. "I figured out there are two things you need to do. Buffalo are herding animals. If you only have a few, they jump a fence to search for a herd. But if you have enough of them, then they want to stay together, and they don't want to stray far. The second thing is to get the buffalo young, so they become adjusted to your land and accept it as their home range." On the ride to see the buffalo, we passed through regular wire gates and electric fences.

Larry had a lot more to say about buffalo: "The meat tastes better if an animal is shot on the pasture. Doesn't get their adrenaline up. You don't know how good meat tastes until you've had it this way. Buffalo meat is low in cholesterol and fat. The buffalo don't marble the meat. They have their fat under the skin, to help keep them warm. These animals get no artificial chemicals."

They found the animals easier to care for than cattle. "Buffalo don't have trouble calving. They don't freeze to death in blizzards. When it snows, they face away from the wind. The wind blows away the ice that forms on their nostrils," Larry said. "Cattle face into the wind, but they suffocate from the ice forming in their nostrils. Most cattle die this way in storms. Buffalo are very healthy. They don't get cancer, as far as we know."

We rode on a dirt track through the rolling terrain to a hollow where the buffalo were herding together. It was calving season and there were three or four puppy-like, snub-nosed, light-brown calves a few days old. When we stopped, the buffalo ambled over to us and Monty took out a bucket full of treats and handed some of them to us. A big bull scratched his back against the haywagon, shaking it on its suspension. He looked up, opened his mouth and put out a long, narrow tongue, and took the cylinder of alfalfa and molasses.

"They're curious animals," Larry said. "You can't leave anything out on the pasture. They come and look at it, push it around." Curiosity and the treats brought them over to us. We sat in the calm quiet and watched the herd. Some grazed lazily. Two young animals pushed at each other, horns locked, for a few seconds until one gave way. In the quiet on the pasture, we heard the low, intestinal-like rumble that is a way the buffalo communicate with each other. Birds called from trees whose leaves were just opening. A gentle wind blew over the pasture. This is nature you can experience when you visit one of the small but well maintained buffalo ranches along the Lewis and Clark trail.

27. Vermillion: On the Wild and Scenic Missouri

In Sioux City, Iowa; Ponca, Nebraska; and Vermillion and Yankton, South Dakota, seek local river guides. There is no formal organization of these guides; check with bait shops, etc.

On August 26, 1804, Clark wrote, "The river verry full of Sand bars," as the expedition passed near the location of modern Vermillion, South Dakota, and moved upstream. They saw "a Island & large Sand bars on both sides" where the river was wide, and the expedition passed white cliffs and elsewhere others of "blue or Dark earth of 2 mile in extent"—cliffs of white chalk estimated now to be late Cretaceous, therefore more than sixty million years old. Two days later they found several sandbars on the river, and Clark reported that "the river here is wide & Shallow full of Sand bars." One of the pirogues struck a snag, which cut through it "and like to have sunk," Clark continued. It was a difficult river, soon to be notorious for its ability to sink boats. These qualities of the river would become all too familiar to steamboat pilots and their passengers.

Steamboats first ran on the Missouri on May 18, 1819, almost fifteen years to the day after Lewis and Clark started their trip. Steamboating as a dominant form of transportation lasted only four decades, ending before the Civil War, replaced by railroads. Yet so treacherous was the Missouri that more than 450 steamboats were lost on the river during that time—a rate of about eleven wrecks a year. Some say that the average lifetime of a steamboat was four trips.

Most of that treacherous, wild Missouri exists no longer, replaced by the Army Corps of Engineers' channelization of the river below Ponca State Park.

Although a hazard to navigation, this original river has a quality of the wild that is little known and little appreciated, except by a few who live along the only downstream reach of the Missouri that has not been channelized. This is the lower, legally designated wild and scenic portion of the Missouri; it extends fifty-nine miles from near Gavins Point Dam to Ponca State Park. It was here that we were fortunate to go out in a small boat with someone who had lived his life on this part of the river.

"I'm just an old river rat," Jim Peterson said. "I was born in Ponca, Nebraska, and my father took me on the river when I was a small boy. Been boating on the river ever since. Don't fish. People ask me what I do on the river. I tell them I just like being on the river." It was a beautiful cloudless spring day when we pushed Jim's outboard boat off the silty bank, a bank that gave way under our feet if we stepped where it was wet—just a little warning by the river about the material that it used to make up its sandbars.

Soon we were out in the middle of the Missouri, passing a large sandbar of the type Clark observed almost two centuries before. After busy days of travel by car and traveling here and there on the channelized Missouri, we felt a wonderful sense of peacefulness in the center of the river. We passed lines of cottonwoods just opening their leaves on the large sandbar/island. An occasional waterbird flew before us. There was no one else on the river. This was the most serene and beautiful of all our experiences on the lower Missouri—the Missouri below the most downstream of the big dams. Jim slowed the boat to see if we could get up a small tributary. The silty sediment of the river scratched against the aluminum bottom of the boat. But for Jim's experience and skill, we might have run aground. Jim backed the boat off. It may sound strange to say that a motorboat ride was serene and gave a sense of wildness, but on this big river, this is exactly what we felt.

"If anybody tells you he never ran aground on this part of the Missouri," Jim said, "he's a liar. I run aground from time to time." Jim was much more than a river rat. He had recently retired as a faculty member at the University of South Dakota and was president of the Lewis and Clark Trail Heritage Foundation. He was a devotee of the Lewis and Clark expedition; his pickup license plate was "LCTHF." Jim knew the river so well that he had navigated the paddle-wheel steamboat, the *Far West*, from Yankton, South Dakota, to

EASTERN RED CEDAR

Ponca—through this untamed portion of the river—when that boat was being moved to Florida, having failed to attract enough customers to maintain a tourist business from Yankton.

We talked about why there was so little tourist business taking people on the river. He said the season was short—June, July, and August—and the liability insurance rates were extremely high for motorboats, and that a federal motorboat license was required. "As soon as Labor Day is past, children are in school and the business dries up," he said. But he also observed that the number of foreign visitors was increasing, and I suggested that this kind of business might begin to attract a different, wider audience as the Lewis and Clark journey became more popular. Jim spoke of the difficulties of navigating the sandbars and snags on the river. That is another reason it is a difficult tourist business. The very qualities that made the Missouri a beautiful and peaceful place to be on that spring day are the ones that make it difficult to be there.

And so it is difficult today to find a way to travel on this wild and scenic reach of the Missouri River. We asked Jim what a visitor could do, because there is no professional organization of river guides here. "Go into a local bait shop, boat dealer, or bar," he said. "Ask around. Usually you can find a river rat like me who will be happy to take you on the river." At least until the river becomes so popular that the boatmen form a professional organization. As the boat eased back against the silty shore, we decided that if your intention was to experience the sense of the river as it used to be, and to seek a place of beauty on the Missouri, you would come here.

28. The Niobrara River Meets the Missouri: Cedars Persist on the Bright Bluffs

From Yankton, South Dakota, take Route 81 south to Route 12, turn right (west), and continue through the town of Niobrara. The road follows a bluff uphill, and a short way beyond the town, on the slope, is the entrance to Niobrara State Park on the right. To canoe on the Niobrara River, continue

Grand Tower on the Missouri Above the Niobrara, watercolor and pencil on paper. From the original by Karl Bodmer. The Missouri looks much the same at this location today.

on Route 12 to Valentine, Nebraska, more than 120 miles to the west. There are several outfitters in Valentine.

On August 25, 1998, a new bridge over the Missouri opened for traffic. It is located about three miles east of Niobrara and will eventually connect Nebraska Route 14 to South Dakota Route 37. The bridge ends in South Dakota at Running Water, about ten miles west of Springfield, South Dakota.

On September 4, 1804, Lewis and Clark were traveling up the Missouri River where it flows generally west to east, upstream about thirty miles from today's town of Yankton, South Dakota, when they reached the mouth of the Niobrara River. That river flows generally from southwest by west, Clark wrote, forming an acute angle with the Missouri River and leaving a peninsula between the two. Clark observed that "Qui courrse," referring to the river by its French name, "Comes roleing its Sands" and was "Throwing out Sands like the Platt (only Corser) forming bars in its mouth." As was his practice, he measured the river and found it "152 yards wide at the mouth & 4 feet Deep." Traveling up the Niobrara three miles to where there had been a Ponca Indian village, he found that "The river widens above its mouth and is devided by Sand and Island, the Current verry rapid." The river was colored light, "like that of the Plat." Along the Niobrara, "on the upper Side," Clark saw "a butifull Plain riseing gradially from the river." Wildlife was abundant.

The next day, September 5, 1804, the expedition headed upstream on the Missouri River and Clark wrote that they "passed a large Island of about 3 miles long in the Middle" of the river, opposite of which was Ponca Creek.

Today the lower Niobrara River is part of the Wild and Scenic River System and famous among boaters as one of the top ten canoeing rivers in the United States. I had wanted to see this river for a long time, partly because it has not been channelized or otherwise altered, except for a small dam near Valentine, Nebraska. Although much smaller than the Missouri, the Niobrara retains the characteristics of a prairie river as Clark described it, flowing rapidly, carrying a heavy sediment load, and divided by sandbars. I had also wanted to see the Niobrara because it is the river of one of my favorite books, which I had read several times since high school—*Old Jules,* by the great Nebraska writer Mari Sandoz. She portrayed a prairie country that was open and lonely, but with a certain special appeal of the Niobrara River. We arrived at the mouth of the Niobrara on a beautiful spring afternoon, full of anticipation, but still greatly surprised by the beauty of the landscape and of the two rivers, the Niobrara and the Missouri, at their confluence.

We stayed at Niobrara State Park in a cabin on a bluff overlooking the confluence and the surrounding rolling countryside. It was the most beautiful place that we stayed on the Missouri River downstream of Montana. Late that afternoon we went out on the river in a Zodiac powered by an outboard motor with Rick Plooster, assistant park superintendent, on a trip available to park visitors during the summer. Here the Missouri River is upstream from Gavins Point Dam and downstream from the other five major Missouri River dams. The river flow is controlled, but otherwise the Missouri has the aspect of the unchannelized river as Lewis and Clark described it.

The Missouri widens upstream from the mouth of the Niobrara into a beautiful stretch of water with extensive sandbars on the northern, South

Dakota side and with beautiful bluffs on the southern, Nebraska side. We passed a large island just as Clark had mentioned, and saw that it was large enough to have several vacation homes on it and to be well wooded. Along the island's shore was a layer of silty and sandy sediment among which large cottonwoods grew, perhaps sixty feet high. We stopped to look at a beaver lodge above the water level. Rick said that the island was used frequently in the summer by deer who browse on its trees.

We moved away from the island. Scaup and mergansers paddled and flew. An immature eagle soared above us. We saw that the land on the southern, Nebraska shore was a series of bluffs and valleys, each bluff like an arch and each valley with seasonal or flowing small drainages. The exposed rocks on the bluffs were yellow chalk, brightening in the late afternoon sunlight. On some bluffs, below the chalk a shalelike rock was wasting away like roof shingles decaying on an old ranch house. Hundreds of swallows' nests clung to the underledges on the bluffs. Red cedars covered the summits of the bluffs, bur oaks grew on the midslopes, and grasses in the valleys. In the angling sunlight, the blue sky, dark green cedars, and yellow sandstones reflected beautifully from the river. Beyond the river the land had the look of dry country and of the West. Rick said he thought this was a hidden jewel of a park and we agreed.

Since cedars come into prairie when fire is suppressed, and since frequent fires keep the cedars out and promote grasses, I thought that the dense stands of cedars on the summits must be the result of fire suppression since settlement and farming of this land. The pattern was well known, and we had seen it at Loess Hills State Recreation Area in Iowa: Where fire has been suppressed and water is abundant, cedars grow and shade out the prairie grasses. But cedars are also relatively short-lived trees, few reaching one hundred years. I guessed that the dense cedars on the bluffs must be an indication that the wildfire suppression began within the last one hundred years.

In the evening, we walked through the park. We saw deer and turkeys in the twilight and heard the turkeys call, joined by the haunting fluting of whippoorwills. After the sun went down, I decided to check the journals of the Lewis and Clark expedition once again. On September 4, 1804, Clark wrote that he saw turkeys, much as we had seen and heard them that evening. But I was surprised to read that upstream a little way from the mouth of the Niobrara, Clark "walked on the top of the hill forming a Cliff Covd with red Ceeder." And here the expedition stopped to make a new mast of cedar. If the red cedar were there almost two hundred years ago just as they were on our visit, then it is unlikely that there has been a change in fire frequency. I had been too quick to attribute causes to human interventions. Perhaps the wildfire frequency was lower here than elsewhere because the two rivers came together at an acute angle, somewhat isolating the land between them from fires. Also, fires were less likely to reach the tops of the bluffs, so the cedars might have been protected that way. But some wildfires had to reach the cedars. Otherwise the cedars would begin to reach their maximum age and die back, and we would have seen many dead cedars and logs, and perhaps other trees like the oaks would have been coming in among the cedars.

Once again, I found that there was much about the natural history of the American West that I could learn from the combination of reading these journals and reading the landscape. The journals were more than the interesting history of an adventure. They provided an accurate account of the landscape and its plants and animals almost two hundred years ago, a description difficult to obtain elsewhere because few made such careful notes as Lewis and Clark. Even today, in our age of information, it is rare to find careful journals about the natural history of a region.

PRONGHORN

The next day we drove to Valentine, Nebraska, rented a canoe, and paddled down the Niobrara for about twelve miles. A stiff wind blew and the water was cold in early spring. It was before the main canoeing season and we saw no other people on the river, famous for its wall-to-wall canoeists in the summer.

In the fast-moving current, we passed sandbars and wetlands as the river took us through a deep valley beside rising bluffs. Once again we were surprised by the beauty of this landscape, a place we hoped to return to one day; a place with the look and feel of the countryside seen by Lewis and Clark and from which we had learned a little more, with the help of Clark's journal, about the natural history of the western landscape.

29. The Confluence of the Niobrara and Missouri Rivers: Lewis and Clark Begin to See the Animals of the West

For directions to this area, refer to the entry for Niobrara State Park.

On September 4, 1804, Clark recorded the expedition's first encounter with mule deer and pronghorn, providing the first written scientific description of the mule deer, whom they so named, and the name stuck. Clark referred to "Several wild goats on the Clift & Deer with black tales." Later, on September 17, 1804, when the expedition neared the location of modern Chamberlain, South Dakota, Clark wrote a longer description of mule deer when one of the men, Colter, shot one. Clark observed that it was "a Curious kind of Deer, A Darker grey than Common the hair longer & finer, the ears verry large & long a Small resepitical under its eye its tail round and white to near the end which is black & like a Cow" but "in every other respect like a Deer, except it runs like a goat" and later that it "jumps like a goat or Sheep" and it was "large."

The expedition was near the hundredth meridian, entering the short-grass prairie and the landscape and wildlife that we identify today as the American West—cowboy-and-Indian country of open plains and big skies. They began to encounter a wealth of new species.

On that day also one of the hunters brought in "a Small wolf with a large bushey tail," probably the expedition's first encounter with a coyote. It was another of their contributions to biological science. A few days later they would find prairie dogs and provide not only their first written description, but the first live specimen to be sent back and reach Virginia. On September

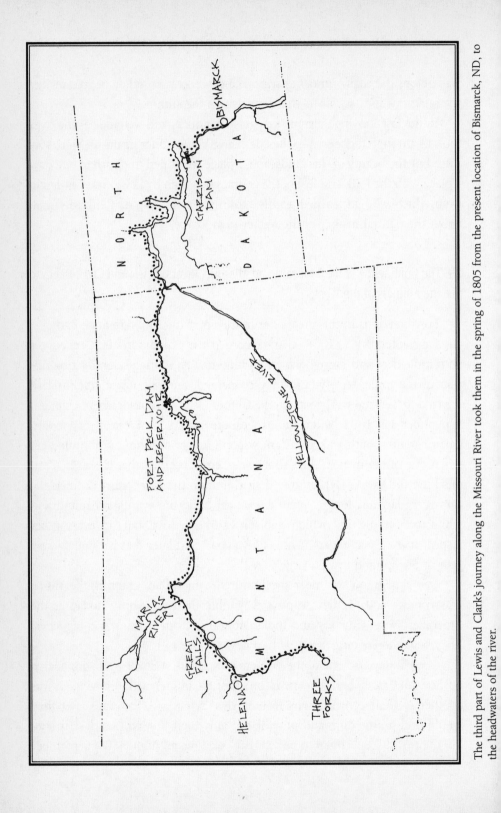

The third part of Lewis and Clark's journey along the Missouri River took them in the spring of 1805 from the present location of Bismarck, ND, to the headwaters of the river.

16, 1804, they saw and shot a black-billed magpie, about which Lewis wrote a detailed description, noting that "the wings have nineteen feathers, of which the ten first have the longer side of their plumage white in the middle of the feather" and the "upper side of the wing, as well as the short side of the plumage" was "a dark blackis or bluish green sonetimes presenting as light orange yellow or bluish tin as it happens to be presented to different exposures of ligt." He wrote that "it is a most beatifull bird" with the outer wings changing in color with different light to be an orange green and then a reddish indigo blue. He was observing one of the many kinds of birds whose plumage color is the result of the way light is refracted from the feathers rather than from an actual dye.

The mule deer is the characteristic deer of the western plains and Rocky Mountains, living in conifer forests, desert shrub lands, and prairies. At the time of Lewis and Clark the mule deer occurred west from the Dakotas to the Pacific coast. Along the coast, they were found from Baja California to British Columbia. In the prairie, they ranged from the south edge of Alaska through Canada, south into central Texas and interior Mexico. Mule deer feed primarily on herbaceous plants including grasses, but also browse on shrubs and trees. The whitetail deer, the characteristic deer of the eastern United States, is more of a forest animal, primarily feeding on leaves and twigs of shrubs and trees, as well as acorns. At the time of the Lewis and Clark expedition, the whitetail had a larger range, and was found in Lewis and Clark's home state of Virginia as well as the entire eastern seaboard. It was absent at that time only from the Rocky Mountains and California. Both deer remain abundant.

The pronghorn antelope is native only to North America. It has been here for about fifty million years, since the Eocene. Pronghorn feed on grasses and forbs during the growing season and shrubs in the fall and winter. Some experts estimate that at the time of the Lewis and Clark expedition pronghorn may have been almost as abundant as buffalo, perhaps numbering thirty or forty million. But soon after the Lewis and Clark expedition, pronghorn became a major item in the diet of pioneers, and was also sold commercially. A creature of the prairie, the pronghorn lost its habitat to the plow and cattle. By the beginning of the twentieth century there were only about ten thousand pronghorn remaining.

Concern about the decline of this species occurred rather early in the history of conservation in America. In the early twentieth century, states began to pass laws protecting the pronghorn and outlawing its hunting. A yearly census of the herds began, as well as collection of information about diseases and predation. In the 1920s the first extensive census was made over the entire range, and there appeared to be about thirty thousand pronghorn. Today these animals number over a million, with the greatest numbers in Montana, Wyoming, and North Dakota. They remain relatively rare in South Dakota— under ten thousand. Pronghorn have increased in abundance over the past eighty-five years, more than doubling between the late 1970s and late 1980s. With care and restoration of prairie habitat, the outlook for the pronghorn remains good. It is possible to see pronghorn along Interstate 90 east and west of Gillette, Wyoming, but most likely you will still have to seek wildlife refuges and prairie preserves to see these animals.

MULE DEER
BUCK

30. Fort Mandan Park, North Dakota: Winter on the Plains

From Bismarck take Route 83 north to Washburn. Do not take the turnoff into the town of Washburn. Go just north of Washburn and take a left turn on Route 200. Watch for a sign on the right that says two miles to the Fort Mandan reconstruction, open 1–5 Tuesday through Sunday. Make an immediate right turn. This road takes you to the edge of the river, and you will be on the east side of the Missouri River. The Lewis and Clark Interpretive Center, dedicated in June 1997, is located here.

An interesting circle route from Bismarck is to go first to the reconstruction of Fort Mandan, then return to Route 83 north and follow it to Route 200 west, to Garrison Dam, which forms Lake Sakakawea. Then drive to

Sakakawea State Park, where there is good viewing of wildlife. From there, return to Route 200 south and visit the Knife River Indian Village National Historic Site. This is an archeological site and a reconstruction of the villages of the Indians that Lewis and Clark would have seen. From there take Route 200 south and east to Route 200A. You can either take Route 31 south to Interstate 94 or, if there is time, take a side trip on Route 200A to Hensier, then a gravel road south a few miles to Sanger, and then a gravel road east a few miles to Cross Ranch State Park on the shore of the Missouri River, a park purchased by the Nature Conservancy. From there return west on the gravel road and continue south on the first gravel road to Route 25, southeast to Interstate 94, and then to Bismarck.

Lewis and Clark reached the Mandan village where the expedition would spend its first winter on October 21, 1804. Auspiciously, the day after they arrived, they saw a beautiful plain "covered with herds of buffalo," one of which they shot for food. Although winter was approaching, their arrival was pretty much as planned. They were still in "discovered" country, land that had become known to Europeans, mainly French-Canadian traders, trappers, and hunters, and the usual raggle-taggle of the curious, the rough, the ill-fit, and the outcasts of civilization. From these, the Mandan villages were known to Lewis and Clark as a place of peaceful Indians where they might overwinter. The maps they saw in St. Louis in 1803 and early 1804, and had copied and carried with them, showed the Missouri up to these villages.

Methodical as always, they had reached this destination just in time before winter set in, and knew that it would be impractical to proceed farther that year. Winter had approached the expedition with a deliberateness recorded firmly in the pages of their journals. Observant of everything and determined in their attempts to record what they saw, Lewis and Clark wrote of the change in the seasons as they approached the area that is now near Bismarck, North Dakota. On the first of October the leaves of ash and poplar and most of the shrubs had begun to turn yellow and "decline." There was a slight "white" frost on the fifth of October, and they saw brant and geese "passing to south"; frost the next night and teal, gulls, and mallards. On the thirteenth the cottonwoods were yellow and their leaves falling; on the fourteenth the leaves of all the ash, elm, and all other trees except cottonwood had fallen; on the seventeenth snow geese passed overhead. Pronghorn antelope passed on their fall migration.

Lewis and Clark brought a thermometer along with them and recorded the temperature at noon and at four in the afternoon whenever possible. During their winter with the Mandans, they recorded temperatures in January 1805 that ranged, within a few weeks' time, from minus forty to plus thirty-five degrees Fahrenheit. The next summer, Clark and Sacagawea were almost drowned by an intense thunder and hailstorm; within a month afterward, Clark walked in dry heat that gave him sunstroke. Extremes of weather seemed to be the rule. Part of the reason for these extremes is that the Missouri River basin lies totally within the interior of a major continent, far from the ameliorating effects of an ocean.

Interiors of continents are notorious for their highly variable climate. Fast changes in temperature, like those Lewis and Clark experienced in January 1805, occur because the Missouri River basin is at the crossroads of major air masses. Some come from the north, some from the south, generally one alternating with the other. This leads to large changes in temperature over a few days, even within a few hours. In the basin as a whole, temperature extremes range from minus 20 degrees in the winter to plus 110 degrees in the summer, although Lewis and Clark measured even deeper cold.

On the nineteenth of October, 1804, there was a hard frost, freezing clay near the river as well as water in containers. The day after they arrived at the Mandan villages, a half inch of snow fell. By the twenty-fifth all the leaves on the trees had fallen, including those of the cottonwoods. Snow fell but did not stay on the ground. Violent winds struck on the twenty-eighth and twenty-ninth, and in this way winter came.

They would stay here until April 7, 1805—more than five months. They began to build their winter camp on the second of November, calling it Fort Mandan, at a site later known as Fort Clark, since believed to have been washed away by the Missouri. In the early summer of 1998, the federal government provided a grant for further work on Fort Mandan. Additional searching is now being conducted for Fort Mandan, and a preliminary site survey has been made. I came to see a reconstruction of Fort Mandan at a small park located about eight miles downriver from the original site. Since

Bismarck, North Dakota, and International Falls, Minnesota, seem to vie for the coldest winter temperatures, I wanted to see the place where Lewis and Clark survived a cold winter with little equipment, and to find out as much as I could about how they did it.

I had spent most of one winter with my wife and newly born daughter in a small, old farmhouse heated only by one wood stove and two fireplaces. The house I stayed in was in Acworth, New Hampshire, far from North Dakota in miles, but with severe winters, perhaps not quite as cold as Bismarck, North Dakota, but chilly enough. The house sat on a slope, so that the winter winds whistled up through thin and worn siding into a partial basement and then into the living room. I heated the house with firewood that I cut and split myself. My daughter was born in the fall and knew her first five months in that house. The memories of the cold and the time spent cutting wood and keeping the fires going in the middle of the night came back to me as we drove out of Bismarck to find the reconstruction of the Lewis and Clark campsite.

We took Route 83 north, through farm country—hay, corn, grain, a few cows—then turned left onto Route 200. A sign pointing to the right said two miles to the Fort Mandan reconstruction. We made an immediate right turn and drove to the river. A flock of magpies scattered in the grass by the road.

A sign at the visitors' center showed a map of the area, indicating that the Fort Mandan reconstruction was several miles down the river from the original Fort Mandan. The original fort was upstream on this side of the Missouri, and almost directly across the river from the present Fort Clark State Historical Site, a site off Route 200 on the west shore. We could see that our circle route would take us to that historical site.

It was noon and there were no other visitors. I hadn't understood from the Lewis and Clark journals that they had camped down on the floodplain, where a modest bluff provided some protection from the winds, and within a grove of cottonwoods along the river that provided additional protection from the winds. The reconstruction had these features, and perhaps the original Fort Mandan was located near the shore for the same reasons, and also because that was where cottonwoods, the only large trees in any abundance in this part of the plains, grew. How much worse the winter would have been in crude huts up above the floodplain, without the protection of the bluffs or the trees.

Lewis and Clark had the men build huts of cottonwood, "this being the only timber we have," Clark wrote on November 6, 1804. Sergeant Gass described the huts as "in two rows, containing four rooms each, and joined at one end forming an angle." The floor was of split planks, covered with clay and grass. The roofs reached about eighteen feet above the ground. Two storerooms were built in the angle formed by the other huts. During the building of the fort, two men cut themselves with axes. Meanwhile, ducks, geese, and brants continued to pass overhead. On November 13, some of the men moved into their huts and began their stay for the winter. The next day Clark wrote that the ice was "running very thick" as the river rose and some snow fell. On the sixteenth "a very white frost" covered "all the trees" with ice, and all the men moved into huts, finished or not.

Along with, and as a consequence of, the varying temperatures, the Missouri River basin has a great variation in wind, reaching one hundred miles per hour. Winds are strongest in the spring as a rule. The high winds increase the rate of water evaporation, making the soil drier than would occur from the temperature and rainfall in comparatively still air. Winter blizzards—snowstorms with strong winds—are a common winter hazard.

With the huts finished enough to protect them from the worst of the weather, the men of the expedition then turned to hunting—out of necessity. On the nineteenth of November the hunters returned with "32 deer, 12 elk and a buffalo," the first mention in the journals of buffalo since mid-October, most likely because Lewis and Clark had been occupied with preparation for the winter, rather than a lack of the animals in the neighborhood. The weather improved toward the end of November. November twenty-third was a "far warm day" as were the next two, but then the weather turned again and became very cold and windy.

On the thirtieth of November the Mandan chief told Lewis and Clark that some of his hunters had been attacked and killed by the Sioux. "We thought it well to show a disposition to aid and assist them against their enemies," Clark wrote. Lewis and Clark took twenty-three men armed and on horseback with a promise to defend the Mandans, but the chief suggested that they wait until spring because the snow was too deep for the horses and it was too cold. Winter was closing in upon them and their crude huts were barely completed, a food supply was not in, but they took up arms and went out with their horses to help their hosts against enemies. So began their first winter on the plains.

On December 7, 1804, the chief of the Mandans told Lewis and Clark that there were "great numbers of buffalo" on the hills nearby. Lewis went with a hunting party of fifteen of his men and killed eleven, "three in view of our fort," but the weather was "so excessively cold and the wolves plenty, we only saved five of them." Clark went with another party on the next day with eighteen men and four horses, when the temperature was forty-four degrees below freezing, and found buffalo about seven miles away. They killed eight, but several of the men suffered frostbite. On the ninth, Lewis went out and stayed out all night, experiencing "a cold disagreeable night . . . in the snow on a cold point with one small blanket." The ice was so hard on the river that the buffalo crossed without breaking through. Lewis and his men killed nine buffalo, but many were "so meager that they [were] not fit for use." On the twelfth, pronghorn were seen but the weather was "so cold that we do not think it prudent to turn out to hunt." Clark, however, with his proclivity to make measurements, paced the width of the river by walking across on the ice; he found it to be five hundred yards wide.

Clark went on a hunting party on December 14 and 15 when there was "much snow" and it was fifty-two degrees below freezing. Buffalo continued to be seen on the eighteenth, but again the weather was too cold for hunting. Thus during this period they appeared to have been visited by a large herd, which remained in the vicinity of the camp for ten days. They next reported buffalo on January sixth, when Clark was out hunting them with sixteen men, killing a total of eight.

On January 14, Clark wrote that one of their hunters, who had been sent out for several days, returned to say that another member of the expedition, Whitehouse, was so badly frostbitten that he could not walk home.

In spite of the cold, Lewis reported on the same day that there was an eclipse of the moon, which he observed with the small refracting telescope that was part of his sextant, having "no other glass to assist me in this observation." He was able to "define the edge of the moon's image." He wrote that clouds interrupted his observations, which made the observation of the "commencement of total darkness" inaccurate. "The last two observations the end of total darkness and the end of the eclipse, were more satisfactory," he wrote. These observations Lewis used to locate the longitude of their winter fort. Thus he continued, in spite of the cold, to carefully map the expedition's course across the continent and to make quantitative measurements, in keeping with the scientific purpose of the expedition.

While we think of "man and nature" as a primitive experience—men pitting themselves against nature without the aid of civilization—in fact technologies played a key role in the success of the expedition, as Lewis's use of his sextant to observe the moon testifies. Most important to the expedition, along with the sextant, were the compass, the gun, blacksmithing, knowledge of surveying, the ability to make wheels, wagons, and ax handles, and of course the ability to write. At times, the blacksmith traded his skills for Mandan corn and repaired many objects. The gun saved several of the men from grizzlies later in the trip, and hunting with guns provided the staple food, meat.

On the fourth of February, Lewis wrote that "no buffalo have made their appearance in our neighborhood for some weeks" and their "stock of meat" was nearly exhausted. Clark decided to take a group of men and go downriver to hunt. They pulled their baggage on small wooden sleighs, and also brought three packhorses to carry any meat they acquired.

Clark returned on the night of the twelfth. He and his men had walked thirty miles on the ice and through the woodlands. In some places the snow was up to their knees. On their first day, the fourth, they had found nothing to hunt and had nothing to eat. On the second, Clark broke through the ice and his feet and legs were wet. On that day they killed a deer and two buffalo, but the buffalo were in too poor condition to eat. They saw buffalo on February 8 but found them again too lean to be worth taking. On the trip they killed elk and deer, which provided their meat until they were able to hunt again. They had killed a total of forty deer, three buffalo, and sixteen elk. They saw no more buffalo that winter.

Today we often romanticize about nature. Most of us see nature on television, in the comfort of central heating and air conditioning. Or we go to the ski slopes or snowmobiling with the best of modern gear. It is cold, but relatively few of us test ourselves against winter as did Lewis and Clark and their men, arriving at a place strange to them, maintaining good terms with the Mandans, building shelter for the winter, and finding food. In the spring, they would move forward into an area completely unknown to the mapmakers who'd come to St. Louis. It is well to remember the difficult winter Lewis and Clark spent with the Mandans when we romanticize about nature and believe that what we may conserve will always be benign for us to visit. It is just as likely to be like Clark's hunting trip, with falls through the ice, buffalo too lean to eat, and the constant danger of frostbite.

31. Knife River Indian Villages: Choosing a Place to Live Within Nature's Constraints and Opportunities

From Bismarck, North Dakota, take Route 83 north past Washburn and turn left onto Route 200. Turn left onto Country Route 37 where there is a sign to the Knife River Indian Village National Historic Site. Or you can make this visit part of a trip to the restoration of Fort Mandan. To do this, take 83 north to connect to Route 1806, a route named in honor of Lewis and Clark's year of return, to Garrison Dam, which forms Lake Sakakawea. Drive to Sakakawea State Park, where there is good viewing of wildlife. From there return on Route 1806 east to Route 200 south and visit the Knife River Indian Village National Historic Site.

Soon after Lewis and Clark arrived near the present location of Bismarck, North Dakota, and began to settle in for the winter, to build their cabins and fort, they went to meet neighboring Indians. Several closely related groups of Indians lived in the area in small villages, some using different if related languages. Lewis and Clark visited the nearby villages, including one on the Knife River, where they spoke with the chief. Today, the Knife River village is a national historic site, historic because Indians lived there at the time of European expansion into the American West, and also a significant archaeological site, because Indians inhabited this village for many generations. Its villagers were Hidatsas Indians known as the Awaxawi, who were close relatives of the Mandans. Charbonneau and his wife, Sacagawea, probably lived in this village before joining the expedition.

The people of the Knife River village were known to later travelers. Karl Bodmer, the famous landscape artist, painted this area and many of the Indians when he accompanied Prince Maximillian, who came from Europe to retrace the travels of Lewis and Clark in 1833–34. Living in the days before photography and being a person of considerable means, Maximillian brought Bodmer along as his personal illustrator of their travels.

I thought of Bodmer's paintings and decided that the Knife River village would be a good place to try to understand how the Indians visited by Lewis and Clark lived within the countryside, in this environment famous for its cold winters. I wanted to see in what ways they made use of the topography and how they located their village in relation to resources.

Lewis and Clark chose to build their fort near a Mandan village but down on the floodplain of the Missouri River. The Mandan and Hidatsas villages were somewhat away from the main channel, up on the prairie. In our day, we are used to housing developed in large tracts where the land is bulldozed and flattened, where water is supplied by a central water authority, trash is picked up, sewage systems take away other wastes, and central heating and air conditioning keep us comfortable. Within this modern environment, it is easy to think that there is no connection between the location of a settlement—village, town, fortification, or city—and its environment. But that wasn't true in the past, and it isn't really true today.

We stayed overnight in Bismarck and drove north early the next day. The countryside to our right, away from the river, was planted in hay, corn, and small grains and looked pretty in the morning summer light. Where a sign indicated a turnoff to the town of Washburn, we saw a dense band of trees covering a number of acres on the far, western shore of the Missouri, which looked less settled and populated.

We reached a parking area marked by a sign that said, "Awatixa X'e Village." We saw a few people walking through the remains of the village. It was a warm summer day with a pleasant steady breeze beneath cumulus clouds. I walked about a half mile to the shore of the Knife River, a small, pleasant stream well wooded along its shores. Along the way, I passed remains of

Indian dwellings, round depressions in the soil. These seemed to fit Clark's description, made on October 27, 1804, when he visited a village of similar design and wrote that "the houses are round and Very large Containing Several families." The dwelling sites were crowded so close together that there was little room between them even to dry corn, suggesting either a close-knit social structure or a need for protection against other tribes. There were fifty-one such depressions visible. At least four hundred people occupied this village from the late 1790s until 1834. At the shore of the Knife River a sign advised us to look for artifacts, and we did, finding bones of animals embedded in the side of the bluff, where one did not have to excavate in order to see them.

I looked at the village setting and asked myself, If I were to settle here and try to survive the winters, and also enjoy the kind of pleasant summer day that we were fortunate to find, would I pick this location? Yes, I decided, I might. It seemed to be a well-chosen place for a village—near water, in a pretty countryside. Game was nearby. We noticed few annoying insects. The streamside was wooded and would provide fuel for the winter. From the village one could see buffalo or enemies in the distance.

Before modern technological civilization, people had to locate their villages and homes to make the best use of the topography and resources. I had a friend who worked as a plumber but was well known for his ability to find Indian artifacts even in a highly settled landscape. One day we got to talking about how he found so many arrowheads and other tools. "It's easy," he said. "I just go to a place and look around and ask myself: If I were going to live here, where would I put my home? Then I go to that spot, and that's where I find Indian tools." The rules are the same, it just takes experience in understanding what makes a good dwelling site. Perhaps his work as a plumber made him more aware of these factors.

When you visit the Knife River Indian Village National Historic Site, you can look around and try to decide if you would want to set a village here, and if so, just where you would put your home. It is a lesson we need to learn again. Even with modern technology, a house will be more efficient in terms of energy use and more comfortable if it is properly situated in relation to its local environment. For thousands of years houses were designed so that they were in the best position to gather sunlight in the winter. The classic Mediterranean houses of Greece and Rome had an enclosed court-yard that faced south so that the sun warmed the house in winter. Recently, the U.S. Environmental Protection Agency supported research that shows that deciduous shade trees planted on the south side of a house cool the house in warm climates significantly in the summer and let the sunlight warm the house in the winter. The early European settlers built sod houses set partially into the ground, because this made them warmer.

Today there is a growing return to the understanding that the location of a house, the compass direction it faces on that location, and the kind of veg-etation planted around it can make a big difference in economics, energy effi-ciency, and the coziness of the house.

My visit to the site of the Knife River Indian village, in a cold climate where people lived for centuries, set me to thinking about this important connection between ourselves and our environment. A breeze picked up and the air felt just a little chilly, a reminder of the cold that was ahead, and of the harsh win-ter that Lewis and Clark spent near here along the Missouri River.

32. Little Missouri National Grassland and Theodore Roosevelt National Park: Prairie Dogs, Black-Footed Ferrets, and the Shortgrass Prairie

Approximately one hundred miles west of Bismarck, North Dakota, and near the North Dakota–Montana border. Take Interstate 94 to exit 24 at Medora, then go south to the grassland entrance; the southern section of the national park is within this part of the national grassland. To reach the north-ern section of the park, take Interstate 94 to exit 42. Go north on Route 85 approximately twenty-three miles to the park entrance. The north section of the national park is also within the national grassland. Route 85 is designated a scenic road.

Lewis and Clark first saw prairie dogs when they went out walking together on September 7, 1804. They had climbed a domelike hill about sev-enty feet high and on their way down "discovered a Village of Small animals

PRAIRIE DOGS

that burrow in the grown," which they estimated covered about four acres with "great numbers of holes on the top of which those little animals Set erect make a Whistleing noise and whin allarmed Slip into their hole." They poured a lot of water—more than five barrels—into a prairie dog hole, and flushed one out, killed it, and examined it.

"Those Animals are about the Size of a Small Squirel," Clark recorded, "& thicker, the head much resembling a Squirel in every respect, except the ears which is Shorter, his tail like a ground Squirel which Shake & whistle when allarmed." Clark described them further: "the mouth resemble the rabit, head longer, legs short, & toe nails long, ther tail like a ground squirel which they Shake and make chattering noise, ther eyes like a dog, their colour is Gray and skin contains Soft fur." These small, social animals were familiar to the plains Indians and to the Canadians. Clark noted that they were called by the French "pitite Chien," or little dog. Lewis later wrote a more complete description that was the first scientific description of these animals.

Once prairie dogs were widespread throughout the shortgrass prairie—the western, drier prairie countryside that does not support the grand, tall grasses of the eastern plains. These animals feed on grasses, but need to see from their burrows to protect themselves, and would not do well in the tall-grass prairie, where they could not see beyond the next clump of grass. At the time of Lewis and Clark, shortgrass prairie extended north-south from southern Saskatchewan, Canada, to northern Mexico, and eastward from Denver to about the hundredth meridian, which has been the traditional dividing line between the deep-rooted tallgrasses with large leaves and the shallow-rooted shortgrasses with small leaves. Along the trail of Lewis and Clark, the hundredth meridian passes north-south near the mouth of the

Niobrara River; that is to say, near where the Missouri River arrives at the Nebraska border and begins to form the Nebraska–South Dakota line. This was near where Lewis and Clark first saw prairie dogs—a location within fifteen miles of modern Fort Randall Dam. But you won't find prairie dogs easily in that area today.

Once individual prairie dog villages covered large areas and had great numbers of animals. At the turn of the twentieth century, an immense prairie dog town in Texas was reported to cover an area 100 by 250 miles and to contain 400 million prairie dogs. Now some say that 98 percent of the prairie dog towns in the United States have been eliminated.

Prairie dogs have been eliminated from most of their range both directly, by poisoning, because they are thought to compete with cattle for grasses and their holes pose a problem to the movement of horses and cattle, and indirectly, through destruction of their habitat via the plowing of shortgrass prairie or the intense use of it for cattle grazing.

Lewis and Clark saw prairie dogs and the shortgrass prairie over a long distance, from the Niobrara River to west of Bismarck, North Dakota. After wintering with the Mandan Indians, Lewis and Clark sent back a live prairie dog specimen, which reached President Jefferson in Washington, D.C.

We set out to find shortgrass prairie and to see prairie dogs and other wildlife of this part of the plains. On a hot, sunny August day we drove into the Little Missouri National Grassland in North Dakota. This grassland is a huge area covering 1,200,000 acres, within which is the Theodore Roosevelt National Park, which itself is made up of two sections totaling more than 70,000 acres.

We had driven here from Montana, following Interstate 94 and the Yellowstone River, the route that Clark took on his return in 1806, when the expedition divided into two parties, one led by Lewis and one by Clark, to see if they could discover a better route across the mountains than the one they had taken westward the year before. Interstate 94 travels along the Yellowstone River, often in sight of it, until the town of Glendive, Montana, where the interstate turns east and the Yellowstone River continues northeast to its confluence with the Missouri River.

The Little Missouri National Grassland extends north from Route 12 in Bowman County, North Dakota, lies east of the northerly coursing Little Missouri River, and reaches almost to the Missouri directly north in western North Dakota. Although this national grassland is near an interstate, we had the feeling that you have to want to get here if you are going to visit the area. It is not the typical way that tourists would travel from coast to coast.

The *North Dakota State Parks and Recreation Outdoor Adventure Guide* that we picked up at a visitors' center stated that this was the largest "and most diverse" of the nineteen grasslands found in the western United States. The guide went on to say that "this 140-mile stretch of rolling prairie, badlands terrain, woody draws and high buttes includes more than a million acres. From the north half, bighorn sheep can be seen in Hank's Gully, Cottonwood Creek, and Lone Butte. In the south half, visitors may view the only stand of Limber Pine in the state, just north of Marmarth." West of Amidon is the only natural ponderosa pine forest in the state. There is a campground at Burning Coal Vein where an underground lignite seam has been burning for over a century. North Dakota has four state forests—with oak, aspen, paper birch, green ash, American elm, poplar, willow, and ponderosa pine. The trees listed are all eastern forest trees, except for ponderosa pine, so we are in an area where the eastern deciduous forest trees reach their western extension.

We passed along the Little Missouri River, North Dakota's only designated scenic river, which flows south to north through the park and the national grassland and extends for a total of 274 miles until it enters the Missouri River. The Little Missouri has carved a kind of badlands through this dry country.

After stopping at the park's visitors' center, we drove a thirty-six-mile scenic loop. The air was hot and dry. The road, paved and two lanes wide, climbed into badland bluffs, eroded by the Little Missouri River. It was a little after noon and we decided to stop for lunch. We found a small picnic ground by a prairie dog town, in a lowland where cottonwoods provided shade and sagebrush grew in the drier areas. We sat in the shade and watched the prairie dogs acting cute, doing what Clark described them doing—sitting erect, whistling, appearing out of their holes and staring at us, moving around to eat.

We were tempted to go over and get acquainted with them, but we noticed a sign at the picnic ground that said to be careful because these animals carry a form of plague spread by fleas from one prairie dog to another, or, if touched by a person, spread to human beings. The sign told us that we should not even dig around in their burrows, as we might come in contact with the fleas this way. So we abandoned our idea to act like Lewis and Clark and decided instead to relax in the shade and watch the animals. Because plowing and grazing and intentional killing have removed prairie dogs from most of their range, what was once a common sight in the western plains is now a rarity, and the chance to watch the behavior of these animals in their village was something to take time and enjoy.

As we watched the prairie dogs sit up, alert, and turn their heads around to look for possible predators, I began to think how well these animals epitomize our society's mixed attitudes and unresolved conflicts about wildlife. Here prairie dogs were protected. But outside national parks and grasslands such as these, the prairie dog was still an enemy. The Web site for the State of South Dakota tells us that "the black-tailed prairie dog is found throughout western South Dakota. It's no secret these small, gregarious rodents are a major irritant to stockmen whose cattle compete with the burrowing grass-eaters for grazing land. There is no closed season, so it's legal to shoot prairie dogs anytime. The ideal time is from May through September." According to the Web site, any caliber rifle or handgun is legal. And "the season is open year-round, and there is no limit on the number of prairie dogs you may shoot. The predator license, small game, waterfowl or big game license is needed to shoot prairie dogs. You can obtain a predator license from a license agent, such as a sporting goods store, when you arrive."

Several issues arise when we talk of hunting prairie dogs. Many tourists like to see them and consider hunting them rather unsportsmanlike. Additionally, some predators of the prairie dogs—animals thus living near or among them—are listed as rare or endangered and are protected by state and federal laws. The two most important of these are the black-footed ferret and the burrowing owl. The South Dakota Web site continues: "Please make sure your target is a prairie dog. Burrowing owls often nest in abandoned prairie dog dens and look similar from a distance. The brownish owls are approximately 8 inches tall. They feed on insects and small mammals. This owl is believed to be declining in numbers, take time to verify your target before shooting. Burrowing owls are protected. If you observe one while you are in a prairie dog town, make a note of the precise location and call one of the contacts below."

Of greatest conservation concern is the black-footed ferret, called the most endangered mammal in North America. According to the American Zoo and Aquarium Association, "the decline of the black-footed ferret is almost entirely due to government-sponsored poisoning of prairie dog towns and development of farms, roads, towns, etc. over prairie dog colonies." Prairie dogs make up about 90 percent of the diet of the ferrets, which live in the prairie dog towns, inhabiting abandoned prairie dog burrows. They depend on the prairie dogs for food and shelter. In contrast to the statements of the State of South Dakota, this conservation association states that "recent studies have proven that the grass-eating prairie dogs are not significant competition with livestock for forage," and the problem is more one of education than of competition.

Once the ferret population had been reduced to very low numbers, it was then in danger of becoming extinct when the few remaining animals contracted canine distemper, which is fatal. The Wyoming Game and Fish Research Facility started a captive breeding program with 18 animals, a population that has increased to about 330 animals. These are now located in a number of zoos around the country and in Canada and some have been released back into grasslands.

On the one hand, money is made available to promote hunting of the prairie dogs, which in turn threatens prairie dog habitat and therefore the habitat of the black-footed ferret. On the other hand, money is made available for captive breeding of the ferret with a plan to reintroduce it into its original habitat. The state government and the ranchers argue that prairie dogs must be reduced because they compete with cattle; conservationists argue that this is not the case, and the U.S. Fish and Wildlife Service has to protect the ferret because it is listed as endangered under the U.S. Endangered Species Act.

So it is with many environmental issues, all epitomized by the cute animal before us who seemed to think, as it scanned around, that its only enemy was a local nonhuman predator and who was, of course, unaware of the complex social context within which its future is embedded.

I thought also about how the problem here related to ecological food chains—the web of life, of who eats whom. The most endangered species of the shortgrass prairie, the black-footed ferret, is near the top of the food chain, as a predator of the prairie dog. The prairie dog eats vegetation for the most part, except for an occasional protein-rich grasshopper. In general, the farther up a food chain, the less abundant a species, and the more likely it is to become threatened and endangered. The ferret's problem was a combination of lack of food and lack of habitat, and that's common for many endangered and threatened species.

Well, the sun began to get too hot for that kind of speculation and reflection, and we certainly were not going to see a ferret. It was time to move on. After lunch, we continued our drive on the scenic route and saw the muddy Little Missouri River once again off to our left. Sagebrush was widespread, but we saw dead cottonwoods and brown, unhealthy-looking cedars on the river's floodplain. Cottonwood is the characteristic tree of floodplains and riparian areas of the dry western plains. Out here, cottonwoods are the only trees that can grow, and it is so dry that they are restricted to watercourses. It's an old rule of thumb in the cowboy country that if you want water, look for cottonwood on the horizon—and even then you may have to dig.

We were more than satisfied with our visit to the shortgrass prairie of this public land. Here is a good place to get a feel for the prairie through which the Lewis and Clark expedition passed during late summer and fall of 1804, the spring of 1805, and after they had crossed the confluence of the Yellowstone and Missouri Rivers on their way back in 1806. And it is a good place to contemplate the mixed opinions and attitudes about wildlife that run through American culture.

33. The Confluence of the Yellowstone and Missouri Rivers: Wolves and the Conservation of Endangered Species

BLACK-FOOTED FERRET

There is no major road that goes directly to the confluence. You can approach the general area from the west by taking Interstate 94, which follows the Yellowstone River from Bozeman to Glendive. Then take Route 16, which follows the Yellowstone to Sidney, Montana.

Near the confluence are Fort Union Trading Post National Historic Site and Fort Buford State Historic Site, both in North Dakota. Fort Union Trading Post National Historic Site is at the location Lewis recommended for a fort. There are interpretive and live history demonstrations. To reach the historic forts, take exit 42 on Interstate 94 in North Dakota; follow Route 85 north to Watford City, west to Rawson, and north on across the Missouri; and then go west on Route 2. At Williston go southwest on Route 1804, which goes to the historic forts. Fort Union fronts on the Missouri and Fort Buford is at the confluence. Route 58, which goes southwest from Route 1804, crosses the Missouri as close to the confluence of the Yellowstone and the Missouri Rivers as any road, and from this bridge is the best view from a paved road of the Missouri near that confluence.

To see the Yellowstone as near to its mouth as possible from a paved road, take Route 200 west from Route 85, before reaching Williston, and go about fifteen miles to the Sundheim Park just west of the bridge across the Yellowstone. At this point you are just a few miles from the town of Fairview, Montana. This route is scenic, passing through the northern portion of the Theodore Roosevelt National Park and the Little Missouri National Grassland for much of the way.

If any location on Lewis and Clark's journey matched the idealized view of the presettlement American West as a Garden of Eden rich in vegetation and wildlife, it was the confluence of the Yellowstone and Missouri Rivers, just east of today's Montana–North Dakota border. The expedition arrived there on April 26, 1805. Lewis took four men and went by foot to explore the Yellowstone River upstream from its mouth. From a hilltop, Lewis wrote, "I had a most pleasing view of the country, perticularly of the wide and fertile vallies formed by the missouri and the yellowstone rivers, which occasionally unmasked by the wood on their borders disclose their meandering for many miles in their passage through these delightfull tracts of country." Below him, "The whole face of the country was covered with herds of Buffaloe, elk & Antelopes; deer are also abundant," he continued, and adding to the sense of a Garden of Eden, "the buffaloe Elk and Antelope are so gentle that we pass near them while feeding, without appearing to excite any alarm among them, and when we attract their attention, they frequently approach us more nearly to discover what we are, and in some instances pursue us a considerable distance apparently with that view."

The vegetation was also rich and abundant. "There is more timber in the neighborhood of the junction of these rivers," Lewis wrote, " than there is on any part of the Missouri above the entrance of the Chyenne river to this place." On the floodplains were cottonwood, "small elm, ash and boxalder;" and "Goosbury, choke cherry, purple currant; and honeysuckle bushes." On sandbars in the river were willows, wild roses, and serviceberry. Where there were no trees, there were many small plants, including "wild hyssop which rises to the hight of two feet" and which was a favorite food of "the Antelope, Buffaloe Elk and deer." Willows filled river sandbars and "furnish a favorite winter food to these anamals as well as the growse, the porcupine, hare and rabbit," he added.

It was an American Serengeti, and everybody was happy to be there. "To add in some measure to the general pleasure which seemed to pervade our little community, we ordered a dram to be issued to each person; this soon produced the fiddle, and they spent the evening with much hilarity, singing & dancing, and seemed as perfectly to forget their past toils, as they appeared regardless of those to come."

But it was also in this region—below and above the confluence—that they saw many wolves. On April 29, 1805, near the mouth of Martha's River, they found themselves "surrounded with deer, elk, buffalo, antelopes, and their companions the wolves, which have become more numerous and make great ravages among them." A week later, on May 5, 1805, Lewis wrote of "Buffalo, elk, and goats or antelopes feeding in every direction" and "a great number of" wolves.

Today, for some people, the presence of wolves would be the final touch in creating a wilderness paradise; for others, the presence of wolves would destroy the very idea of such a place. People have hated wolves throughout most of western history, and the desire to conserve wolves is relatively new in western civilization. Ancient Greek and Roman writers, including Aristotle and Plutarch, mention the evil and dangerous nature of the wolf. In Dante's *Inferno,* the wolf represents human greed. In contrast, some American Indian tribes had wolf clans, considering the wolf to be a fetish and a "brother."

Today the wolf represents a powerful symbol of the character of wild nature. In its wariness of people, the wolf epitomizes our predominant contemporary image of nature: nature as separate from human beings and human beings as divorced from nature. Where we are, there are no wolves; where the wolf lives, there is wilderness.

Because of the ancient symbolic meaning to people, wolves, perhaps more than any other large animal of the American West, force us to ask why we should save endangered species, why we should extend large sums and restrict land use, hunting, fishing, and other activities on behalf of certain species. The great diversity and abundance of life at the confluence of the Yellowstone and Missouri Rivers makes the question all the more compelling. The controversy has focused upstream, in Yellowstone National Park, where wolves have been reintroduced where they had been locally extinct for sixty years, as part of a plan to help conserve this endangered species.

One standard answer why we should save any species from extinction is utilitarian: A given species has direct benefit to people or might in the future. One of the purposes of the expedition was to find such benefits, including determining the potential for fur trade with the Indians of the West. Therefore Lewis and Clark carefully recorded the distribution and abundance of beaver—of major economic importance at the time—often through the occurrence of beaver lodges, dams, and tree cutting.

Even grizzlies, so dangerous to the expedition, had a use—their hides were used by the expedition. In contrast the wolves, the other big mammalian predator commonly seen by the expedition, were neither of use nor a threat. If there were then or is now a reason to conserve wolves, it would seem to lie beyond some direct, practical benefit of the wolves to people.

The second standard argument for biological conservation is that each species plays some essential role in its ecosystem. It is an ancient question, found in Greek and Roman writings, why there should be predators—referred to as vile and vicious creatures—on the Earth. The answer has always been that these animals control the abundances of their prey. This argument was picked up by the modern science of ecology and formulated in terms of the mathematics developed for mechanical systems and the physics of mechanics. Hence, wolves are seen as mechanical devices, personality-less entities that bang into their prey at random.

The theory, still prevalent, predicts that such predators and their prey will function together to control each other's numbers with great precision and pre-dictability. According to this theory, the prey species would increase uncon-trollably without its predator. The prey would overeat its food supply and its population would crash, perhaps leading to its extinction. But with both predator and prey present, the two would achieve a constant abundance that would persist indefinitely, or the two would oscillate forever, exactly out of phase, like two guitar strings tuned to the same note and the second plucked exactly at the moment when the first reached its peak of vibration. The only problem with this theory is that it fails completely to predict anything real. All field studies show that real predators and prey do not follow these rules. Big game predators can reduce the numbers of their prey, but they have never been observed to control the abundance in the precise way the theory predicts.

This theory arises from the same world view that led to the belief that we could channelize the Missouri River, run it as if it were just a hydrological machine, and that we would receive only benefits and suffer no ill effects. It is the same world view that ignores the connection between human settle-ments and the river, that has led us to lay big interstate highways between cities and their riverfronts. It has failed with predators just as it has failed with rivers and cities.

The other standard reasons for the conservation of endangered species are aesthetic and moral. Wolves are social animals, a species with highly

WOLF

developed social behavior and signs of individualistic behavior that appeal strongly to many people. Such social behavior and individualism is a primary argument behind the conservation of whales and porpoises, whose care for their young and apparent intelligence leads to moral arguments that these creatures have a right to exist. Wolves share these qualities. They live in packs of typically four or five to twenty. There is a rigorous social structure, with a lead male and female who breed and whose pups are cared for by other adults as well as by the parents. The lead male affirms his dominance through his posture and, when challenged, in fights. The personality of the lead male seems to be able to influence the behavior of the entire pack. He does not happen upon his prey at random.

It is my opinion that the aesthetic justification is the underlying rationale for most people. I have worked in wilderness areas where there are wolves, and what I remember most about the wolves is their calls at dusk and during the night. Few other sounds bring out the primitive wildness of the woods as do these haunting sounds, evoking the essence of wilderness and the connection between human beings and nature. People shy away from the aesthetic argument like a wolf shying from people, as if nobody would take this argument seriously. For me, these are powerful justifications to save the wolves. And my guess is that, down deep, it is this aesthetic rationale that underlies the impetus of most people who work to save endangered species. However, most discussions place emphasis on the utilitarian and the ecological, both mechanistic approaches. They are echoes of the machine age of the nineteenth and early twentieth century, when the science of ecology first attempted to explain how nature works. To limit our justification for or against big predators like wolves to these echoes is to debase the deep connection between the human spirit and nature. We have passed through a machine-age era of arguments limited to the utilitarian, and seen the consequences of it in our rivers, our cities, and here, in the diversity of life.

New developments in ecological science point to ways we can deal with the complexities of real predators, with their individual behaviors, social interactions, and effects on their environment. And so the question before us at the confluence of the Yellowstone and the Missouri Rivers is whether there is a place, in our imaginations and in our realities, for the wolves in the idealization of the American West. Do we want to envision the richness of life as Lewis and Clark found it there with wolves or without them? When you visit the confluence and see the still well-watered bottomlands and the Yellowstone River, neither channelized nor dammed and therefore more in its presettlement condition than the Missouri, it is a time to reflect on this question.

34. Fort Peck Dam and the Milk River: How the Ice Ages Altered the Course of the Missouri River

To Fort Peck Dam: From the north take Route 2 to Nashua, Montana, then Route 117 south to Route 24, which goes along the reservoir, Fort Peck Lake. Turn left to the dam. From the south take Route 200 to Route 24; take Route 24 north to the dam.

To see the Milk River: Take Route 2 west from Nashua. The route passes now and again near the river. Route 24 northwest from Fort Peck Dam goes to Glasgow, where it passes a park along the Milk River in that town.

The Hewitt Lake and Bowdoin National Wildlife Refuges are near Malta, Montana, and are reached by following Route 2 west from Fort Peck. Bowdoin National Wildlife Refuge is off Route 2 one mile east of Malta. There turn east onto Old Highway 2. The refuge headquarters is six miles down this road. To reach Hewitt Lake National Wildlife Refuge, from Malta take Route 2 east, then take a side road north toward Cree Crossing. Then take a gravel road west across Nelson Reservoir. The refuge is two miles west. It is advised that you use USGS or BLM local maps for details to reach this refuge.

A curious change occurs on the Missouri River between Fort Peck Dam and Loma, near Fort Benton, Montana. The river you can see at Fort Benton or on a float trip through the white cliffs—a portion of the Missouri River that's designated wild and scenic—is very different from the river both upstream of Great Falls and downstream of Fort Peck Dam.

Lewis and Clark saw this change in the Missouri River as they slowly moved upstream in the spring of 1805. On May 7, 1805, the expedition was just downstream from the location of modern Fort Peck Dam, where Lewis wrote that "the country we passed today on the North side of the river is one of the most beautifull plains we have yet seen." He saw that the land rose "gradually" away from the river "to the hight of 50 or 60 feet, then becoming level as a bowling green." That green landscape extended "as back as far as the eye can reach." But the floodplain of the Missouri changed abruptly upstream. Four days later, on May 11, 1805, when the expedition was a little way upstream from the present site of that dam, Clark wrote that the "high land is rugged and approaches nearer than below, the hills and bluffs exhibit more mineral . . . Salts than below." Lewis's journal confirms this change with almost identical wording. Below the site of Fort Peck, the Missouri flowed then, as it does today, in a wide and gently sloping valley. Above the site of that dam, the river flowed through a narrow and steep valley. Today, this change is not visible in a single view, because the upstream portion at Fort Peck Dam is covered by water. But you can see the change when you compare the Missouri River that you see from the causeway below Fort Peck Dam with the Missouri you can see when you visit Fort Benton, Loma, Judith Landing, or Virgelle, Montana, and especially if you are able to take a boat trip down the famous white cliff section of the river.

I wondered why the river was so different in these two sections. I thought perhaps it was simply because the upper Missouri section was relatively near to the headwaters and the Rocky Mountains, where the river still carried a heavy load of sediment that could knife a steep edge into the countryside. But the Missouri upstream from Great Falls flows in a wider valley, not so steep as in the white cliffs section, so this explanation couldn't be right.

A key to the reason that the upper Missouri River is so different from the lower is found in a visit to the Milk River, a tributary that flows into the Missouri just below Fort Peck Dam. That river has a different look and a different setting from the Missouri upstream of the dam.

Lewis saw the difference when he walked upstream on the Milk River. The expedition arrived at the mouth of the Milk River on May 8, 1805. "We nooned it just above the entrance of a large river," he wrote, continuing on to say that he "took the advantage of this leasure moment and examined the

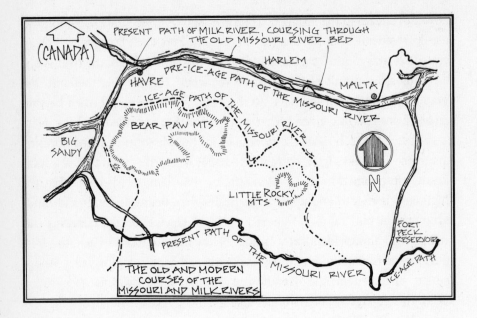

THE OLD AND MODERN
COURSES OF THE
MISSOURI AND MILK RIVERS

river for about 3 miles." He found the Milk River to be deep and gentle with a "large boddy of water." But, most important, he saw that "the bottoms of this stream are wide, level, fertile." He named it the Milk River because the water had "a peculiar whiteness, being about the colour of a cup of tea with the admixture of a tablespoonfull of milk."

Lewis and Clark observed each of the rivers they came across carefully. They wrote down each river's characteristics and gave the rivers names. Theirs was a careful examination made in the interests of natural history. This is not the way most of us view rivers in the countryside. Most of the time when we travel we accept the countryside as it is, as a static picture passing by us, without questioning how it came about. But a river on a landscape is telling us a story—a story about its history, why it is the kind of river we see. Now here was a curiosity: two rivers coming together on the same landscape at the same location, but one, the Missouri, had cut itself steeply between bluffs, while the other, the Milk River, flowed in a wide and gentle floodplain. What caused the difference?

An important principle in geology, uniformitarianism, says that the processes that exist today existed in the past, and also that the processes that occur in one place occur in another. That is, the physical, chemical, and biological processes that create a landscape have to follow the same rules of nature everywhere, in time and in space. Given that, and given the two rivers' close proximity to one another, one might expect the Milk and Missouri Rivers to look the same and to flow in similar-looking valleys. Then how is it that these two rivers are so different?

It's a curious question, and the answer lies in effects of the great continental ice sheets on the Missouri River tens of thousands of years ago. During the last ice age, the ice sheet pushed down from Canada all the way to the Missouri River in this part of Montana. The ice was an irresistible force, and the Missouri, that mighty river, was not quite an immovable object. The ice pushed the river out of its old bed along a section between Loma and Fort Peck. The ice began to melt back about 15,000 years ago.

When we see a great river, it appears to us as a permanent and unchanging part of the landscape. But a river has a history and goes through stages from young to mature. When a river first starts to flow on a landscape, it cuts straight down. The sediment that it carries wears away at the land. A young river flows in a narrow valley with steep sides. But over a much longer time, the river keeps undercutting the bluffs along its narrow valley. The bluffs collapse. Lewis and Clark saw cliffs that had fallen into the Missouri just this way. The river then moves the debris from those fallen bluffs downstream. Slowly the valley widens. The slopes become gentle. When the valley is wide enough, the river can meander over it, and over the years it shifts its channel, creating oxbows, oxbow lakes, backwaters. It becomes a mature river in a mature river valley.

The Missouri is an ancient river, and for most of its length it flows through the wide and gently sloping valley that characterizes such a river. But when the ice sheet pushed the Missouri out of its old bed, the river was forced to create a new one. During the height of the ice age, the Missouri was pushed south and forced to flow just to the south of the ice, where it began to cut a new valley into the countryside. Once that valley was formed, the river was captured by it. When the ice sheet retreated, it left debris in the Missouri's old channel. The river had cut its way down into the new one and continues to flow through it today, from Loma to Fort Peck. From Great Falls to Loma, the Missouri flows through a wide valley. But because of glaciers long ago, at Loma the

Missouri begins to flow through a narrow canyon and continues to do so past where Lewis and Clark noticed the change in the countryside.

As the ice sheet melted, it left debris of boulders, rocks, sand, silt, and clay everywhere, helter-skelter, mixed together, but also somewhat smoothed out. The beautiful plain that Lewis saw where the Milk River flows into the Missouri, at the site of present-day Fort Peck, was bulldozed by the glaciers to create the rolling but relatively flat and pretty countryside that Lewis found so beautiful. Huge boulders, dropped here and there by the glaciers, are markers and testimony to the powerful work done by the moving sheets of ice. They stand along the roadside to remind us of that awe-ful geologic history.

After the ice sheet retreated, the Milk River began to flow in part of the Missouri's old channel. A smaller river, it passes through a plain too big for it to have created. It is a young river in an old river's arms.

From Fort Peck Dam, you can travel to see the Milk River by going up to Nashua, Glasgow, or Malta, and visiting the Hewitt Lake National Wildlife Refuge, which is on the big bend of the Milk River, or the Bowdoin National Wildlife Refuge. When you do this, you are seeing the original valley of the Missouri. Just imagine a bigger river in this valley and you will be able to imagine the way that this countryside would look today if there had never been the great climate change of the ice age, a time when ice hundreds of feet thick pushed aside the landscape in its path, scraped and eroded mountains and hills, dumped the rocks and soil it had cut into valleys, disrupting the rivers, covering the forests. As I traveled along the upper Missouri, I thought about the great irony of this history: the arrival of a huge sheet of ice that persisted for thousands of years, causing an incredibly large-scale change in the land—an environmental change that we would not want to happen now that we are occupying the land; we would do whatever we could to prevent the migration of the Missouri River into a new channel that is now considered its most beautiful stretch.

35. Fort Peck Dam and the Pines Recreation Area: Grizzlies and the Conservation of Endangered Species

To Fort Peck Dam: From the north take Route 2 to Nashua, Montana, then Route 117 south to Route 24, which goes along the reservoir, Fort Peck

Lake. Then turn left to the dam. From the south take Route 200 to Route 24; take Route 24 north to the dam.

To the Pines Recreation Area: From Fort Peck take Route 24 west to Maxness Road, then go about four miles west to Willow Creek Road. Take this road west to the Pines Road. Go south on the Pines Road to the recreation area, at the end of the road on the reservoir.

On May 11, 1805, when the expedition was northeast of what is now the Pines Recreation Area near Fort Peck Dam in eastern Montana, Bratton, one of the members of the expedition, went for a walk along the shore. Soon after, he rushed up to Lewis "so much out of breath that it was several minutes before he could tell what had happened." Bratton had met and shot a grizzly bear, he told Lewis, but the bear didn't fall; instead it ran about half a mile and was still alive.

Lewis took seven men and trailed the bear about a mile by following its blood in the shrubs and willows near the shore. Finding it, they killed the bear with two shots through the skull. Upon cutting it open, they found that Bratton had shot the bear in the lungs, after which the bear had chased him a mile and a half.

"These bear being so hard to die rather intimidates us all," Lewis wrote. "The wonderful power of life which these animals possess," the journals continued, "renders them dreadful; their very track in the mud or sand, which we have sometimes found 11 inches long and 7 1/4 wide, exclusive of the talons, is alarming."

Not far from this location, Lewis wrote the first scientific description of the grizzly, although it did not receive its scientific name, *Ursus horribilis*, until 1815. Lewis described a male "not fully grown" that he estimated weighed three hundred pounds, which they had killed after shooting it many times. He wrote that the grizzly had longer legs than the black, that its color was "yellowish brown, the eyes small, black, and piercing; the front of the fore legs near the feet is usually black; the fur is finer thicker and deeper than that of the black bear."

Their first encounter with a grizzly had taken place the previous fall, on October 20, 1804, when they were near Bismarck, North Dakota, and about to set up their winter camp. That location, in the Great Plains hundreds of miles east of the Rocky Mountains, considerably extends the eastern range assumed for this animal.

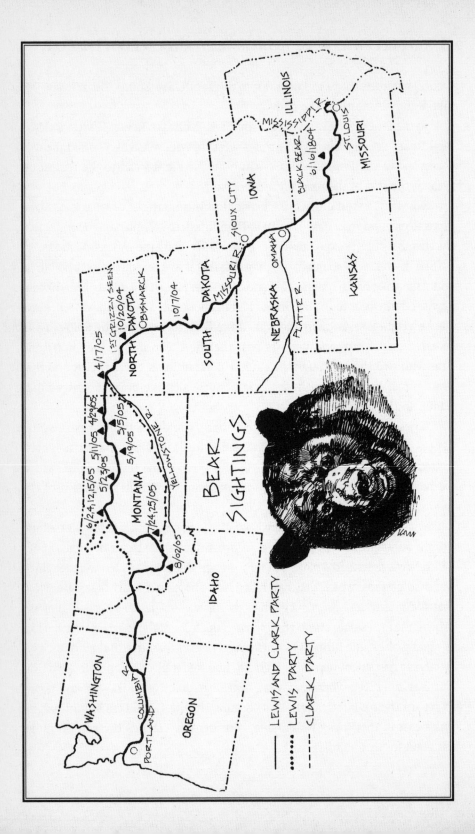

BEAR SIGHTINGS

LEWIS AND CLARK PARTY
LEWIS PARTY
CLARK PARTY

WASHINGTON
OREGON
IDAHO
MONTANA
NORTH DAKOTA
SOUTH DAKOTA
NEBRASKA
KANSAS
MISSOURI
IOWA
ILLINOIS

PORTLAND
COLUMBIA R.
YELLOWSTONE R.
BISMARCK
MISSOURI R.
SIOUX CITY
OMAHA
PLATTE R.
ST. LOUIS

8/02/05
7/24/25/05
6/24,12,15/05
5/23/05
5/19/05
5/11/05
4/29/05
4/17/05
1ST GRIZZLY SEEN
10/20/04
10/7/04

MISSISSIPPI R.
BLACK BEAR 9/16/1804

Lewis and Clark saw grizzlies during the next spring and into the summer. Approximately twenty times between April 17 and the end of July they saw these bears—about one encounter or sighting every five days. They were especially troubled by them when they were portaging their equipment around the Great Falls. Their last sighting was near Three Forks, Montana, the headwaters of the Missouri. No grizzlies were found east of Pierre, South Dakota, or west of a north-south line passing through Missoula, Montana; the grizzlies were confined to two regions of the trip: the upper Missouri and adjacent shortgrass prairies, and the Rocky Mountain forests—the dry plains and the cold mountains.

Because grizzlies are so big and dangerous, Lewis and Clark recorded the number of bears (usually one) in each encounter. Reading their accounts, I realized that it was possible to use the journals to estimate the original abundance of these dangerous animals and to learn about their original range. The expedition encountered a total of thirty-seven grizzlies over a distance of approximately one thousand miles, or an average of about four grizzlies per hundred miles traveled. The area known to have grizzlies today, 20,000 square miles, is 6 percent of the presettlement range of the bear, based on the journals of Lewis and Clark. Today, grizzly habitat occurs mainly on government land, mostly U.S. Forest Service land, in four states. Only 5 percent is private land. Much of the rest is in four national parks: Glacier, Yellowstone, Grand Teton, and North Cascades. Habitat in and around Yellowstone National Park that appears to have grizzlies at present is about 7,800 square miles. You are very unlikely to see a grizzly. But you can, at the Pines Recreation Area and elsewhere, see grizzly bear habitat. The rare encounter with a grizzly today would occur if you go cross-country backpacking in one of the national parks or national forests. You are more likely to see them in the Canadian Rockies, although there too the chances are low, or in Alaska, where the chances are greater.

Why would anyone want to know how many grizzlies there were? Grizzlies are listed as an endangered species, and the U.S. Fish and Wildlife Service has a recovery plan for the grizzly bear. But recovery to what? Under present interpretation of the Endangered Species Act, a species can be listed as threatened or endangered if its numbers drop to less than one-half of the estimated "carrying capacity"—the maximum number of animals that a habitat can support. And the carrying capacity is typically taken to be the estimate of presettlement abundance. That number can be estimated from the Lewis and Clark journals.

Assuming on average that the men of the expedition could see about a half mile on each side of the river, then the density of the bears was about four for every 100 square miles. Multiplying this by the assumed presettlement range of the bears, about 530,000 square miles, suggests that there might have been as many as twenty thousand.

Although it is legally required to restore the grizzlies, and an estimate of the presettlement abundance is the usual method for determining how many would constitute "restoration," I was surprised to find that there are few other studies that provided any useful estimate of this abundance. One of these few was by the Craighead brothers, two of America's experts on grizzly bears. Their study was limited to Yellowstone National Park, where they reported sighting an average of 230 grizzlies between 1959 and 1967, which works out to an average density of three bears per 100 square miles in Yellowstone National Park, similar to my estimate from the Lewis and Clark journals.

Strangely, with the sole exception of information gathered in Yellowstone National Park, our present knowledge about the abundance and density of grizzlies is not much better than what someone could have surmised by a careful reading of Lewis and Clark's journals when the expedition returned to St. Louis in 1806.

If this is what we know about one of the most famous, most readily reported, legally threatened and therefore protected species, whose abundance and whereabouts are of considerable interest to outdoorsmen as well as government agencies, what could be our knowledge of other species? The answer is, in most cases, much worse.

But is striving to restore the abundance of an endangered species to a single presettlement number the right thing to do? To do so is to assume the constancy of nature—to believe that before the influence of European civilization, the abundance of grizzlies and everything else in nature never changed from year to year. This doesn't make much practical sense and all the evidence available about wildlife suggests that this has never been true; populations of wildlife change all the time. Such a belief, while consistent with the ancient idea of a perfect balance of nature, contradicts the inherent changeableness of the environment, which Lewis and Clark came to know all too well in their travels on the Missouri.

Scientists now know that populations of grizzlies and other animals and plants are, like the Missouri River, always changing. There is no single "natural" abundance. There is a range of abundances, all of which are "natural" in the sense that the population was at each level within the range at some time during the past, prior to the effects of modern civilization. This has become known as the "historic range of variation."

When we recognize this, a plan to return the grizzlies to their original "abundance" becomes more complicated. We begin to wonder not what the right population number is, but what the right conditions are—what is the key to their ability to persist as a species.

Some more recent programs to restore endangered or threatened animals have begun to focus on this more realistic goal of a self-sustaining population. Apparently, this was the goal for the Fish and Wildlife Service's Grizzly Recovery Plan. Its objective was "to establish viable, self-sustaining populations in areas where the grizzly bear occurred in 1975." To accomplish Fish and Wildlife's recovery plan for the grizzly bear, we must understand much more about the requirements of this species than a single number. We must understand what it needs from its habitat—the physical structures of the places it lives—and the ecosystems—the food chains, the other species, the changes occurring over time—within which it lives. We have to obtain estimates of the abundances of the bears before and after settlement by Europeans, and, if possible, obtain estimates at different times so we can calculate the range of variation.

To believe that there is a single magic number that is the only sustainable one is to believe that a species is fragile and that individuals within a population are not resourceful. This seemed hardly the case with the grizzlies that met Lewis and Clark. The grizzlies were fearless, strong, able to withstand a number of bullet wounds; they seemed quick to respond, resourceful. A population that persists and prevails over a long time must have abilities to respond to change. We understand now that to be sustainable is not the same thing as to continue to exist at a single abundance; and that to exist at a single abundance may not be the best way for a species to persist.

THE MIGHTY GRIZZLY

On June 28, 1805, the expedition was camped and in the midst of portaging around the Great Falls of Montana. Lewis noted in his journal that "The white bears have now become so troublesome to us that I do not think it prudent to send one man alone on an errand of any kind, particularly where he has to pass through the brush." The bears were bold enough to "come close around our camp every night, but have never yet ventured to attack us and our dog gives us timely notice of their visits, he keeps constantly patrolling all night." It was so dangerous, Lewis believed, that "I have made the men sleep with their arms by them." Reading this and the other accounts of the expedition's experiences with grizzlies, I was at first caught up in the excitement at the danger that the bears posed, and in the bravery with which the men responded. Lewis and Clark's encounters with grizzly bears were their most dangerous encounters with any animal and among the most dangerous of all their experiences. But the meaning of these encounters to us in our search of nature is much greater, much deeper.

From their encounters with the grizzlies, we learn much. We learn about the limits of our present knowledge. We learn that, in spite of much emotion and desire directed toward the conservation of rare and endangered animals during the last thirty years, our knowledge remains terribly limited. We discover that we know little more now about the range and density of the grizzly bears in the lower forty-eight states than one would have known from reading Lewis and Clark's journals in the early nineteenth century. We discover that clear, objective, written historical records can be a great help to us. And, in the end, we discover that we have a much longer journey ahead of us than Lewis and Clark had, if we are to be able to predict the results of our attempts to conserve endangered species.

36. Judith Landing: How Early People May Have Affected Wildlife

From Great Falls take Route 87 northeast past Fort Benton to Big Sandy. Take Route 236 right (southeast) to the mouth of the Judith Landing Recreation Area. This road crosses the Missouri River to the mouth of the Judith River.

On May 29, 1805, the expedition reached the mouth of the Judith River where that river enters the Missouri in Montana. Clark named the river for Judith Hancock of Fincastle, Virginia, whom he would marry in 1808. On that day, Lewis wrote that near this junction they passed the "remains of a vast many mangled carcases of Buffalow." He attributed these carcasses to hunting by Indians who drove the animals over the cliffs, and records in considerable detail the methods by which this kind of hunting was done.

Clark makes a simpler note, mentioning that he walked on the shore and "saw the remains of a number of buffalow, which had been drove down a Clift of rocks." He does not go further in attributing the cause of these deaths. This method of killing buffalo was one of the few available to peoples without guns and horses, and was a well-known practice among the plains Indians. Lewis notes that "in this manner the Indians of the Missouri distroy vast herds of buffaloe at a stroke." However, some experts familiar with the method suggest that the broken country back of the bluff on the Judith River is not of the right shape for concentrating and stampeding buffalo, and therefore the large number of dead buffalo, which Clark estimated to be about one hundred, was more likely due to drowning during spring thaw and flood—due to a weather-induced natural hazard rather than human impact.

This incident epitomizes a question that has intrigued naturalists, ecologists, and anthropologists for decades: What was the relative impact of the Indians on buffalo compared to the effects of natural environmental change? In the nineteenth century, the famous British biologist, Alfred Wallace, wrote that an examination of the fossil record since the end of the last ice age suggests that the "biggest and hugest and fiercest" animals had died off, such as the saber-toothed tiger and the hairy mammoth. Some speculate that the changing climate at the end of the ice age was the cause. But the cause is unclear because the time these extinctions occurred is also around the time that the Indians were migrating to North America from Asia. Paul Martin, an American anthropologist, suggested instead that perhaps these extinctions were due to hunting by the newly immigrating Indians. They would have been an introduced predator whose methods would have been unfamiliar to the native animals. Martin suggested that a densely populated, moving wave of peoples coming down from the north could have used just this kind of method to kill vast numbers of the big animals and lead to their extinction. The matter, like the cause of the death of the buffalo that Lewis and Clark found near the Judith River, remains unresolved.

In his journal for that day, Lewis described this method of hunting buffalo. "One of the most active and fleet young men is selected and disguised in a robe of buffaloe skin," he wrote. This man then positions himself near the herd and the precipice. "The other Indians now surround the herd on the back and flanks and at a signal agreed on all shew themselves at the same time moving forward towards the buffaloe." This causes the animals to stampede. Then the man disguised in the buffalo skin reveals himself to the animals and runs ahead of them to get them to stampede toward the precipice. Blinded by fear, the buffalo keep going and fall over the cliff. Meanwhile, this man has to be careful not to be run over by the buffalo. "If they are not very fleet runers the buffaloe tread them under foot and crush them to death, and sometimes drive them over the precepice also," Lewis wrote.

Could the Indians have caused the extinction of such huge animals as the mammoth and the saber-toothed tiger with this method, along with killing individuals here and there with bows and arrows? There is no doubt that the Indians had large effects on the native animals, including buffalo. But it is my guess that the biggest impact was through alteration of the habitat—in the case of the plains Indians, the frequent setting of fires, which would have improved the habitat for grass-eating grazers like buffalo, and made it poorer for woodland feeding animals. We know today that it is generally much harder to cause the complete extinction of a species by hunting down and killing all of the individuals. Such hunting can greatly reduce the numbers of a species, but it is very hard to get the very last animal—especially if the tools available are stone arrow points and wooden bows and arrows, and the method of transportation is the human foot.

A much easier way to alter the abundance of an animal is to affect its habitat. Most of the extinctions that modern technological civilization has brought about have occurred through habitat change, including physical alteration of the habitat and the introduction of exotic predators, competitors, and parasites.

At the time of Lewis and Clark, the number of buffalo on the plains was immense. Estimates, based on the density of herds and the area a herd covered, suggest that there could have been 60 million of these animals in 1804.

With the coming of European technology and the introduction of the horse, and then with the invention of the train and telegraph, the potential to kill off the buffalo through hunting increased greatly and almost succeeded. But this required a major intentional effort to destroy the buffalo in order to eliminate the primary food source of the Indians, as well as to supply a voracious American and European market with buffalo hides. The economic pressures to hunt buffalo and the intentional destruction of the herds by the military almost succeeded in causing the extinction of this species. It might have, except for the work of a very few people who, seeing the demise of the great herds, began to collect small numbers of these animals and conserve them. Ironically, Buffalo Bill was one of these, as were some Native Americans.

Elsewhere, with other species native to North America, hunting often came close to causing extinctions but did not. Typically, when a species is reduced to a very small number, individuals become hard to find, and the cost to collect those few exceeds the value of the return from the sale of a small number, so the chase is abandoned. This happened with the bowhead whale, hunted from 1840 to 1920 by Yankee whalers out of New Bedford, Massachusetts. Often the hunters, no longer able to find the few that remain, believe that the species is extinct while in fact a few pockets of the animals remain. This was the case with the sea otter and elephant seal, also hunted in the nineteenth century.

Our relative effect on the environment and its animals and plants is a major question for today as well as yesterday. The challenge is to sustain these wild living resources in the face of much smaller habitats and much greater human population pressures.

When you visit the confluence of the Missouri and Judith Rivers, take some time to look around the countryside and see if you think it might be possible to ambush a herd of buffalo and drive them over the cliffs, or whether the topography of the river might be one in which the animals could drown during spring ice breakup and floods.

37. The Mouth of the Marias River: Which Was the Best Way West?

To the confluence of the Marias and Missouri Rivers: From Great Falls take Route 87 northeast to Loma (eleven miles northeast of Fort Benton). The highway crosses the Marias River at the confluence with the Missouri.

To go near the location upstream that Lewis reached in 1805: From Great Falls take Route 87 to Fort Benton, then take State Secondary Route 223 north from that city to where it crosses the Marias River.

On June 3, 1805, the expedition was camped at what we now know as the mouth of the Marias River, but which appeared to Lewis and Clark as the junction of two large rivers. The problem was that they weren't sure which of the rivers was the real Missouri—the river that flowed in from the north, or the one that flowed in from the west. In a certain sense this is arbitrary, because at the confluence of two major waterways, you can call either one the upstream continuation of the main river. But for Lewis and Clark, the question was: Which river would take them the farthest into the mountains and give them the best route over the Rockies to the Columbia? The Indians had told them to search for a river that had some great falls on it. This would lead them to the trails the Indians used for passing over the mountains. This is the river they would call the real Missouri.

Choosing the wrong river and following it would have serious consequences for the expedition. "To mistake the stream at this period of the season, two months of the traveling season having now elapsed, and to ascend such stream to the Rocky Mountains or perhaps much further before we could inform ourselves whether it did approach the Columbia or not, and then be obliged to return and take the other stream would not only lose us the whole of this season but would probably so dishearten the party that it might defeat the expedition altogether," Lewis wrote.

Although the future of the expedition, even perhaps their lives, depended on the right choice, Lewis took a detached, almost scientific approach, as if he were a modern scientist sitting in a comfortable laboratory office, rather than at a rough camp in bad weather. He pursued the problem with a seeming academic curiosity, writing, "An interesting question was now to be determined: which of these rivers was the Missouri."

In a sense, the expedition was lost and needed directions. We are all familiar with this problem. Perhaps you are lost at this very moment while you read this section of my book, trying to follow the directions at the top of this section. But the trouble was, in Lewis's time, there wasn't anybody handy to give them directions. Today you can stop at a gas station, use your car phone if you have one, or even rely on the GPS device some cars now have.

The problem the expedition faced was one of their own uncertainty. The rivers were set in their directions and were not about to move at random over the next few days.

And so Lewis proposed an experiment: "To this end an investigation of both streams was the first thing to be done." He recognized the need to measure things about the river, making observations quantitative, to "learn their widths, depths, comparative rapidity . . . and thence the comparative bodies of water furnished by each," and by these means attempt to infer which was the main stream.

Like a modern scientific team, the camp divided into two groups, each examining the available evidence and each proposing what we would refer to today as a hypothesis. Most of the men believed the north fork was the main river and therefore the one to follow. Lewis reviewed the evidence on their side: The north fork was deeper but not as swift. However, its waters ran "in the same boiling and rolling manner which has uniformly characterized the Missouri throughout its whole course." The waters were brown, thick, and turbid—the big muddy, so it seemed. The bed of the river was also mainly mud, so that the "air and character of this river" seemed "precisely that of the Missouri below." For these reasons, most of those on the expedition were convinced that the north fork was the Missouri. On the other side were Lewis and Clark who, Lewis wrote, were "not quite so precipitate."

They decided to explore both forks, what scientists would call testing the two hypotheses. The next morning Clark led a group up the left fork, while Lewis took a group on the right. The rest of the expedition remained at the base camp where the two forks joined. Lewis traveled up the north fork from June fourth to the sixth. He found that this fork continued northward toward what is now the border between Montana and Alberta, Canada, and he became convinced that this direction was too far to the north to be the route to the Pacific.

After taking time to attempt a reading of the latitude and longitude (which failed because of cloudy weather) he began his return on June 7 to the junction of the two forks to rejoin the main body of the expedition. Lewis was correct; the north fork was a small tributary, which they named the Marias River (actually Maria's River, in honor of Lewis's cousin, Miss Maria Wood, but after a while, people dropped the apostrophe).

By waiting a few extra days on the Marias River to try to take measurements to determine his latitude and longitude, he was trying to reduce the uncertainty about the position of the expedition. But a change in the weather, something he could not make accurate predictions about, prevented him from making the measurements.

In deciding which was the right river, Lewis and Clark were confronted simply with a lack of information. They were uncertain about what to do and wanted to avoid making a crucial error. The error they faced at the junction of the two rivers was what scientists call an error of uncertainty of the first kind—a problem regarding a situation that already exists or, given present conditions, that must occur. Resolving such an uncertainty becomes a matter of learning more facts about the situation. One of the channels was the main river—a fact that was not going to change during the time of the expedition. There was only one correct river to take. They could do something direct and simple to resolve this uncertainty—explore the two rivers and determine by direct observation which was the correct one.

The complex quality of nature, however, often presents us with a second kind of uncertainty that we can resolve only to the degree of knowing the probability of an event, not exactly where or when it will occur. I call this the Las Vegas uncertainty: Will you place a bet on dice that haven't been rolled yet? Unlike the first kind of uncertainty, the second kind is not resolved so directly and simply. You can't pick up your car phone, call the weather bureau, and ask to know with complete certainty whether a thunderstorm will strike Loma exactly where the two rivers come together. The best a weatherman can do is give you the odds on whether or not it will happen. We cannot reduce the uncertainty of this kind of future event by studying it. This is the problem with the flooding on the Missouri River. It is an uncertainty of the second kind that leads us to build levees and dams.

We can, however, learn the odds—or at least get an estimate of the odds—and decide if we want to accept those odds. Because people have rolled dice for a long time, and through mathematical analysis of probabilities, we know what the chances are that any given number will come up with a legitimate pair of dice, and we know that the number seven is most likely. But we can't find a route to always getting the number seven the same way we can take Route 87 to Loma.

Traveling on Route 87, the countryside appeared similar to the badlands that Lewis and Clark described along the Missouri breaks, near to where we were driving. Another historic marker told us that we had reached Marias River and that "the Lewis and Clark expedition camped at the mouth of this river just east of here, June 3, 1805." A land of good directions, maps, and apparent certainty.

But Lewis and Clark saw it very differently. Pushing up the river in a slow-moving boat against a six-mile-an-hour current, sleeping on its banks, studying the land through which it flowed, Lewis and Clark experienced a Las Vegas–style river full of chance and uncertainty, risks that were possible, but whose location and timing were not knowable. Perhaps our problem with this kind of error in our knowledge is a matter of relative time scales. Lewis and Clark spent more than a year on the Missouri, a time as long or longer than it takes the river to perform some of its variations. In this day of satellite and aircraft observations, automobile travel, and vacations that are quick stops here and there, our time of observation is much shorter. Most of us have just one shot to see the Missouri River of Lewis and Clark. If it is flooded, well, we may lose that chance. If it's a dry year, we will remember the river as it looked that year and it will be fixed in our imagination as if it were always and forever that way.

On Lewis's return, following the Marias River downstream, it began to rain, and the peculiar clay soil of the floodplain turned into a slippery mess, difficult to traverse. After a "most disagreeable and restless night" camped in the rain, Lewis and his small band set off downriver to join the rest of the expedition. The clay soil prevented the rain from soaking in, and the surface became so slippery that it was like "walking over frozen ground which is thawed to small depth." We know today that they were walking on a clay derived from glacial till and shale, commonly called gumbo, a clay that turns into a plastic and sticky material when wet.

Lewis slipped on this soil while walking on a bluff above the river, but managed to save himself from falling ninety feet to the water. Just after he had saved himself, he heard one of his men, Windsor, cry out, "God, Captain, what shall I do?" Lewis saw that Windsor had slipped on the clay and slid so that his right arm and leg hung over the bluff and he was holding on to the edge with his left arm and leg. "I expected every instant to see him lose his strength and slip off," Lewis wrote, but "I disguised my feelings and spoke very calmly to him and assured him that he was in no kind of danger." Lewis then astutely told Windsor to take his knife out of his belt with the hand that was hanging over the precipice, dig a hole in the bank for his right foot, and by such effort work his way up, which Windsor did, and in that way he was saved.

Searching for the correct fork is inherently a different problem from try-ing to avoid slipping on wet clay and falling into a river. The second kind of uncertainties are referred to today as problems of risk, because the event has not yet happened and its occurrence has to do with inherent chance or with processes whose causes, for all practical purposes, we cannot distinguish from true chance events. Translated into human events, risk becomes a matter of prediction, forecasting, luck, and fortune, the latter two of which were also constant companions of the expedition.

Our modern environmental problems confront us with both kinds of uncertainty. And it's important that we understand which kind we are facing. The floods on the Missouri in the 1990s showed us that we cannot treat uncertainties of the Las Vegas kind as if they were uncertainties of route directions. We do not seem to have trouble accepting the idea of our own errors—that we might not know which river to take. But we have a great difficulty understanding and accepting the second kind of uncertainty—that there may be some inherent chance in nature.

On the level plain we passed fields of hay and wheat, and we saw mountains along the horizon. About forty-six miles from Great Falls, we passed over a bridge where we saw the Marias River. Here the river appears as a small, meandering current in a floodplain of cottonwoods. I thought about the irony of what geographers say today: If Lewis and Clark had followed Marias River, they would have found a better pass through the mountains, the one eventually used by the railroad. It crosses the divide in Wyoming and would have taken them more easily to the Columbia River.

If you have the time to take a canoe trip through the wild and scenic portion of the Missouri, you may have a chance to experience the river at the Lewis and Clark time scale. When a friend of mine did this during a five-day trip, he got caught in an intense thunderstorm, and experienced the second kind of uncertainty directly. Another friend canoed the region slightly upriver from Loma, and he was caught in a strong easterly wind, a headwind, so he and his companion had to canoe hard against that wind in spite of the fact that the river was flowing with them.

The Missouri's refusal to stay put and stay constant has been the source of many a good story and pithy saying, but this quality has also interfered with our society, with commerce, and with our conservation of nature. Most of our past methods to conserve and manage environmental factors assume the constancy of nature—except for human intervention. But the reality is the other way around. We try to fix a naturally varying environment, believing that our interventions are the causes of variations in an otherwise static structure of environment. Like the fickle Missouri, all of nature changes at many scales of time and space. We have longed for and tried to create an environment that is fixed, like the channelized Missouri downstream. Having lost our cultural heritage and our detailed, repeated experiences about the river and the prairie, directly and in story and song, we seem to have ignored their important message.

38. Fort Benton, Montana: Caches, Geology, and the Location of Cities

From Great Falls take Route 87 east. Follow 87 past the towns of Carter and Kershaw. Watch for a sign and turn right on Route 386 to reach Fort Benton. It meets Route 80 in the town and Route 80 continues over the Missouri River.

When Lewis and Clark approached the Rocky Mountains, they realized that it would be necessary to leave some of their equipment behind. They had to lighten their load as much as possible to get over the mountains, and there were some things, such as their boats, that they could not bring up the Rockies. They had to cache their heavy equipment, and the location they chose was near the present site of Fort Benton, Montana. On June 10, 1805, downstream a little way from this town, they dug a large hole, like a house basement. "To guard against accedents," as they noted in the journals, they stored some gunpowder and lead—in case they lost the rest and needed more on their return. They also left two of their "best falling axes, one auger, a set of plains, some files, blacksmiths bellowses and hammers Stake tongs &c. 1 Keg of flour, 2 kegs of parched meal, 2 kegs of Pork, 1 Keg of salt, some chissels, a cooper's Howel, some tin cups, 2 Musquets, 3 brown bear skins, beaver skins, horns of the bighorned anamal, a part of the men's robes clothing and all their superflous baggage of every discription, and beaver traps." They tied a boat, their red pirogue, on a small island in the river and covered it with brush.

The first steamboat to navigate the Missouri, the *Independence*, moved up her waters on May 28, 1819, only twelve years after Fulton's steamboat sailed on the Hudson River and only thirteen years after Lewis and Clark returned to St. Louis. As the Pacific coast opened up and people sought better ways to travel west, steamboats began to take people and materials up the Missouri. In 1846 a town, first called Fort Lewis but renamed in 1850 for Sen. Thomas

Hart Benton of Missouri, was located here and became the terminus of steamboat travel. The town boomed during the California gold rush as people rushed to get to the West Coast, and as cattlemen began to use steamboat transportation for supplies. From here, travelers took the Mullan Wagon Road, 624 miles between Fort Benton and the head of navigation on the Columbia River, and for years it was the fastest route, taking forty-seven days.

Why did this location in particular become a common place to stop and cache excess baggage, a place where large boats went no farther? Why did Lewis and Clark not wait until they reached the great falls, the truly impassible section of the river, and make a cache just below that? Or why not leave things farther downstream than the area near Fort Benton?

For the expedition, as for steamboats, any location for many miles downstream from Fort Benton would have been difficult. At the site of modern Fort Peck Dam, the Missouri River begins its passage through steep bluffs and cliffs, and these continue to Virgelle. Even if Lewis and Clark had found a place to cache their goods in that section of the river—a place that would have been safe from flooding and where the soil was deep enough—they would have had a difficult time finding a good trail that led down to the river on a gentle slope.

Knowing that the Rocky Mountains could not be too far in the distance, it would be a natural decision for explorers to stop and make a cache as soon as the land began to flatten out again after that difficult section. This is what happens near Fort Benton.

Thus the geology of this location made it a good place to take things *to*, traveling up the Missouri, but not to take things *farther*. The expedition, as well as later travelers going west, were affected by the geology and the geological history of the Missouri River basin.

So it is with most major cities. Today, we travel often unaware of these factors. Most major cities around the world are located at crucial locations along rivers. There are three kinds of these locations. The first is the ocean mouth of a river, as with New York City and New Orleans. The second is the junction of two major rivers, as with the site of St. Louis where the Mississippi and Missouri come together, and the site of Omaha, Nebraska, where the Platte River flows into the Missouri. The third is at what is called the "fall line," where a river passes on its way downstream from harder, more erosion-resistant rock into softer rock. Waterfalls or unnavigable rapids are the result. The fall line is a natural location to create a city and a natural place for a city to succeed. Not only is the fall line the farthest inland that a steamboat or ship can navigate, but a fall line is also typically far enough upstream to be easily spanned by a wooden bridge, important before the invention of modern steel suspension bridges. And the falls are a good site for water power. Great Falls, Montana, is just upstream of the fall line; Fort Benton is well situated not far below it.

Usually, the fall line is relatively near the ocean—within a few hundred miles. This is the case with many major cities of the east. In Jefferson's Virginia, the city of Richmond is on the fall line, as are most of the inland cities of the East Coast and south central plains: San Antonio and Fort Worth, Texas; Little Rock, Arkansas; Montgomery, Alabama; Columbia, South Carolina; Washington, D.C.; Baltimore, Maryland; and Philadelphia, Pennsylvania. On the Missouri, the only odd thing is the long distance from the ocean that the fall line occurs, at Great Falls.

The environment of cities and towns, and the reason that cities succeed in a location, had long been a curiosity of mine, and I wanted to see this town that was the steamboat terminus on the Missouri. On an August day, we left Great Falls and drove north on Route 87 to Fort Benton. It had been a wet summer, and as we entered Chouteau County we saw that the bottomlands were flooded in many places. We passed some pretty farms, pretty because there were many trees providing shade and variety on the landscape. About fifteen miles from Great Falls the road reached a crest and from there we viewed a sea of wheat. The wheat was being harvested in strips and we saw long rectangles of golden wheat and brown soil stretching for long distances.

Soon we reached Route 386, where a sign said to take the next right to Fort Benton. We passed through tree-lined streets until we saw a sign announcing, "Upper Missouri National Wild and Scenic River, Lewis and Clark National Historic Trail, 1963." With the building of the railroads, Fort Benton diminished in importance as a transportation terminus and transit point. It has become a pleasant small town—one of the nicest places to view the upper Missouri in Montana.

We turned left to see a park with big cottonwood trees growing on a lawn beside the fast-flowing river. Fort Benton is dominated by a main street that parallels the river. We walked several blocks down and saw a sign for the Grand Union Hotel, which opened to the public on November 1, 1882, a "haven of relaxation" in this "boisterous frontier town at the head of navigation on the Missouri." At a cost of $200,000 it was "the finest hostelry between Seattle and the twin cities." Here "steamboats blew for the landings and great cattle herds crossed the Missouri within sight and sound of the guests." Now Fort Benton is a town that remembers its past and perhaps will grow a little more as tourism becomes a more important business in this region. Geology created a location for this hotel, at least for a brief while until railroads came and made fast travel to the coast possible, ending the era of the Missouri steamboats.

39. Ryan Dam: Scenery and Electricity

In Great Falls take Fifteenth St. north, which is Route 87 north, crossing the Missouri River. Take Route 87 north six miles and turn right at a sign for Ryan Dam onto a paved road; follow signs, taking the right-hand road where it forks. The road descends deeply through the bluffs by the river to a parking lot where a sign says "Montana Power Company Welcomes You." The total distance from Great Falls is fifteen miles. Walk across the footbridge to a park on the island in the river.

Lewis described the five falls on the upper Missouri River, for which the city of Great Falls is named, as one of the most beautiful scenes he had ever witnessed. I had been fascinated by his long description of these falls ever since I first read the Lewis and Clark journals, and was anxious to see what remained of that scenery. Having spent the night in Great Falls, Montana, we drove on an August afternoon to Ryan Dam, the site of one of those falls.

"From the extremity of this rolling country I overlook the most beautiful and level plain of great extent for at least fifty or sixty miles," Lewis wrote on June 13, 1805, and within this plain "were infinitely more buffalo than I had ever before witnessed at a view." Just as Lewis had described it, we saw a rolling but rather level plain, now cattle-grazing land but with the same general aspect. The river has incised itself into this landscape, cutting through the level plain, so that a person traveling away from the river, on a main road such as Route 87, is not aware that one of the greatest rivers of the world is nearby. It isn't visible.

Lewis saw "two curious mountains" rising out of this plain, which were "square figures," probably the buttes just south of Black Horse Lake that we could see as we drove on Route 87. Lewis describes these as having perpendicular sides rising to a height of 250 feet and appearing to be formed of yellow clay.

On that same day, Lewis found the first of the great falls, which is now at the site of Ryan Dam. He was traveling with four of the men of the expedition: Fields, Drewyer (one of the main hunters of the expedition), Gibson, and Goodrich, and he sent the first three to kill some game for meat and then join him and Goodrich at the river for dinner.

"I had proceeded on this course about two miles with Goodrich at some distance behind me when my ears were saluted with the agreeable sound of a fall of water and advancing a little further I saw the spray rise above the plain like a column of smoke which would frequently disperse again in an instant caused I presumed by the wind which proved pretty hard from the southwest," Lewis wrote, and "soon began to make a roaring too tremendous to be mistaken for any cause short of the Great Falls of the Missouri." This was a welcome sound because the Indians had told them earlier that the true Missouri River, the river that would lead them as far into the mountains as possible, had great waterfalls on it.

Walking sixteen miles, he and Goodrich reached the falls at noon. There they were, a small party in the midst of a huge region that was unmapped and unknown to his civilization. Reading his accounts, I admired the energy and ambition with which he rushed to see a place of beauty, when the expedition was about to be confronted with one of their most difficult tasks—portaging their equipment around these falls, which would take them about a month. But this was not what was in Lewis's mind at the moment. He heard the sound of a great fall of water and rushed to see what he hoped would be a beautiful view.

At a fork in the road, a sign directed us to the right, and the road descended steeply along a sheer, almost vertical sandstone bluff to the riverside and a parking lot.

As he neared this point Lewis wrote, "I hurried down the hill which was about 200 ft. high and difficult of access to gaze on this sublimely grand spectacle. I took my position on the top of some rocks about 20 ft. high opposite the center of the falls."

We parked and joined a summer crowd and strolled along a tree-shaded walk to a suspension footbridge that led over the river to Ryan Island. We walked over the bridge and strolled up the path to where we could watch the water cascading from the dam.

When Lewis descended the steep slope, he saw a double falls, one just behind and above the other. The second, which he wrote was "an even sheet of water falling over a precipice of at least 80 feet," formed, with the first, "the grandest sight I ever beheld." The second falls was especially beautiful, because "the irregular and somewhat projecting rocks below receive the water in its passage down and breaks it into a perfect white foam which assumes a thousand forms in a moment, sometimes flying up in jets of sparkling foam to the height of 15 or 20 ft. and are scarcely formed before large rolling bodies of the same beaten and foaming water is thrown over and concealed them," he wrote. The rocks appear to be perfectly placed to break up the water most beautifully.

Below in the river he saw an "abutment of rocks" that "defends a handsome little bottom grove of about three acres" and which was "agreeably shaded with some cottonwood trees. In the lower extremity of the bottom there was a very thick grove of the same kind of trees which are small." The land was not uninhabited; he saw among the trees several Indian lodges "formed of sticks."

The view that we saw at the dam was pretty, and there were people taking pictures, eating snacks, and enjoying the coolness of the air that rose from the river. I thought about Lewis's extensive and detailed descriptions of the falls, most of which were now no longer visible because they were under the water of the reservoirs behind hydroelectric dams.

For most of the journey, Lewis and Clark had maintained a rather distant and professional tone in their notes. Once in a while one of them would write that they saw a beautiful prairie or a wonderful and amazing number of animals, but these expressions about the beauty of nature were usually brief and reserved. At the time of their expedition, a great change was taking place in western civilization concerning the idea of natural beauty. The romantic poets of England—Wordsworth and Coleridge especially—were writing that the wildness of the Alps, with their fearsome heights, cliffs, ice, and wind, were objects of beauty.

Only a few decades before, mountains were perceived, as they had been since Greek and Roman times, as horrible places, out of symmetry and therefore ugly. Until Lewis reaches the great falls, a reader of the journals would hardly know that Lewis was aware of such a debate over aesthetics and nature. But something happened to him at the falls, and he opened up and wrote at considerable length about his own wonder at the beauty of the scenery, in the style of his time. On that summer day, now long ago, he was responding to what you and I seek today when we go to Yosemite, to the Grand Canyon, to the Tetons, or why people ski at Lake Tahoe rather than at more convenient locations, why vacationers travel from Europe and America to Fiji and Tahiti—to find a place of beauty in which they can enjoy nature and better enjoy themselves. Sent by President Jefferson to find a route to the Pacific and to observe the condition of the countryside, its plants, animals, and minerals, traveling as military captains in charge of a group of rough men through unknown country fraught with great dangers, for the most part the two leaders do not admit in their notes that they have these sensitivities; they do not take the time, or have the time, to just plain wonder at the beauty of the American West.

But at this first set of falls, Lewis saw a rainbow in the spray as the sun reflected off the water. This, he wrote, "adds not a little to the beauty of this majestical grand scenery." And for once he sought within himself an ability to express the beauty of the landscape, not just its capabilities. "After writing this imperfect description I again view the falls and am so much disgusted with the imperfect idea which is conveyed in the scene that I determine to draw my pen across it and begin again, but then reflected that I could not perhaps succeed better," he wrote. He wishes for "the pencil of Salvator Rosa," a seventeenth-century Italian landscape painter of wild and desolate scenes, and for "the pen of Thompson," an eighteenth-century Scottish poet who was one of the forerunners of the Romantic movement. He wishes that he had a camera obscura—the precursor of a photographic camera, basically a small room open only to the light outside through a lens that cast the image of the outside scene on a wall, and which artists could then trace exactly.

We walked around the entire island, enjoying the shade of the trees and looking at the Missouri River from all sides. It was the kind of pleasant afternoon outing depicted by the French Impressionists in their paintings of Sunday strollers carrying parasols along the Seine River.

The next day, June 14, 1805, Lewis reached several more of the falls and was most impressed with one he called Rainbow Falls, which is now much altered by Rainbow Dam. This is "one of the most beautiful objects in nature," he wrote. Lewis spent some time trying to decide which of the two, the falls he had seen the day before or this one, was the most beautiful. "At length I determined between these two," he wrote, that Rainbow Falls was "pleasingly beautifull," while the one he saw the day before was "sublimely grand." These are the turns of phrase that were in use among the Romantic poets and their predecessors to describe aspects of beauty. "Beauty" was used then to refer to the classic Greek and Roman idea of beauty through symmetry, perfection in geometry. "Sublime" had come into fashion among the Romantic poets to refer to the awe-inspiring scenery of the great mountains in the Alps. Lewis was using phraseology that would have been familiar in the aristocratic drawing rooms of England, and in Jefferson's Monticello mansion; but such a distinction would be unlikely to occur to other explorers of the American West in Lewis's time or for decades to come—perhaps not until the great nineteenth-century landscape painter Thomas Moran reached some of the great scenery of the American West after the Civil War. Moran popularized the awe-inspiring scenery of the American West to the point of probably helping the movement that created American national parks.

Clark arrived at the falls a few days after Lewis, on Monday, June 17, 1805. In contrast to Lewis, Clark remained true to his propensity to report directly and to make quantitative measurements—the first step in the scientific process. "I beheld those Cateracts with astonishment," he wrote, "the whole of the water of this great river Confined in a Channel of 280 yards and pitching over a rock of 97 feet 3/4" and also that the mist extended "for 150 yrds. down & to near the top of the Clifts" so that the "river below is Confined to a narrow Chanel of 93 yards haveing a Small bottom of timber."

This point kept sticking in my mind as I looked at the tumbling waters coming down from Ryan Dam. For one of the few times in the entire journey, Lewis revealed here, at this very spot, that he knew about art, literature, and the culture of Europe and the eastern United States. He stepped out of his role as military captain charged with getting across the Rocky Mountains, to reveal himself briefly as a young man greatly affected by nature's beauty and educated about the philosophy of aesthetics. Reading his accounts, I found this section of his journals an amazing release and admission of his humanity and personality. His attempt to describe nature's beauty, and his frustration with that attempt, is as impressive to me as the scene he described.

Soon he would be directing the movement of all the goods on which the expedition depended. In fact the next morning, June 15, 1805, Lewis "set one man about preparing a saffold and collecting wood to dry the meat." He sent a message back to Clark to start searching for the best location to camp at the base of the falls for the portage around them. A few days later he would have a dangerous encounter with a grizzly bear. A month in the future he would be searching for Indians from whom to buy horses and guide them over the Rocky Mountains before winter was to set in. The entire expedition was at a crucial juncture. But that was put aside when Lewis looked at the falls. "I hope still to give to the world some faint idea of an object which at this moment fills me with such pleasure and astonishment, and which of it's kind I will venture to ascert is second to but one in the known world."

The afternoon sun was hot and the crowd was beginning to thin out as people returned to Great Falls. This was one of the prettiest places we had seen on our travels, modern dam or not, and it was also one of the more obscure, not well marked on maps or in the available tourist material. We lingered a long time on the island while I thought about the entire rationale behind the conservation of nature. There are usually four reasons given for conservation: utilitarian, ecological, aesthetic, and moral.

Conservationists usually tend to rely on the first and the second, the utilitarian and the ecological, which are the practical reasons to maintain nature. It is my belief that most people who want to conserve nature want to do so, down deep, because of nature's beauty, and because of the importance of that beauty to them. And here I was standing where Lewis had stood, after he had traveled more than a thousand miles by boat, by horse, and by foot; after he had wintered under the most difficult conditions, in rough huts that he and his men had built; after the death of one of the party; after many other trying experiences. And on this day aesthetics was his preoccupation. I began to realize why this portion of his journals had left such an impression on me. The beauty of nature is a powerful argument, and one with often considerable financial payoff. There was no need to shy away from that reason to want to sustain aspects of our environment.

40. Giant Springs and Great Falls: Huge Quantities of Fresh Water Rise and Descend As Hail and Rain

Giant Springs is in Great Falls, Montana. From Interstate 15, take the Route 87 exit north, then take the east fork just before the bridge over the Missouri River (so that you stay on the city [south] side of the river). Follow 87 until Giant Springs Road veers to the left and Route 87 goes away from the river. Giant Springs is in the state park near this intersection.

On June 18, 1805, Lewis and Clark were approaching and scouting out the great falls on the Missouri River to prepare for portaging their materials around the falls, a task that was to take them about a month, from June 21 to July 14, 1805. Clark set out early and, after passing the second of the great waterfalls, came on "the largest fountain or Spring I ever Saw." He made an estimate that this was "the largest in America Known." He was correct; the giant spring has been measured to discharge as much as 389 million gallons a day, with more recent measurements of 174 million to 213 million per day. This is enough water to cover one to two square miles a foot deep every day! "This water boils up from under the rocks near the edge of the river and falls imediately into the river 8 feet and keeps its Colour for ½ a mile which is emencely Clear and of a bluish Cast," he wrote.

Eleven days later, on June 29, 1805, Lewis set out to see the same spring with the hunter and French-Canadian, Drewyer. On his way, Lewis described the countryside as "a level beautiful plain for about Six miles." Lewis too concluded that the fountain, as he called it, was "the largest I ever held." More likely than Clark to dwell on aesthetics, Lewis wrote that "the hadsome cascade which it affords over some steep and irregular rocks in it's passage to the river adds not a little to it's beauty." But like Clark, he also makes measurements, writing that the spring was about twenty-five yards from the river, "situated in a pretty little level plain, and has a suddon decent of about 6 feet in one part of it's course." He noted, as did Clark, that the water was "extreemly tranparent and cold; nor is it impregnated with lime or any other extranious matter which I can discover, but is very pure and pleasent." There was so much water moving so quickly out of the ground that Lewis observed "the water of the fountain boil up with such force near it's center that it's surface in that part seems even higher than the surrounding earth which is a firm handsom terf of fine green grass."

Today Giant Springs is in a state park within an urban setting. In the twentieth century, Great Falls developed around the production of electricity from Ryan Dam downstream, whose reservoir flooded and covers the great falls for which the city is named and around which the expedition portaged. At one time, Anaconda Copper had a large refining plant here to convert ore to metal, using the electric power from Ryan Dam. Great Falls is a combination of pleasant residential, tired-out industrial, and pretty riverfront. All the riverfront is public land, and there is a marina and walkways and picnic tables here and there.

We visited the spring in early August. The city's River's Edge Trail goes from the center of the city to Giant Springs. Along this trail botanists recently have found fifty-five of the plant species collected by Lewis and Clark. The spring, the trail, and the Great Falls Interpretive Center celebrate the Lewis and Clark expedition. It was near sundown and families with small children strolled along the riverfront path. A tern flew overhead. Canada geese and a gull were at the spring. A steady breeze blew downriver. We watched the natural, but incredible amount of bubbling water spewing out alongside and into the Missouri River, creating rapids that spread into the river. For a good distance the clear waters of the spring flowed alongside the muddy waters of the Missouri without mingling.

And where does all this water come from? we wondered. A sign at Giant Springs told us about the geological processes that created the spring. A formation of limestone, called Madison limestone, lies under most of eastern Montana. It was formed about 250 million years ago from the deposits of shells and other biological processes in the bed of an ancient sea. Since the formation of the Rocky Mountains, which began about 90 million years ago, each year rainfall and snow soak into the limestone where it is exposed on the slopes of the Little Belt Mountains. From there the water drains downward and then flows through openings in the limestone to the Great Falls area. Next, under pressure because the water starts at a high elevation, the water flows upward and out at Giant Springs. A fracture in this limestone allows the water to be pushed up. The spring is a giant artesian well. As it flows through the limestone, the water dissolves calcium and magnesium, which it brings to the surface.

On their way to the Giant Springs, Lewis and Drewyer were "overtaken by a violent gust of wind and rain from the S. W. attended with thunder and Litning." They took shelter "in a little gully wher there were some broad stones" that Lewis thought he could use to protect his head from hail. They remained for about an hour "without shelter and took a copious drenching," Lewis wrote.

At the same time, Clark was ascending the riverside along the series of falls, so that he could retake some notes about the river that he had lost on his previous ascent. With him were Charbonneau, the French-Canadian interpreter, his Indian wife, Sacagawea, her baby boy, and York, the only black person on the expedition. They too saw the black cloud coming from the west. Clark "looked about for a shelter but could find none without being in great danger of being blown into the river should the wind prove as violent as it sometimes is on those occasions in these plains." Clark found a deep ravine with "shelveing rocks" where they took shelter. He put his guns and the compass under one of these rocks. "Soon after a torrent of rain and hail fell more violent than ever I Saw before," Clark wrote.

The intensity was so great that it "felt like one voley of water falling from the heavens" and produced a flow of water into the ravine where he and Sacagawea had taken shelter "with emence force tareing every thing before it takeing with it large rocks & mud," he continued. It was clear that they had to get out of the ravine, which was flooding rapidly. He took his gun in his left hand and used his right to help Sacagawea, who was carrying her baby. Charbonneau, meanwhile, was also trying to pull his wife up. "Before I got out of the bottom of the revein," Clark wrote, "the water was up to my waste & wet my watch."

By the time he reached the top of the ravine, he estimated at least fifteen feet of water had risen. Sacagawea's baby had lost his clothes; she was wet and cold and "just recovering from a Severe indispostion." Clark was "fearfull of a relaps."

We read this account from the journals that evening; we then went back the next day to look at the Giant Springs again. It was an unlikely setting for one to imagine the incredible storm of rare intensity that had struck Lewis and Clark at slightly different locations near the spring. On this day, all seemed as quiet and peaceful as the design of human artifice could hope.

But other members of the expedition also suffered from that storm as they moved materials on the portage. "Some nearly killed one knocked down three times and other without hats or any thing on their head bloodey & Complained verry much," Clark wrote. He gave everybody a little grog.

In the midst of the escape, he had lost the expedition's large and best compass, which was a "serious loss" he wrote. Fortunately, the next morning two of the men went to the falls and found the compass covered with mud and sand, but everything else, including a tomahawk, a shot pouch, powder and balls, moccasins, and the baby's clothes and bedding, were gone. These men found that the place where Clark had sought shelter the day before was "filled with huge rocks."

Such rare events not only threatened the lives of Clark, Sacagawea, and her baby, but they also cause major changes to natural areas, leading to new channels in a river, clearings in a forest. These rare, not often seen, events can play a major role in the dynamics of life on the Earth, resetting the ecological clock to start natural processes of restoration and recovery, to which many species are adapted. It is well that we be aware of them though we rarely experience them.

41. Gates of the Mountains: Continents Collide and We Are Rafted Along in Their Wake

Traveling south on Interstate 15, about sixty-five miles south of Great Falls, take the exit to the Gates of the Mountains Recreation Area. Drive east on a paved road about four miles to the recreation area. The area between Great Falls and Helena is an excellent place to experience the river where it has cut a broad and scenic canyon—either by following an access road and trail system along the river or by boat or raft. This is also a good area for bicycling and picnicking. There are several good locations between Great Falls and Helena to launch and take out a boat, among them Craig and Wolf Creek. Boat trips into the Gates of the Mountains are available at the recreation area (406-458-5421).

On July 19, 1805, the expedition neared the location of modern Helena, Montana, and came to an area of impressive scenery. In the evening Lewis wrote that "we entered much the most remarkable clifts that we have yet seen." They seemed to "rise from the waters edge on either side perpendicularly to the hight of about 1200 feet." It was impressive and a little forbidding. "Every object here wears a dark and gloomy aspect. The tow[er]ing and projecting rocks in many places seem ready to tumble on us," Lewis continued, then discussed the geology of the location, as Jefferson had instructed him to do. "The river appears to have forced it's way through this immence body of solid rock for the distance of 5¾ miles and where it makes it's exit below has thrown on either side vast collumns of rocks mountains high," he wrote. It was so steep that for more than a mile there was only "a few yards in extent on which a man could rest the soal of his foot." Then Lewis notes, with a bit of understatement, "It was late in the evening before I entered this place and was obliged to continue my route untill sometime after dark before I found a place sufficiently large to encamp my small party."

The rocks were of many shades and hues, from black to "yelloish brown and light creem coloured yellow." Clark described the hills as made up of "a dark grey Stone & a redish brown intermixed and no one Clift is Solid rock, all the rocks of everry description is in Small pices appears to have been broken by Some Convulsion." The snow-capped mountains were in view, so Lewis wrote that "from the singular appearance of this place I called it the *gates of the rocky mountains*."

Today the land nearby the river is little developed and, in spite of the fact that Gates of the Mountains is now between the reservoirs of Holter and Hauser Dams on the Missouri, this area looks much as Lewis and Clark saw it. Large areas are coming under protection for conservation. The Montana Land Reliance has obtained conservation easements on twenty-four ranches, totaling 73,000 acres, protecting almost 150 miles of streams and riverbanks.

In early May the daunting mountains are snow-capped, while the land just above the river is stark and dry, after an exceptionally warm early spring. At the Gates of the Mountains Recreation Area it is hot, just the way Lewis described it. "Whever we get a view of the lofty summits of the mountains the snow presents itself," he wrote, "alto' we are almost suffocated in this

confined vally with heat." Above the river Lewis saw Douglas fir and ponderosa pine, a "scattering of timber on the river and in the valley." There were
bighorn sheep, beaver, and otter. These are still found in this area today and
if you are lucky you will see one of them. The area also remains a prime habitat for many birds, including pelicans, gulls, bald eagles, merganzers, mead-
owlarks, osprey, loons, Canada geese, peregrine falcons, and the turkey
vulture—to name a few of the 118 species spotted over a year by Tim Crawford, director of the Gates of the Mountains Foundation.

Crawford maintains the recreation area and conducts boat tours on three
large open-air riverboats. Tours run several times a day from Memorial Day until
October; during this time you can travel on a boat through the same passage
between the cliffs where Lewis and Clark came. A tour lasts close to two hours
and includes a stop at Meriwether picnic area, where Crawfold speculates the
expedition camped for a night. From there, hikers may choose to explore the
Gates of the Mountains Wilderness Area, catching a later boat ride back to shore.

We're a little early for a tour, but we watch as people prepare their boats for
the season. The day is warm with a light breeze, the sky a deep blue. Despite
activity in the area, as we look out on the expanse of Holter Lake the scene is
one of peace and tranquility, unlike the feeling Lewis must have had as the expedition fought its way through the canyon to find a safe place to spend the night.

The power of the river and the even more powerful forces that created the
surrounding mountains capture your attention when you visit this location. If
you take a boat tour, you might experience the power of the river as it cuts
through the mountainous canyons and get a sense of the awe men of the
expedition must have felt as they saw the nearby canyon opening up to the
valley in the distance and snow-capped mountains beyond. Crawford tells us
the tour boat runs in a sort of circle within the close canyon area, giving the
impression to passengers of the mountains opening and closing, like a gate.

"The river appears to have woarn a passage just the width of it's channel
or 150 yrds," Lewis wrote. Confronted with such an amazing landscape, one
can't help wondering what brings us the mountains. Since the early nineteenth century, soon after the Lewis and Clark journey, early geologists recognized the processes of mountain building and mountain erosion. But no one
had an explanation about how this mountain building came about; whence

came the energy for the incredible forces that must have been involved. The answer is one of the great discoveries of twentieth-century geology.

In 1914 Alfred Wegener, a German scientist, proposed as evidence in support of a radical theory that continents moved—drifted—the fact that similar fossils of animals and plants were being found on different continents, and that the coastlines of Africa and South America are largely parallel. But at the time the theory was dismissed; no one could conceive of a source of energy for that process, and it was too radical an idea for the dominant theories about the constancy of nature. As the understanding of radioactivity increased, it became clear that the decay of radioactive elements deep in the Earth provided a source of energy. It further became understood that, with intense heat and pressure, the material forming the crust of the Earth could act as a semi-liquid. Today this theory of plate tectonics is well accepted.

The term *tectonics* comes from the Greek word for carpenter or builder. And if the river is the painter, the continents are the carpenters. Mountains come about from the collision of the gigantic continental plates in motion. The deep earth acts as a semiliquid and the cooler, lighter continents float on the surface, drifting about over time. The "solid" earth on which we stand moves. Heated from below, the continents are to the rest of the Earth as the skim that forms on the top of chocolate pudding. The depth of the continents are no thicker relative to the rest of the planet than the skim on the pudding. When the huge continental plates collide, mountains form as mere wrinkles on the surface.

The plates move slowly, but not so slowly that the movement cannot be measured. The average rate is about three and a half inches a year—108 inches in the two hundred years since Lewis and Clark passed by the Gates of the Mountains. So, where we stand today, the Missouri River is nine feet farther west, in terms of a fixed longitude on the Earth, than it was when Lewis and Clark were here.

Mountains form wherever continental plates collide, and some mountains are old, like the Appalachians of Virginia—the home of Lewis and Clark. The Rocky Mountains, which Lewis and Clark confronted at the Gates of the Mountains and were soon to cross, are comparatively young mountains, too young to have been worn smooth by rivers like the Gallatin, the Jefferson, and the Madison—the rivers that form the Missouri. That geolog-

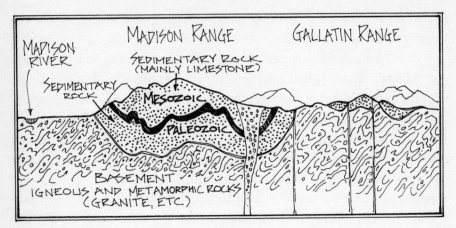

The underlying rocks near the headwaters of the Missouri are folded and make a complex pattern.

ical youth means that in 1804, as in our time, the Rockies were still high, steep, and rough, a challenge unexpected by the expedition.

Geologist Brian Skinner has written that "it is not just the continents that move, it is the entire lithosphere. The continents, the ocean basins, and everything else on the surface of the Earth are moving along like passengers on large rafts; the rafts are huge plates of lithosphere that float on the underlying convecting material."

The colliding continental plates that formed the Rockies began their mountain building here near the end of the age of the dinosaurs and at the beginning of the age of mammals, more than 60 million years ago. They are built from even more ancient deposits. The lighter, brighter-colored rocks are ancient limestones that are part of what geologists call the Madison formation. These formed in a seabed, the deposits of ancient seashells and other materials from biological processes, in the Mississippian period, more than 300 million years ago, when shallow seas were common on many continents, especially in North America. The darker gray rocks that Clark described are even older. They are Greyson shale formed more than 600 million years ago.

Before the Rocky Mountains began to rise, when dinosaurs roamed this country, most of Montana was coastline—near sea level or under water, part of a shallow sea that covered two-thirds of the state. After a continental plate previously in the Pacific Ocean collided with the plate that formed North America, several things happened: The colliding westward plate formed the land that is now Washington and Oregon, where Lewis and Clark were soon to go. The Rockies began to rise; the land to the east that had been seashore rose also above sea level, and the sea was forced to retreat eastward.

Before the Rocky Mountains there was no Missouri River, and without the Rocky Mountains there would still be none. A river is a necessary consequence of a mountain range. Water must flow downhill and as it does it begins to carry sediment and erode a path. Tributaries begin to come together and form a young river. The young river cuts steeply through the rocks. But just how a river will form depends on bedrock, climate, and the stresses and strains, the cracks and bends, to which the rocks have been subjected over their longer history on the Earth.

And so at Gates of the Mountains you have a dramatic view, as did Lewis and Clark, of these primary forces that bring us the landscape from which begins the river that drains one-sixth of the continental United States. If you are able to take one of the excursion boats through Gates of the Mountains, you can imagine that you are on the continental raft being carried on a journey into the collision of continental plates. This is part of the new view of our planet, one of constant motion at all scales, all materials, all levels. It is a great journey, symbolized by the travel of Lewis and Clark up the Missouri River through the Gates of the Mountains.

42. Three Forks, Montana: Headwaters of the Missouri River

Take Interstate 90 to exit 278 and go north to Missouri Headwaters State Park. You can take this route south to the town of Three Forks, a pleasant village.

As the expedition reached the headwaters of the Missouri, traveling on the river became more and more difficult. The river was ever more shallow, and the men had to drag the canoes over the rapids. The river current, descending from the steep mountains, was so swift that it was impossible for the men to paddle upstream even where the water was deep enough for the canoes to float. It took great energy to advance the canoes with line and poles.

Lewis and Clark divided the expedition into an advance group that went ahead on foot to explore the river and decide the best route, and a main group that pulled and poled the boats upstream. The exertion became exhausting and dangerous. Charbonneau sprained an ankle hiking in the rough country. Sergeant Gass fell in one of the boats and injured his back so that he could not help pull or push the boats. Lewis assigned him to the advanced party on land.

During the winter at Fort Mandan, the Indians had told Lewis and Clark that when they followed the Missouri River they would arrive at "three forks," where three smaller rivers came together and flowed as one downstream. Clark took a small group of men and headed upstream and, on July 25, 1805, was the first to arrive at this location, which he called Three Forks. Lewis arrived with the main party two days later. Not far downstream from the three forks, the river passed through a narrow channel "hemned in by high cliffs." Lewis climbed to the top of one of these cliffs, a "beautifull spot" where he "commanded a most perfect view of the neighbouring country." Below he could make out the three branches that flowed toward each other and met, two meeting upstream and then the third, the southeastern fork, joining the others a little farther downstream. Each passed for many miles through large green meadows—riverside wetlands and floodplains. Between the southeastern branch and the middle branch he saw "a distant range of lofty mountains" with "snow-clad tops." The mountains that would be one of their greatest tests, and which they hoped would provide a short route to the Columbia, were near.

Rejoining the main party, he found that the cliffs soon opened up. He passed the southeastern fork and followed the southwestern one for only one and three-fourths miles, where he set up camp. "Beleiving this to be an essential point in the geography of this western part of the Continent," he wrote, "I determined to remain at all events untill I obtained the necessary data for fixing its latitude Longitude." They settled in, unloaded the canoes, secured their goods onshore, and several men went out to hunt.

Having settled his men in camp, Lewis walked through the streamside meadows and examined the middle and southwestern forks, whose junction was upstream from the location of where the southeastern stream joined the main river. Once again, a question that had caused the expedition considerable time came to the fore: Which was the Missouri? "I walked down the middle fork and examined and compared it with the S.W. fork," Lewis wrote, "but could not satisfy myself which was the largest stream." He decided that neither could be called the Missouri in preference to the other because "they appeared if they had been cast in the same mould," and there was "no difference in character or size." Each was about ninety yards wide.

Clark soon after rejoined the main body, having explored the southwestern branch some twenty-five miles above, during which he suffered from sunstroke and lack of water and was sick at the camp for several days. Reflecting on the similarity among these three branches, Clark and Lewis decided to call none of these the Missouri and instead consider them separate rivers and give each its own name. They decided that the confluence of these three streams would thereby be marked as the headwaters of the Missouri. They named the southwest fork the Jefferson, the middle fork the Madison, and the southeast fork "Gallitin's River in honor of Albert Gallitin."

In a sense, the decision not to call any of these three tributaries the Missouri was arbitrary, as events of the next weeks demonstrated. After several days' stay at Three Forks, they decided that the southwestern fork, the Jefferson, was most likely the river that would take them farthest west and into the mountains, and chose to follow it to its headwaters. Once again the expedition divided into groups.

Lewis took a few men and followed an Indian trail into the foothills, where they experienced great difficulties. At one height of land, Drewyer "missed his step and had a very dangerous fall, he sprained one of his fingers and hirt his leg very much," Lewis wrote on August 5. Meanwhile the body of the expedition, still trying to proceed upstream by boat, had its own accidents. One of the canoes overturned on August 6 "and all the bagage wet, the medecine box among other articles." In addition, "two other canoes had filled with water and wet their cargoes completely," Lewis wrote, wetting their cornmeal and many presents they had for the Indians. One of the men, Whitehouse, was thrown from a canoe which then turned and came over him and "pressed him to the bottom as she passed over him," Lewis wrote, "had the water been 2 inches shallower he must have been crushed to death."

But they persevered, crossing small streams and rough country until on August 12, 1805, they reached what Lewis concluded was the very beginning of the Jefferson. And there he stopped and drank the water. "Judge then of the pleasure I felt in allying my thirst with this pure and ice cold water which issues from the base of a low mountain or hill," he wrote, for he had reached "the most distant fountain of the waters of the mighty Missouri in search of which we have spent so many toilsome days and wristless [restless] nights. Thus far I had accomplished one of those great objects on which my mind had been unalterably fixed for many years."

Others of the crew were equally joyful. "Two miles below McNeal stood with a foot on each side of this little rivulet and thanked his god that he had lived to bestride the mighty & heretofore deemed endless Missouri," Lewis noted, using that name for the first of the headwaters that he had been calling the Jefferson. Having decided that this stream took them the farthest into the Rockies and the nearest to the continental divide, Lewis could have named the southwest branch the Missouri River. But he did not; the name Jefferson River remained. No matter; it is arbitrary. The feat, the struggle, the long and dangerous trip had accomplished its first major objective.

Having drunk from the Missouri's first water, Lewis walked up to the top of this eastern slope, crossing the continental divide—the location where all rivers to the east flow into the Missouri to the Mississippi and to the Gulf of Mexico (or, in the north, to Hudson Bay), and all the rivers to the west flow to the Pacific Ocean. He walked a short way down the western slope. "I now decended the mountain about 3/4 of a mile," he wrote, "to a handsome bold running Creek of cold Clear water. Here I first tasted the water of the great Columbia river." He was drinking out of Horseshoe Bend Creek, a tributary of the Lemhi River, which in turns flows into the Salmon and Snake and then into the Columbia. The trip up the Missouri was completed.

As they had traveled from the great falls upstream to the continental divide, the expedition passed through an ecological transition, from the Great Plains to the eastern slope of the Rocky Mountains. New animals and plants appeared on the landscape. On August 1, 1805, Clark shot a bighorn sheep—which they ate—and Lewis saw "a flock of the black or dark brown pheasants," the blue grouse, one of which they shot, examined, and described. It was a new species, "fully a third larger than the common phesant of the Atlantic states," Lewis wrote, and then set down the first scientific description of this bird. The same day Lewis saw "a blue bird about the size of the common robbin," whose call and behavior he described. It was the pinyon jay, and his description of this bird was also a scientific first. On August 3, Fields killed a mountain lion. The animals of the plains were in their past, behind them; the animals of the mountains were coming into view.

Lewis was wary of this change, because it meant a transition from the abundant big game of the plains, especially the buffalo, to the wildlife-poor forests and mountains. The wealth of the wildlife in this country was in and near the streams—beaver and otter in great abundance, along with fish and water birds. On August 3, Clark noted that they saw "great numbers of Beaver Otter &c. Some fish trout & bottle nose." This change in the abundance of big game animals was characteristic worldwide of a transition from grasslands to forests. The greatest abundance of big game wildlife occurs in grasslands, as on the Serengeti Plains in Africa, declining rapidly in abundance with forest cover, as occurs in Africa when one travels west to the tropical rainforests. Forests, whatever else their beauty, ecological value, and economic worth, are meager in meat for people to eat.

Although they were entering the mountains where forests usually dominate, they found few trees. "The mountains are extreemly bare of timber," so they were forced to hike "through steep valleys exposed to the heat of the sun without shade and scarecely a breath of air," Lewis wrote on August 1, 1805. The east slope of the mountains was in the rain shadow of the Rockies. A rain shadow occurs where moisture-laden breezes from the Pacific Ocean flow inland and are pushed upward by the mountains. Rising, this air cools, and the water it holds condenses and is released as rain that falls on the western slopes and the mountain summits. The air, thus dried, descends down the eastern slope and, sinking, is warmed and expands, and is able to absorb moisture from the land. Dry itself, it makes the land below it even drier. The rivers and streams were fed by the snows on the summits, but the surrounding, lower elevation countryside was dry. As a result, the expedition forced their canoes upstream against strong water currents but hiked through dry country.

Not only did the mountains create a dry, tree-poor climate, but the Indians may have had an additional effect. "The Indians appear on some parts of the river to have distroyed a great proportion of the little timber which there is by seting fire to the bottoms," Lewis wrote on August 4.

Their diet began to shift from meat of the plains to mountain fruits—berries and currants. "We feasted suptuously on our wild fruit particularly the yellow courant and the deep purple servicebury which I found to be excellent," Lewis wrote on August 2, 1805. Everything that was happening to them was influenced to a great degree by the natural history of the location, by the geological formations that influence the climate, by the vegetation that was in turn influenced by that climate, by the change in wildlife that was a result

WOOD DUCK

of the change in vegetation and the decrease in rainfall. The steepness of the streams, their rapid and dangerous currents, and the steep and rough country were the products of the ancient and great mountain building events that began about 90 million years ago to form the Rocky Mountains and, as a result, to produce the Missouri River. Ancient geological processes and modern ecological processes combined to challenge the expedition with tough going, little water except in the streams, and less and less game.

It was thus a location of great peril to the expedition, in which the Indians had to—and would—play an important role. As Lewis wrote on July 27, 1805, "we begin to feel considerable anxiety with respect to the Snake Indians. if we do not find them or some other nation who have horses I fear the successfull issue of our voyage will be very doubtfull or at all events much more difficult in it's accomplishment."

Lewis understood the changes to be expected in the transition from plains to mountains. On foot and by stream, Lewis and Clark had developed their own understanding of the natural history of the Missouri River. That learning was now at an end, to be replaced by the harsh lessons of the mountains and the Columbia River to the west.

Afterword

■　■　■　■　■　■　■　　■

by Robert Redford

As we approach the bicentennial of Lewis and Clark's Passage of Discovery, Dan Botkin's book reveals that the original Missouri now exists mainly on the pages of their journals. Were the two explorers with us today, they would hardly recognize most of the Missouri River. Just think about that for a minute. The same exquisite, natural, wild places and wild inhabitants that provided these great explorers the challenges and adventure, wonderment and inspiration, human and spiritual fulfillment so vividly brought to life in their cherished journals would simply be *unrecognizable* to them.

It goes without saying that their loss is our loss. But it is also the loss of generations to follow, who will not have the opportunity to reap the same challenges, inspiration, and fulfillment that Lewis and Clark did from their exploration of America's longest and once great river. The renewal of the soul and spirit that came with their adventures will be something only to be imagined rather than to be experienced.

The picture painted does indeed have strokes of bleakness. But there is also hope in its broad canvass. While certain remnants of the Missouri River of Lewis and Clark can never be brought back to their original natural wonder, and some of its wild inhabitants will never be seen there again, there's still an opportunity to bring significant portions back to their original glory. It's not too late to restore some of what Lewis and Clark witnessed and explored for our children, and theirs.

The approach of the bicentennial of Lewis and Clark's journey can do more than remind us of what has been lost—it can serve as a *national call to action* to restore as much of the original greatness as possible, using the pages of their journal as our blueprint. This may be a once-in-a-lifetime opportunity for all of us to not only honor the memory of these phenomenal men, but to also honor those that follow us in this world by leaving a source of inspiration that might not exist otherwise.

To begin this national call to action American Rivers has proposed a four-part strategy to restore the Missouri and revitalize riverside communities:

RESTORE NATURAL PLACES

Riverside communities and resource managers can create a string of natural places along the Missouri—including pockets of floodplain forest and prairie, side channels, sandbars, and islands. Restoring shallow water and floodplain habitat will help meet the needs of river wildlife by providing nesting, foraging, and spawning areas.

MANAGE DAMS FOR WILDLIFE AND PEOPLE

The Missouri's dams should be operated to provide rising flows in the spring to trigger fish reproduction and cottonwood regeneration, and declining flows during the summer to support nesting wildlife and recreation. Releasing more water in the spring will trigger reproduction by river wildlife, build sandbars, and aid cottonwood regeneration. Reducing flows in the summer will aid young fish and birds like terns and plovers.

REVITALIZE RIVERFRONTS AND IMPROVE RIVER ACCESS

Communities can revitalize their riverfronts in order to attract businesses, residents, and tourists, helping boost the economic health of cities

and towns along and near the Missouri. Today, many towns and cities are recognizing the river's potential as a community center, creating riverside parks and nature preserves connected by trails and greenways.

REDUCE IMPACTS OF GRAZING

Ranchers and land managers should work together to reduce the impacts of grazing along the designated wild and scenic segment of the Missouri in Montana. Scientists predict that cottonwoods will soon be virtually absent unless action is taken.

The work has already begun, as evidenced in the many illustrations in Dan Botkin's book of communities taking action toward the renewal of the Missouri River. While we should find inspiration in this, we cannot afford to be complacent. Whether or not we live near the once great Missouri, we can embrace it as an important part of our national heritage and the heritage we will leave for future generations. Each and every one of us can make a difference as we begin our very own voyage, the voyage of recovery. Supporting the efforts of American Rivers in the launch of this modern-day voyage is a good first step.

Additional Sites to Visit

■ ■ ■ ■ ■ ■ ■ ■

For people setting out to retrace the expedition of Lewis and Clark, there are many places to visit in addition to the ones listed as main entries in this book. Some of these are not locations where Lewis and Clark went, but have related historic or natural history features. Some locations are listed for those whose routes of travel bring them closer to one of these rather than one of the major entries. These are cross-referenced to the main entries.

This list is a selection out of many, and as the interest in the Lewis and Clark expedition grows, the number will increase, so it is wise to check with local chambers of commerce, parks, and wildlife departments in the states along the route, as well as Bureau of Land Management, U.S. Fish and Wildlife Service, and U.S. Forest Service offices. On the way up the Missouri River, Lewis and Clark passed through lands that are today part of the states of Illinois, Missouri, Kansas, Nebraska, Iowa, South and North Dakota, and Montana, and information about natural history areas can be obtained from each of these states. *The Lewis and Clark Trail Map*, published by the National Park Service, can be obtained from the U.S. Government Printing Office or from many locations along the trail.

The locations that follow are on public lands or otherwise have public access. On a map you may see other locations that are closed to the public, including research areas. Some wildlife refuges that are remote and have few visitor facilities are also not included. This is not a list of accommodations, restaurants, and other facilities. There are many other travel guides that provide such information.

If you dig around in a big library, you can find two hundred or so accounts of people who have tried to follow the entire Lewis and Clark expedition from beginning to end, and to do it exactly as Lewis and Clark did. Such trips are more for adventure and verisimilitude. This book is meant to guide the traveler to experience nature as Lewis and Clark did, as much as is possible today, given the great changes our society has wrought on the countryside. It is also meant to guide the traveler to understand these changes for what they are, both positive and negative. To this end, I suggest some places for you to go that, though not exactly where the expedition passed, are the best remaining places to see a certain kind of countryside or a certain kind of wildlife in a natural or naturalistic setting. Some sections of the Missouri are so altered by dams or are relatively inaccessible that I suggest you do not try to follow these unless you are intent on the adventure of reproducing their exact pathway, whatever has happened to that path.

The list is from east to west, with some side excursions; *statements in italics refer to main entries in the book.*

1. Jefferson National Expansion Memorial National Historic Site at Gateway Arch, St. Louis, MO An extensive information exhibit about the Lewis and Clark expedition. Jefferson National Expansion Memorial is located in the heart of downtown St. Louis on the Mississippi River. Interstate Routes 44, 55, 64, and 70 converge near the park. The address is 11 N. Fourth St., St. Louis, MO 63102 (314) 655-1700.

2. Missouri History Museum in the Jefferson Memorial Building at Forest Park, St. Louis, MO The museum houses many historic documents and artifacts related to the Lewis and Clark expedition and their time. It is preparing a major exhibit about the Lewis and Clark expedition, including some of the natural history collections. You can contact them at P.O. Box 11940, St. Louis, MO 63112-0040 (314) 746-4599.

3. Missouri Botanical Garden, St. Louis, MO One of America's preeminent botanical gardens, a place to begin learning about plants and their role in nature. Location of the new Flora of North America project. For more information contact Missouri Botanical Garden, 4344 Shaw Blvd., St. Louis, MO 63110 (800) 642-8842 or (314) 577-5100.

4. Columbia Bottom, near St. Louis, MO Drive north on Riverview Drive; the road's name changes to Columbia Bottom Road, follow for approximately one mile; at a sharp curve the name changes to Strodtman Road; follow road to gate. For information contact the St. Louis Chamber of Commerce at (314) 444-1150.

5. Missouri Botanical Garden Arboretum, St. Louis MO Location of restored prairie and oak woodlands using prescribed fires. Thirty miles west of the St. Louis Gateway Arch on Interstate 44, at exit 253. P.O. Box 38, Gray Summit, MO 63039 (314) 451-3512.

6. Katy Trail from St. Charles to Columbia, MO A rails-to-trails, biking and hiking trail to view the countryside. The trail passes along the floodplain of the Missouri River. You can see limestone, dolomite, and sandstone bluffs. There are picnic tables and other facilities along the trail. The easiest access from the St. Louis area is River Front Park, near the historic Main Street in nearby St. Charles. However, you can intersect the Katy Trail at a number of locations. An alternative from St. Charles is to take Interstate 70 west to State Route 94 along the river and stop at the parking areas along the Katy Trail. You can start bicycling on the trail from any of these locations. A pleasant location is at Portland, Missouri, on the north shore of the Missouri River just east of Jefferson City. For information contact the Department of Natural Resources Division of State Parks, P.O. Box 176, Jefferson City, MO 65102 (800) 334-6946.

7. Jefferson City, MO One of the access points for Katy Trail State Park. For information contact the Department of Natural Resources Division of State Parks, P.O. Box 176, Jefferson City, MO 65102 (800) 334-6946.

8. Boone's Lick State Historic Site, Boonville, MO Clark mentions salt springs in this area, and these are probably the same springs that the sons of Daniel Boone used between 1806 and 1814 to produce salt as a commercial product. They heated the saltwater and produced five hundred pounds of salt a day. The historic site is ten miles north off of Route 87. (Boone's Furnace Creek flows into the Missouri east of Boonville.) The town of Boonville was important after Lewis and Clark as part of the Santa Fe Trail. There are historic buildings there. Contact The Friends of Historic Boonville, 614 Morgan St., Boonville, MO 65233 (660) 882-7977.

9. Baltimore Bend, MO One of the last remaining original bottomland forests. *Discussed in more detail in Arrow Rock State Park (entry 5).* For information about this and other conservation areas managed by the Missouri Department of Conservation, including Blind Pond Lake Conservation Area, Fount Grove, and Bunch Hollow, contact Grand Pass Conservation Area, Route 1, Box 62, Miami, MO 65344 (660) 595-2444.

10. National Frontier Trails Center, Independence, MO A museum about the trails west, especially the Lewis and Clark, Oregon, and Mormon Trails. 318 W. Pacific, Independence, MO 64050 (816) 325-7575.

11. Leavenworth Landing Park, Leavenworth, KS Located on the Missouri River, this was a major landing site for boats. It is a good place to walk along the Missouri River shore. Take Route 73 into Leavenworth to Spruce Street (Route 92), turn east and go to the river shore, which will take you to the park. Located at the crossroads of Esplanade and Choctaw Streets. For more information contact Leavenworth Park Community at (913) 651-2203.

12. Sugar Lake, north of Atchison, KS Sugar Lake is an oxbow lake; perhaps the lake Lewis and Clark called Gosling Lake, where they saw clear water and great quantities of fish and geese. Most oxbow lakes have been drained and converted to farmland. *Discussed in more detail in DeSoto Bend*

National Wildlife Refuge (chapter 21). For information, call Atchison Chamber of Commerce (913) 367-2427.

13. Lewis and Clark State Park, south of St. Joseph, MO Location of an oxbow lake formed when the river cut off a meander. A full-scale replica of the Lewis and Clark keel boat is at the park. The park is located east of where State Route 59 crosses the Missouri River. *For further discussion, see DeSoto Bend National Wildlife Refuge (chapter 21).* 801 Lakecrest Blvd., Rushville, MO 64484 (816) 579-5564.

14. Squaw Creek National Wildlife Refuge, near Mound City, MO, and Big Lake State Park The largest oxbow lake along the Missouri River is located here. This area is used by more than 275 species of birds, including migrating waterfowl: white pelicans, great blue herons, pintails, teals, mallards, snow geese, Canada geese, and cormorants. Squaw Creek is a place to see many of the species of wildlife that Lewis and Clark saw in the easternmost part of the journey, and it is also one of the southernmost areas of loess hills. From Interstate 29 take exit 79 (forty miles north of St. Joseph, MO) to Route 159 west, which goes to the Squaw Creek National Wildlife Refuge Headquarters. Squaw Creek National Wildlife Refuge, P.O. Box 101, Mound City, MO 64470 (816) 442-3187 or Big Lake State Park (660) 442-5432.

15. Museum of the Missouri River History at Nebraska State Recreation Area, Brownville, NE Location of the steam-powered side-wheel dredging boat, the *Captain Meriwether Lewis,* one of the boats that channelized the Missouri River between 1932 and 1969 and is now a designated national historic landmark. Located just off of Route 136, south of the bridge across the Missouri on the west side of the river. *Discussed in more detail in Columbia and the Big Muddy (entry 4).* For additional information, contact Indian Cave State Park, RR 1, Box 30, Shubert, NE 68437 (402) 883-2575.

16. Indian Cave State Park, Brownville, NE This 3,000-acre park has excellent views of the Missouri River and its floodplain. There are twenty miles of hiking trails, horseback trail rides, and cruises on the Missouri River. It is located ten miles south of Brownville and five miles east on S-64E. For more information write or call Indian Cave State Park, RR 1, Box 30, Shubert, NE 68437 (402) 883-2575.

17. Nebraska Mitigation Projects These are supported by the Nebraska Department of Game and Parks. At this time, Hamburg Bend is functioning, while the other six are in a planning stage; for some, land acquisition has been completed. The other six are: Blackbird-Tieville-Upper Decatur Bends; Middle Decatur Bend; Tobacco Island ($3\frac{1}{2}$ miles south of Plattesmouth, NE); Kansas Bend (north of Peru, NE); Langdon Bend (near the Cooper Nuclear Power Station); and Rush Bottom Bend (near Rulo, NE). *For further discussion, see Columbia and the Big Muddy (entry 4); Pelicans and Grand Pass (entry 6); and Hamburg Bend (entry 11).* These will develop over time. For their status and visitor facilities, contact the Nebraska Game and Parks Commission, 2200 N. 33rd St., P.O. Box 30370, Lincoln, NE 68503-0370 (402) 471-0641.

18. Wabash Trace Nature Trail, on the way to Omaha, NE The trail, sixty-three miles long, proceeds from Council Bluffs, IA, southeast to Blanchard, IA. It winds through river valleys that are tributaries of the Missouri, through hills and fields, sometimes within a few miles of the Missouri River. For information contact Bill Spitznagle (president) at (402) 280-6835. SWINT, P.O. Box 524, Council Bluffs, IA 51502-0524 (712) 325-1000 or The Council Bluffs Chamber of Commerce (712) 325-1000.

19. Loess Hills Scenic Byway Two hundred twenty miles of paved roads more or less paralleling Interstate 29 and offering "a mosaic of designated roads through the heart of the scenic Loess Hills region of western Iowa." *For more detail, see The Allwine Prairie (entry 16) and Loess Hills (entry 20).* A brochure including a map can be obtained from Welcome Centers in Iowa or by writing to the Harrison County Museum, RR #3, Box 130A, Missouri Valley, IA 51555 (712) 642-2114.

20. Papillion Creek Dams, Omaha, NE These dams were built by the Army Corps of Engineers for flood control and recreation, within the city limits. Cunningham Lake is at 90th and State Streets (712) 444-5900. Standing Bear Lake is at 138th and Fort Streets. Chalco Recreation Area (712) 444-5900 and Wehrspann Lake (800) 444-6222 are at the junction of State Route 50.

21. Joslyn Museum, Omaha, NE The museum has major collections of the paintings Karl Bodmer made during his trip with Prince Maximillian in the 1830s, perhaps the first tourist trip to rediscover the journey of Lewis and Clark. Lacking photographic cameras, the prince brought along his own landscape painter. The museum is located at 2200 Dodge St., Omaha, NE 68102 (402) 342-3300.

22. N. P. Dodge Memorial Park, Omaha, NE This is where the expedition camped on July 28, 1804. The park is located at 11000 N. River Dr. For more information, contact the Omaha Visitors Bureau at (800) 332-1819.

23. Neale Woods Nature Center, Omaha, NE The nature center's emphasis is on prairie restoration. *For more detail, see Fontenelle Forest Preserve (entry 15).* For more information contact Fontenelle Forest Nature Center, 14323 Edith Marie Ave., Omaha, NE 68112 (402) 453-5615.

24. Hayden Prairie State Preserve in Howard County Site of original tallgrass prairie. *For more detail, read entries on Allwine Prairie and Loess Hills.*

25. Hitchcock Nature Center, Honey Creek, IA The nature center includes eight hundred acres with hiking trails through loess hills with wooded bluffs and native prairie. *For more detail, read The Allwine Prairie (entry 16) and Loess Hills (entry 20).* You can reach the center from Interstate 80, exit 40, or call (712) 545-3283 for more information.

26. Boyer Chute National Wildlife Refuge near Omaha, NE Fishing and hiking are available within 2,000 acres of woods, wetlands, and croplands. Boyer Chute has more visitor facilities than most national wildlife refuges. There is a two-mile reconstructed chute—a slow-moving water channel of the Missouri River—and restored wetlands. *For more detail, read Columbia and the Big Muddy (entry 4); Hamburg Bend (entry 11); and Pelicans and Grand Pass (entry 6).* Boyer Chute is located three miles east of Fort Calhoun. Information about the chute can be obtained from the Fontenelle Forest Association, which is a partner in its development and management (402) 453-5615.

27. Plattsmouth, NE An interesting side trip is to follow the Platte River to Lincoln, NE. The Platte has not been channelized, but its flow is less than in 1804 because much of the water is diverted for irrigation. However, the Platte retains much of the scenic aspect of a prairie river, with sandbars and cottonwoods. *For more detail, see Along the Platte River (chapter 13).* Lincoln Chamber of Commerce (402) 436-2350.

28. Nine Mile Prairie, Lincoln, NE This is one of the earliest attempts at prairie restoration and the subject of early ecological research. Relatively little used for scientific research at present, it offers an opportunity to see some of the prairie grasses and forbs. From the center of the city of Lincoln go west on "O" Street to Northwest 48th, travel north about four miles to Fletcher Avenue, then turn west on Fletcher Avenue and drive about one mile. There is parking on the right; the prairie is to the left. For more information contact the Wachiska Audubon Society at 4547 Calvert St., Suite 10, Lincoln, NE 68506-5643 (402) 486-4846.

29. Grand Island, NE This is a worthwhile site to visit during the sandhill bird migration, because as many as a half million of these birds stop here to feed. *For more detail, read Pelicans and Grand Pass (entry 6).* Grand Island is located west of Lincoln on the Platte River. For more information, contact the Grand Island Visitors Bureau at P.O. Box 1486, Grand Isle, NE 68802 (800) 658-3178.

30. Riverton Wildlife Refuge, IA One of the locations along the Loess Hills Scenic Byway trip. See Additional Site 19 (p. 220). *Also see Loess Hills State Recreation Area (chapter 20).*

31. Midland Marina, Sioux City, IA The marina is near the mouth of the Big Sioux River, one of the major rivers that flows from Iowa and South Dakota into the Missouri River. Even though the hills are low in Iowa, there is a definite state divide, separating east from west. The rivers to the east flow to the Mississippi River, the rivers to the west flow into the Missouri River— the rivers and countryside of Lewis and Clark. 1100 Larsen Park Rd., Sioux City, IA 51102 (712) 258-2000.

32. Sioux City Recreation Trail and Greenway, Sioux City, IA Fourteen-mile trail along the Missouri and the Big Sioux River, which can be reached from the riverfront park in Sioux City.

33. Sioux City Park, Sioux City, IA Fifty-seven city parks are located in and around the Sioux City area. For more information, write to Sioux City Parks and Recreation, P.O. Box 447, Sioux City, IA 51102 (712) 279-6126.

34. Sioux City Stone State Park, Sioux City, IA Has excellent views of the Missouri River Valley and three states. For more information, write to the park at 4500 Sioux River Rd., Sioux City, IA 51109 (712) 255-4698.

35. Loess Ridge Nature Center, Sioux City, IA Site of a walk-under prairie and a 400-gallon aquarium of native fish. Located at 4500 Sioux River Rd., Sioux City, IA 51109 (712) 258-0838.

36. Clay County Park, Vermillion, SD Camping and boat-launching facilities on the wild and scenic stretch of the Missouri River. For further discussion, see *Vermillion: On the Wild and Scenic Missouri (entry 27)*. Located two miles southwest of Vermillion off South Dakota Hwy. 50 (605) 987-2263.

37. Bike Trail, Yankton, SD This bike trail has waterfront views of the Missouri River. For further discussion, see *Vermillion: On the Wild and Scenic Missouri (chapter 27)*.

38. Riverside Park, Yankton, SD On the Missouri River, a place where you can consider how cities and towns treat their waterfronts. From Route 81 go east on W. Fourth Street and south on Douglas Avenue to the park.

39. Missouri National Recreational River, Gavins Point Dam to Ponca, NE, State Park Fifty-nine-mile unchannelized stretch of the Missouri River from Gavins Point Dam to Ponca State Park—the longest remnant of the original Missouri except in Montana. For further discussion, see *Vermillion: On the Wild and Scenic Missouri (chapter 27); Omaha, Nebraska (chapter 14); and Columbia and the Big Muddy (chapter 4)*. N.P.S. P.O. Box 591, O'Neill, NE 68783 (402) 336-3970.

40. National Fish Hatchery and Aquarium, Yankton, SD The hatchery for native fish, including those of the Missouri River. For further discussion, see *Hamburg Bend (entry 11)*. Located three miles west of Yankton on Route 52. For more information call (605) 665-3352.

41. Gavins Point Dam, between Nebraska and South Dakota The most downstream of the major dams on the Missouri River. The dam is earthen, 74 feet high and 8,700 feet long. The Lewis and Clark expedition held a council at Calumet Bluffs in the vicinity of Gavins Point Dam with Yankton Sioux on August 28, 1804. This council meeting is noted by interpretative signs at the dam and at Lewis and Clark State Recreation Area (see Additional Site 42, p. 225). *For further discussion, see Omaha, Nebraska (chapter 14) and Columbia and the Big Muddy (chapter 4)*. Gavins Point Dam is located on Nebraska Route 121, two miles south of Yankton, SD. The visitors center is four miles west of Yankton in Nebraska at the south end of Gavins Point Dam. For more information, call (402) 667-7873.

42. Lewis and Clark State Recreation Area at Gavins Point Dam, SD The recreation area has boat ramps on the reservoir formed by the dam, called Lewis and Clark Lake. The lake is used for recreation and is a place to see the benefits and alterations of the landscape created by such a reservoir. It is located five miles west of Yankton on Route 52. For more information call (402) 688-2985.

43. Ponca State Park, NE The park is at the lower end of the 59-mile stretch of the Missouri National Recreational River area and is one of the best public locations to see this section of the Missouri River from the shore. The channelized river begins here. Look upriver to see the "wild Missouri," downstream to see the channelized river. Some of the wildlife you can see include wild turkeys, eagles, and deer. For more information, contact Ponca State Park, P.O. Box 688, Ponca, NE 68770 (402) 755-2284.

44. Blue Bluffs area, NE Historical marker locating the Lewis and Clark campsites of August 23–25, 1804. For further discussion, see *South Sioux City and the Bluffs on Fire (chapter 24).*

45. Lewis and Clark Lake near Yankton, SD The reservoir behind Gavins Point Dam where you can see bluffs overlooking the lake. The lake can be reached by following Route 12 to S54 to Santee, NE, the headquarters of the Santee Sioux Indian Reservation. For more information, call (402) 388-4169.

46. Fort Niobrara National Wildlife Refuge near Valentine, NE Site to view prairie terrain and drive through and see penned-in buffalo (about 375), elk (about 70), prairie dogs, and Texas longhorn cattle. For further discussion, see *Vermillion, South Dakota, and Dixon, Nebraska (chapter 26).*

Located five miles east of Valentine, NE, on Route 12. For more information call (402) 376-3789.

47. Valentine National Wildlife Refuge, Valentine, NE Approximately twenty miles south of Valentine, NE, on Route 83. More than seventy thousand acres with many ponds and small lakes in the Sandhills and many water birds. *For further discussion see Pelicans and Grand Pass (entry 6).* Refuge Manager, Fort Niobrara–Valentine National Wildlife Refuge Complex, HC 14 Box 67, Valentine, NE 69201 (402) 376-3789.

48. Niobrara River Wild and Scenic section, Valentine, NE Famous as one of the top ten canoeing rivers in the United States, a way to experience a prairie river with sandbars and snags from the water. *For further discussion, see The Niobrara River Meets the Missouri (entry 28) and The Confluence of the Niobrara and Missouri Rivers (entry 29).*

49. Big Bend Dam near Chamberlain, SD One of the six major dams on the Missouri River. *For further discussion, see Omaha, Nebraska (entry 14).* To visit the dam, take Interstate 90 west of Chamberlain to Route 47 north to Fort Thompson. For more information, call the Army Corps of Engineers at (605) 245-2255.

50. Akta Lakota Museum, Chamberlain, SD The museum is a good source of information about the Sioux Indian culture, which Lewis and Clark encountered on their journey. For more information, contact Saint Joseph Indian School, Attention Akta Lakota Museum, N. Main St., Box 89, Chamberlain, SD 57325 (605) 734-3455.

51. Native American Loop Tour, Chamberlain, SD A driving tour through the Crow Creek and Lower Brule Indian Reservations. Loop attractions include the Akta Lakota Museum, the Big Bend Dam, and the Lower Brule Game Lodge. Self-guided brochures and audiocassettes are available. For more information, contact the Chamberlain Chamber of Commerce, 115 W. Lawler, Chamberlain, SD 57325 (605) 734-6541.

52. Farm Island and Pierre, SD Lewis and Clark hunted elk here. It is the site of South Dakota's first continuous settlement (started in 1817). Today there is fishing for walleye pike and hunting for geese. From the town of Pierre, take Sioux/Wells Ave. This road connects with Hwy. 34. Farm Island is three to four miles east of Pierre off Hwy. 34. For more information, call (605) 224-5605 or write to Farm Island, 1301 Farm Island Rd., Pierre, SD 57501-5829.

53. Fort Pierre National Grassland, Pierre, SD *For further discussion, see Little Missouri National Grassland (chapter 32).* Drive south on Route 83 from Pierre. Or, from Chamberlain, take Interstate 90 west to exit 212, then go north on Route 83 to Fort Pierre National Grassland. P.O. Box 417, Pierre, SD 57501 (605) 224-5517.

54. Samuel H. Ordway, Jr., Memorial Prairie, Eureka, SD Seventy-six hundred acres with more than 300 species of plants as well as water birds and buffalo. *For further discussion, see Vermillion, South Dakota, and Dixon, Nebraska (entry 26).*

55. Oahe Dam, Pierre, SD One of the major dams on the Missouri River. *For further discussion, see Omaha, Nebraska (entry 14) and Columbia and the Big Muddy (entry 4).* Located four miles north of Pierre on Hwy. 1804. For more information, contact the Army Corps of Engineers, 28563 Powerhouse Rd., Pierre, SD 57501 (605) 224-5862.

56. Ashfall Fossil Beds State Historical Park, Royal, NE You can see fossil rhinoceroses, horses, and camels, from ten million years ago when this area was a tropical grassland. There are also interpretative programs and nature trails to teach you about the geology, animals, and plants of the Great Plains. Located south of Niobrara State Park near the junction of Routes 59 and 14. For more information, write to Ashfall Fossil Beds State Historical Park, P.O. Box 66, Royal, NE 68773 (402) 893-2000.

57. Mouth of the Bad River, Fort Pierre, SD Location of the Teton Council Site, where Lewis and Clark held a council with the Teton Sioux on September 24, 1804. There is river access and a waterfront park here.

58. Custer State Park, Custer, SD Tours of free-ranging buffalo herds provide one of the best locations to see buffalo. *For further discussion, see Vermillion, South Dakota, and Dixon, Nebraska (entry 26)*. Take Route 385/16 toward Hill City, go into the town of Custer, make a left on Mt. Rushmore Rd., which will take you directly to the park. For information contact Custer State Park, HC 83, Box 70, Custer, SD 57730 (605) 255-4515.

59. Roughrider Trail, Bismarck, ND Seventeen miles for hiking, horseback riding, and snowmobiling, paralleling the Missouri River. *For further discussion, see Fort Mandan Park (chapter 30)*. Roughrider Trail is located south of the city of Bismarck.

60. Fort Abraham Lincoln State Park, Bismarck, ND This is near the site of a Mandan village where Lewis and Clark spent a winter. When they arrived on October 21, 1804, they saw a beautiful plain "covered with herds of buffalo," one of which they shot for food. *For further discussion, see Fort Mandan Park (chapter 30)*. Located seven miles south of Mandan on Hwy. 1806. For information contact the park at 4480 Fort Lincoln Rd., Mandan, ND 58554 (701) 663-9571.

61. Garrison Dam, Bismarck, ND One of the six major dams on the Missouri River. There is an exhibit area, camping, and fishing. Lewis and Clark stopped here on August 13, 1806 on their return trip. *For further discussion, see Fort Mandan Park (chapter 30)*. Army Corps of Engineers Hwy. 200 West, Riverdale, ND 58565 (701) 654-7441 or (701) 654-7411.

62. Sakakawea State Park, Pick City, ND The park is located on a peninsula that extends into Lake Sakakawea, the reservoir behind Garrison Dam. The park is primarily for RVs and motorboats. *For further discussion, see Omaha, Nebraska (chapter 14)* (701) 487-3315.

63. Four Bears Museum, northwest of Bismarck, ND An interpretative center discusses the Lewis and Clark expedition, but focuses on the Indians of this region—the Arikara, Mandan, and Hidatsa. This area was visited by Lewis and Clark. *For further discussion, see Knife River Indian Villages (chapter 31).*

64. Lewis and Clark State Park, ND Located on Lake Sakakawea, and therefore a place where you can see one of the large reservoirs resulting from a major dam, in this case Garrison Dam, on the Missouri. The park is sixteen miles west of Williston, on Route 1804 (named for the Lewis and Clark expedition's first year). *A visit to this park could be part of a circle route linking entries 30, Fort Mandan, and 31, Knife River Indian Villages.* For information call (701) 859-3071.

65. Loma Ferry Crossing, MT A put-in location for boat trips down the Missouri River and a place to view the white cliffs region of the river. This is an area where the river still follows its natural course. Nearby is the Richard E. Wood Wildlife Viewing Area. *For further discussion see Fort Peck Dam and the Milk River (chapter 34) and The Mouth of the Marias River (chapter 37).*

66. Black Eagle in the vicinity of Fort Benton, MT An opportunity to see farm country of Montana. It was named Black Eagle by Lewis and Clark because the Indians told them they would see a black eagle at the falls of the Missouri. Located about thirty-six miles from Fort Benton.

67. Fort Belknap Indian Reservation of the Gros Ventre and Assiniboine Tribes, MT There are guided tours to various buttes and canyons and to a buffalo range. About 300 buffalo on a 10,000-acre reserve can be seen on daily guided tours. *For further discussion, see Vermillion, South Dakota, and Dixon, Nebraska (entry 26).* From Great Falls, MT, take Route 87 north to Route 2 east, then drive south on Route 66 to the Fort Belknap Reservation Visitor Center. Or you can drive north from Billings, MT, on Route 87 to Route 19 and on north to Route 191 to Route 66. For more information, contact Tribal Buffalo Tours, RR 1, Box 66, Fort Belknap Agency, Harlem, MT 59526 (406) 353-2205.

68. Charles M. Russell National Wildlife Refuge, MT On their journey west, Lewis and Clark spent thirteen days within today's Charles M. Russell Wildlife Refuge. The second largest wildlife refuge in the continental United States, it contains some original prairie as well as sagebrush and ponderosa pines. A visitor can see raptors, antelope, deer, grouse, and prairie dogs, and one of the largest remaining prairie elk herds. The U.S. Fish and Wildlife Service warns that the gravel roads of the tour route may become impassable during extended periods of rain, so use proper caution. *For further discussion, see Little Missouri National Grassland and Theodore Roosevelt National Park (entry 32).* The refuge has a twenty-mile auto tour route that begins fifty-five miles south of Malta off Route 191 and ends one-half mile north of the Missouri River on Route 191. P.O. Box 110, Lewistown, MT 59457 (406) 538-8706.

69. Crooked Falls, MT Located in Cascade County, north of Malmstrom Air Force Base at Great Falls, MT.

70. Upper Missouri National Wild and Scenic River, MT One of a handful of stretches where the river is neither dammed nor channelized, you can go on a canoe camping trip and see the Missouri River much as it appeared in this area to Lewis and Clark. There are various put-in locations, and detailed maps are available for boaters from the Bureau of Land Management. A growing number of outfitters provide guided trips down this portion of the Missouri River, including Missouri River Outfitters, Fort Benton, MT (406) 622-3295; and Missouri River Canoe Company, Virgelle, MT (800) 426-2926. *For further discussion, see The Confluence of the Yellowstone and Missouri Rivers (entry 33); Fort Benton, Montana (entry 38); Ryan Dam (entry 39); and Fort Peck Dam and the Pines Recreation Area (entry 35).* This 149-mile stretch of the Missouri River is located between Kipp State Park and Fort Benton, MT.

71. Geraldine and Square Butte, MT Wildlife viewing area. This natural area, under the jurisdiction of the Bureau of Land Management, is located on Route 80 between Fort Benton and Loma, MT.

72. Earth Science Museum, Loma, Mont. The museum has gems, minerals, fossils, and Indian artifacts. Located ten miles past Fort Benton off Hwy. 86 on Main Street.

73. Lewis and Clark Pass, Great Falls, MT Location of the footpath that follows the Indian trail around the Great Falls that was used by Lewis and Clark for their portage.

74. River Edge Trail, Great Falls, MT The trail passes by Crooked Falls, the only remaining undammed falls that Lewis and Clark portaged around. Seven miles of paved trail run along the Missouri River from Gibson Park at Tenth Avenue South in downtown Great Falls to Giant Springs Heritage State Park; close by is a new interpretive center. For more information contact Giant Springs Heritage State Park, Giant Springs Rd., Great Falls, MT 59408 (406) 454-5840.

75. Lewis and Clark National Forest, Great Falls, MT There is a scenic byway through this park. From Great Falls take Route 89 southeast to the forest. Contact the Forest at 1101 Fifteenth St. N., Box 869, Great Falls, MT 59403 (406) 547-3361.

76. Canyon Ferry Lake, Helena, MT Numerous state recreation areas are in this region. Some have Lewis and Clark interpretation markers. *For further discussion, see Gates of the Mountains (chapter 41).*

77. Ulm Pishkun Buffalo Jump, Ulm, MT *For further discussion, see Judith Landing (entry 36).* From Great Falls take Interstate 15 west twelve miles to the exit for Ulm. Follow signs to a monument and picnic area. The picnic area is four miles from the interstate exit. For more information con-

tact Montana Fish, Wildlife and Parks at P.O. Box 6609, Great Falls, MT
59406 (406) 454-5840.

78. Vicinity of Three Forks, MT The forests up the slope from the Missouri River provide an introduction to the forests and the geology of the
Rockies. *For further discussion, see Three Forks, Montana (chapter 42).*

79. Madison Buffalo Jump State Park, Bozeman, MT Near the mouth
of the Judith River, downstream from Great Falls, Lewis and Clark found
what Lewis described as a buffalo jump. But there has been a disagreement
as to whether this countryside could have been a location for such an activity. This method of killing buffalo was common, however, and at this site you
can see a buffalo jump used for 2,000 years. *For further discussion, see Judith
Landing (chapter 36).* From Three Forks take Interstate 90 east to Bozeman
and take exit 283 south, following signs for the buffalo jump. From the exit
on the interstate, the park is a seven-mile drive; six miles of the drive is on a
gravel road. For more information contact Montana Fish, Wildlife and Parks
at 1400 S. Nineteenth, Bozeman, MT 59715 or call (406) 994-4042.

80. Pompey's Pillar, Billings, MT This national historic landmark,
administered by the Bureau of Land Management, is the only known existing
location where Clark inscribed his name. It is located about thirty-five miles
northeast of Billings. Take exit 23 north on Interstate 94. On July 25, 1806,
Clark wrote in his journal that the rock he named Pompey's Pillar was "200 feet
high and 400 paces in circumference and only accessible on one side. The
natives have engraved on the face of this rock the figures of animals, etc., near
which I mark my name and the day of the month and year." Many birds come
through this area, including bald eagles and white pelicans. From this location
you can see the cottonwoods along the Yellowstone River. *For further discussion, see The Confluence of the Yellowstone and Missouri Rivers (entry 33).*

81. Gallatin National Forest, Bozeman, MT Clark passed through the
area where Bozeman is now on July 14, 1806. *For further discussion, see*

Three Forks, Montana (chapter 42). For information contact Gallatin Canyon Campground (406) 587-9054.

82. Greycliff Prairie Dog Town State Monument Wildlife Viewing Area, Billings, MT This 98-acre park is open year-round. There are many interpretive displays that introduce the visitor to the black-tailed prairie dog community. *For further discussion, see Little Missouri National Grassland and Theodore Roosevelt National Park (entry 32).* Located off Interstate 90 about seventy-seven miles west of Billings, MT. For more information, contact Montana Fish, Wildlife and Parks at 2300 Lake Elmo Dr., Billings, MT 59105 or call (406) 446-4150.

Entry Notes

■ ■ ■ ■ ■ ■ ■ ■

All quotations from the Lewis and Clark journals are from the edition edited by Gary Moulton and published by the University of Nebraska Press, volumes 2 through 8, with various publication dates beginning in 1986.

Additional background to the ideas discussed in the entries can be found in my other books: Botkin, D. B., 1990, *Discordant Harmonies: A New Ecology for the 21st Century*, Oxford University Press; Botkin, D. B., 1995, *Our Natural History: The Lessons of Lewis and Clark*, Putnam (paperback 1996, reissued 1998); Botkin, D. B., and E. A. Keller, 1995, *Environmental Sciences: The Earth as a Living Planet*, John Wiley & Sons (second edition 1997); and Skinner, B., S. Porter, and D. B. Botkin, 1999, *The Blue Planet*, John Wiley & Sons.

LEWIS, CLARK, NATURE, AND US

Record the mineral productions . . . The letter from Jefferson to Lewis was dated April 1803 and is quoted in the Coues edition of the Lewis and Clark journals, first published in 1893, as Coues, E. (ed.), *History of the Expedition under the Command of Lewis and Clark,* reprinted 1965 by Dover Books, on pp. xxiv–xxxiii.

THE MISSOURI RIVER: NATURE'S LANDSCAPE PAINTER

I thank Brian Skinner and Steve Porter, my coauthors of another book, *The Blue Planet* (1999, John Wiley & Sons), for the idea that we can speak of rocks as nature's books, and minerals as its words. I have expanded on this idea liberally. The discussion of plate tectonics is based on a chapter by Brian Skinner in the same book.

The river is the central fact . . . Missouri Basin Survey Commission, 1953, "Missouri: Land and Water," U.S. Government Printing Office, p. 34.

Thousand years. All this here water just a-going to waste . . . Woody Guthrie, "Columbia Talkin' Blues," in Murtin, B. (ed.), 1991, *Woody Guthrie Roll On Columbia,* Sing Out Publications, p. 57.

The Missouri drains waters . . . *Encyclopedia Britannica,* 1997, 24: 1038–40 (CD-ROM version).

THE NATURAL HISTORY OF SPECIAL LOCATIONS ALONG THE RIVER

1. Camp Dubois: Preparing for the Journey

Going up that river . . . The quotation from Joseph Conrad is of course from his famous work, *Heart of Darkness.*

Accept no soft-palmed gentlemen . . . Lewis's letter to Clark about the selection of the members of the expedition is quoted in Dillon, R., 1965, *Meriwether Lewis: A Biography,* Coward-McCann, p. 58.

2. Cahokia: Clark Discovers an Ancient Indian Mound

Information about Cahokia is from the visitors center at the Cahokia Mounds Historical Site and from Mink, C. G., 1992, *Cahokia: City of the Sun,* Cahokia Mounds Museum Society, Collinsville, IL.

4. Columbia and the Big Muddy National Wildlife Refuge: Approaches to Meeting All the Uses of the River

Information about the Missouri River and its channelization and dams is based on conversations with: J. C. Bryant, director, and Jim Milligan, project leader, Big Muddy National Wildlife Refuge, U.S. Fish and Wildlife

Service, Columbia, MO; Stephen R. Earl, Missouri River project engineer, U.S. Army Corps of Engineers, Omaha District, Operations Division, Omaha, NE; as well as references and data provided by Jim Milligan.

5. Arrow Rock State Park: Cottonwoods and the Resiliency of Life
Calculations about land required to produce the world trade in timber are from Sedjo, R. A., and D. B. Botkin, 1997, "Using Forest Plantations to Spare the Natural Forest," *Environment* 39 (10): 14–20.

6. Pelicans and Grand Pass: The River and Migrating Birds
Information about the migration of birds on the Missouri River is from conversations with Rob Leonard, wildlife management biologist, Missouri Dept. of Conservation Grand Pass Wildlife Area, Miami, MO.

8. Weston, Missouri: Where the River Meandered Away, Leaving the Town Without a Waterfront
Some people would think . . . The river runs crooked . . . Steward, C. D., "A Race on the Missouri," *The Century Magazine,* LEX (4) February 1907, p. 588, quoted in Vestal, S., 1945, *The Missouri,* Farrar & Rinehart, p. 13.

Eating all the time . . . Vestal, S., 1945, p. 13.

9. Benedictine Bottoms: Pollution As a Problem of Landscape Design
Information on non-point-source pollution is based on discussions with Jim Milligan, project leader, Big Muddy National Wildlife Refuge, U.S. Fish and Wildlife Service, Columbia, MO; Mark Brohman, environmental analyst supervisor, and Gerald Mestl, Missouri River program manager, Fisheries Division, both of the Nebraska Game and Parks Commission, Lincoln, NE. Data for non-point-source pollution was obtained from the U.S. Geological Survey Web site.

10. Atchison, Kansas: Commerce in Beaver
The quote about the disappearance of beaver, *have not know[n] them . . .* Burroughs, R. D., 1961, *The Natural History of the Lewis and Clark Expedition,* Michigan State University Press, p. 107.

11. *Hamburg Bend: The River Farms the Prairie and the Prairie Feeds the Fish*
Information about the ecology of rivers is based on discussions with Mark Brohman, environmental analyst supervisor, and Gerald Mestl, Missouri River program manager, Fisheries Division, both of the Nebraska Game and Parks Commission, Lincoln, NE; Jim Milligan, project leader, Big Muddy National Wildlife Refuge, U.S. Fish and Wildlife Service, Columbia, MO; Kenneth Cummins, South Florida Water Mgt. District, West Palm Beach, FL; as well as the following publications: Hynes, H. B. N., 1970, *The Ecology of Running Waters,* Liverpool Press; Allan, David, 1995, *Stream Ecology: Structure & Function of Running Waters,* Chapman & Hall; Boon, Callow, and Petts (eds.), 1992, *River Conservation & Management,* John Wiley; Callow and Petts (eds.), 1992, *The Rivers Handbook: Hydrological and Ecological Principles,* Blackwell Scientific, London; Hauer and Lamberti (eds.), 1996, *Methods in Stream Ecology,* Academic Press; Fontaine and Bartell, 1983, *Dynamics of Lotic Ecosystems,* Ann Arbor Science Publications.

14. *Omaha, Nebraska: Down the River with the Army Corps of Engineers*
Information about the Missouri River and its channelization and dams is based on conversations with: J. C. Bryant, director, and Jim Milligan, project leader, Big Muddy National Wildlife Refuge, U.S. Fish and Wildlife Service, Columbia, MO; Stephen R. Earl, Missouri River project engineer, U.S. Army Corps of Engineers, Omaha District, Operations Division, Omaha, NE; as well as references and data provided by Jim Milligan.

15. *Fontenelle Forest Preserve: Killing Nature with Kindness*
Information about Fontenelle Forest and the deer was obtained from Gary Garabrandt, chief ranger, Fontenelle Forest Association, Fontenelle Forest Nature Center, Bellevue, NE, and from the association's newsletters and other publications provided by him.

16. *The Allwine Prairie: Once-Vast Prairies Are Now Rare*
The home of the Apache, Assiniboine, and Cheyenne . . . Garrett, W. E., and J. B. Garver, Jr., 1988, *The Historical Atlas of the United States,* Centennial Edition, National Geographic Society, p. 68.

North America's characteristic landscape . . . Whitman, W., 1879, *Specimen Days.*

The biggest sky anywhere . . . Stegner, W., 1992, *Wolf Willow,* Penguin, p. 7.

The drama of this landscape . . . Stegner, W., 1992, *Wolf Willow,* Penguin, p. 7.

19. Ledges State Park: Reading Ancient History in Tiny Grains of Pollen

Information about the geological history of Ledges State Park is based on conversations with Dr. David Glenn-Lewin, now dean of Wichita State University, Fairmount College of Liberal Arts and Sciences, Wichita, KS. Other information on the history and vegetation of Iowa is from: Prior, J. C., 1976, *A Regional Guide to Iowa Landforms,* Iowa Geological Survey Educational Series 3, Iowa Geological Survey; Webb, T., III, E. J. Cushing, and H. E. Wright, Jr., 1983, "Holocene Changes in the Vegetation of the Midwest," chapter 10 in Wright, H. E. (ed.), *Late-Quaternary Environments of the United States,* vol. 2, *The Holocene,* Univ. of Minnesota Press; Baker, V. R., 1983, "Late-Pleistocene Fluvial Systems," in Porter, S. C. (ed.), *Late-Quaternary Environments of the United States,* vol. 1, *The Late Pleistocene,* Univ. of Minnesota Press; and Transeau, E. N., 1935, "The Prairie Peninsula," *Ecology* 16 (3): 423–37.

20. Loess Hills State Recreation Area: To Keep a Prairie, Disturb It with Fire

He was near the location of modern Nebraska City . . . The location is given in GM 2:394; note 2, 397.

22. Sergeant Charles Floyd Monument: Medicine and Nature

Calomel . . . Calomel is mercurous chloride (Hg_2Cl_2). Camphor is a terpene ketone ($C_{10}H_{12}O$). Copperas, ferrous sulfate ($FeSO_47H_2O$), is a bluish green crystal, salty-tasting material; it was also called green vitriol. Ipecac comes from *Cephaelis ipecacuanha,* a plant of the madder family. Niter, also known as saltpeter, is potassium nitrate (KNO_3).

26. **Vermillion, South Dakota, and Dixon, Nebraska: Buffalo Demise and Recovery**
A great store of cattle . . . Haines, F., 1970, *The Buffalo*, Thomas Y. Crowell Co., p. 73.

In 1701 there was an attempt to domesticate buffalo . . . Haines, 1970, p. 74.

One herd was reported in southwestern Georgia in 1686 . . . Haines, 1970, p. 32.

Fossils of bison . . . Haines, 1970, p. 1.

Their number was variously estimated . . . Haines, 1970, p. 33.

A "dark blanket" of buffalo . . . and subsequent estimate of the number, Sandoz, M., 1954, *The Buffalo Hunters*, University of Nebraska Press, p. 102.

A train traveled one hundred twenty miles . . . Sandoz, 1954, p. 83.

Kill every buffalo . . . Sandoz, 1970, p. 88.

Estimates range to 3,500,000 . . . Sandoz, 1954, p. 50.

1,500,000 hides were shipped . . . Haines, 1970, p. 197.

In 1871, the U.S. Biological Survey sent George Grinnell . . . Sandoz, 1954, p. 127.

Fewer than 5,000 reached the border . . . Sandoz, 1954, p. 349.

27. **Vermillion: On the Wild and Scenic Missouri**
More than 450 steamboats were lost . . . Vestal, S., 1945, *The Missouri*, Farrar & Rinehart, p. 43.

29. **The Confluence of the Niobrara and Missouri Rivers: Lewis and Clark Begin to See the Animals of the West**
Information about the geographic distribution and feeding habits of some of the animals was augmented from my own knowledge by Martin, A., H. S. Zim, and A. L. Nelson, 1951, *American Wildlife and Plants: A*

Guide to Wildlife Food Habits, Dover Books. Information about the history and present status of the pronghorn is from Yoakum, J., "The American Pronghorn," in Chandler, W., L. Labate, and C. Wille (eds.), 1989, *Audubon Wildlife Report 1988–89*, Academic Press, pp. 637–50.

30. Fort Mandan Park, North Dakota: Winter on the Plains

Temperature extremes . . . Missouri Basin Survey Commission, 1953, "Missouri: Land and Water," U.S. Government Printing Office, p. 38.

A site later known as Fort Clark . . . Coues (1893) identifies this site in vol. 1, p. 179.

31. Knife River Indian Villages: Choosing a Place to Live within Nature's Constraints and Opportunities

Information about the Knife River villages is from the visitors center and brochures of the restoration.

32. Little Missouri National Grassland and Theodore Roosevelt National Park: Prairie Dogs, Black-Footed Ferrets, and the Shortgrass Prairie

An immense prairie dog town in Texas . . . Digital West Digest Web page.

98 percent of the prairie dog towns . . . American Zoo and Aquarium Association Web site.

33. The Confluence of the Yellowstone and Missouri Rivers: Wolves and the Conservation of Endangered Species

Some American Indian tribes had wolf clans . . . Young, S. P., 1970, *The Last of the Loners*, MacMillan, London.

34. Fort Peck Dam and the Milk River: How the Ice Ages Altered the Course of the Missouri River

At Loma the Missouri begins to flow . . . Alt, D., and D. W. Hyndman, 1986, *Roadside Geology of Montana*, Mountain Press, p. 313.

Other information about the ice-age history of the Missouri River is from the above book and Hunt, C. B., 1967, *Physiography of the United States*, Freeman; and Thornbury, W. D., 1964, *Principles of Geomorphology*, John Wiley & Sons.

35. Fort Peck Dam and the Pines Recreation Area: Grizzlies and the Conservation of Endangered Species

Information on the standard range of the grizzly bear is from Seevheen, C., 1985, "The Grizzly Bear," in *Audubon Wildlife Report*, pp. 401–15; and Storer, T. I., and L. P. Tevis, 1955, *California Grizzly*, Univ. of Nebraska Press.

There are few other studies that provided any useful estimate . . . Mace, R. D., S. C. Minta, T. L. Manley, and K. E. Aune, 1994, "Estimating Grizzly Bear Population Size Using Camera Sightings," *Wildlife Society Bulletin* 22: 74–83.

Three bears per 100 square miles in Yellowstone National Park . . . Craighead, F. C., 1979, *Track of the Grizzly*, Sierra Club Books; and Craighead, F. C., 1982, "A Definitive System for analysis of grizzly bear habitat and other wilderness resources utilizing LANDSAT multispectral imagery and computer technology," Univ. of Montana, Missoula.

37. The Mouth of the Marias River: Which Was the Best Way West?
On a clay derived from glacial till and shale . . . This clay is so described in a note by Moulton (and T. Harrison) in GM 4:264, note 1.

38. Fort Benton, Montana: Caches, Geology, and the Location of Cities
The first steamboat to navigate the Missouri . . . Vestal, S., 1945, *The Missouri*, Farrar & Rinehart, p. 52.

39. Ryan Dam: Scenery and Electricity
The pen of Thompson . . . GM 4:283–88, including notes on p. 288.

40. Giant Springs and Great Falls: Huge Quantities of Fresh Water Rise and Descend As Hail and Rain
389 million gallons a day . . . GM 4:308, note 5.

41. Gates of the Mountains: Continents Collide and We Are Rafted Along in Their Wake
The discussion of plate tectonics is based on a chapter by Brian Skinner in Skinner, B., S. Porter, and D. B. Botkin, 1999, *The Blue Planet*, John Wiley & Sons.

Index

INDEX

Daniel B. Botkin is an ecologist with a lifelong interest in the character of nature, wilderness, and their exploration. He has directed research in many parts of the world, from the Serengeti Plains of Africa to the forests of Siberia. He has published research about forests, whooping cranes, salmon, bowhead whales, moose, and African elephants. He is well-known for his books about the idea of nature in Western civilization, including *Discordant Harmonies: A New Ecology for the 21st Century* and *Our Natural History: The Lessons of Lewis and Clark*. He has advised many federal, state, and county agencies and organizations about the conservation and management of our wild living resources, from forests to whales. Among his awards are the Fernow award for Outstanding Contributions in International Forestry, given by the American Forests and German Forestry Association; election to the Environmental Hall of Fame, housed at California Polytechnic Institute, Pomona, California; and the Mitchell International Prize for Sustainable Development. He has been a fellow at the Rockefeller Bellagio Institute, Bellagio, Italy, and the Woodrow Wilson International Center for Scholars, Washington, D.C. He is president of The Center for the Study of the Environment, Santa Barbara, CA. He has been on the faculty of Yale University, University of California, Santa Barbara, and George Mason University.